The Women's Courtyard

The Women's Courtyard

KHADIJA MASTUR

Translated from the Urdu by
DAISY ROCKWELL

PENGUIN BOOKS
An imprint of Penguin Random House

PENGUIN BOOKS

USA | Canada | UK | Ireland | Australia
New Zealand | India | South Africa | China

Penguin Books is part of the Penguin Random House group of companies
whose addresses can be found at global.penguinrandomhouse.com

Published by Penguin Random House India Pvt. Ltd
7th Floor, Infinity Tower C, DLF Cyber City,
Gurgaon 122 002, Haryana, India

First published in Urdu as *Āngan* by Sang-e-Meel Publications 1962
Published in English in Penguin Books by Penguin Random House India 2018

Copyright © Sang-e-Meel Publications 1962, 2018
English translation copyright © Daisy Rockwell 2018

ISBN 9780670091362

Typeset in Adobe Caslon Pro by InoSoft Systems, Noida
Printed at Replika Press Pvt. Ltd, India

www.penguin.co.in

Contents

The
Women's
Courtyard

Past

1

A winter's night grows desolate so quickly. Today as well, clouds had been gathering since evening. There was a chill in the air now, and the electric street lamp burned silently. Across the gali, an owl hooted from the thicket of trees near the half-built school building, its ominous voice adding to the bleakness of the night. It was a bit quieter in the large room next door now—she could no longer hear Chammi tossing and turning.

She's sleeping soundly, Aliya thought with longing—she herself couldn't get to sleep. Not being able to sleep at night is so very painful—even worse in a completely new place. Perhaps first nights in new places must always be spent sleeplessly like this. She tried once again to fall asleep, casting the room in darkness by pulling the shutters partly closed, then covered her face with the quilt and lay down as though she were actually asleep.

After lying there motionless for a long time, she felt the whole effort had gone to waste. Sleep was nowhere in sight and memories of the past kept whirling through her mind. She sat up on her bed, cross-legged, feeling helpless. She opened the shutters and began to look outside. The school building on the other side of the gali, the dense mango and pipal trees—all were shrouded in darkness. Everything had looked so clear and lovely in the evening. She had sat at the window and gazed out with some interest then; but now, in the darkness, the trees looked like black mountains, and when a sharp gust of wind blew, they looked frightening, like something out of the ghost stories she'd heard in childhood.

I'll never get to sleep this way, she thought, and pulled the shutters closed again. Her body ached as she lay down. The anxiety of a full day's journey had drained her.

'Oh my!' she moaned. 'Now I can't sleep—so long as I can't clear my mind there'll be no room for sleep!' Memories rushed in from all sides. People say you should forget the past. What's the point of turning and looking back? Just keep moving forward. But her past was all she'd inherited. Her past, from which she'd learnt so much. How could she wrench herself away from it now? And now, ever more memories filled her head because of how she'd come to be here.

She had no idea if Amma was also asleep—the house had grown so silent. Someone passing through the lane in the chill night air sang out in a shivering voice:

For you, darling, I was needlessly disgraced . . .

Would this night ever end? 'Abba, how are you spending your nights in jail?' She clutched her knees to her stomach anxiously. From somewhere far off came the sound of the bell striking eleven.

A light rain began to fall. Gusting drops blew against the shutters, thrumming a faint melody.

What would life be like now? She was frightened at the thought. It was so dark in the room. She felt as though her question was similarly shrouded in darkness as she closed her eyes fearfully. Sleep was still far off, but memories of the past settled in to help her pass the night.

2

The new district had looked quite bleak. Red-brick houses were arranged in no particular order, as though someone had just picked them up and scattered them about. But there had been so many temples for such a small place! The golden spires lifted their heads as though praying to God. The faint sounds of priests singing hymns and ringing bells could be heard in the house from morning till evening.

And there had been so many trees there. Both sides of the dusty dirt roads were lined with dense mango, jamun and pipal trees. Wayfarers would spread their turban cloths out in the shade of those trees, lay their heads on their travelling bundles, and sleep soundly. It had been spring then. The mango flowers had already blossomed. The cuckoos sang all day.

When Abba had been transferred to that new place she had found it so lonely and sad, yet it was there that her intellect had awoken and she had developed a new-found capacity for thinking and understanding.

Large bundles of their belongings had been left all about the courtyard on the day they moved into the new house, and Abba started opening these with the help of the chaprasi he had been assigned from the division. Amma seemed totally disconnected from the house and the luggage, but all the same she kept walking about the house, gazing at the high-arched veranda, the rooms, the bathroom and so on. Aliya's elder sister, Tehmina, went about picking up small items with downcast eyes and placing them in various rooms. Amma lay half-reclining on an easy chair, a look of distinct displeasure on her face. Aliya's cousin Safdar squatted under the arch of the veranda, his weak shoulders sagging.

'You help your uncle too,' Amma had said, gazing over at Safdar scornfully.

'Leave him be, he's still weak from the fever, and he's also tired from the journey,' Abba had said softly.

'That one is always tired,' grumbled Amma, and she angrily began to help Abba open the bundles. Tehmina glanced nervously at Safdar, and then gazed down again with a frightened look.

That day it had seemed to Aliya that the atmosphere of the house was terribly strained. The grimaces on everyone's faces upset her all the more. She missed their old place.

There, all the officers' yellow bungalows had been built in a row, and there had been a mango orchard close by, as well as a small pond, where children and buffalo bathed together. There had been many girls and boys her age to play games with all day long. And when there was nothing else to do, they would throw mud balls at the buffalo. They'd slip into the garden and steal small unripe mangoes, and when they were caught in the act, the groundsman wouldn't scold them at all, instead picking up fruit that had fallen on the ground and giving it to the children himself.

'You are our masters' children,' he'd say affectionately, patting their heads. Kamala and Usha would make faces at him, taunting him for his large teeth, but he never got angry.

At night, Aliya would demand that the cook, Khansaman Bua, tell her stories, such as the tale of the prince and the princess who slept in the same bed with a sword lying between them. This story always worried her greatly. What if the prince or the princess shifted in their sleep and someone got cut? 'Sweetheart, people in stories don't get cut,' Khansaman Bua would explain to her, but that did nothing to lessen her anxiety. As she herself was falling asleep she dared not move at all. Who knew if that sword might have made its way into her own bed?

Khansaman Bua told her many amusing tales, such as the story of Raja Bhoj and Gangu Teli, and the tale of the puppet that ate up everything in the king's palace. The puppet's story was so entertaining. When the king received word of the puppet's evil deeds, the news was sung very sweetly:

That wooden puppet, oh, king, she's gone and devoured all the horses!

'Khansaman Bua, when they sang that to the king, didn't he get angry?' she would ask with astonishment.

'No, dear, kingly folk have very delicate temperaments, you must tell them everything nicely. Otherwise they might throw you and your whole family into the oil press.' And when Aliya felt scared, Khansaman Bua would hold her to her chest, sticky with sweat.

The only connection she had with Amma was that she'd hug her when she came inside from playing. Amma would speak affectionately to her and tell her to go play again. Abba she saw only from a distance. He went to the office in the morning, and in the evening the sitting room would fill with his friends. They all talked and laughed loudly, and Khansaman Bua would make them cup after cup of tea.

After Aliya was enrolled in school, her world became broader. Several of her girlfriends had also started school and she made friends with new girls as well. When she came home after school, Safdar would call her to him, ask her questions about her studies, and laugh heartily at her every response— 'Oh my, you know absolutely nothing!' he would tease. She didn't like it one bit and would attempt to run away from him as soon as possible.

When she entered class five, she began to play more refined games on the advice of Khansaman Bua. A large doll's house was built in one corner of the yard, where the dolls would get married and wedding processions would depart with great fanfare. The dolls would have babies, and she would stitch them clothing from piles of scraps Tehmina had given her. Khansaman Bua always served sweets on special occasions, such as weddings and births. Sometimes she would even make zardah. On such days, Kamla, Usha and Radha would not observe the rules of untouchability and openly consume the sweet rice.

But here there was nothing. She walked outside and looked all around: some shepherds drove their goats along and a handful of naked children sat playing in the dirt. She could see two small mud huts. There was only one two-storey house near theirs, and the chaprasi's yellow mud hut. She stared for a long time at the tall two-storey house but she saw no girls that she could make friends with. A man came out and walked quickly down the steps, holding up the hem of his brilliantly white dhoti, and strode away. After that she could hear someone singing and playing a harmonium from the upper storey. She repeated the verses of the song to herself but found them boring.

Birds twittered loudly from the trees. She went and sat dully in the doorway to the sitting room. She felt like sobbing loudly, tearing at her clothes and running away.

'Sweetie, come over here to me!' The wife of the chaprasi was leaning over the low mud wall surrounding the yard, calling out to her.

'Humph!' she said, and went back inside.

Quite a bit of their luggage had been put away by now. The easy chairs had been set out in the courtyard and the chaprasi had made tea. Tehmina, Safdar, Abba and Amma were all sitting around silently, looking tired. No one said anything to her. There was a small henna plant in the middle of the yard with leaves that were turning bright green. She filled a pot with some water and began pouring it over the plant.

'Drink some tea, Aliya.' Safdar spoke to her so affectionately for the first time that day that she went over and sat down on the chair next to him.

'You feel anxious, Aliya, it's a new place, and you don't even have anyone to play with.' She burst into tears when Safdar patted her on the head. He was the only one who understood how she felt. She leant over and lay across his lap.

When Amma looked over at her sternly, she closed her eyes to protect herself. Amma began ordering the chaprasi around in a harsh tone: 'Your responsibilities are outside the house. You can't do any inside work. Arrange for a maid for us right away, but make sure that she isn't young; such women don't do a bit of work.'

'As you wish, ma'am. It will be arranged by tomorrow.'

Evening was falling and Abba picked up his thin cane to go outside for a walk. Amma stared once at Safdar from the corner of her eyes. 'Go now, play,' Amma said mechanically, as she grabbed Aliya's hand and lifted her up. Aliya went back outside to the doorway and stood there. Smoke rose from the upper storey of the house across the way. She could hear the clanging of temple bells.

'Humph! Play? Play with whom! Who is there here in this jungle?' She felt overwhelmed with grief. 'She's telling me to stay in the house or sit in this doorway and play,' she muttered. On top of that, everyone else was sitting inside, looking grumpy. She began to choke up.

'Come, sweetie, have some chapati.' The chaprasi's wife leant over the wall again. Aliya quickly wiped away her tears and turned her face away.

'Aliya.' Tehmina had come to stand behind her, her huge eyes downcast. 'Come inside, it's getting dark now. My, what a beautiful place this is, isn't it?' She sighed deeply and looked far off, then wrapped Aliya's arm around her waist and brought her inside. As they passed by the small room near the sitting room, she stopped for a moment and stood still. Safdar was hunched over a book spread out on the table, reading near the lantern.

The beds had been set up in a row in the courtyard. Tehmina's bed was next to the henna plant, and Aliya's was next to that. She lay down silently on her bed. The moon was rising. The sky was still light, but she could see Tehmina's face even more clearly than the sky in the faint darkness of the yard. She had realized for the first time that day that Tehmina was distracted all the time. At that moment too, she sat on her bed tearing up the leaves of the henna plant and scattering them about in a preoccupied manner.

The wick of the lantern beneath the arch of the veranda was set very low. The chaprasi was cooking in the kitchen. Amma walked from room to room with the other lantern held high.

'When you enter school, you'll make friends with many girls.' Tehmina turned towards Aliya and reached out to hold her hand, caressing it softly. But Aliya was too upset for Tehmina's affection to make any difference. She pulled her hand back and looked away. Then she began to watch the birds flying in the sky and, somehow, she didn't even notice that she had drifted off to sleep.

'Oh my, Aliya, you went to sleep without any dinner?' Aliya started and opened her eyes. Safdar was leaning over her.

'Why did you need to wake her?' Amma spoke in the same tone she used to scold the chaprasi. Safdar was about to walk away when Aliya grabbed his hand, leant over and wrapped herself around his legs. He glanced over at Amma a few times, then sat down and laid Aliya's head in his lap.

'Tell me a story, Safdar—there's not even any Khansaman Bua here,' she said tearfully.

'What story do you want to hear?'

'That one about the princess whose father puts her in a palanquin and sends her off to the jungle.' She requested the story without caring what Amma might think. Tehmina sat up on her bed respectfully.

'I'll tell you a different story. It's about a poor boy who loves a princess. Yes, so listen, there once was a boy . . .'

Tehmina looked around nervously.

The rain had grown stronger. The wind seemed to knock at the door. Chammi was mumbling in her sleep. Aliya hid her face in the quilt as all different insignificant details came back to her . . .

Safdar looked so handsome, but so meek. Amma's extreme hatred was the cause of that meekness. Abba loved him every bit as much as Amma hated him. He was always considerate of even his smallest needs. Tehmina did not speak to Safdar, but she looked after him secretly as well. Amma was very upset that Safdar's education was being paid for out of her husband's money, and that despite earning an FA degree, all he did was lie around comfortably, reading frivolous books, with no thought of earning a living. She was always enraged at him. 'How will he make a living off those books?' she'd cry. 'This wretch won't leave until he's ruined me.'

This was when Aliya had also started hearing a new name: 'Najma Aunty'—Abba's youngest sister, who studied at Aligarh College and lived there in the hostel. During the holidays she would visit her eldest brother's home. Najma Aunty loathed Amma, and whenever Amma thought of her, the snake of her hatred hissed loudly. Though Najma Aunty was far from Amma's sight, Safdar was always right before her, and Amma did not know how to get rid of him.

Amma was totally absorbed in her troubles, and Abba was lost in his own world. When he came home from the office, he'd spend only half an hour or so there. Amma would quarrel over something or other and Abba would immediately leave the house; but he had all sorts of friends who came by to have animated discussions with him.

One time, Aliya had tried to listen to what Abba was saying but she couldn't understand a thing besides words like 'freedom', 'Gandhi' and 'Azad'. She grew bored and moved away from the door. Safdar was quite interested in such things himself, and he'd sit and listen with his head bowed for hours. She'd stand behind the door and try by gestures to get Safdar's attention, but to no avail. This would make her peeved with him. After all, Safdar was the only one who could cheer her up in those days.

She was quite familiar with Safdar's story, as Amma liked to tell it frequently in a particularly haughty tone. One day, when she and Tehmina were sitting by Amma, Amma brought up the tale yet again:

'Your cousin Safdar's father was low-born—he was the son of a poor farmer. His father and grandfather worked on your grandfather's lands, and they also performed chores for your grandfather's household, like servants. Somehow these two wretches got into your grandmother's good graces to the extent that no one even kept purdah from them in the house. And your grandmother's temper was famous throughout the village. She was so severe when she got angry with a servant, she'd get a twisted rope and practically flay them alive. Oh my, what pride she had! What dignity! Everyone shuddered with fear in her presence, but she always addressed your cousin Safdar's father and grandfather with kindness. That was what your grandmother was like—yet she spoke harshly to her own husband. May God have mercy on the deceased, but he did put your grandmother through much hardship too. He had two mistresses, who had three sons. Your grandfather built separate homes for his mistresses, but they didn't have permission to enter your grandmother's mansion. Yes, their children would come into the house, and your grandmother would call them by their names, adding "*haraami*", or bastard, at the end. But in those days it wasn't considered such a bad thing to keep mistresses, so your grandmother put up with all that. The mistresses only increased her prestige as the legitimate wife. All the work of managing the lands was entrusted to her as well, and she would have all the food and drink for the mistresses divided in front of her, then sent over to their homes.

Your grandmother also arranged all the marriages herself. She arranged the marriages of your father and uncles according to her wishes. She kept the daughters-in-law firmly under her thumb, but she was never cruel to me. I, like her, was the daughter of an important family; my brother was studying in England. And I commanded just as much respect as your grandmother. Your two older uncles' wives wouldn't say a peep before her. If ever your grandmother bowed before anyone, it was your youngest uncle. When the Khilafat Movement was going on, he travelled to Turkey. After that, no one knew what happened to him. Nonetheless your grandmother never shed a tear before anyone. She didn't sigh once in remembrance of her son lest her dignity be diminished. But Allah had something else in store, as your aunt Salma, when she was fourteen, blackened your grandmother's face. Your grandmother one day witnessed Salma Aunty with her own eyes, holding Safdar's father's hand, and whispering. That day she locked Salma Aunty up in her room and beat her black and blue. When I sat down to rub a turmeric poultice on her body, I trembled. All the same, this punishment was much too small for your Salma Aunty. She should have been buried alive.

'The next day, she turned Safdar's father and grandfather off the lands and called the Chamars and ordered them to beat them with shoes before everyone and throw them out of the village. That same day, in the evening, the barber's wife came to call, wondering what terrible deed Safdar's father and grandfather had committed to be beaten with shoes in front of everyone—the two of them had even left the village! When she heard the news, your grandmother puffed up with such pride that everyone trembled before her, but your Salma Aunty might as well have been dead. After all this happened, she stopped dressing properly and never touched a comb to her hair. Your grandmother kept her under watch at all times.

'One day I saw your Salma Aunty in a very strange state. It was wintertime and she had gone out on the roof to sit in the sun. A pigeon sat near her on the roof cooing, and Salma was saying to it, "Oh, pigeon! You carry messages for princesses; have mercy on my plight and carry a message of mine as well. Tell him that Salma trembles in his absence."

'The pigeon just fluttered off, but I informed your grandmother of Salma's shameless words. She patted my head affectionately and told me to make sure the other daughters-in-law didn't hear about such things. But everyone did find out—God only knows whether that was an ordinary pigeon or a jinn.

'That day, your grandfather went out of town somewhere and said he'd stay the night at a guest house. Before going to sleep that night, your grandmother locked the house up completely and hid the keys under her pillow. But when her eyes opened in the morning, both the bunch of keys and your Salma Aunty were missing. Your grandmother was dumbstruck. She glared at everyone as though to say, "If you say one word, I'll bury you alive. I'll set the dogs on you." The next evening, when your grandfather returned, she spoke to him for a long time behind closed doors. When he came out his face was red with shame and anger.'

At this point in her tale, Amma remarked regretfully, 'If only Salma had been my daughter! I would have fed her poison with my own hands right away!

'Who knows what your grandfather would have done next, but your father had come that very day on leave, and he shamelessly quarrelled with his father on Salma's behalf. My modesty was greatly offended. If only I hadn't been married to your father. Your grandmother paced about angrily, but to shield your father from humiliation, she said nothing. And who knows what happened to your grandfather—he immediately had his mistresses turned out of their homes and ordered that they leave the village. When your grandmother found out, she demanded that only the mistresses go, but not their children, as they were her husband's flesh and blood.

'All three of the mistresses' sons came to the house. My God, the sight of their faces disgusted me so! The two younger boys were so greedy that during the monsoon they sucked fruit from discarded mango pits contaminated by flies and died of cholera. Thank God they died, otherwise who knows, your father might have taken a liking to them and paid for their college education.

'Salma ran off and eloped. Your grandfather did nothing openly, for fear of your father's threats, but he made sure that Salma's husband was fired from every job he took. He and Salma were starving to death. The truth is that they should have starved like dogs but your father let them die like humans. When Safdar was born, Salma came down with tuberculosis and passed away after much suffering a few days later.

'When your grandmother heard news of Salma Aunty's death, she somehow lost her own sense of shame. She beat her breast and fell to weeping at the death of her shameless daughter. I, on the other hand—I swear to God, not a tear fell from my eyes. I was staring at your grandmother in astonishment—she was sobbing and rolling around on the ground right in front of the servants! That very moment she wired all three of her sons. Your father and eldest uncle came running at the death of their disgraceful sister, but your middle uncle maintained the honour of all. He refused to come home just for the death of that wretch.

'Your grandmother wept and wailed and then fell silent, but I no longer felt even one shred of respect for her, though I was forced to remain silent. Your father and eldest uncle went to the village where Salma lived, and when your father returned, he was carrying your vile cousin Safdar.

'Salma hadn't been dead forty days when your grandfather went to meet his Maker as well while prostrate in prayer. The whole house was being ruined right before our very eyes. None of the three sons liked living in that village, so they sold off the lands immediately to a nawab and returned to their jobs. If that property still existed, today I would be mistress in place of your grandmother, but such was not written in my fate. Now your grandmother is ailing, living off scraps from her eldest son, and the evil root from this whole crisis is ruining my life—it's so awful!'

Whenever Amma told Tehmina this story she watched her closely, and Tehmina would look frightened and glance away. Amma wouldn't say anything to Tehmina but she would instruct Aliya, 'My darling, please do not spend too much time with that disgusting boy. His father and grandfather stole my kingdom from me.'

This admonition of Amma's had absolutely no effect on Aliya. Instead it made her angry that Amma was always enraged at Safdar when he was so nice.

One day she even wanted to complain about Amma to Safdar, but when she went to him she couldn't bring herself to say anything.

'Safdar, *I* like you very much,' she began.

'Ah, then who is it that dislikes me?'

'No one!'

And she ran quickly away.

03

Someone was rattling the chain on the door downstairs. She peeped out from under the quilt. The room was completely dark. She could hear her aunt's voice.

'It's these horrible poets, why do these people leave their homes so late at night when it's cold?'

It was thundering outside, and she couldn't hear anything more.

'By Allah,' she thought, as she turned over restlessly, 'I wish I could fall asleep!'

4

The canvas easy chairs had been arranged with a small table covered by a cloth embroidered by Tehmina. The maid was setting the tea things out on the table, while Amma delivered an endless stream of instructions.

Tehmina sprinkled water on the little henna plant, then came and sat near Amma. Safdar sat on the seat next to Abba. Aliya stood near Abba as well, but no one was paying any attention to her. They were all out of sorts. She placed her hand on Abba's several times, but all he did was smile. Amma was staring hard at Safdar.

Tehmina drank her tea quickly as though she had some urgent business to attend to. But Aliya's tea just sat there growing cold. She was so angry, she hadn't even touched the cup. She felt extremely irritable. What kind of a home was this, where everyone just sat around looking angry? She wished they hadn't come to this place. Since coming here, all she'd seen were angry faces, she thought. Now she felt more upset with everyone. She walked away from Abba and started to tear leaves off the henna plant.

'Don't you want any tea, dear?' asked Abba.

She remained silent, radiating displeasure. She wanted to scream loudly, 'I won't drink it, what does anyone care if it goes cold, anyway?'

'Why are you making a fuss?' asked Amma sternly.

Aliya got up and followed Tehmina who was walking quickly towards her room.

'Everyone here just frowns all the time!' she complained sadly. 'There aren't even any girls here for me to play with and have fun.'

'Oh, my, Aliya, you're getting so big and you can't even tell when there's a fight going on in the house. That's why everyone is sitting there silently. Amma and Abba had an argument this afternoon.' That day for the first time Tehmina considered Aliya old enough to discuss things frankly.

'Why did they argue?'

'Oh, it's just that Amma hates Safdar. As long as he stays in this house the fights will never end.'

In the semi-darkness of the room, Tehmina sat Aliya down by her side and began to whisper to her: 'When Safdar was studying in class four—I was very small, but I remember everything—one time, Amma beat him very badly. When Abba found out, he was very angry with her and went away to Thakur Sahib's house. Thakur Sahib managed to reason with Abba somehow and sent him back home. Ever since then Amma has hated Safdar even more. How shameless he is! Safdar won't leave, even though he could earn money now. I remember well the servant lady would give Safdar spoilt leftover food in the summer on Amma's instructions. And she mixed tons of water into the small amount of milk she gave him to drink, and cut the scraps from the meat and

ground it up and made him keema out of that. But Safdar
never complained to Abba. One day, for some reason, Abba
sat down to examine Safdar's food. After that he began to
have Safdar eat by his side. But even so, Safdar has always
been in poor health.'

'What? Scraps are fed to dogs! Remember our little dog,
Tommy, Tehmina? How we used to boil the scraps and
give them to him?' Aliya said this just for the sake of it, but
Tehmina began to sob and Aliya was so astonished that she
stopped speaking.

'Don't talk to Safdar too much,' said Tehmina quickly,
wiping away her tears, and then she began to laugh.

Aliya paid Tehmina's instructions no mind, and went
outside. Everyone was still sitting there listlessly, as before;
the sound of the call to prayer came from somewhere far off.

'Safdar, should we go out for a walk?' she asked, without
looking at Amma, but Safdar remained totally silent.

'Get her enrolled in school now, otherwise she's just going
to wander around idly like this,' observed Amma tartly.

'I'll find out about it; I've heard there's only a mission
high school here, and only English is taught there, and it's
a mission school for teaching their religion. I'm strongly
opposed to such schools run by the English. They take as
much advantage of our slavery as they can.'

'You're just against the English—you'll work for them
but you won't let your daughter study in their schools! Only
your sister and your nephew are allowed to study in this
family! One of your daughters was only allowed to study
up to class ten and now she just sits around the house—and
this one's ruined her with all the absurd books of stories

and tales he's given her. And now you want to sacrifice the other one to your hatred for the English!' Amma was furious.

Aliya glanced anxiously over at Safdar. He was the one who had given Tehmina those books. Safdar looked flustered and rushed off to his room, and Abba leant back in his chair and closed his eyes. He looked so wounded at that moment.

Aliya went outside, fearing a fight. There were two easy chairs on the terrace in front of the sitting room. She sat on one and began to swing her legs. She could hear someone singing a hymn to Krishna and playing the harmonium in the two-storey house:

> *Oh, where has my Shyam gone, will nobody tell me?*
> *I searched all of Kashi, I searched Brindavan*
> *It's evening now in Gokul*
> *Oh, where has my Shyam gone, will nobody tell me?*

Aliya quietly repeated the verses to herself. She really liked to sing, but she never even mentioned it for fear of Amma. She'd always heard Amma say that girls from respectable homes did not sing.

Evening began to fall as she sat on the terrace. The temple bells were ringing and flocks of birds chirruped loudly in the trees as they settled down for the night. A herd of goats stirred up clouds of dust as it passed by on the dirt road outside. She tried to count the goats but it wasn't any fun. She was too upset after witnessing the quarrel in the house.

'Come inside, Aliya, night is falling.' Safdar came and pulled her up, and she hugged him and began to cry.

'When you start school you'll feel much better.' He held her tightly to his chest with an almost fatherly affection.

The maid was wandering about, lantern in hand, doing something or other. Amma and Abba were still sitting there angrily.

'Did you take a walk?' asked Amma sternly, and without waiting for Aliya's answer, she addressed Abba: 'I'm telling you, you should enrol her in school right away. I plan to have all my hopes fulfilled in this girl. You set your hopes in your sister and your nephew.'

'Safdar, son, please go to your room,' said Abba gently, and when Safdar had gone off to his room, Abba turned to her angrily. 'I loathe mission schools—I will not send her there, better for her to remain ignorant.'

'We'll see about that; we'll see whether she remains ignorant or whether she studies! You just hate the English for the sake of it—you always punch holes in the plate you eat from!'

Amma's tone was so bitingly sarcastic that Abba leapt from his chair.

'All I have to say to you is this: Why did you send my money to your brother without my permission? Now I have no way of helping my children and I'm forced to work at this job. If you hadn't hidden that money I could have started a business with it.'

'What money?' whimpered Amma.

'My share of what came from the sale of the land.'

'Oh, fine! That money is for Aliya and Tehmina; why would I keep it here? So you could use it for your sister and nephew? I'm not such a fool any more,' Amma said with a laugh.

'I'll sue your brother.'

'You do know that my brother's wife is English,' said Amma, raising her head proudly.

'Yes, I do know that—your brother was just wandering about, poor thing, but after bringing home an English wife he certainly rose in the ranks.' Abba spoke so angrily it sounded like he was cursing.

'You've been working at a job for nearly fifteen years but you still haven't risen in the ranks, so of course you're jealous,' replied Amma scornfully.

'My God!' Abba turned away angrily, then picked up his walking stick from the corner of the veranda and went outside. Amma covered her face with the edge of her dupatta and began crying softly. When Tehmina came and tried to calm her, she wiped away her tears.

'I've saved up that money for you two sisters so that it won't get wasted on Safdar and Najma,' said Amma tearfully, and she sighed deeply.

Right at that moment, Aliya felt as though Safdar was some kind of ghost that would eat up everything in the house. Suddenly, she felt very sorry for Amma. She wanted to go and hug her, but she felt too anxious and went and lay down on her bed.

The full moon had risen, and she could hear the faint sounds of someone singing to the harmonium:

If I had known I would be separated from my beloved
I would have set fire to my veil

She fell asleep listening to that song. As she slept, she felt at one point as though someone were trying to wake her up, but she didn't get up. Who knows if anyone even ate dinner that night.

Abba's sitting room began to fill with visitors within just a few days of their moving in. The Hindu family from the two-storey house across the way began to visit, including Kusum and her father, Ray Sahib; Amma was endlessly enraged.

'These people are useless. They have absolutely nothing at all to do in the world. The daughter sings day and night and the father goes about talking politics.'

Amma did not like Kusum one bit. The greatest cause for Amma's hatred was that her father was against the British Raj, and on top of that, they were Hindus, and also, his widowed daughter, Kusum, sang and played an instrument all the time.

Amma had absolutely no sympathy for Kusum, even though Kusum had told her the whole tale of her misfortunes on the very second meeting: 'I was fourteen or fifteen years old at that time. I'd been married only three months. In those days he had been transferred to Amritsar. The day he went to take part in the rally at Jallianwala Bagh, my mother- and father-in-law tried their best to stop him, but he just laughed at them. I went mad listening to what they said to him, but I was too shy to say anything. I just watched from beneath my veil as his feet walked away. He used to say, "I love you very much." But he never asked me before he left what I wanted him to do. He was laughing as he walked away, and he never turned back. I wore myself out waiting for him to return. When people learnt I was a widow they all avoided me. But for some reason, I still don't consider myself a widow. Am I a widow, Aunty?' Kusum asked, looking at Amma, and then, for some reason, she began staring at the ceiling. Amma pulled the paandaan over, and then Aliya hugged Kusum, though she didn't know why.

'If he had loved me, he would never have gone, but he only loved his country. Now what should I do with my love? He never thought about how I would feel—that I have a heart too,' Kusum lamented, and she hid her face in the edge of her sari. Amma looked away, perhaps shocked at Kusum's shamelessness.

The first time Kusum had come to their house, Aliya felt as though a fairy had suddenly appeared before her—straight out of the stories. She'd been sitting on the front terrace, fed up with the household. Safdar had taken her that day to get enrolled in school, after a fierce battle. It was perhaps the first time Safdar had done anything against Abba's wishes, but Abba had not reprimanded him at all, instead he had just ignored Amma. Whenever she spoke to him, Abba looked away.

Kusum had walked down the steps of her two-storey house and come to stand before them. Her tiny pale feet looked like two bits of moon, and her wide, haunted eyes revealed an obsessive nature. She smiled sweetly as she held Aliya's hand affectionately.

'I am Ray Sahib's daughter, I've come to meet your mother,' she said softly, and Aliya recalled the fairy-tale princess whose mouth blossoms with flowers whenever she speaks.

Tehmina and Kusum became such close friends that the two of them would talk in the room for hours about all sorts of things. Amma would wander about enraged the entire time, and after Kusum returned home, Amma was always sure to have something negative to say.

'What a terrible tradition those wretched Kaffirs have of not remarrying. Keeping young women locked up—it's like torture! Oh yes, we know how these young widows sweeten their pots with sugar.'

Tehmina would listen to everything Amma said with her head down, but Aliya didn't like it one bit, and anyway, Kusum had also secretly started to teach her the harmonium.

'Kusum hardly eats sugar that she would use it to sweeten a pot, she hates sugar!' she shrieked angrily and Amma burst out laughing. That day Aliya didn't even talk to Tehmina. 'What's the use of your silence? You don't even speak up for your friend. After all, you're the big sister,' she muttered secretly to herself.

6

That evening, a fierce dust storm blew in and clouds gathered in the sky. It must have been the end of June. The night was shrouded in dense clouds and occasionally a light rain fell. Amma and Abba were asleep in their room. Aliya slept with Tehmina on the veranda. At times the wind was so fierce the rain blew in as far as the foot of the bed, and Aliya would open her eyes for a moment. At one point, she opened her eyes and found that Tehmina was not in her bed. There was a faint rumble of thunder. She felt afraid, but Tehmina returned in just a few moments. She was not alone, however—Safdar was with her. Aliya was astonished: was Tehmina talking to Safdar in the middle of the night? Was she that afraid to speak with him in front of Amma?

Tehmina crept along softly, and when she was about to get into bed, Safdar hugged her. Then he stayed bent down over her face. Aliya held her breath in astonishment, as she recollected the story of Salma Aunty. It all felt so strange to her.

In the morning, when Tehmina was getting her ready to go to school, Aliya asked softly, 'Tehmina, where did you go last night?'

'What?' Tehmina's lips went blue with fear.

'I won't tell Amma anything, of course not,' she reassured her—just like a grown-up lady—and Tehmina hugged her, her whole body trembling.

'If you told Amma, who knows what she would do, even worse than what happened with Salma Aunty. Aliya, it's just that I like Safdar, that's all it is.'

'I like him too, and of course I won't tell Amma—she might get the chaprasi to beat him with shoes . . .'

Tehmina quickly covered her mouth with her hand. Her face had turned turmeric-yellow. 'I will chase him away,' she said.

'That's a good idea.'

Safdar was waiting for her on the veranda. She went to school with him, but she didn't enjoy herself there either. Safdar had said that if she went to school she'd feel better, but she was getting older now. Everything was bothering her—she kept thinking about what had occurred the night before, and was so fearful of what might happen she couldn't read a single word.

7

The school headmistress had said she would visit Aliya's home that day. Amma and Tehmina spent the whole day sprucing up the house. They even swept away the spiderwebs hanging from the walls. Safdar brought marigolds and *gul-e-abbasi*s and arranged them in blue vases. The maid filled the buckets, washed the yard and set up the easy chairs and table near the henna plant. Tehmina's most beautiful embroidered tablecloth covered the table. The new Japanese tea set was taken out. That set was only brought out at times when very special guests were expected. Fried snacks were prepared to go with the tea. Amma seemed exceptionally happy and busy that day. That afternoon she neither rested nor let the maid rest her back.

'Well, well, I must say; she's English and she said she was coming over to our house,' Amma kept repeating joyfully to Tehmina. Aliya had the impression that every time Amma said that, Safdar had to screw up his mouth to keep himself from smiling.

'What I think is that not many people should take part in tea. She's English, so she might not like it,' said Amma at four o'clock, when it was nearly time. She raised her eyebrows as she expressed what she felt was common sense. Safdar immediately went into his room.

At exactly four o'clock, Mrs Howard arrived. Amma and Tehmina welcomed her. Mrs Howard's round blue eyes looked like marbles as they rolled about evaluating the house. The moment she sat down on her chair, she began to speak rapidly in her broken Urdu.

'I'm verry plaised to meet you all, you have a lovely home. Verry clean. Other peoples here keep their home quiet filthy. Even prominent ladies don't keep his home clean. I'll chertainly come to visit you again,' she said.

'Yes! The people of this country are quite filthy. My sister-in-law—my brother's wife—is English,' Amma remarked with pride.

'Really!' The two glass marbles looked as though they might crack from astonishment.

Mrs Howard's deep blue eyes looked so lovely to Aliya. In school, when she went into her office, she would secretly stare at them.

'Women here raise chickens, and they're just so filthy.'

Who knows what else Amma would have said, but Tehmina interrupted.

'Please have some tea.'

Tehmina had grown listless ever since Safdar had gone into his room after Amma's hints. Suddenly signs of fatigue had appeared on her face.

'Yes, yes, Tehmina dear, do tell the maid.' Amma was startled at the mention of tea. Her face went white. As Abba had been leaving for his office, Amma had reminded him several times to come home by teatime so he could please Mrs Howard by speaking with her in English.

'Aliya, does you want to sit by me?' Mrs Howard looked at Aliya kindly, and Aliya slipped away from Tehmina and went to sit by her, but just then the teacups were filled and she quickly stood and picked up a cup. Amma stared at her but she rushed off to Safdar's room.

Safdar was lying in his room, face down, lost in thought. How quickly evening fell inside their rooms! His room was already cloaked in darkness.

'Safdar, tea,' she said. She placed the cup on the table.

'Oh my,' he said, sitting up. 'Aliya, you drink with me as well.'

'No! I have to drink my tea with Mrs Howard.'

She came back outside. Mrs Howard was gobbling down the shami kebabs, her eyes watering from the chillies.

"Your girl is very clever, she study lots,' said Mrs Howard praising Aliya. Aliya felt embarrassed.

'Yes, our daughter is very clever, and anyway the girls around here are quite idiotic; they flee at the mere mention of studying. Indian people are happy to keep their daughters ignorant.' Amma was on a roll again.

'*Idio tick*?' asked Mrs Howard, confused by the Urdu word.

'Exactly.'

'And how much has your elder daughter studied?' asked Mrs Howard smiling.

'Till class ten, then she fell ill,' said Amma.

Tehmina had been silent this whole time. She had not said one word to Mrs Howard. Dusk had fallen. Lines of birds flew off to their nests. Mrs Howard started and stood up.

'Your husband hasn't come. I was so hoping to met him. He must have gone somewhere for work?'

'Yes, yes, a friend of his died today, so he must have gone to his home.'

What better excuse could Amma have made than this? There could only be a serious reason for not being able to take tea with an Englishwoman.

As soon as Mrs Howard left, Amma blew up. 'Did you see? He didn't come home for tea. Thank God I came up with a good excuse, isn't it? Otherwise what would Mrs Howard have thought? Just watch! He'll end up acting on his hatred one of these days. I'd like to know who could be a better ruler than the English! Our people are the sort to slit one another's throats—but who will ever make that man listen to reason?'

'He must have had some work to do,' Tehmina suggested on Abba's behalf.

'Work?' Amma boiled over. 'I doubt he had any work to do. Really, that man . . .'

Who knows what else Amma would have said—Aliya rushed off to see Safdar. The cup of tea still sat on the table and had grown cold. Safdar looked odd in the yellowish light of the lantern.

'Safdar, you didn't drink your tea?'

'Oh my, didn't I drink it?' He picked up the cup and drank it down like water.

'I'm not talking to you, what's the point of drinking it now?' As she left the room, Safdar called out to her but she didn't reply.

When it had grown quite dark, the maid pushed aside the table and chairs and set up the beds. She was exhausted and her eyes were half-closed from opium intoxication. Her only cure for every illness was opium; as soon as she swallowed those tiny black pills she forgot all her troubles. Her exhaustion would disappear and she would fall asleep with the grandeur of a queen.

After the maid had set up the beds and gone into the kitchen, Abba came home. Amma flew into a rage the moment she saw him. 'Oh, so now you've come, Exalted Master! Of course she'll figure out you didn't like her coming here. There's a limit, I must say! She's English and came to our home, and the gentleman of the house doesn't even care. If she reports that Your Excellency behaved rudely to her, maybe you'll come to your senses.' Amma slammed the lid of the paandaan shut so loudly she frightened the maid, who came running out of the kitchen.

'Those days are gone when people trembled at the mere mention of the English; even if I can't do anything about them, I can at least hate them!' retorted Abba harshly. 'Forget these godawful businessmen, these rulers! I hate them all. If I were like my elder brother, I'd do something, but my hands are tied. I'm forced to do my job.'

'Humph! One thing I do know is that you are hell-bent on making us all die of hunger.'

'That's the exact reason why I'm still working, otherwise I'd run a shop like my elder brother. Oh, but you sent all the money to your brother. "He's a man of great integrity, his wife is English!"'

'I've told you again and again not to speak ill of my brother and sister-in-law!' Amma broke down sobbing.

Tehmina sat on the bed totally silent, her legs hanging down. There were tears in her eyes. Her tears looked so painful in the dingy moonlight.

Go on, cry about everything, fight over everything, I'll just run away from home, Aliya thought to herself with the wisdom of an elder. The fighting and tears caused her very soul to tremble.

She lay face down on her bed and began to sob loudly.

'Now see what you've done, what are you doing to these children? They'll all be ruined and . . .' Abba went into his room to change his clothes. Amma wiped away her tears.

'Maid, bring the food before Aliya falls asleep,' Amma called out.

'I won't eat,' screamed Aliya and she began to cry again.

When dinner came, she felt the soft palms of Abba's hands on her forehead but she pretended to be asleep. Today, she was announcing her annoyance with everyone.

∽

The days continued to pass by. The atmosphere of the home changed like the flickering of sunlight and shade. Abba spent his evenings in the sitting room, where he had loud discussions with his friends. The maid kept on making tea and bringing it out as she muttered softly, and Amma wandered about restlessly, or set about redoing some task that had already been completed. Tehmina was silent all the time and sat reading the same page of a book over and over.

God only knows why Tehmina spoke so infrequently, Aliya wondered. *Does love render people mute? Does love put all speech to death? And if so, why then do people chase after such a wretched thing? Tehmina, you were so innocent.*

Upset by this painful atmosphere at home, Aliya would go and stand in the doorway of the sitting room. Besides the names of Nehru, Jinnah and Gandhi, all she understood was that everyone was speaking ill of the British. She heard nothing interesting, or fun, at all. When he saw her, Abba would order her to go back inside. Safdar would refuse to pick up on her hints. Even he wouldn't hear of leaving the sitting room in the evening.

She'd grow disconsolate and go outside to sit on the terrace and begin to think of their old house. How far off it seemed now. She had sat near the window of the train as they were leaving, and counted so many trees she lost count.

It was the summer month of Jeth now. The scorching loo wind blew. The birds hidden in the mango and pipal trees kicked up a ruckus all day long. The small henna plant in the yard had dried up. The maid poured loads of water on to it but the leaves sagged. On moonlit nights when they could hear Kusum singing and playing her harmonium at Ray Sahib's house, Tehmina would get up and start to pace. In those days Kusum sang the same song over and over.

Amma would grow weary of waiting for Abba and start talking to Tehmina, recounting those same old tales of enmity with Safdar's family, stories of Najma Aunty's self-interestedness, or loving hymns in praise of her brother and sister-in-law. Tehmina would listen to it all, blinking but saying nothing herself. When Abba's sitting room was empty, he'd go off to some friend's home and not return home before ten or eleven at night.

Before going to sleep, Aliya would visit Safdar. His bed was made up outside on the terrace, where he'd be lying quietly, thinking.

'Safdar, please tell me a story,' she'd immediately request when she went to him and leant against him. And Safdar would begin to remember the stories he'd heard as a child, and when he'd recollect a good one, he'd laugh out loud. He'd start every story with a princess and a poor man, and when the poor man was not able to win the hand of the princess, he'd always die of grief.

'Safdar, will you die if you don't marry a princess?' she asked once with great concern.

'Heaven forbid, why would I die, Aliya?' And he laughed so much it annoyed her. The summer vacation was passing by. She was happy that school days were drawing closer. When time passed at school, she felt happy; she could forget the entire world.

That afternoon, when she was sleeping, the sound of Amma talking loudly woke her. Abba's voice was soft but angry. She panicked and went out to the hallway where Tehmina was standing. She couldn't understand what was going on.

A short while later, Ray Sahib's voice came from outside and Abba left. Tehmina had already returned to her room.

'Safdar will marry into our family when my dead body is carried out of this house!' cried Amma as Abba was leaving. He listened for just a moment, then continued on his way.

As soon as Abba went into the sitting room, Amma came and hugged Tehmina.

'Look, he's thinking of marrying you to that low-life Safdar, but I will swallow poison first. Honestly, he must have gone mad! To marry you to a person whose father and grandfather destroyed the honour of our family and stole my glory.' Amma sat down on the bed weeping. 'Now he's sending that good-for-nothing to Aligarh to study for a BA. I'll write to my brother today, then we'll just see if all this comes to pass.'

Aliya was worried what her uncle might do, but then she was encouraged by the thought that Amma was always writing letters to her brother but he only ever answered two or three months later.

'It was shameless of your grandmother to remain living even after Safdar's father became her son-in-law; I would have immediately taken poison.'

'Why are you so upset, nothing's going to happen.' Tehmina spoke as though from the bottom of a well. Her face had gone quite pale.

'Oh, would that our Heavenly Father put an end to the quarrels in our home!' Aliya prayed silently as she went into Safdar's room. This prayer that Miss Mercy had taught her freed her of many sorrows.

As she entered the room she saw that Safdar was crying too. 'Even the Heavenly Father does nothing,' she said, now cross with Him as well. She wept and hugged Safdar.

'Everyone's crying, I wish I could die,' she said sadly.

'But the reason why I'm crying is that I'm going to Aligarh and I'm going to miss my little Aliya.' He laughed as he wiped away his tears. 'Now that you're ten or eleven you're so big,' he chuckled.

'I know everyone is lying.'

Safdar was leaving for Aligarh in only one week.

One week was quickly over, like a setting sun in December, and Aliya was counting the days on her fingers. How sad she felt. She believed that besides Tehmina, only Safdar really cared about her. Tehmina loved her silently, but Safdar was her play companion who told her stories. What would she do if he left?

ক্ষ

Safdar had passed that day shut up in his room. The sky was shaded with clouds in those days and the air was full of dampness.

Amma refused to even look at Safdar's face. Abba had stopped speaking to Amma. He'd begun to openly express his animosity for the British until ten or eleven every night. Tehmina's reading habits had improved a great deal. She would study thoroughly whatever she read. She would sit and stare at the same page for hours.

The atmosphere in the house made Aliya anxious, so she went to sit on the front terrace outside, where the chaprasi sat sucking on his hookah. She began chatting with him.

'What's your salary?'

'Five rupees.'

'Why didn't you build your house out of bricks?'

'Because we're poor, see, we can't very well build a house with bricks like other people.'

She immediately recalled Safdar's father, who couldn't get anyone to respect him in his lifetime. She began to think of that entire story that had been told to Tehmina so many times. Whenever her heart ached, she'd get up and go to Safdar, but he'd forgotten how to talk these days.

The next day, in the morning, Safdar was going to Aligarh. His luggage was all packed. The room felt completely deserted. That day, Amma wandered listlessly about the house. She'd scold the maid at the slightest excuse and kept muttering to herself, 'He's being sent off to college instead of being thrown out of the house, he's paying this dog's tuition with our money. He wants to foist him on us forever—please, God, may he never return!'

In the evening, Abba went into Safdar's room and re-emerged after a very long interval, then went to his sitting room. In the meantime, Amma had been working herself into a rage.

It was a very dark night. There were signs of wind and rain. That night the beds were set up in the veranda. After dinner everyone lay down. They lowered the wick of the lantern in the large alcove.

Before going to sleep, Aliya prayed fervently that the Heavenly Father would stop Safdar, and morning would never come. After this prayer, she went to sleep. At one point in the night, her eyes flicked open for fear of morning. Then she saw Tehmina tiptoeing from Safdar's room. She came and lay down on her own bed, and Aliya could hear the soft sound of her sobbing as she fell back to sleep.

In the morning, Safdar climbed into a tonga and left, but before leaving he went to see Amma. He stood still before her for some time but when Amma would not look at him, he left after taking blessings from the maid.

Aliya went with him as far as the door. When the tonga set out kicking up dust on the dirt road she wrapped herself around Abba's legs and began to weep. It was the first time that she had hugged Abba's legs, and he patted her on the head; otherwise when did Abba ever have the time to show affection to anyone?

In the afternoon, Kusum came and talked quietly with Tehmina. In the evening, after tea, Abba spoke to Amma for the first time in a week.

'After he's done with his BA, that thing is going to happen, understand?'

'We'll see about that,' announced Amma defiantly.

As the days slipped by, memories of Safdar dimmed. Aliya would go to Kusum's after school and practise the song 'Oh, where has my Shyam gone . . .' on the harmonium. She was so happy when she was at Kusum's. She didn't care for the atmosphere in her own home one bit. These days Amma was fretful and irritable all the time, and Tehmina still read with her gaze buried in just one page of a book, or sat with eyes downcast, or helped Amma out around the house. Aliya decided that something else was wrong at their house besides Safdar.

A takht was placed in Safdar's room, covered in a sparkling white sheet. When it was time to eat, this was covered with a tablecloth. Ever since they'd started eating in Safdar's room, Tehmina's diet had grown quite spare.

Safdar had written only one letter since leaving for Aligarh. He'd not written any after that, and when Abba had sent him a money order, he'd returned that as well. That day Abba was very upset but Amma looked thrilled.

She laughed sarcastically and Abba avoided eye contact with her.

'He knows you hate him because of that money,' said Abba, finally forced to speak up.

Amma was beside herself with rage. 'So I am to embrace the son of a low farmer! Don't we have children of our own to spend money on? That good-for-nothing, he's slapped you in the face by returning your money. What does he need you for now? He'll get a BA and live it up. Someone told the truth when they said that true blood never fails, and a low-born is never faithful.'

'So the son of my sister is low-born and your brother's wife isn't! She's probably descended from some sweeper. When your brother married her, he slapped his people across the face. Oh yes indeed, thanks be to God, a British sweeper is also our ruler.'

'If you say anything about my brother and his wife it won't turn out well for you! She knows you well enough, doesn't she? That's why she doesn't give a damn about you, she keeps silent for my sake, else she'd long since have had you thrown in jail!' Amma's voice was tearful.

'That sweeperess would have me thrown in jail?' screamed Abba angrily.

Amma began to weep loudly. Tehmina had gone pale and Aliya cried silently. The older she grew, the more sensitive she became. She loved Abba fiercely, and was increasingly distressed by Amma's cantankerousness, but when she saw her crying she felt agitated. She longed to hide Amma away in her heart.

'Now let your low-born nephew come, if he doesn't get beaten with shoes by a sweeper, my name's not . . .' Amma lashed out at Abba as she wept.

'Certainly he will come, and he'll come directly here in a groom's procession,' declared Abba, before quickly walking outside.

Amma muttered for a long time, 'One day this household will come to a very bad end.'

Aliya went into her room. Tehmina lay face down on the bare bed.

'Aliya, I'm going to write him a letter and tell him never to come here again.' Tehmina lifted her head and looked at Aliya. Her skin looked so sallow.

'But Abba says you'll be married to Safdar?' Aliya asked, as she leant over Tehmina.

'Hah! Amma will never allow the marriage, and I'm very frightened of dishonour, so nothing can happen,' cried Tehmina, her face hidden in her arms. Aliya sat down quietly and stroked her hand.

What bitter thoughts she was thinking right at that moment. Safdar must be having a wonderful time studying, and he wasn't giving them a moment's thought, but everyone here was thinking of him and fighting bitterly. It was all so absurd. Safdar hadn't written Aliya a single letter. Did he even miss Tehmina?

'Don't tell Amma that I'm crying,' said Tehmina, lifting her tear-stained face to look at her.

'When have I ever told Amma anything?' Aliya was annoyed.

Kusum had entered the room so Aliya got up and went out on to the veranda. She knew what sort of things the two of them would discuss now. Even so, everyone hid everything from her, just because she was younger, despite her being fairly old by now. No one even knew the state of her heart. No one even wondered what she might be thinking. No one made any effort to understand her. No one knew that now in school she even prayed to the Heavenly Father to have mercy upon her home.

8

Several autumns and springs came and went, but in Aliya's home, autumn never turned to spring. No matter how Tehmina watered the henna plant in the yard its thirst was never quenched; the thin green branches had turned black. Tehmina had grown thin and weak over those few years. Abba seemed completely detached from the household; after he returned home from the office, his sitting room would fill up, and his voice, full of clear hatred for the British rulers, was the loudest of them all. At such times, Amma would pace restlessly about the yard.

'Oh, what a cursed day it was when I married! All is lost— and what little is left is bound to be lost as well,' she'd say to Tehmina as she paused her pacing. On receiving no answer she'd set to mumbling again.

At least she was to some extent at peace with Safdar now. He had completely disappeared after completing his BA at Aligarh. Try though he might, Abba was unable to learn anything about his whereabouts. Amma was in a great hurry to get Tehmina married off somehow. She felt there was a danger that Safdar's ghost might suddenly reappear.

Whenever the maid finished cooking, Amma would discuss the wedding arrangements with her. Abba no longer took any interest in household matters. When he came to bed at night, he'd pick up a book. If the topic of marriage came up he'd grunt and put it off.

One day, when Amma heard from Kusum that a friend of Abba's had been arrested, she fell to trembling with dread.

'You'll send us all out begging. If anyone arrests you what will happen to us?' Amma whimpered and cried that night.

Abba sat up, agitated. 'I won't do anything myself because of you people, and anyway there's nothing I know how to do, there's just this hatred that cannot be concealed.' Then Amma wept a long time and talked and talked, but Abba spoke not one word.

After the arrest of Abba's friend, Amma became even more anxious about Tehmina's marriage. She had no family herself, besides her brother and his wife, but there were loads of boys in the families of Abba's relatives. Amma had also written a letter in those days to her brother, asking him to arrange Tehmina's marriage. In response, her brother wrote that his wife had said that girls should marry as they chose, so she should introduce Tehmina to boys in the family and marry her to whomever she preferred, and his wife said that they would certainly come for Tehmina's wedding.

Upon reading this, Aliya was aghast but Amma smiled the whole day. She was elated and kept saying, 'Look, how could my poor sister-in-law know that we don't observe such customs here?'

Though Amma was herself so pleased on reading this, she didn't even mention it to Abba, though she did keep after him to arrange Tehmina's marriage. Abba either kept quiet or tried to get out of it by saying she could arrange the marriage with whomever she liked. At this, Amma would settle in for a fight.

'Then why don't you go ahead and say you're not her father! Then I'll go out myself and search for a boy?' she'd cry.

Abba would call out to Tehmina to avoid these conversations, and ask her to come sit by him. Then Amma would have to keep quiet.

Around that time, a letter came from Big Aunty requesting Tehmina's hand for her son Jameel. Such a letter at a time like this seemed a blessing to Amma and she wrote to accept after asking Abba's permission.

That very same day it was Holi. The next day, Kusum brought many tasty treats to their house and when she hugged Tehmina, she smeared her face with Holi colours. Then she rushed over to Aliya, who managed to escape her clutches. Amma burst out laughing when she saw Tehmina's colourful face; perhaps she'd forgotten for just a moment that she considered Holi sinful.

'But, Kusum, you didn't play Holi?' Amma asked.

'I'm a widow, Aunty!' Kusum's smiling face fell.

'Humph!' said Amma, paying close attention to her for perhaps the first time.

'How I wish I could really play with the colours, Aunty, and wear a colourful sari, it's such hard work to restrain myself. But my husband never considered any of this.' Kusum burst into tears.

'Hush, hush, Kusum, it's inauspicious to cry on a festival day,' said Amma, trying to calm her down, and Kusum quickly wiped away her tears and turned to chat with Tehmina.

The next afternoon the maid told Amma, her eyes bulging, that Kusum had run off. Amma's eyes opened wide with astonishment.

'What, did Kusum truly run away?' Aliya was also startled and stared at Amma. There was not the slightest trace of surprise on Tehmina's face, however, as she watered the henna plant, the leaves of which had now turned green.

'Oh, my, Sahib has been shamed; such respected people they were.' The maid beat her brow as she spoke.

'Now she really will play Holi and wear colourful saris; her parents have been shamed, but who cares! Of course, if it were up to me I would bury all elopers alive. Gracious! She turned out just like Salma. Don't go and get remarried, they say— oh, no! Well, they can have their religion, their daughter was singing constantly and no one read the signs.' Amma stared hard at Tehmina as she spoke—'Oh dear, oh dear, if only I'd known, I wouldn't have let my Tehmina spend a single minute in her company.'

'What difference does it make if I spent time in her company or not, Amma?' Tehmina spoke sharply for perhaps the first time in her life.

'God willing, Kusum will be happy in her new home,' Aliya kept praying, and she thought of Salma Aunty as well.

For a few days, Ray Sahib did not even come to Abba's sitting room, and when he did come, he kept telling everyone that Kusum had gone to visit her maternal grandmother, that she'd left in a huff, and that was why he hadn't been going out anywhere because he was feeling gloomy.

Kusum's mother also told Amma, 'Kusum has gone off sulking to her granny's house in Haridwar. Won't I give it to all the rumour-mongers when she comes back!' But when Aliya said the same thing to Tehmina, she blanched. 'God willing, she'll never come back,' she said softly.

After Kusum had eloped Amma's worries only increased. She wanted to marry Tehmina off somehow or other. All day long Amma spoke of cousin Jameel's good looks and many virtues. Aliya would listen with great interest but, for some reason, Tehmina would become extremely involved in housework at such moments. She'd rush about rearranging things all around the house.

'Tehmina, you've seen cousin Jameel, what's he like?' asked Aliya, who was getting extremely curious about her sister's groom-to-be.

'Who knows!' Tehmina burst out laughing at her question. She looked fairly cheerful at that moment. 'But, Aliya, don't you ever miss Safdar?'

'Not a bit! He's turned out to be an extremely heartless man, I only miss those who miss me,' Aliya responded bitterly. 'I only miss my cousin Jameel now.' When she looked at Tehmina mischievously, Tehmina began to laugh heartily.

'Tehmina, I hope you get married after my exams, otherwise all the fun will be spoilt,' said Aliya anxiously. Studying in class nine had made her very earnest.

'There's no way I can get married before your exams, because you're the one who will make me a bride,' responded Tehmina staring at her hard; then she left the room.

9

In those days the leaves of the henna plant were turning a deep shade of green. Tehmina would fill a pot with water in the morning and evening and water the plant. The maid gazed upon Tehmina with great tenderness and laughed. 'Water them well, my daughter, we will need this henna for your hands.' And Tehmina would smile quite shamelessly. What strength did she have left to be embarrassed by anything anyone said? She intently prepared her dowry in front of Amma. The tablecloths and pillowcases she was embroidering were so lovely it made you want to kiss her fingers. Aliya was not being asked to do anything because she was burdened with her class-nine schoolwork. The atmosphere in the house in those days was as cool and calm as a moonlit night. Amma had so forgotten Abba's presence that she didn't even think of quarrelling. The tailors and the goldsmiths rushed to and from the house all day long. Amma's eyes never tired of poring over books of patterns and Aliya happily read to herself.

But oh, my, how short-lived that happiness was! Early one morning, the maid came in and said that Tehmina's friend Kusum had returned.

'Get out, liar!' Amma screamed with astonishment.

'I swear to Allah, Bibiji, she's returned. My sister-in-law saw her herself. There's a man with her and they've rented a house.'

'My God, what shamelessness, first she runs off, then she comes back to rub it in her parents' faces! Really, couldn't she find some other place to live? If she ever tries to come to my house I'll rip off her legs and throw them away!' declared Amma, glancing over at Tehmina. Tehmina's face went turmeric-yellow. She set aside her tablecloth, stood up, and quickly rushed off to her room.

When Aliya went to see her, Tehmina was anxiously rubbing her hands together.

'Oh dear, Aliya, why did she come back here? Everyone will insult her here. Why did that idiot bring her back here?'

'Maybe she came to see her parents; it's been six months, after all. Maybe she wants to ask their forgiveness,' Aliya suggested.

'Oh, you idiot!' retorted Tehmina; then she began to think about something.

'Who knows what house Kusum must be in—how can I go see her without Amma finding out?' Aliya desperately wanted to see Kusum.

'Don't you go see her, or Amma will kill you!' Tehmina objected, but Aliya continued to plot: if she could find out where the house was, she could definitely go see her on the way to school.

That night Tehmina was extremely anxious. There was such silence at Ray Sahib's house that one couldn't even hear anyone speaking. Tehmina must not have slept that night; in the morning her eyes were red.

When the maid came to work she again relayed startling news: that man had left Kusum in the dead of night! Kusum had wept for the rest of the night. All the people nearby had gathered around. He had brought her there on the pretext of visiting her parents and asking their forgiveness. Ray Sahib had refused to see her, but his wife had gone to Kusum's house this morning when it was still dark.

'This is the punishment for such vixens! It was quite right of him to leave her and go away; after all, she had been dreaming of running away and becoming a wife. She did it and now she's paying the price,' declared Amma venomously. Tehmina looked like she was in shock.

'I'll tell Abba to make Ray Sahib understand that he must bring Kusum home. Oh dear, what will she do alone?' asked Aliya excitedly. She was feeling such intense hatred towards that man. What calamity he had unleashed in bringing her here! If he had left her far off in some strange place, she could have beaten her head in and died, but at least she wouldn't have to be insulted by her own people.

'What will you say to your Abba? That Ray Sahib should take his runaway daughter back in? Won't you be ashamed of yourself saying such things?' asked Amma, enraged.

'Yes, that's what I'll say!' cried Aliya as she ran away from her mother.

That evening, when Abba came home from the office, she went and stood before him. 'Abba, Kusum is crying alone in her house. Please go talk to Ray Sahib—tell him to bring her home. Someone has run off and left her there!'

'I know everything—I would have reasoned with Ray Sahib before you said so, but you're very intelligent, my dear.' Abba patted her on the head and smiled.

'Why must she take part in such shameful things?' asked Amma, livid with rage.

'Why shouldn't she? You have her study at the mission school but you don't even give her the right to speak.'

'Why don't you just come out and say that you think the English are shameless?' Amma was spoiling for a fight so Abba rushed off to the sitting room.

That night Abba quietly told Aliya that Ray Sahib had agreed, that he'd bring Kusum back home, and perhaps he already had. She was very pleased at Abba's handling of the situation, and got a sense of her own importance that day. All the same she was not able to go see Kusum despite her best efforts.

10

That night dragged on and on. Aliya couldn't get to sleep. When would morning come, so that she could go to school and visit Kusum on the way? The barking of stray dogs rendered the night all the more bleak. The next morning, she went to Kusum's house before going to school. Kusum's mother was in the kitchen. Ray Sahib was reclining in his easy chair, his eyes closed. He pointed towards the room where she would find Kusum.

She went into the room but Kusum was not there. She peeped into a small room, and saw her lying there, dishevelled, on a bare string bed. When Kusum saw Aliya she shrank back. Aliya went over and hugged her.

'I missed you, Kusum,' she said, examining her closely. The crop had been harvested and the field lay empty.

Aliya grabbed Kusum's hand and tried to pull her up. 'Why did you sneak into this dark little room? Why don't you come on out and sit with me?'

'When I sit out there, everyone comes to look at me. Mother says to hide myself, and then Father feels depressed when he sees my face. I've been dishonoured, after all. How is Tehmina?'

'Come to our house and see her, Kusum.'

'I can't go anywhere now.' Her haunted eyes filled with tears.

'Then I'll take you myself.'

It was nearly time for school, so Aliya promised to come back in the evening and then left. The whole way there she kept cursing Kusum's lover. When she returned home Tehmina grabbed her and asked her all sorts of questions about Kusum, but what could she say? She had hardly talked to her at all.

'You should go over there and see her, Tehmina.'

'Now if I see her, people will point at me; she's become a famous runaway.'

'But why don't people say that man who ran off and left her is bad?'

'They just don't, that's all, they only think of the girl as bad. You're a big girl now, so don't go over to her house or people will start talking.'

That evening, Aliya felt herself in a quandary for the first time. She felt bewildered by the emotions of love and romance. What is this thing called love for which humans were willing to lose so much, and why? She just couldn't understand, and became exhausted thinking about it. She'd eaten dinner before anyone else and then gone and lain down on her bed and got caught up in her course books. She had no idea when she fell asleep after that.

She woke up once during the night. Outside she could hear dogs barking and wailing. The night was truly filled with foreboding. Suddenly she looked up. The rooftop room at Ray Sahib's house was clearly illuminated in the moonlight, and she could see the flames of clay lamps moving about up there. Then she saw a figure covered in white clothing from head to toe. She closed her eyes with fear. No one stayed in that room at all. Kusum herself had told her that the room had been locked ever since her grandfather had died in it. Everyone was afraid to go in there.

She worried that perhaps the soul of Kusum's grandfather had returned, but then she remembered that in Hindu homes, they had ghosts instead. She cried out to Tehmina in fear, but Tehmina had turned over and gone back to sleep.

A little while later, when the light went out and the wraith-like figure had disappeared, she heaved a sigh of relief. The next morning, everyone was drinking tea when the sound of weeping and wailing came from Ray Sahib's house.

'I bet that Kusum has run away again,' declared Amma. The maid ran outside with great excitement, and Abba rushed out at the same time. Abba came back a few minutes later and fell into his chair.

'What a tragedy! Kusum drowned in the pond, no one knows when she went out last night,' he told them. All day long people came to see her and find out what had happened. Perhaps they were eager to learn if the runaway had grown horns.

'Bring me my clothes, I need to go to Ray Sahib's,' said Abba.

Amma was totally dumbstruck. Tehmina was weeping and Aliya sat shaking from head to toe as she leant on her father's shoulder. Abba stroked her head. Despite his consoling her, she was unable to even weep for some reason.

Kusum had already been brought home on a cot. Aliya pushed through the crowd of women. When she saw Kusum's uncovered face, she shrieked. Her blue, swollen face was devoid of emotion. Everyone was staring at Kusum, but she refused to return their gazes. Her mouth was curved in an odd smile, as though she were just about to sing the song *'Oh, where has my Shyam gone, will nobody tell me?'* before she had died. The end of her white sari hung from the cot, as the last drops of water dripped into the dirt of the courtyard.

11

It was the month of October. It had started to get a bit cold. The veranda had been shut up and people were now sleeping indoors. Aliya usually slept wonderfully in winter, but for some reason Tehmina was spending most of her nights awake. Her health was poor—her colour was dull and the skin on her face was dry. Amma monitored her nutrition closely: in the mornings she fed her sweet almond milk instead of tea.

Tehmina's dowry was all sewn and Amma was anxious that the date of the wedding be fixed. In the meantime, Big Aunty had also been sending letter after letter asking to set the date quickly, but Abba was stalling. 'When Tehmina is doing better, we'll see,' he said.

Once, when a letter came from Big Aunty, there was a picture in it of cousin Jameel. Aliya took the picture to show Tehmina, but Tehmina looked away.

'One can only belong to one person,' she said angrily, then burst out laughing. 'And anyway, I will see Jameel in person once I marry him.' There was something so helpless about her laughter.

'Tehmina, do you miss Safdar?' asked Aliya anxiously.

'Of course not! Why would I?' Tehmina picked up the book at the head of her bed.

When Abba came home from the office, he seemed very upset. The maid set out the tea things on the table but Abba just lay back in his easy chair.

'Won't you take any tea? It's getting cold. Also, you must find a good date for the wedding today; your sister-in-law is sending letter after letter.' Amma dragged her chair over to Abba.

'It was because of you that he left this house. Now he's joined the wrong sort of party and ruined himself. You're the one responsible for his ruin.'

Tehmina's face went white. Everyone realized whom Abba was talking about.

'Which scoundrel have I ruined?' demanded Amma.

'I'm talking about Safdar; now do you understand?' Abba snapped back.

'Mercy, even after leaving the house, he's not really gone— we'll never be rid of him!' Amma wept, her tears a ruse.

'Rest assured, now he'll never return,' said Abba softly, and he went into his sitting room without drinking tea. When Aliya brought him his tea, he was lying on his takht with his eyes closed. He sat up when he saw her, and smiled. 'How can I explain to your mother that she's ruined your cousin Safdar? A friend of his has come from Calcutta, he told me all about it. Safdar was asking after you quite a bit too.'

'Abba, which party did he join?'

'Daughter, it's a party of atheists,' Abba sighed. 'And I thought of him as my own son.'

But clearly he never considered anyone to be his father—he hasn't written a single letter after he left; he doesn't value our love, thought Aliya. She felt that Abba was needlessly losing his head over him, but she couldn't say anything to him.

'How are your studies going?' Abba asked her.

'They're going well, Abba.'

'And you're not being influenced at all by the religion of the British?'

'God forbid!'

'Excellent! You're very intelligent. All my hopes are pinned on you. You do know, don't you, that I loathe those dishonest businessmen. They've made slaves of us.'

'I loathe them too, Abba!' she said, to make him happy.

Abba watched her as he placed his cup on the teapoy. His eyes sparkled with happiness. She was wondering why Abba hated all the English. Her own headmistress at the school was kind and sweet. How exactly was she ruling their country?

'God willing, they'll all go back to their own country some day; I can't do anything out of concern for all of you, but we have such a great country, don't we?'

'Yes, Abba, it's a very large country!' she replied foolishly, making her father smile as well. Just then someone knocked on the sitting-room door, so she took the tray and went quickly back into the house.

'I know what's going on, I know why he's ruining himself,' Tehmina whispered to Aliya that night. Aliya didn't reply. *Kusum's gone and drowned, but Tehmina still misses Safdar*, she thought with revulsion.

The next evening, when Abba came in to eat dinner, Amma was sitting in the veranda writing a response to Big Aunty's letter.

'I've written to your sister-in-law to set the date for the tenth of Eid month,' Amma announced. Abba was silent. He didn't respond at all. He looked rather sad in the dim yellow light of the lantern.

12

The wedding date was drawing nearer. Amma was getting busier and busier. At around twelve or one o'clock in the afternoon, the chaprasi's wife would wrap herself in a burqa and come over to pick the unhusked rice from the clean. And there were seers of dry fruits and nuts to be chopped! Amma looked quite merciless when overseeing the chaprasi's wife. The exhausted woman would be limping when she headed home after a full day at their house.

It was the end of January. The day before, the rain had been mixed with hail. That night was so cold they felt like they were sitting on icicles. The temple bells fairly shivered as they rang. They talked until late that night, and then Tehmina turned away from her. Aliya was just about to fall asleep, when Tehmina began talking again. Somehow her sleepiness had disappeared.

'It feels as though I am sitting in wait, like a traveller,' she murmured in a faraway voice.

'Well, you are a traveller—in just a few days, you'll become a bride and then leave. You'll be such a beautiful bride!'

'And don't my hands look lovely?' Tehmina took her tiny hands out from under the quilt and waved them about.

'They'll be decorated with mehndi then; this was the day I watered that small mehndi plant for, and now it's grown so large—I wish I could lie in its shadow and sleep. And isn't mehndi such a strange thing too? It carries the fragrance of a blissful marriage, the coolness of love, and from its red colour, you do get the sense of the death of desires.'

'Oh my! What are you even talking about, Tehmina!' Aliya stared at her sister in confusion. At that moment she realized that Amma was right when she said that Safdar had ruined Tehmina by giving her trashy books.

'What am I talking about?' Tehmina smiled. 'All sorts of things—such things made me a traveller in the first place, and they can end my journey too.'

'Tehmina, are you missing Safdar? Tell the truth.'

'Safdar who? Oh you silly, you don't have a bit of sense.' Tehmina slapped her hand, laughing. 'Come on, let's go to sleep now; it's so late.'

There were only a few days left for the wedding. Amma was extremely busy and happy. At times, she also worried that her brother and sister-in-law might not make it for some reason, although they'd written to say they would arrive a week beforehand. She talked of them continuously. 'The changing seasons of this country don't agree with my sister-in-law's health. She gets colds so easily, and her stomach is always bad too. And the poor thing is always having to eat chillies at parties. After all, are chillies really a thing one should eat?' Amma tried to get Tehmina to respond, but she was silent.

Tehmina had stopped coming out of her room. Whenever Abba came home she'd shut the door. Amma just adored this bashful behaviour of hers. 'That's what modesty is like!' she'd say with pride. Aliya searched Tehmina's face for modesty, but she didn't find a drop of it. When Tehmina felt shy, she turned pink, like a Japanese doll, but nowadays she was ashen. There was such depth in her eyes, such darkness, that Aliya felt she was peering deep into a well when she looked at her.

When there were only seven days left for the arrival of the groom's procession, Tehmina was bathed and scrubbed in turmeric paste and dressed in special yellow clothing. That night, the *mirasi*s and *domni*s brought drums and sat on dhurries spread out in the veranda and began to sing different songs, all filled with poignant longing and desire. It was as though each and every verse was sung with outstretched hands full of longings that were not fated to ever be fulfilled in the bride's life.

The songs continued on and Tehmina wiped away her tears with her yellow dupatta. Though Abba's friends' wives requested to hear each song twice, the singers' throats never tired. From time to time during the singing, the audience would drop two- and four-anna coins on the dhurrie in praise.

ଓଃ

Amma was taking her afternoon nap, sound asleep after staying up later than usual the night before, and the maid had gone home for two hours, having got some free time for the first time in many days. Tehmina was lying down but she didn't feel sleepy. She kept tossing and turning. A crow sat on the low wall across the yard, its cawing only deepening the silence of the afternoon.

'Guests are about to come, that's why the crow is cawing,' Aliya told Tehmina happily.

'And guests are also about to leave.' Tehmina was starting to look happy and peaceful after quite a while, but then she suddenly thought of something and sat up. 'What do you know, Aliya? My tiny life has crept by like a tortoise.' Her face turned red.

'You've always been better off than me, I've never been more than a leftover piece of junk, tossed in a closet, Amma always . . .' Aliya's lips began to tremble.

'Amma scolds me as well, but I always stay happy. Everything she's done has been out of animosity for Safdar. He was in danger because of me, wasn't he?'

'But now you will be free, now Safdar won't come back to make your life difficult. May God take him to task for what he's done.'

'Aliya, don't curse!' Tehmina left the room on bare feet to get a drink of water.

When she returned, her eyelids were damp. She closed her eyes the moment she lay down.

Enough, Tehmina is still thinking of that rascal. She still hasn't come to her senses after seeing what happened to Kusum, thought Aliya.

Aliya was trying to fall asleep when the chaprasi came with the mail. Tehmina woke up as well. She picked up one letter and turned it over and looked at it: it was addressed to Amma, and 'Safdar' was written in one corner. Tehmina opened the letter with trepidation and after reading it, she held it out to Aliya. What she read made her writhe with fear:

Dear Aunt,

Congratulations on Tehmina's wedding. It doesn't
matter whom you give her to, she'll always belong to
me. She is mine alone.

An expression of immense peace came over Tehmina's face,
as though she'd just received all the wealth in the universe.
She quickly ripped up the letter and threw the scraps into the
grate. The other letter was from their mother's brother; that
she placed carefully at the head of the bed.

'Come on now, let's go to sleep. I'm feeling really
sleepy.' Tehmina lay down and very craftily acted as
though she were asleep, but Aliya lay there cursing Safdar
to herself. What would have happened if Amma had got
her hands on that letter? The very thought filled her with
dread.

'Tehmina, Safdar is such a rascal!' she said, shaking
Tehmina.

'Of course he is, but for God's sake, don't mention it to
Amma, or who knows what will happen,' Tehmina replied
softly.

After dinner, the dhurrie was spread out in the veranda.
The maid tightened the drum and pushed it into the middle
of the veranda and hung the rented gas lantern in the
middle—a little while later the guests began to arrive.

After eleven o'clock at night, when the mirasis had
finished singing and gone home, Tehmina softly emerged
from her room and into the veranda. The drum looked so

lonely lying on its side on the wrinkled dhurrie. The maid was taking the chairs away and putting them back in the rooms, while searching for something at the same time.

'Oh dear, oh dear, where could it have gone? I can't find it. Blast my memory!'

13

'Aliya, sweetheart, listen, if you ever see Safdar after I leave, tell him this message from me. You will tell him, won't you?' asked Tehmina helplessly as she lay down in the bed.

'What, Tehmina?' Her heart broke to see Tehmina in such a strange state.

'Tell him I never forgot him, that's all.'

'Go to sleep now, Tehmina.'

Outside, they could hear the dogs barking. Aliya had no idea when she fell asleep.

ෆ

In the morning, when Aliya opened her eyes, Tehmina was still sleeping soundly. She went about getting herself ready for school, but Tehmina did not get up. When everyone was up for tea, Amma sent the maid in to wake Tehmina and serve her tea.

As she entered, the maid screamed, and Abba and Amma came running as well. There they found the maid beating her breast and crying, 'Our darling Tehmina is no more!'

'Where did she go, where has she gone?' Aliya wondered, as she began to tremble with fear. Somehow she made her way to the room where Abba stood holding up Amma, who had fainted. He looked as though he might collapse as well.

Tehmina truly was no more. Her mehndi-lined hands had turned yellow and fragile, and her lips looked black, as though they'd been smeared with *missi* powder. As soon as Amma came to, she began to flail about in a fit. Abba wept like a child and Aliya wrapped herself around Tehmina's cold body and whimpered.

Abba quickly dried his tears. 'She always had a weak heart, so it must have just stopped beating. Go heat some water, Maid. All is as Allah desires,' he declared in a shaky voice.

As soon as the maid left the room, Abba whispered to Amma, 'Be brave—this is a disaster! We must bury the body immediately.' He let go of Amma to put his arms around Aliya and lead her into the other room.

'You are very intelligent, you sit out here,' he said.

Abba left her there alone and went away, but she didn't have it in her to obey his orders at that moment, so she went and stood behind the door. Abba was reasoning with Amma. There was a scrap of paper in his hand which he burnt with a match; then he led Amma out on to the veranda.

The maid filled a metal pot with water and rolled out the dhurrie much earlier than usual, but she didn't tighten the drum and set it out. Abba's friends' wives came, but no one would be throwing money on to the carpet; everyone wept, and Amma kept fainting. Tehmina was quickly cleaned, bathed and dispatched. Amma ran after her like a madwoman.

'Darling, your big sister has been carried off,' said the maid. 'Sing:

Why did you marry me so far from home, my wealthy father?'

The maid's words unleashed chaos inside Aliya. She ran into Tehmina's room and collapsed on the ground where she unburdened her heart by weeping, as burnt scraps of paper flew about her.

'Oh dear, oh dear, and she departed so full of desires!' murmured the maid as she came into the room and began searching about like a madwoman. 'I haven't been able to find my opium box since yesterday, if I just eat a little I always feel better.'

⍥

Big Uncle, Big Aunty and Amma's brother, Mamoo, came and stayed for two days of mourning, and then they all went away. Mamoo's English wife had not been able to come because she was pregnant in those days and cousin Jameel had not come either. He could at least have come to see the tomb of his intended bride.

Amma was silent and withdrawn after this episode, and it was only to Aliya that she showed any affection. She kept her eyes on her at all times; if Aliya was away from her for a short while, Amma started throwing a fit.

Abba had grown so distant from Amma. When he came home from the office he'd just wash his face and hands in his sitting room, drink his tea there, and after eating, sit and debate in gatherings of his friends until eleven or twelve at night. At night, after everyone had gone to sleep, he'd come quietly and lie down on his bed. Since Tehmina's death, the silence had become oppressive and nothing seemed to break it.

Nothing more was heard from Safdar. He'd been swallowed up by the earth or the sky. Aliya longed to find out where he was. She wanted to send a message to him, to tell him there was plenty of room next to Tehmina's grave. *Come back if you really loved her.*

∽

One day, when Abba came home to the sitting room, there was no one with him. Aliya went quickly to his side. How long it had been since she'd been able to sit by Abba! She'd had no chance to talk with him about anything.

'Abba, you never come into the house, you never talk to anyone,' she said as soon as she came in, her voice tearful. Abba started and hugged her to his chest.

'Your mother has pushed me far from the house, you know how it is.'

How she wished that Amma hadn't driven anyone from the house; it was Safdar who had divided everyone, and then Abba was so busy with his animosity towards the English that he wouldn't even turn and look at anyone. He didn't even acknowledge her love. But she couldn't say any of this out loud. She herself wondered why, despite Abba's indifference, she still loved him the most. Abba's affectionate eyes were so expressive. She'd never been able to say even one word against him.

'Your mother has never understood me; she's never shared any of my aspirations. If I had the courage of my elder brother, I wouldn't be so helpless today.' Who knows what else Abba would have said, as Ray Sahib had just arrived.

Aliya had aged ten years with Tehmina's death. She wished she could make Amma happy and was anxious to bring Abba back into the home. She wanted to get him away from politics. After she had complained to him, Abba began to spend some time in the house, but he still seemed to avoid Amma, and when Amma's eyes met his, her face would contort with memories of bygone days and Aliya would think of Safdar. How heartlessly he had shoved Tehmina into the maw of death with just one letter!

A few months had passed since her death, but Amma hadn't moved any of Tehmina's things. Her bed was right where it had always been—all her books were still out. Whenever Aliya went into the room, she felt her heart sink. Amma had even stowed her dowry chest in that room. Aliya was overwhelmed when she saw it there. Soon enough, crickets would get into the chest and chew everything up; all the tinsel and gold embroidery would go black come the rainy season, she thought.

She had been totally idle since taking the matric exam; she had nothing to do all day. One day, she began to leaf through Tehmina's books absent-mindedly. Such tales of love and fancy! Women would commit suicide for love and depart as examples of perfect fidelity, and then, some dark night, men would appear to momentarily light a lamp over the tomb, then leave, and that was that. She threw the books back in the cupboard and cried tears of rage, as she felt Tehmina watching her with disdain from the other side of her curtain of tears.

14

Abba had been extremely busy for the past two or three days, and was even coming home very late from work. His superior officer was due to visit for an inspection. Abba was not only setting everything in order, but was also arranging for his stay in the Dak Bungalow. The chaprasi had even come and asked for some of the tablecloths and pillowcases that Tehmina had embroidered.

'Great! He curses the English and now that an Englishman is coming, His Excellency is out of his mind with fear. How quick people are to waste their words.' When Amma laughed sarcastically, Aliya burned with rage. If only she could become Amma's mother for just a short while, she could tell her there was no use needling him. Abba was growing further and further removed from the household, and Amma was enjoying herself mightily.

When Abba returned home that night, exhausted, he said to Aliya, 'Can you have something a little special arranged for dinner tomorrow night, dear? Just dinner for six or seven. He's coming tomorrow morning for the inspection, then there will be a dinner party at our house that night.'

'Well, I must say, you go around with a heart full of hate, and now all of a sudden you're kissing up to him! Hmm . . . why didn't you talk to me? I'll arrange it all myself,' retorted Amma, who did not even flinch before Abba.

'If I didn't kiss up to him you'd have to go begging,' snapped Abba, as he walked out quickly. Aliya couldn't say one word to Amma. When she saw the devastation on her face, she pitied her.

The next day, Abba rose under the shadow of the stars and went to the station. Amma sat at the edge of her bed with her feet dangling, laughing sarcastically, but Abba didn't look at her.

By one o'clock in the afternoon, Abba still hadn't come home for lunch. Aliya remained busy helping Amma prepare for the night's feast. She decorated the sitting room in a new way and ordered two gas lanterns and cleaned them nicely. Amma was having several types of koftas and kebabs prepared and carrying on about how the spices must be ground without chilli peppers. Amma had never prepared a meal for anyone with such devotion.

The food was only just ready when the chaprasi, a look of alarm on his face, slipped into the house without calling out first to announce his presence. It seemed as though he'd come running from a great distance.

'Begum Sahiba, the police have arrested Babuji; he got angry with the officer during the inspection and smashed him over the head with a ruler.'

Amma stared at him, eyes bulging, as though darkness had fallen all around her. Then she tried to scream but her mouth just opened and froze. Flies buzzed around the dinner party dishes.

'Where is Abba, I will go to him!' Aliya got up and ran forward like a lunatic, but the chaprasi blocked her path. 'Where will you go, Baby?' he asked.

'How dare you stop me!' She held up her fists and tried to hit him.

'I am Baby's faithful servant, but where will you go? Babuji is in jail.' He covered his eyes with the tail of his turban. 'He called our Babuji a *damn fool*, a bastard.' He stared at her, his eyes red. 'If I find them, I'll sacrifice a thousand and one Englishmen to protect our Babuji and throw them off! I'll kill them all!'

In a short while, Ray Sahib came over. Amma stood behind the door and spoke with him. She gave him her brother's address so that he could send a telegram, but Aliya quickly gave Big Uncle's address as well. She had fast become attached to Big Uncle after seeing him just twice . . . *And if it hadn't been for him*, she thought, *what would have happened to us?* For Amma's brother, Mamoo, had made it clear in his reply that attempted murder was an enormous crime, and that sheltering the wife and child of such a man would put him in danger. Amma had hidden this from Aliya, but she had heard it with her own ears, standing in the veranda. Since that day, she'd come to hate both Mamoo and the English so deeply she wished they'd all be destroyed.

When Big Uncle had arrived, he placed his hand on everyone's heads, promising protection. In just two days, all their baggage had been packed and loaded on tongas. Uncle freely cursed the British throughout. What had happened to

Abba had only increased his anti-British fervour. After he had taken leave of Abba's friends, and Aliya's tonga had begun to move along slowly, she saw the headmistress of her school rushing over. Mrs Howard was out of breath as she ran up to the tonga, and held on to Aliya's hand affectionately.

'You people be happy, don't be sad, your father was a very good man, your country will surely find freedom,' she cried. As the tonga pulled away, she called out, 'Goodbye, goodbye!'

છ3

Oh, Abba, what will life be like for you behind the bars of your jail? As Aliya sat up in her bed and opened the shutter, a puff of cool air greeted her. She felt her head would explode in pain. If only she could fall asleep, morning would finally come, she thought as she lay down again.

Present

1

Morning had come, the clouds had dispersed and now the sun's rays shone through the open window. Her eyes felt irritated after sleeping only half an hour, as though eyelashes had fallen into them.

'Oh my! You're still sleeping!' declared Shamima, looking bright and cheerful. Aliya stared at her very hard: she had such an innocent face, as though she were protected by angels.

'Oh, no, I've been awake for a long time!'

Aliya jumped up from the bed, but then suddenly remembered she was in a new place; this was a new world, and the soothing shade of Abba's affection lay far away.

'I haven't had breakfast yet. I was waiting for you; everyone else ate long ago,' said Shamima proudly.

'Silly girl, you should have eaten breakfast too, Chammi,' said Aliya, as she quickly joined her.

'But why would I have eaten breakfast without you? No one here cares about anyone else, they're all selfish.' Chammi made a face.

The two of them made their way downstairs together. Smoke floated through the holes in the canvas curtains that hung in the veranda. Amma and Big Aunty were seated on the takht with the tarnished paandaan, preparing and chewing paan. The dirty sheet spread over the takht was covered in hundreds of paan stains. Kareeman Bua was seated on the low stool by the hearth talking non-stop in a cloud of smoke.

'You got up, Aliya! I didn't wake you earlier because I didn't know if you'd slept well in this new place or not.' Big Aunty had Aliya sit down beside her.

'But I did sleep well, Aunty.' She looked over at her mother, about whose face hovered traces of sleeplessness and the dust of worries.

'Oh my God, the parathas I set aside for you are all dried out, they probably have no taste by now!' Kareeman Bua put the pan back on the fire to warm the parathas. 'If you knead puris in ghee they don't dry out all day; it's really just a sign of the times,' sighed Kareeman Bua sadly.

'All the bags are still packed. After you've finished breakfast, go ahead and unpack them,' said Amma softly to Aliya.

'Come now, how can she unpack them herself? Jameel and Shakeel will do it all when they get home. Aliya will take the upstairs room. It will be easy for her to study alone up there. Jameel used to sleep there, but he said last night to give that room to Aliya and her mother; but you'll stay down here with me, won't you?' Big Aunty asked Amma.

'Yes, I'll stay here,' Amma said after thinking it over for a moment. Perhaps she was remembering those days when she hadn't even cared to set eyes on Big Aunty; poor Aunty had come from a home that had been financially ruined. She was already engaged to Uncle, so Granny had no choice but to get them married because Uncle insisted, even though Granny was firmly of the opinion that engagements should be broken if the bride no longer came from money.

As she ate her dry roti, greasy with ghee, and sipped her tea boiled in only a little bit of milk, Aliya could sense that this household had fallen on hard times.

'What a great paratha, amazing! Just as dry as Kareeman Bua's skin. Don't you think so, Bajiya?' This last was said so softly by Chammi that Kareeman Bua couldn't hear it.

'They are great, Chammi,' Aliya said trying to stop her laughter.

'God willing, Aliya and Mazhar's wife will have no trouble here, the good days may be gone, but if Jameel passes his exam, things in this house will turn around, and our Mazhar will also be freed.' Aunty fell silent as she spoke.

'If he cared about his family why would he be in jail today? After all, what did the English ever do to him?' Amma sighed deeply, then looked down and quietly wiped away her tears. For a little while everyone fell silent as though they were all recalling painful memories.

'May God preserve this home from misfortune as well,' Kareeman Bua murmured softly.

Just then, an exceedingly feeble voice came from the sitting room: 'Kareeman Bua, it's getting late to go to the shop, could you send in my breakfast?' Kareeman Bua jumped in irritation, banging her tongs on the floor. She picked them up and snatched a roti from a small basket, then spilled some tea into a filthy cup and withdrew from the veranda bent over double.

'Oh, what a fine one he is, that Asrar Miyan. I mean to say, there's a limit to shamelessness, there is. There is no way to keep him patient until he gets his food. Only Kareeman Bua can fix him!' laughed Chammi loudly.

'Oh, so he's still here? Must be thanks to his elder brother,' said Amma.

'Yes, that's him. Where would the poor fellow go, anyway? And anyhow he does look after the shop.' Aunty hung her head like a criminal and glanced over at Amma from lowered eyes.

'Great!' Amma retorted sarcastically and began chopping betel nut. She seemed aloof and proud in this house.

Aliya listened to all this silently and felt a wave of sympathy. Oh dear, if only poor Asrar Miyan's brothers had not sucked on filthy fly-infested mango pits perhaps they'd be alive today, and companions to Asrar Miyan. How alone he must feel among all his legitimate relatives.

'Go sit with Granny a little,' Amma told Aliya. So she quickly got up to go. Tehmina's death and Abba's arrest had made her very dutiful. Perhaps that would make Amma happy.

The evening before, they hadn't spoken to Granny at all, as they were exhausted from the journey, and anyway, Granny had been suffering from an asthma attack. Now, when Granny saw Aliya, she held out her hands. The flesh sagged from her thin withered arms, but even in this state of extreme weakness, grandeur still emanated from her person. Aliya respectfully clasped her outstretched hands and rested her head gently on her chest. Chammi was tidying up her messy bed. No one had even blown out the lantern in the alcove from the night before.

'Mazhar never comes! My eyes long to see him,' sighed Granny. Aliya pursed her lips. Everyone had hidden from

Granny that her son was in jail and that too for attempted murder.

'He never gets time off, Granny, and now his workload has increased and that's why he sent us all to stay here.' She looked about, avoiding Granny's gaze.

'Thank goodness, everyone is gathering together again, who knows, perhaps your youngest uncle will come home as well.' Granny's eyes shone at the thought.

Chammi raised the chimney of the lantern and blew out the flame. There was nothing in the long room but two high black beds and two chairs. On the wall hung a portrait of Maulana Muhammad Ali Jauhar, its frame caked with the grime and dust of countless storms.

'Has my dear Mazhar sent a letter?'

'No, Granny, he's always so busy.' She felt pained at the thought of Abba.

'That's fine, that is the glory of men, that they work; now your youngest uncle . . .' Granny propped herself up a bit on her bolster. 'You do know, don't you, that he went away during the Khilafat Movement and never came back. The Khilafat Movement was all the rage back then. I don't like such things, but in other homes, women were embroidering caps and gathering donations. They wrote songs too. What was that lovely song?' Granny pressed her temples as she tried to recall. 'Yes, I remember: "Don't worry about your old mother / Put your life into the Khilafat, my son." But all these are senseless things; that's how your big uncle got caught up in his ridiculousness. But who listens to me now, anyway? Perhaps he'll come to his senses some day and . . .'

'Oh my, this room is getting so dirty and on top of that, the smell of Granny's spit and pee! But I'm not about to let my granny stay in some other room! This is my own room—Big Aunty says that I was born in this very room,' said Chammi, as she rushed out, soon returning with a broom. Today she was suddenly thinking a lot about cleaning. She felt embarrassed by the filthy room and kept glancing over at Aliya, and Aliya was wondering to herself where Abba might be, which jail he might be in, when a letter from him might arrive.

Granny was out of breath after even this small amount of conversation, but when Chammi started kicking up dust with her broom, she had a violent asthma attack. She coughed so much she couldn't breathe. Aliya was alarmed and began stroking her chest, but Chammi continued to sweep in a leisurely fashion. Sweat poured from Granny's face and her eyes popped in distress. Aliya stood up in alarm. Kareeman Bua bustled in and sat by Granny, her hands covered in flour.

'Mistress, Mistress . . .' said Kareeman Bua, in an agitated attempt to soothe Granny. She held one hand on her own breast as though to stop her heart from sinking.

'Oh dear! Chammi, quickly tell Aunty to call the doctor,' cried Aliya, who was seeing a strong asthma attack for the first time.

'Enough, you are too much, Bajiya! Does the doctor come for such a little thing? Granny gets these attacks all the time. There's a sweet paste in a small box at the head of her bed. Give her a little pinch of that. Who has the money to call the doctor every time? You're getting upset for no reason.' Chammi hid her face in her dupatta to stop her laughter.

Aliya gazed at her with astonishment as Chammi pushed the dirt out of the doorway and into the courtyard. What if she fell ill herself, she worried. Abba always called for the doctor at the slightest sneeze, but here Chammi laughed at the mere mention of a doctor. The sound of coughing echoed throughout the house, but only Kareeman Bua seemed to hear it. Everyone else was engaged in their own activities. No one came rushing in. A little while later, Granny's breathing returned to normal, and she lay down, exhausted. Kareeman Bua wiped the sweat from her face.

'Now how are you feeling, Mistress?' What pain there was in Kareeman Bua's eyes! When Granny said, 'Hmm,' and closed her eyes, Kareeman Bua suddenly remembered she'd been kneading dough.

'Call for Chammi,' said Granny softly; so Aliya went to the doorway and called out to Chammi.

'Tell her I'm coming after I wash my face; she calls for me all the time.' Chammi was sitting on a stool in the yard washing her face and hands, muttering to herself. All the stories of Granny's grandeur collapsed right before Aliya's eyes.

'Come quickly, Aliya, set the luggage up properly,' called Amma from the veranda. So Aliya quietly slipped away. Granny was now sleeping peacefully, her eyes closed.

Cousin Jameel squatted out in the courtyard under the arch of the veranda. He looked exhausted after putting away all the luggage. She examined him carefully for a moment. He was good-looking, but his eyes were small and sunken. There was such depth in his eyes that one felt embarrassed examining them too closely.

Amma seemed irritable, as though she was on a long journey and her final destination still lay far off.

And when will this journey end? Aliya asked herself, as she walked over to her bedroll, which lay on one side in the yard. Her trunk and bedding had to be carried to the small room upstairs.

'I'll take it up, Bajiya!' cried Chammi. The tattered hem of her skirt dragged along the ground as she began to pull the strap of the bedroll.

'Get out of the way, you idiot.' Jameel got up and began forcefully pulling the straps from Chammi's hand.

'Watch what you're doing, Jameel! I don't want to respond to you because Aliya is here, otherwise . . .' Chammi's face had turned red. 'Out of the way, please, I'm going to take her bedding up myself.' Chammi jerked Jameel's hand away and dragged the bundle up the stairs. Jameel sat back down on the chair and began to watch the spectacle with great relish. Dust swirled all about as Chammi dragged the bedroll.

'Oh, no, Chammi! You'll fall! Why do you always invite trouble for yourself?' Big Aunty stopped making paan and got up anxiously.

'Let her fall, Amma, let me see her helpless too sometime,' Jameel laughed awkwardly.

Oh my, how amazing! thought Aliya. *It makes you happy to see her helpless, Jameel? Then you must be thrilled with me and Amma.* She glanced at Jameel sarcastically and then looked down again. He'd been watching her out of the corner of his eye since they'd got there. She quickly followed Chammi up the stairs, but she'd already got the bedroll up. Chammi smiled very proudly when she saw Aliya.

'Look, Bajiya, I brought it myself. Jameel thinks he's so great, he just brought a little bit of luggage up and now he's sitting down all tired; if he'd carried up the bedroll he'd be panting away.' She laughed loudly. 'Oh no! This hem ripped too,' she exclaimed examining the hem of her pyjama as though she'd only just noticed it. How could she admit that the hem had already been torn when she'd taken the pyjama out of her chest to put it on. This ancient fabric that now protected her body had belonged to her late mother.

Aliya began to unroll the bedding with Chammi. Twilight had fallen, but the street lamp had not been turned on yet. She rolled up the bedding she'd slept on the night before and then made her bed with her own. In the meantime, Jameel had brought her trunk.

'Aliya, this room will be good for you, won't it? I used to sleep here before. Its greatest advantage is that you get the electric street lamp for free here. This is where I prepared for my BA—and if it weren't for that I would probably have ruined my eyes with lantern light. The large room next door was always empty as well. No one ever came up here . . . just a bat every now and then.' Jameel glanced over at Chammi out of the corner of his eye, but she had very quietly left the room and walked out on to the open roof.

Was Tehmina really supposed to marry this creep? Aliya thought with disgust. Really, she wouldn't have lasted more than a few days with him. Was this the same person she used to enjoy discussing with her sister?

Aliya set up her chest and, without saying anything to Jameel, went over to Chammi. She turned to look as she went; Jameel was rooted to the spot.

'I can't tell you how excited I was to meet you, Bajiya,' said Chammi. 'Uncle and Aunty had said such wonderful things about you. You're educated, right? That's why Uncle wanted to marry Tehmina to Jameel. But I'm completely ignorant, aren't I, Bajiya?'

'You are already sweet, Chammi. You don't need to study! I'm happiest of all to have met you,' she said.

'I can write letters, and read too, I just haven't been to school,' Chammi told her proudly.

'You're not at all happy to meet her, you'll never be happy to meet anyone here, you're just showing off and trying to act like educated girls do,' said Jameel with amusement, and he began strolling about the roof, swinging his arms. Neither of the girls had even noticed him walking over and standing behind them.

'Who knows what has happened to Jameel today. Now that he's seen you he's been putting on airs. Bajiya, it used to be he couldn't do anything without me.' Chammi glanced at Jameel sideways.

'I'm telling you to go downstairs now, Chammi.' For some reason Jameel had suddenly turned serious.

'Why should I? My father also owns a share of this house! I can go where I want to, you think you're so . . .'

'Okay, then I'll leave,' Jameel said, and strode off downstairs.

All this conversation seemed quite odd to Aliya. She looked at Chammi with surprise.

'Bajiya, don't let it bother you, things like this happen here every second.' Chammi looked quite embarrassed.

'All right then, I think I'll set up my books now,' said Aliya. Suddenly the thought of her education began to worry her. Dear God, how would she study now? Where would the money come from? But then she recalled that Amma had stored up quite a bit of money with her brother and she breathed a sigh of relief.

Chammi suddenly remembered something she had to do for Granny and quickly ran downstairs. As Aliya arranged her books on the table, she was pleased to see that Jameel had spread a tablecloth on it. It was the same tablecloth that had been on Jameel's table the night before. Well, then, he did respect her.

Once her books were arranged, she started gazing out of the window into the gali below. A circle of light lay beneath the street lamp and a hawker was coming from the other end of the lane. On his head he balanced a tray decorated with a lamp with two wicks.

'Come downstairs, Aliya, dear!' She heard Aunty call out in her heavy voice and stood up quickly.

Downstairs, Amma was coming out of Granny's room.

'It's got colder since last night's rain,' she said, 'so Granny's health is worse. Cold is the worst enemy of that illness.'

Aliya went into Granny's room as well. Chammi was sitting on her bed, mending old clothes and happily humming an old ghazal:

These are pieces of my heart that are emerging as tears

She suddenly forgot her song when she saw Aliya, and tried to hide the pile of old clothing under the quilt. 'Granny is totally fine now, Bajiya,' she assured her.

Aliya perched on Granny's bed frame. Granny lay motionless with her eyes closed. Her chest still rose and fell. Aliya was reminded of a blacksmith's bellows she had seen as a child. Who knew when the fire of life would be extinguished? Tears of sympathy came to her eyes. The light from the lantern in the large alcove was growing dim. Aliya quietly hid Granny's hands beneath the quilt.

Kareeman Bua came into the room, bent over double, and leant forward to examine Granny.

'Mistress,' she called softly. On receiving no answer, she padded softly away. Her hands were smeared with damp ash.

'Is Granny sleeping?' Shakeel asked as he peered in from the doorway.

'If she's sleeping, what's it to you?' Chammi replied jeeringly.

'Shut up, hotshot,' Shakeel snapped.

'Come on, Granny is sleeping, do be quiet, dear Shakeel,' said Aliya anxiously as she stood up.

'Aliya Bajiya, I need some money, I have to buy books.'

'Granny's not well right now,' said Aliya, trying to reason with him.

'Of course she'll give you money, she's got piles! You've taken everything while pressing her feet, he's a swindler, he is,' Chammi snapped. 'There were so many guineas, and you spent them all, every one.'

'But you've never pressed her feet; poor Granny is lying there in pain, and this one lazes around like a queen,' Shakeel retorted.

'Don't talk to me, you wretch, just wait and see what I'm going to do to you.' Chammi jumped up from her bed. Granny opened her eyes for a moment and then moaned and turned over. Aliya pulled Shakeel outside. Kareeman Bua was setting out the lantern on the stool in the yard. She muttered something to herself and then went into the veranda.

'Really, Shakeel, you're growing up now, but you still quarrel; Chammi is much older than you,' Aliya pressed his shoulder, but he said nothing. He wiped a tear with his sleeve and stood with his head down.

'It's wrong to quarrel, my brother,' said Aliya giving him a hug.

'Granny loves me, she says that I'm like our youngest uncle—that's why Chammi gets jealous of me. Also because Granny keeps giving me money for books. Chammi hates that most of all; but who else can I ask, you tell me? My father, Jameel, Amma—all of them just start yelling if you bring up money.' Shakeel began sobbing like an innocent child.

'I have two rupees. Will you take them?' asked Aliya. Shakeel hugged her tightly for joy. 'You can get the money from me in the morning and go buy your books.'

'Okay, Bajiya.'

She pushed aside the canvas curtain and entered the veranda. Amma and Aunty were sitting on the takht. Amma was totally silent, but Aunty was cheerfully chopping betel nut. The moment she saw Shakeel, she turned towards him. 'Do you even study or do you just wander about? I'll be surprised if you don't fail your exams.'

'I don't wander about, I study with my friend. I don't even have all the books! You're always scolding me for no reason,' retorted Shakeel. Aliya saw that Amma was regarding Shakeel with alarm and disgust.

'Bajiya, when I take my Middle Exam, I'll study at the school across the street; it's such a big school!' Shakeel sat down next to Kareeman Bua near the hearth.

'Spring is coming,' said Kareeman Bua, as she lit the lantern and went to put it in the sitting room. When she returned, she sat down to knead the dough. 'May Allah keep Master well; even if he's not here, there still should be light in his room.'

'When will Uncle come home?' asked Aliya.

'When his rally is over.' Aunty laughed helplessly. 'If Jameel comes home soon, at least he'll get a warm roti to eat.'

'God willing, Master Mazhar will send a letter from jail telling us he's well. Lord, you alone can protect us.' Kareeman Bua kneaded the dough and placed the chapati pan over the fire.

Aliya felt her heart ache. She loved Abba so much, though she'd never known a cheery home, and she understood Abba to be responsible for Amma's bitter existence. She'd come to hate politics—Abba's goals were so crude, but all the same, she loved him dearly. She felt so peaceful under his protection, but now she was bereft of that protective love.

'Bajiya, you won't study in college now?' Shakeel looked very cheerful now that he knew two rupees were coming to him. The new red school building across the gali was the object of his aspirations. He had high hopes for fleeing his own run-down middle school.

Aliya remained silent, and Amma glanced at her sadly. There was resolve in Aliya's eyes. Thoughts of Abba made her so uneasy that, despite the insistence of Kareeman Bua and Aunty, she just couldn't eat much, and got up from her dinner quickly. Kareeman Bua continued to mumble, 'Everyone in the house now only eats like a bird and that lout Asrar Miyan eats so much, my hands ache from cooking, and . . .'

2

In a few days, Aliya knew all of what went on in the house. Uncle, after selling off his estate, had opened two large fabric shops, which at some point he used to run himself. He had built this beautiful house with great pride. In those days there was much bounty, and everyone had been happy, but when his passion had turned to politics, the running of the shops had grown sluggish under Asrar Miyan's supervision. And whatever earnings they had were now squandered on donations and various other political activities. Uncle had already gone to jail several times and had been chained up and sentenced to solitary confinement. There were huge black callouses on his ankles, and when he washed his feet he'd gaze at those callouses with pride and affection. He was such a stalwart Congress member that he could not tolerate any Muslim-only parties. He even doubted that they were true Muslims. In his eyes, anyone who was a member of any party besides Congress was a traitor to the country.

Uncle was so wrapped up in his own world that he'd forgotten all about his household. He'd married off his first-born and only daughter to an ordinary boy, simply because he was a Congress man. From that time until the present moment, his daughter had spent her life patting out dung cakes in her courtyard and raising her four children. After all, when did Uncle have the time to worry about his daughter's future or find her a well-to-do family? Aunty had fretted when the daughter had reached a marriageable age, but Uncle could think of no better man than his political comrade. But after just a short while, Uncle had come to loathe that worthy young man, because he'd left politics and got caught up in his few acres of land and his wife and children. Uncle never went to his daughter's home again.

He'd enrolled Jameel in a free primary school and had not the slightest notion how his eldest son had studied his way to a BA. When Shakeel was old enough to go to school, Jameel had beaten him soundly, and then forcibly enrolled him in the same primary school where he himself had studied.

Jameel did not get along with his father. He just wrote bad love poetry, attended poetry recitations and roundly cursed editors on receiving rejections for ghazals he'd submitted to their journals.

Whenever Uncle was at home, Aunty and Kareeman Bua spent the entire day preparing food for guests. Beef was fried in mustard oil in enormous metal pots, and for the Hindus they ordered puris and vegetable tarkaris from a shop. Kareeman Bua would mutter as she cooked piles of rotis, and tears would come to her eyes when she remembered the sweet scent of pure ghee from the good old days. All the same, the household did function, and everyone certainly ate their fill.

Whenever household needs were mentioned to Uncle, he'd blush. For some reason, he'd look at everyone with embarrassment, rub his growing belly and then passionately try to reason with everyone.

'When the country becomes free, all our troubles will go away; you all must think a bit more deeply.'

'How deep should we go?' Aunty would snap sometimes.

'What Uncle means is, go jump in a well!' When Chammi heard such things, she'd be sure to crack a joke, and Uncle would ignore her words as though he hadn't heard a thing. Uncle somehow had infinite patience; whenever he was at home, someone would think up a real zinger for him, but he'd just laugh it off and put up with them, or go back out to the sitting room.

To Aliya, Aunty was the cautionary tale in that house. Her eyes seemed filled with centuries of grief. She alone had taken on the burden of worrying about all these people. Asrar Miyan would sometimes manage to cut a bit of money from the shops to lessen her worries, but he himself would lie in the sitting room until late, calling out for a few rotis like a beggar.

Despite all these things, Aliya liked Uncle very much, just as she deeply loved her own father, despite all her complaints. She could not understand why she still felt the stirrings of love in her heart towards these agents of the households' sorrows and ruination. What sort of affection was this, what sort of love was this, that made her long for them at the slightest prompting? Whenever Uncle came home, she would drop everything she was doing and put out water on the stool for him to wash his hands and face. When he lay down exhausted on his bed after washing up, she'd sit by his side and gently massage his head. Uncle would embrace her and bless her, and then close his eyes peacefully, and Chammi would stuff the end of her dupatta into her mouth to stop her laughter, and cry, 'Oh, my, Uncle is wiped out with exhaustion, work must have been so hard!'

Aliya found life in this house more contentious and tiring than in her own home, but she kept herself occupied somehow or other. Uncle had given her the keys to his bookcases so that she could read his books and enlighten herself. Along with this he had also instructed her not to let Jameel get his hands on the keys. These books were of no importance to that useless hack, in his opinion. In the silence of the afternoon, she'd take out the books with great care and read them one by one. Her heart felt the greatest sympathy for all the characters in the books who had been shot in the struggle for freedom, fighting for the welfare of man, but she also feared them. She believed that such people loved no one: they got married, had children, then destroyed them. Their own homes had no part in the world. Their families were not mankind, they were thorns in the feet of love that injured you in just a short while. The fates of Amma, Aunty, Kusum and Tehmina all flashed before her eyes. At the age of seventeen or eighteen she'd already become so wise. How quickly worry and sorrow had snatched away her childhood.

3

A letter had come from Mamoo. He wrote to Amma that he wouldn't send all the money at once, as per his wife's advice, but rather, he'd send thirty rupees a month for Aliya's education, and this could also be used for clothing and such. One shouldn't have too much money on hand in bad times, he cautioned, or everyone else would have their eyes on it.

Amma was very pleased with this letter and her hands shook with joy on receiving the money order three months later, but Aliya felt angry that for one thing he'd responded only after three months, and on top of that he'd decided to send only thirty rupees per month. Would she end up being a burden on Uncle during these hard times? It was useless saying anything to Amma. She didn't want to upset her by criticizing Mamoo. She slipped off silently to her room, but she was enraged by his letter, and the letter she was longing to receive had not arrived. In those three months, Abba had written only one letter, in which he'd expressed his happiness that they'd gone to Uncle's house and instructed Aliya to continue with her studies. But he wrote not a word about himself.

She was just thinking about this when Amma came upstairs. She was out of breath from climbing the stairs, but her face was pink with happiness. 'My sister-in-law is so clever,' she said. 'She must know, after all, that everyone here is naked and hungry, and that we'd be robbed,' Amma whispered. 'Ask Jameel to arrange a teacher for you and you can take the exam from home.'

'But, Amma, what can we afford with that money? We should shoulder all our own expenses. It won't be long before Abba's back; Uncle's got him a very good lawyer. Abba will get the shortest possible sentence.'

'Who knows? That officer didn't even die, but the charge is murder. Who knows when he'll come home? Oh dear, if he had any decency, he'd have spared a thought for his family . . .' Amma was perhaps recalling bitter bygone days. Aliya had no way of knowing what she was thinking.

'Mazhar's Bride! Oh, Bride!' Aunty called to Amma from the courtyard. Her cry was mingled with the voices of Shakeel and Chammi bickering.

'Coming! Allah, what a disaster . . .' Amma muttered. 'We won't ask them for more money than this. It's your Uncle's duty to look after our needs; after all it's his brother's fault we're here. We didn't come here of our own accord . . .' Amma went downstairs without waiting for Aliya to reply.

∞

It was late afternoon. The sun was already low in the sky. Aliya lay face down on the bed for a long time. Outside, a toy seller shook a rattle and sang sweetly, 'Rubber dolls! Buy a rubber doll! Buy a fun doll!' Chammi was done quarrelling now and was playing a record on the gramophone with a worn-out needle. Aliya imagined that all the records would be ruined this way, and she resolved to tell Shakeel to get a new box of needles for Chammi.

The sunlight had turned yellow by now. Kareeman Bua was noisily calling people to tea, but Aliya didn't feel like going downstairs. She went on to the open roof and lay down on the bare cot, now burning hot from lying in the sun all day. The shouts of children playing on nearby roofs grew louder, and the sky was turning grey from the smoke that rose from nearby houses.

The cot was still a bit too warm, so she got up and began to stroll about. She felt so dejected. Right then she wished she could just leave the house and go somewhere else. But where? Since she'd arrived here, she'd not once set foot outside the house. Whenever Chammi was in the mood, she'd throw on a burqa and wander from house to house, though only to Muslim homes, because she absolutely loathed Hindus. In this home, Aliya's world was limited to books. She had taken the key to Uncle's bookcase and hidden it in her bed. Kareeman Bua was calling out that it was time for tea, so she really had to go downstairs. But just then, Chammi came up with her teacup, her round face looking so grave it was almost foolish, and her eyes slightly pink.

'What's wrong, Chammi?' asked Aliya as she took the cup.

'Nothing, I just got a letter from my father.'

'So everything's okay, isn't it?' Chammi's seriousness made her feel fearful.

'No, Bajiya, He's written that now he'll send only ten rupees a month. I've got another little brother that was just born, so expenses have also increased. That's why he's reduced it by a full five rupees.'

'Oh, so that's what's wrong! Congratulations on your new brother, Chammi.'

'Why have I started having brothers! God willing he'll die; all my brothers and sisters died with my mother. Now I'm all alone, I have no one.'

'Don't say such things, Chammi.'

'Then you tell me, no matter how many times my father marries, no matter how many of his wives have spawn, will they all still be my brothers and sisters?' Tears had started in her eyes. She looked so innocent at that moment—she had the sort of face that looked terribly innocent even when she was fighting or going red with rage.

Aliya hugged Chammi. At that moment, Chammi's father seemed the most heartless creature in the world. He'd pursued no other occupation in life besides changing wives. After the death of Chammi's mother, he'd married twice and divorced both wives over the slightest things. He also had a strange way of getting divorced. He'd go into the sitting room and write out his divorce papers, then sent them to his wife. After that moment he'd begin to observe purdah from her. But the fourth wife had caused him a world of trouble. After giving birth to an endless succession of children, she had pinned him down so that he was powerless. In the meantime, Chammi had become a nuisance to all of them—her father ceased to shower her with affection and instead made her the scapegoat for his sorrows.

'I'm totally alone, Bajiya! But everyone likes you, even Jameel. Whenever he comes in, he just hangs around you.' She laughed sarcastically.

Aliya trembled and glanced at Chammi. She saw in that moment Tehmina's lush green mehndi plant dried up and turned black, and the last drops of water from Kusum's white sari soaked into the ground. *My heavens, I won't be stupid as they had been. No such thing will happen to me, least of all with that idiot! Why, Uncle wouldn't even give him the keys to his bookcase.*

'Chammi, you're such a child! What must you think of me? Even if ten Jameels came along, do you think I'd let them ruin me?'

Chammi stared hard into Aliya's eyes as though searching for the truth; then feeling reassured, she hugged her. 'That's what I thought. I thought, our Bajiya could hardly be like that.' She laughed very proudly. 'But, Bajiya, tell me, how am I to survive now with so little money?'

'Nobody ever even sends me ten rupees, Chammi,' she said, thinking of Abba.

'What, won't my ten rupees belong to you as well, Bajiya?' Chammi pouted and picked up the teacup.

'Sure, that's fine. But then I won't give you one paisa of it,' said Aliya to cheer her up.

'Oh, and Bajiya, there's going to be a rally tomorrow in my room.' It seemed Chammi had already forgotten everything.

'What sort of rally?' Aliya looked at her with surprise.

'Why, a Muslim League rally, of course, Bajiya!'

'But Uncle will be angry—why don't you just join the Muslim League as a member in your heart?' asked Aliya, trying to reason with her.

'Who is he to get angry with me? Do I forbid him from going to Congress Kaffir rallies?'

'But what good will come from you being in the Muslim League?' asked Aliya. She felt sad that everyone here was quite mad.

'None—I'm just a Muslim, so I belong in the Muslim League.' Chammi laughed proudly. 'I'll give people sweets—bataashey—Bajiya, those will be good, won't they?'

'Chammi, you've got so little money, and you need to make it last the whole month; why are you pointlessly getting involved in such things?' Aliya again tried to reason with her.

'What? What does this have to do with money? I would sacrifice my life for the Muslim League, our Kaffir uncle will see!' Then she suddenly dashed downstairs, as though she'd just remembered something.

'Oh, Chammi! Why are you trying to get yourself in trouble?' Aunty was calling from downstairs. Aliya moved away from the roof and stood by the window in the large room. From there she could see the courtyard downstairs.

'She's an extremely disobedient girl. I've seen the new way of women also going to rallies—have men not ruined enough homes that way?' Amma was sitting on the bed in the yard, chopping betel nut.

'I do what I want,' said Chammi in her peculiar way, and she put on the burqa she was holding and went outside.

'What can I do? Even when her uncle gets mad at her, I feel sad.' Aunty was perched beside Amma. Granny began to cough loudly, so Kareeman Bua quickly rushed off to her room.

4

In the evening a long, threadbare dhurrie was rolled out in Chammi's room and all the mohalla's children started coming in and sitting down. Granny's bed had been moved to a corner of the courtyard. Kareeman Bua had sprinkled water around it. Granny held a small fan in her hand and gently waved it as she listened to the din of Chammi and the children in disapproving silence. There were signs of distress on her face. Aliya sat down at the head of the bed and took the fan from her hand and began fanning Granny herself.

'Come, Bajiya, you come to my rally too,' urged Chammi, as she grasped Aliya's hand and tried to pull her away.

'Not me, Chammi, I don't like such things at all.'

'Then don't come, the rally will hardly be ruined without you,' said Chammi with a pout. 'I always knew you'd take Uncle's side!'

'If you knew, then good. Aliya doesn't go in for such foolish things,' Amma snarled at Chammi, but Chammi gave no answer and her face fell as she quickly went into her room and started shouting slogans with the children.

'Oh dear, now what am I to do, Mazhar's Bride, her uncle's in the sitting room; if he hears the slogans, what will happen? I've told her again and again, "If you hold a rally, at least read Milad at the beginning," but she doesn't listen to me,' fretted Aunty, who seemed quite upset by Chammi's rally. 'Really, what was her father thinking; why doesn't he just have the marriage vows read over her and get her settled?'

'Let he who enjoys it get married,' retorted Chammi from the doorway, before getting back to work.

'Oh dear, Shakeel, do get up and close the sitting room door so the noise doesn't reach there.' Despite the fact that Aunty disliked what Chammi had said, she still seemed to be protecting her.

'Why should I close it? If Abba breaks her bones one of these days, it'll be a good thing,' snapped Shakeel, jumping up excitedly. He had been sitting and patching his school bag nearby.

'You're talking nonsense. Chammi is much older than you.' Aunty stared at him angrily and Kareeman Bua got up to put the tea things on the tray. She closed the door of the sitting room and then began again to set the tea out. After shouting slogans, the children were singing along with Chammi:

> The tulsi was planted in Kashi; the goats ate it all up
> Mourn, Gandhiji, the Hindu grandmother's dead!

At this spontaneously composed song, Aliya burst out laughing, but when she saw Uncle standing by the door of the sitting room, she got worried and called out to Chammi. Chammi turned and saw, and then began calmly handing out bataashey to the children.

'Good God, this mad fool of a girl won't listen to reason. I'll break her bones one day.' Uncle stormed out into the yard, his face pink with rage, and the children took off in a swarm. One of the children's sweets fell to the ground and broke into pieces and he gazed up at Uncle with frightened eyes as he picked it up.

'Oh, well, you're very intelligent, aren't you? Are you taunting me for my ignorance after giving me such a wonderful education?' Chammi saw no reason to keep quiet.

When Uncle lunged towards her, Aunty intervened. 'Mercy! What is this madness? You'd raise your hand against a young girl?' She began to hyperventilate.

'Oh, come on, Aunty, let him beat me, it will make him feel so much better,' challenged Chammi obstinately.

Aliya wanted to grab Chammi's hand and take her back to the room but Chammi pushed her away. Kareeman Bua stood there dumbstruck and Granny's breathing became laboured as she attempted to say something, but Amma just sat there on the bed, watching it all like a spectator.

'Chammi, go inside, sweetie, won't you listen to me?' Aliya attempted to coax Chammi, but Chammi just looked at her strangely, before going back into her room.

'What should I do? How everyone frustrates me, Aliya dear! You try to reason with these people,' said Uncle sadly as he looked over at Aliya. His anger had dissolved; he felt powerless and wanted encouragement. A short while later, he returned to the sitting room with his head down, and for a while there was silence all around.

'Oh dear, oh dear, that I should be forced to witness such things in my own lifetime!' Kareeman Bua sat down on her stool and was speaking to herself. 'And this is the family of the late Master Muzaffar; he must be rolling over in his grave, right now!'

As night began to fall, Kareeman Bua lit the lanterns and placed them all about and made up the beds in the courtyard. Chammi could be heard sobbing softly in her room.

'What will become of Chammi?' Granny asked softly, looking at Aliya. By now her breathing was under control. 'My love for everyone doesn't let me die.'

Aliya didn't know what to say. She held on to Granny's hand. Life was so full of confusion. Chammi didn't care about Granny at all, but even when she was lying on her bed, she was a support to Aliya.

'What's happened, Aliya Madam?' asked Jameel when he entered the house. He came and sat down on the rusty metal chair. 'Everyone's so quiet right now.'

Hearing Jameel call her 'Aliya Madam' made her feel as though he were spewing venom. She remained silent.

'There was a Muslim League rally here; then your father scolded Chammi. That's all,' replied Amma rebelliously.

'Great! Great!' He laughed loudly. 'Then I imagine my father must be livid right now. Amazing! What a great man he is, my father, isn't he? And this home is a wonderful example of that. He's been a slave to the Congress for years and hasn't been able to get me a job even though we have Congress rule now.' Jameel laughed again.

'Yes, why don't you start another fire now? You have no respect at all for your father,' snapped Aunty. 'Certainly, he serves the Congress but he hardly does it out of greed.'

'Amma, what do you know? Oh God, I'm so hungry. If there's anything left from Abba's guests, please feed me too.' Jameel was bent on making a joke of the matter.

'You're constantly talking nonsense and nothing else! I suppose you've got so large eating somewhere else, since you just die of hunger here,' shrieked Aunty.

'Amma! No need to get so angry.' Jameel burst out laughing. 'Okay, you tell me, Aliya Madam, are we not all members of the world my father is so worked up about creating? Then why does he need to ruin us too? And your father, Uncle Mazhar, who's gone to jail for bashing in the head of an Englishman, how has he helped things, exactly? Hasn't he ruined everything for you? How you'll suffer in this house, after leading such a splendid life. Right now, I'm not good for anything, otherwise . . .' He stopped for a moment and stared at Aliya.

'Don't say such things, Jameel; what if Granny hears while she's sleeping?' Aliya spoke softly to Jameel, as she quickly drew near him.

'Who knows how your mother puts up with all this. I wore myself out fighting with him. After all, what did he get out of his enmity with the English?' Amma sighed deeply and put a paan gilori in her mouth.

'Will you not eat with me, Aliya Madam?' asked Jameel, taking the tray from Kareeman Bua's hands.

'No, thanks, I'm not hungry right now.' She got up and went into Chammi's room. Chammi was still lying face down on her bed, sobbing.

'Come on, let's go outside, Chammi, it's so hot in here.' Aliya pulled her up. 'Let's go up to the roof and stroll about.'

Chammi came out of her room, but immediately sat down when she saw Jameel. 'You go ahead and stroll, Bajiya.'

Aliya felt great peace on reaching the open air on the roof after the fetid atmosphere downstairs. Even in the dusty summer heat, there was a sweet coolness in the dim moonlight up here. Children were happily playing train in the gali down below. Whenever they were especially pleased, they'd shout 'Long live the Muslim League!' and 'Long live Congress!' a couple of times. Then they whistled like a train, cried 'Chug chug!' and ran off. After that, all was silent.

Standing by the rooftop wall, she saw that the high-school building was obscured by darkness because of the dense shade of the trees. She stared at the building vacantly for a while— one day Shakeel would study there. Surely he would achieve his dream. But her own dreams had all evaporated. Now she wouldn't be able to study at a college. All the same, she must study. She had to stand on her own two feet. No one knew when Abba would return, and Uncle seemed so hopeless. When she'd speak of her father's case, he only replied in a roundabout manner. Aliya gazed at the sky as she thought; the moon looked so muted and drab.

'Aliya.'

She started and turned around. Jameel stood behind her.

'What are you doing up here alone?' he asked.

'Nothing.'

She felt nervous being there alone in her cousin's presence. Jameel looked around.

'You must feel anxious here, Aliya. If Tehmina were alive, perhaps you'd be happy and perhaps we'd have already married. Believe me, the wedding was taking place despite my extreme opposition. Nonetheless, when she died, I felt as though I had become a widower.' Jameel closed his eyes as though in pain.

'But why are you bringing this up now?'

'Just because I felt sympathy for her. I knew everything, and I also don't believe she died of natural causes.' Jameel looked into her eyes.

'This is your home; you may say whatever you wish.'

She turned her face away from him, but Jameel came and stood before her again.

'But listen, Aliya, I'm not all that bad,' he continued. 'The thing is that I got a letter from Safdar, and he said, "Don't marry Tehmina. I'm in love with her." But all the same, I couldn't stop the marriage. I still feel like a criminal because of that. If I could have, I would have done anything in my power to arrange their marriage but . . .' He fell silent for a moment. 'You don't consider me a criminal for it?'

What, he knows so much? She looked at Jameel with astonishment and then looked down again. Now that Tehmina's secret was revealed she began to loathe the very sight of Jameel. His words had pierced her heart like an arrow.

'If I want, I can leave and go to Mamoo's home right now.' Aliya knew the truth about her maternal uncle, but where else could she threaten to go?

'But you can't go! I'm in love with you—what would I do then?' Jameel blurted out.

He grabbed her hand and squeezed it. It was damp and cold and she felt as though she was rooted to the floor. She felt too weak to extricate herself, and stared helplessly at his clammy hand, which immediately brought to mind a frog that had once leapt on to her hand during monsoon. She shut her eyes for fear and shrieked. And then, who knows what happened to her, she kept on screaming, and she must have passed out as she screamed. When she opened her eyes again, everyone had gathered around her. Amma was weeping and Uncle was holding out a medicinal paste, but Jameel was nowhere to be seen.

'Those horrid wicked Hindus live nearby—you must have seen a ghost!' Chammi suggested as soon as Aliya opened her eyes, and Amma kept kissing her hand, overwhelmed with emotion.

'Again with your ignorant ideas!' Uncle lashed out at Chammi. 'No, no, she must have had some frightening thought; it's clearly a mental illness. Just make sure to eat this electuary every day, and your mind will grow stronger, dear,' he advised Aliya. He was so intent, he didn't even notice how desperate Chammi was to take revenge for his remark about her ignorance. But then for some reason she didn't say anything.

'But what happened, Aliya?' Aunty asked.

Aliya felt alarmed at this and closed her eyes as though she wished to go to sleep. After all, what could she tell them?

5

Abba's legal case had come to an end. He was sentenced to seven years' imprisonment for attempted murder. Afternoon had already faded when the news came. After a light drizzle, the sky had gone absolutely clear. When Uncle entered the house he looked ill, as though the strength to speak was somehow beyond him. Amma clutched at him.

'Please tell me some good news, my brother,' she pleaded, as she stared up at him, eyes full of hope and fear. Uncle slowly sat down on the stool in the courtyard, and Aliya filled the pot with water and set it by him. His face was pale and he began to sprinkle drops of water on it mechanically, while avoiding everyone's glances. Amma's patience finally gave out. The bad news was clear from his eyes. She burst out weeping as she stared at his face, and Aunty and Kareeman Bua rushed over to support her.

'Close your grandmother's door so that she won't hear the sounds of weeping,' Uncle said, looking over at Aliya. Then he turned to Amma and said, 'Bride of Mazhar, please be patient; these seven years will pass by too, and it could also be that he won't be in jail a year before we get independence.'

'Useless words! He destroyed an entire household! How are we to bear seven years? Seven years won't just pass quickly by,' sobbed Amma.

'My God, these British rulers didn't recognize how old our family is; they don't realize whose son he is. Our departed Master used to save people from the gallows. Important men used to live off his gifts; but now those times are gone,' wept Kareeman Bua as she recalled the bygone era, her face red with tears. She embraced Amma and tried to take her inside the room.

'We've been uprooted, we're ruined, why did he hate me so much that he would do this to me?' Amma screamed, out of control and breaking free of Kareeman Bua's embrace.

When Amma had been taken forcibly into her room, Aliya was left standing alone in the courtyard. Because of Amma's wailing no one had looked at Aliya, no one had even seen what was happening to her heart. She felt as though a well had been dug beneath her feet, and that she was slowly falling. Somehow, she managed to walk forward and grab on to the metal chair. A heavy silence had descended over the courtyard. A few moments later, she climbed the stairs, went to her room and fell upon her bed, where she began to sob in earnest.

After a good cry, her heart had calmed, but she felt totally devoid of thought. She picked up her course books mechanically, then put them down again. Her tutor would come to teach her at five o'clock. She set her pillow on top of the books as though today she hated even the sight of them. But what was the date today? She searched her memory— tonight would count as the first day of his sentence; evening was coming. She pushed one day forward, full of hope.

Then she heard footsteps on the stairs and saw that Uncle was coming towards her; so she sat down on her bed. She gazed patiently at his morose face, but when he began stroking her head and peered into her eyes, she trembled. Everything looked blurry on the other side of her curtain of tears.

'You must look after your mother, dear. Be brave, I have hope that the jail walls won't hold him for long, all right?' Uncle sighed deeply. The confidence in Uncle's eyes made her lower her eyes in acceptance. After he left, she wiped away her tears and lay down peacefully.

Evening was falling and each hawker of jasmine garlands shouted out as he passed by. The shadows had deepened in the room, but Aliya still lay on her bed with her face hidden. Aunty, Chammi, Kareeman Bua—each had come to her in turn, insisting on bringing her downstairs, but how could she go? How could she even look at her mother? Amma, who had been sitting in that house for one year, waiting like a traveller. And now their journey had been brought to a halt by this sad news; their luggage must now be unpacked.

The electric street lamp in the gali came on. She walked out of her room and on to the roof. Tonight she liked the darkness very much. The stars looked so bright in the dark night, like sorrows sparkling in the dark of sadness. There was a great din coming from nearby rooftops. Children quarrelled. Gramophone records played. Someone sang the bhajan '*Meera's lord, the lifter of mountains*'.

'Aliya, can I talk to you? You won't scream, will you?'

When had Jameel crept up on her on cat's feet? He looked quite anxious at that moment. This was the first time that he'd spoken to her since that bitter moment when he'd revealed his love several months earlier. He had even been coming home less frequently, and generally keeping to himself. Aunty had been worried by her son's state—she thought it was because he couldn't find a good job and was earning his living by tutoring a few worthless girls.

Aliya remained seated, lost in her thoughts.

'Do you hate me so much that you won't even answer me?' He reached out to her spontaneously and then withdrew his hand, embarrassed. Perhaps he remembered what had happened before. 'Won't you go to see your father in jail?'

'I can't see Abba in jail. Could I bear to see him as a criminal?' she spoke softly.

'Come now, since when is he a criminal? How is striking a British man a crime?'

'Humph!' She looked up at Jameel, startled. Even in that darkness, he looked so headstrong and earnest. She said nothing. A light mist filled the air and a few shreds of clouds swam about in the sky.

'Come on downstairs, please; if you sit with everyone else, you'll feel better,' Jameel said as though the feeling better part was a complete lie.

'You go ahead, I'll come in a little while.'

Jameel stood there for a few moments in silence, and then went away. She went into her room, pulled the table towards the bed and sat down to write Abba a letter. She wrote with a great deal of thought—the glimmering hope of a meeting would always eclipse the seven years of separation. 'I will wait for you every minute,' she wrote.

After finishing her letter, she rested her head on the table. How long seven years seemed at that moment. *Allah, how could Ramji have borne those fourteen years of exile in the forest?*

'Kareeman Bua, tell the household that I am deeply saddened by the news of my brother Mazhar's jail sentence. If someone could send me to jail in his place, I'd be prepared to go immediately. My own useless life is only . . .' She heard Asrar Miyan's tearful voice clearly from the doorway of the sitting room, as it pierced through the silence of the house. She lifted her head from the table and tucked the letter into an envelope.

There was no reply to Asrar Miyan's message, only the clanking of Kareeman Bua's tongs. God willing, Asrar Miyan would become deaf before he reached old age, like Granny. Then he would always think that the answer had been given but he just hadn't heard it.

She glanced out of the window of the large room and looked below. The beds were set up and everyone was seated quietly in the courtyard. Only Uncle was lying down, stroking his chest. Aunty's betel-nut cracker slowly clipped away, and Kareeman Bua was briskly toasting rotis. Jameel was seated on the metal chair, twisting his fingers about. Who knows where Chammi was. After that incident, one didn't even hear her voice. She'd forgotten all her quarrelling.

Aliya tiptoed downstairs. Amma looked so helpless in the yellow lamplight. She quickly went to sit by Uncle, but she didn't even stroke his head.

'Your tutor comes every day, right?' asked Uncle. He'd finally come up with a topic to discuss and the pall of silence lifted.

'Yes, he does.' She slid over and began stroking his head.

'If you don't work hard on your studies now, what will become of us? It's not like I have a son to help make these years pass by.' Amma was again overcome with weeping. Aliya got up quickly and went into Granny's room. Ever since the nights had grown dewy, Granny's bed had been moved back into her room. She spent all her time in that room, except during May and June.

Aliya perched on the edge of Granny's bed. Chammi lay on her own bed with her face covered. She had seen Aliya, then covered her face.

'Has any letter come from my son Mazhar?' asked Granny, attempting to bring her irregular breathing under control. She'd been having asthma attacks all the time recently.

'A letter did come, Granny; he has a lot of work and can't take a vacation.' Aliya's voice choked. When Chammi raised her head for a moment, Aliya saw two tears roll from her eyes, then disappear into her pillow.

'It feels as though life is ending now, who knows when your youngest uncle will return, he loved me very much. He was already eighteen years old, but he still slept with his head resting in my lap. Who knows when he'll . . .'

Granny's breathing grew rapid and she held her knees to her stomach.

'Aliya, Chammi, come and eat!' called Aunty from the yard. Aliya stood up as Kareeman Bua entered with Granny's food.

6

Amma had accepted her fate. Yes, she had tumbled down from her highest perch, but not so very far that she would consider Aunty her equal. Her face still reflected the pride she felt at receiving thirty rupees a month and the comfort she felt at the knowledge that she had money kept in trust by her brother. She also felt the shadow of protection conferred upon her by her only brother's high social standing and that of his English wife.

After the court ruling, Amma had written Mamoo several letters in which she had spoken ill of Uncle's home and its atmosphere. She expressed her wish to come live with him, but Mamoo responded helplessly that if they moved in, he too would be under government scrutiny and his status would be imperilled. Aliya did not mention to Amma the letter he had written to Aliya, in which he clearly acknowledged that his wife had been brought up in a liberal atmosphere. In her country, he wrote, it was not the custom to make life difficult by getting involved in pointless family squabbles. That was why it was important she try her best to convince her mother to stay there.

She'd read the letter and ripped it up. She didn't want to break Amma's heart. What have we left when we've lost faith? Even if faith in another finally proves deceptive, it can come in handy for a while. She had come to hate Mamoo deeply. *This crow with the gait of a swan has forgotten how he used to walk*, she thought disdainfully after reading his letter. One day, when she had made something of herself, she would rip up that faith he was sending to Amma and throw it far away. She resolved that from now on, she would work even harder at her studies.

In those days, it was extremely cold. All the same, she'd study until midnight, and when Shakeel came home late after loafing about all day and tapped softly on the front door, she'd go on tiptoe and unlock it. By now, Shakeel had enrolled in high school. She'd hidden the money for his fees from Amma and given it to him, but where would she get the money to buy all those books he needed? This was Shakeel's excuse for meeting up with friends to study. His eyes were full of impudence these days. Sometimes Aliya would admonish him as she opened the door, but he would burst out laughing carelessly.

There had been a knock at the door while she was studying this evening as well. She set down her books and walked quickly down the stairs. As she was opening the door, Jameel emerged from his room with a muffler wrapped about his ears. When he saw Aliya, he hesitated a moment, then grabbed Shakeel's arm and slapped him across the face a few times.

'There you go, make sure you remember this well.'

Shakeel glared at Jameel defiantly, but went quickly into Aunty's room.

'What's the use of hitting him? Buy him books; then he won't need to go study with his friends,' she said softly.

'Books? Nobody gave me books either, but I wasn't like this. This big lout of a camel doesn't think about anything. He could still come home at a reasonable time after studying a couple of hours. And don't you wonder who's had a silk shirt made for him? I've never had a friend like that.'

Jameel was angrily rubbing his hands together and she just gaped at him like an idiot. 'So what if his friend had a shirt made for him?' she retorted.

Jameel stood with his head bowed. She began to feel compassion for him. He hadn't even been able to get any job training due to a lack of funds. He didn't have a proper job at all. Even the money he earned from tutoring he handed over to Aunty, and on top of this, that lout Shakeel annoyed him and didn't listen to anything he said.

When she turned to go upstairs, Jameel came with her. 'Shall I come up with you as well, so we can talk for a little while?'

'What sort of time is this for talking? Go to sleep,' she said quickly and placed her foot on the stairs.

'Oh my, what are you up to at this hour, Bajiya?' asked Chammi, popping out of her room.

'I came down to open the door for Shakeel.'

'Oh, great! You both came to open the door—well, well, what a tough lock that must be.' She laughed sarcastically. 'Do you feel embarrassed to be talking to Bajiya in front of everyone else?' she asked Jameel.

'Chammi, don't talk nonsense,' Jameel pleaded.

'Don't be fooled by him, Bajiya, he used to be in love with me, and now he is with you . . .' Chammi stopped in the middle of the sentence.

Aliya rushed up the stairs. She was out of breath. Good God, what a disaster. Was this why Chammi always followed Jameel around? And now Jameel had left her and come after Aliya. She began to tremble from the cold and hatred. She slipped under the quilt and picked up her book again, but she couldn't read a word. Jameel's silence and seriousness and the respect it had earned him over the past few months had all been destroyed. The dogs in the gali barked and howled so loudly she began to feel a dread of the night.

In the morning, Chammi did not come to wake her lovingly as she did each day. Aliya lay there for quite some time waiting for her. The newspaper salesman was wandering about the gali, shouting: 'Iron will clash with iron in Europe! War is imminent! It's here, it's here! Today's paper—no one can stop the war—a fourteen-year-old girl has been abducted!'

She got out of bed in annoyance. What did it have to do with her if there was a war in Europe? Which of Amma's sister-in-law's loved ones would be killed, and are women good for nothing but falling in love and eloping or getting abducted? *Everyone can go to hell*, she thought sadly as she walked down the stairs. But why did Chammi distrust her? God, she was such a crazy idiot.

Chammi was seated on the takht nibbling a paratha. Her eyes were swollen. When she saw Aliya, she turned away and drank down all her tea in one gulp. Aliya was amused at Chammi's foolishness, but when she slipped over and sat next to her, Chammi looked upset and moved to the other side. Then she got up and went into her room.

'What time did Shakeel come home last night, Aliya?' asked Aunty.

'Around twelve o'clock. Jameel also woke up, and he slapped Shakeel.'

'That boy is not showing much promise,' said Amma with disgust.

'What can I do, Mazhar's Bride? I'll go mad,' lamented Aunty, sighing deeply.

'His father should take his own child in hand,' goaded Amma. But Aunty was not easily goaded. She herself quarrelled with Uncle only when she wished.

'It's a generational thing. Time was when none of Master's children would set foot outside the house after seven o'clock,' murmured Kareeman Bua, haunted by the past.

Aliya went into Chammi's room after she finished her tea. Granny was asleep. Her laboured breathing gave her no rest at night. Aliya tiptoed over to Chammi and sat down. Chammi lay covered in a quilt from head to toe. The quilt had holes in places, making it look like the rags of a fakir.

'Come and sit upstairs in the sun, Chammi,' suggested Aliya, sliding the quilt off her face.

'I'm not speaking to you.'

'Come upstairs, silly, and we'll talk there.'

Chammi got up and came with her. Her eyes had a look of distress in them.

'Why haven't you spoken to me all morning?' asked Aliya, as she sat Chammi down in her quilt.

'What do you mean? Why would I stop speaking to you? It's not like I'm in love with that ass that I would be jealous of you!' she exclaimed, making a face.

'You decided all by yourself that Jameel was in love with me. I told you even before that I despise such things, and he has never even said anything to me,' she lied.

'Jameel used to love me. I didn't even know what love was, but now if he's changed, let him change, since when do I love that idiot?'

'Whether you're in love with him or not, I do know how much you used to love me,' Aliya said with a reproachful look at Chammi. Then Chammi fell into her arms.

'Of course I don't suspect my bajiya, I was just sad about something.'

She was touched by Chammi's innocence and wanted to hold her close to her heart; all the same, she continued to act sulky with her.

'Listen, I'll tell you everything,' said Chammi, turning Aliya's face towards her.

'The year Jameel was studying for his FA exam, he asked me for money. When I refused, he looked at me with such eyes that I gave him all my savings, and then he hugged me tightly . . . and I really liked it.' She turned pink with embarrassment.

'Then what happened?'

'Then, Bajiya, I started to fall for Jameel. I gave my five rupees for food to Aunty, and all the rest to Jameel. I didn't have a single piece of clothing made in those three years; haven't you seen, all my clothes are falling apart!' She thought for a moment. 'Before you came, Jameel slept in this room. I used to come visit him at night, but, Bajiya, I swear to God, he never did anything improper. One time I lay down next to him, but he sat up. He only showed me affection.' Chammi's face was turning red.

'Then what happened, Chammi?'

'Then, Bajiya, Aunty arranged his marriage. She thought that if Jameel became Mazhar Uncle's son-in-law, he'd pay for his MA and also get him training. But just between us, I'll tell you that Aunty is very fearful of your mother, that's why she asked, without even an engagement, to please help continue with his studies, because her own husband was useless. Aunty requested the engagement with Tehmina very fearfully, and the day your mother sent the acceptance letter, she wept with joy, and even I cried, but out of shock. After all, how could I say that I had paid for his BA, and that I'd also pay for his MA? Who knew what I'd suffered?' She put her head down and began thinking about something.

'Then, Chammi?'

'The world is a terrible place, Bajiya. After he finished his BA, Jameel began to change. If I sat by him for too long, he'd make some excuse to make me go away. He'd forgotten everything, hadn't he? And now he remembers nothing at all! He makes fun of me in front of everyone and says mean things. Well, let him. I'm not some bitch that I'll just go following him around.' Chammi suppressed a sigh and looked at Aliya in such a way that she felt miserable. She thought of Tehmina. What if Chammi were to do something stupid too? Then what would happen?

'Who knows, Chammi, maybe Jameel does love you, or maybe he doesn't. Can't humans be happy without love?'

'Does that mean I should go around throwing myself at him? You know what? We should return the love of those who love us, that's a fair exchange; give with one hand, take with the other.' She got up, laughing. 'Granny's health was very bad last night, Bajiya, I couldn't sleep at all.'

After Chammi left the room, Aliya sat for a long time, swaying from side to side, wrapped in the quilt. Then she got out her books and went and sat in the sun. *Oh dear, what does Jameel get out of that poor girl with his games! But then, why are all these women so hungry for love, Allah?*

7

The clock was striking midnight. Aliya had grown exhausted from studying and put her books on the table. She wanted to go to sleep, but she couldn't. And when sleep wouldn't come, so many other things began to twist about in her mind. Why had no letter come from Abba? Tehmina had thrown her life away for love, and now Aliya was all alone; there would be no companionship in her fate. Amma was embroiled in her own sorrows—she'd never even peered into the heart of this child of hers, never thought about her—and Jameel was becoming an obstacle in her path for no good reason. Had he nothing else to do in life, for God's sake? But why was she even thinking about him? The light from the street lamp coming in through the window was preventing her from falling asleep, so she closed the shutters.

But suddenly she heard everyone talking downstairs. She lay still and tried to hear what they were saying. It was midnight—perhaps Shakeel had come home and everyone had been waiting up for him. Then there was the sound of footsteps on the stairs, and she panicked and sat up. Jameel was coming towards her.

'Aliya, Granny's health is much worse,' he said, 'please come downstairs for a little while.' He was quite serious. 'I hope you don't feel anxious; one day this will happen to all of us.'

Her heart beat fast. She understood everything now. She felt her legs trembling, but she gathered up her courage and went down with Jameel. He was holding on to her hand, but she couldn't even tell if this hand was her own or someone else's. Granny's bed had been brought into the middle of the room and her face had been turned towards the Kaaba. Amma, Aunty and Uncle stood silently around the bed. Granny's laboured breathing was so peaceful now. There seemed to be no spark of life at all. Her eyes were glued to the door, still full of expectation. Chammi had wrapped herself around Granny's feet and lay there sobbing. Aliya thought of that wretch, her youngest uncle, whom she had never seen. She wished she could scream—'Granny, stop waiting for that useless child now!'

Kareeman Bua paced around the bed muttering prayers. 'Oh Lord, give Mistress her health, and take me instead. Oh Lord, oh Lord.' Emperor Babur had requested the very same exchange for his son Humayun's life. Oh, Kareeman Bua, what was this love that still raged in your heart? Aliya wanted to step forward and make Kareeman Bua sit down; she tried to embrace her, but Kareeman Bua freed herself and began praying again, 'Oh Lord, oh Lord.'

Just then, Granny's breath caught in her throat, and with that she found eternal peace. Kareeman Bua clasped her hands together and stood up. There wasn't a single tear in her eyes. Uncle took his hand away from his mother's pulse, wrapped her hands across her chest and covered her face with the quilt. Kareeman Bua left the room, her head down.

'Get up now, Chammi,' said Aunty, lifting Chammi up. But Chammi lost control when she saw Granny's covered face.

Uncle's face was turning pink as he tried to control his emotions. Poignant memories of his mother passed before his eyes as he shook with the shock of eternal separation. He went into the sitting room, his head bowed, perhaps in order to inform Asrar Miyan. Amma and Aunty tried to hush Chammi, though she kept getting away from them. But when Jameel came forward and placed his hand on her shoulder, Chammi laid her head against his chest and fell silent as though she'd never been weeping at all.

Aliya left the room. Kareeman Bua had made a hearth of bricks in the courtyard and was heating water in a large pot, and Aliya, who had not yet been able to shed one tear for her grandmother's death, heaved a sob when she saw the flames leaping in the dark. Kareeman Bua looked up at her and then looked down again.

The night was spent sitting by Granny's bed. Amma and Aunty had forgotten all of Granny's crimes and tortures and wailed at her memory, as though the world had become empty without her. As long as Granny had lived, she had tormented everyone, and when she had reached old age, everyone had taken their revenge. They had picked her up like some useless object and thrown her aside, and then got wrapped up in their own lives, and Granny could do nothing but stare on.

Aliya wished she could stuff her ears with cotton. She couldn't bear to hear tales of Amma's and Aunty's great love for her. Why was it that no one could remember Granny's cruelty at this moment? She preferred Chammi, who wasn't saying anything and, after crying for a little while, lay in one corner of the dhurrie sleeping very peacefully as though her head still rested on Jameel's shoulder. And Kareeman Bua, who sat across from her in the cold breeze, blowing on the damp wood and swaying as she read the holy Quran in her lap—how calmly and quietly she had endured Granny's death. Kareeman Bua, who had served her body and soul for six years, hadn't shed a single tear.

Aliya wished she could curl up in a corner somewhere and sleep. She had neither extreme love for Granny nor any special complaints. She was just her grandmother, that was all. Nonetheless, she couldn't lie down now. When Chammi had fallen asleep, Amma had criticized her spitefully.

At last, morning came. Kareeman Bua spread the dhurrie out in the courtyard and the women of the mohalla came and gathered there. Each remembered their own sorrows and wept, and Chammi, on seeing them, felt overwhelmed with grief herself. When Granny had been bathed and prepared for her final journey, all the women on the veranda fell silent behind the canvas curtain. Only Kareeman Bua stood by the corpse with her hands clasped, muttering to herself. When the men came in to take out the bier for the funeral procession, Asrar Miyan stood in the very front.

'You watch yourself! Mistress never once looked upon you in your life, and now you've come to befoul her corpse!' Kareeman Bua shrieked at Asrar Miyan, who hid behind Jameel like a thief. Everyone stared questioningly at him.

'Oh dear, where is Shakeel? He should have come to take his Granny to her grave,' worried Aunty, as she looked for Shakeel through a hole in the curtain. Where was he?

'Go inside, Kareeman Bua!' said Uncle, placing his hand on Kareeman Bua's shoulder.

'Mistress, we have entrusted you to God, we have entrusted you,' murmured Kareeman Bua, as she walked out of the yard and into the veranda.

As Granny's corpse passed out of the house through the front door, everyone shrieked and burst into tears, but Kareeman Bua, head down, was gathering up all the debris scattered about the yard.

A little while later, after the guests had left, the house seemed to grow totally deserted. Aliya had no idea what to do now.

That night, Uncle left for Kanpur at nine o'clock on business. The Non-cooperation Movement was at its height, and he would be busy for many days. Aliya was extremely offended that he had left that very same day. Could he not stay at home to mourn his own mother for a couple of days? Couldn't he take even a small rest from his political activities? But when Amma objected to his leaving, Aliya just listened silently. Who knows why she couldn't say one word against Uncle.

Jameel had sent telegrams to Najma Aunty, Abba and Chammi's father, and now everyone awaited their replies.

Starting the next day, life went back to normal as though nothing had occurred at all. Perhaps the only time there was a sense of Granny's death was when Kareeman Bua would finish up her chores and sit down to read the holy Quran; but no one else read even a verse. Aliya began to envy Kareeman Bua's love. She'd wanted to read some fragments of the Quran so many times and pray for Granny's soul, but she didn't have time. Thoughts of exam preparation weighed upon her and she desperately wished she could study attentively again. She wasn't prepared to lose an entire year to Granny's memory. She considered her own love inferior to Kareeman Bua's and consoled herself with this thought.

For a few days Chammi was fearful of going into her own room. Perhaps it seemed desolate after losing her old companion. She just wandered about idly or sat on the stool in the courtyard and mended her clothes. Then she'd water the flowerpots and beds, and when she got bored of even that, she'd put on a burqa and wander from house to house in the neighbourhood.

Then one day, she picked up the broom and began cleaning out her room again. She swept out all the cobwebs, dusted off the portrait of Muhammad Ali Jauhar, patched the old embroidered white sheets and spread them over the two beds. Then she lay down on her neat and tidy bed and began to sing like always:

Māl-e-soz-e-gham hai! Nihānī dekhte jāo
Behold, o beloved, the consequence of searing hidden sorrows

Chammi knew all the songs on the gramophone records and all the ghazals sung by the fakirs by heart. She had a talent for singing the right ghazal or song for every occasion.

That day, as Chammi lay singing in great style, Aliya wished she could go and hug her, but Chammi still wasn't speaking to her directly. Despite telling her everything, a splinter remained in her heart that wasn't in Aliya's power to remove.

Letters had arrived from Najma Aunty and from Chammi's father. They had both written that since Amma had already departed, there was no point in coming home. If only someone had told them beforehand! Chammi was beside herself after reading her father's letter. 'Yes, now what's the point in coming? However could he find peace being separated from his wife's side for even a moment? If I could, I would strangle my dear respected father's throat with my own two hands!'

'Chammi, do try to hold your tongue,' Amma chided her. Then Chammi broke down weeping. For some reason, she was wary of talking back to Amma even after she had known her so long.

Abba had also received the announcement of Granny's death and sent a letter.

'No jail can imprison a man's imagination,' he had written. 'It cannot be locked up. I carried my mother's bier, and I lowered her into her grave. But don't despair, my daughter. You should not feel heartbroken. Death is also a fact of life. Study hard and send me the good news of your passing your exam.'

Aliya sat with her head bowed down for a long time after reading his letter. It was afternoon, but she didn't feel like studying. For one thing, Abba's letter had made her depressed. For another, in the silence of afternoon, the sound of Kareeman Bua softly reading the holy Quran sounded to her like a lamentation.

She came out of her room and went downstairs to sit next to Kareeman Bua on the takht. Amma and Aunty must have been sleeping because she couldn't hear either of them speaking. She sat by Kareeman Bua with her head down for as long as she read, and when she wrapped up the holy Quran and began praying, tears came to Aliya's eyes—what a great example of love Kareeman Bua gave her! She could just as well take a nap during the day when she grew tired from work.

'You didn't sleep, Aliya dear?' asked Kareeman Bua after she had finished her prayers.

'I wasn't sleepy, Kareeman Bua, and . . .' She fell silent.

'Do you feel hungry, sweetie? I'll start the fire and toast up a roti for you.'

'No, Kareeman Bua, I was feeling sad listening to you read.'

'Chammi's father and Najma should have come as well. Chammi would have seen her father, and then, if nothing else, they would have laid eyes on the bed where their mother breathed her last. It's the changing times—time was they couldn't rest until they saw their mother,' lamented Kareeman Bua.

'You loved Granny so much, Kareeman Bua, I bet she felt the same way about you.'

'Did Mistress love me?' Kareeman Bua turned the question around. 'You weren't around for your granny's time, my dear. Who knows if she loved anyone or not! Yes, it was only her youngest that she loved, the one who disappeared off to who knows where; the Khilafat Movement took him—but I was just a servant. Me, Aliya my dear, what standing did I have?' Kareeman Bua pulled her kameez up as she sat down with her back to Aliya. There were black spots on her back, and white flesh protruded from one of these.

'What's this that's happened, Kareeman Bua?' asked Aliya. Kareeman Bua quickly pulled down the kameez.

'My mother came in Mistress's dowry; my father had died, and I was small. When I grew up a little, Mistress had me married to another servant in the house. It was a brand-new marriage. Because of this I made a slight error in my care of Mistress—this was my punishment for that, that's all.' Kareeman Bua bowed her head in thought.

Allah, what a puzzle was this Kareeman Bua. Even after enduring so much torture, she had been devoted to Granny as long as she'd remained alive, and even now she didn't speak ill of her. Aliya stared at her in amazement.

'I had eaten her salt my entire life and even now I eat the salt of her children. Salt carries great obligations, Aliya my dear. My mother, may God give her the fate of paradise, used to say that he who does not repay the obligations of salt will not be excused by God. Mistress, if I did any wrong, please do forgive me, so I can breathe happily in the next world.'

Kareeman Bua got up and began tidying the dirty pots and pans, and Aliya felt as though she had overturned an entire container of salt into her mouth and that it tasted more bitter to her than poison.

8

As the sun set, the hawkers swooped in for the kill, each shouting louder than the last. Children and men called out from rooftops and open windows, as everyone hailed their favourite hawkers to break their fasts. Aliya opened the window and glared out into the gali for a moment. The black gate of the high school across the way was closed, and a cuckoo sang from the thicket of trees. *Who knows if Shakeel even goes to school or not*, she thought. But who would care? If Uncle paid the slightest heed to the household, it wouldn't fix everything, but . . . suddenly she missed Abba. She would definitely send him an Eid card this year. When she closed the window and came out on to the roof, she felt a slight chill in the air, but all the same she began to stroll about. Children shouted and flew kites from the roofs. Aliya remembered how, as a child, she'd once tried to fly a kite with the child of a Bhangi, and Abba had scolded her sternly. But she was still very fond of kites.

'Aliya . . .' Aunty came panting upstairs and stood by her, her face pink with effort. This happened to her every time she climbed the stairs; the very thought of it sent her into palpitations. 'Here you go, your clothes,' said Aunty. She laughed after her breathing had returned to normal and held out a bundle. 'Dye the dupatta and pleat it, then stitch up the pyjamas on the sewing machine—you already have kurtas.'

Aliya opened the bundle with great interest and examined its contents. Inside gleamed a muslin dupatta from Dhaka and blue satin fabric for pyjamas.

'But, Aunty, how could this be . . .?'

'Hush, hush, put it on for sure tonight and enjoy your Eid.' She turned to go. 'It's almost time to break the fast, you're not coming downstairs?'

Allah, where had this clothing come from, who had bought it? No one in the house had clothing made for Eid at all. Aunty had brought it up with Uncle a couple of times, but every time he'd been embarrassed and retreated to his sitting room. So then who had brought this clothing for her? Had Jameel spent his tutoring money on her? Or had Uncle taken Abba's place and bought it for her? Her heart began to beat with happiness. It must have been Uncle who had bought it.

But in just a short while, she found out who it was. She could hear Shakeel speaking very clearly downstairs: 'Jameel had clothes made for Bajiya, but nothing came for me. Do I have to get my Eid gift from my friends as well?'

'Don't talk rubbish, you good-for-nothing!' Aunty scolded him. 'Is she not your sister? Why don't you buy clothes for her yourself? Really, many boys like you feed their entire families.'

'Yes, when you spend so much time outside the house, wear the clothes there—Jameel is a very good boy,' said Amma, picking on Shakeel as well.

'What have I ever got from this house? I guess my friends will have to give me my clothes too!' Shakeel responded brashly.

'If you too become like Bajiya, I swear to God, Jameel will make you ten suits of clothing, but no one's going to care about you when you're like this.' Chammi let fly a volley of arrows that pierced Aliya's heart.

Aliya laid the clothing down on the bed. For a moment, she felt that these were a gift of Jameel's deep love, but the very next moment they felt clammy and shroud-like to her. A blue-lipped face peered out from the pile of clothing. She trembled, gathered it up and went into her room, stuffing everything into the trunk and locking it. God forbid—could she too be made a fool of? They're all the same! Men are like quicksilver by nature. All they need is a bit of warmth, and then they climb and climb. Yesterday it was Chammi, now she was the beloved. After that, it will be someone else's turn.

When she went back downstairs, everyone was basking in the afterglow of their iftar. Kareeman Bua was busy making rotis for dinner. Aunty and Amma were sitting on the beds in the veranda preparing and chewing paan, and Jameel was seated out in the cold on his metal chair, reading something by the light of a lantern placed on a stool. That chair seemed especially vacant during winter evenings; on winter afternoons, Chammi sat on the chair and sunbathed; and during summer and monsoon, the chair sat abandoned near the flower beds.

For a moment, Aliya worried Jameel might catch a cold. By now it had got quite chilly.

'How are your studies going now? The exam is just around the corner,' Jameel asked, walking over to her in the veranda.

'They're fine.'

Aliya had gone to sit by Amma. She did worry about what would happen if Jameel tried to test her. Even if Uncle didn't give him the key to his library, she was still convinced of his intelligence.

'Jameel, you should take a look at Aliya's studies,' said Amma.

'Yes, I'll definitely take a look, but of course these days I'm also preparing for the MA,' replied Jameel, encouraged. He gave Aliya a sidelong glance.

Chammi had wandered out at some point to sit in the doorway of her own room.

'Come over here, Chammi, it's cold! Come sit in the veranda,' urged Aunty.

'I'm fine over here,' retorted Chammi.

'Last time too this happened—when war broke out it got expensive here, but that was a different time,' said Aunty, 'we didn't even notice it in our homes. And if we did notice, in those days, my brother . . .' She suddenly paused, then sighed deeply and continued. 'In those days, Jameel here was already born, when we got news of my brother's death.' Aunty looked around at everyone, but they all sat silently, eyes downcast. 'But now we feel the expenses . . . now circumstances . . .' Aunty fell silent because Amma was frowning. Whenever Aunty spoke of expenses, Amma frowned.

'Everyone eat dinner, otherwise it will get cold,' said Kareeman Bua, spreading out the tablecloth.

Chammi suddenly leapt from her spot, and taking her portion from the plate, she rushed back into her room. Aliya was shocked when she saw her face. Oh my, why did Chammi get angry so quickly? If she had a cause to be angry that would be understandable. How she wished Chammi would just once go back to the way she'd been. Now there was no one to lovingly call her 'Bajiya'. She glanced reproachfully over at Jameel, but he was staring at her. She started and looked down. Perhaps he'd begun to consider her his property after buying her clothing. Now she wished she could throw a really stinging barb right in his face.

'But why is this war happening anyway?' asked Aunty, looking over at Jameel. 'There's been a one- or two-paisa rise in the price of everything and that's made the quality of food even worse.'

'If you're such a great supporter of Abba, why do you start quarrels with him?' Jameel shot back.

'And you're an enemy to your father!' retorted Aunty.

'Look, it's obvious, whenever their interests are hurt or they feel greedy, there's war,' replied Jameel, speaking as though Aunty was two years old.

'Oh, cut it out, look at you, just talking nonsense! You've never spoken properly; always been a joker.' Aunty laughed.

'What does any of this have to do with interest and greed, Jameel Miyan? It's just a sign of the times—everything's changed,' interjected Kareeman Bua. Why should she keep quiet, after all?

'This is all the fault of people like your father and Aliya's father. It's people like them who mess up and cause war, why wouldn't there be war, when Aliya's father is turning against the English?' said Amma, expressing her opinion as well.

Jameel laughed heartily. 'You've got that right; you're so right, Aunty.'

'If everyone's eaten, please send in some dinner for me too, Kareeman Bua,' called out Asrar Miyan faintly from the desolation of the sitting room.

Uncle was dining out somewhere, so had already departed with his guests, and now Asrar Miyan was languishing in there, waiting for his dinner after breaking his fast with a couple of chickpea-flour phulkas.

'Hold your horses just a little bit, Asrar Miyan Sahib! I suppose I should decorate your tray and send it in before the family's eaten?' snapped Kareeman Bua.

There was such sarcasm in the way she called him 'Asrar Miyan'. The mock respect was thick with ridicule, but somehow, when Uncle called him Asrar Miyan, the words carried with them a sense of sincerity and equality. Aliya had no idea why all these people didn't spare a thought for Asrar Miyan.

Oh, Asrar Miyan, if I could, I would decorate the tray myself and send it in to you first of all, said Aliya to herself. She finished her dinner quickly and fled upstairs. Jameel had been eyeing her constantly and she felt incredibly oppressed. She couldn't even eat in peace.

Once on her bed, she peacefully gathered her books, slid her pillow over and lay down in such a way that the street lamp in the gali would shine directly on her book. When she heard a tread on the stairs, she turned and looked. It was Jameel.

'I thought I'd test you today,' he said, sitting down near her.

'I know it all; don't waste your time. If I fail, don't worry, next year is fine too,' answered Aliya abruptly. The look in Jameel's eyes spoke fluently of what subject he had actually come to test her on.

'Will I be wasting my time by testing you, Aliya? Just think how much you upset me by saying such things. If you can't love me, at least don't cause me pain.'

'Cousin Jameel,' she said in a scolding tone, 'don't you feel ashamed when you say such things? Have you forgotten Chammi? She lives with you in this house too. I know everything.'

'Chammi!' Jameel looked down. 'If you know, that's for the best, but I will tell you truly that I never had any such love for her, I only love her as a sister. You must know that Abba has destroyed this household for politics, but I was not prepared to destroy it myself. Somehow I managed to keep my studies going. Some money Asrar Miyan saved up for me and some that Granny gave me secretly came in handy, but by the time I got my FA, the household had been ruined. Chammi bore all my remaining expenses. I'll never forget it, but she began to take it the wrong way, and I was too fearful to make her see reason, and . . .'

'And then suddenly after your BA you started making fun of her and making her see reason that way, right?' she shot back. Despite having some pity for Jameel she didn't back down.

'Now what can I do?' he asked.

'Marry her, Jameel, she's in love with you!'

'Marry her?' He jumped up. 'I had no idea how much you hated me, Aliya, I've never loved anyone but you. Look into my eyes, Aliya.' He grabbed hold of both her hands and placed his head in her lap.

'I can leave for my mamoo's house today, understand, Mr Jameel?' Whom else could she name who would have any importance to him? She felt completely powerless.

'You can't go anywhere, Aliya Begum. Just today my mother was saying to Kareeman Bua and your mother that you would live in this house forever.'

'Who said that? Who are they to decide such things?' cried Aliya, pushing Jameel away from her like a madwoman. She stood and pulled him up from the bed. 'Nobody can push me around. I am not Tehmina! Everyone thinks they're so important.'

Jameel gazed at her red-hot face with astonishment, then quietly turned away, mortified. As he was going down the stairs, Aliya muttered to herself, 'Useless sham poet—Uncle won't even give you the key to his library!'

9

Tomorrow it would be Eid. Today, Chammi's father's money order had come. Chammi rushed eagerly to sign for it, but when she saw it was only five rupees, her face went red. There was a note on the coupon telling her to have her Eid clothing made with the money. Chammi accepted the five-rupee note and then, standing right in the middle of the courtyard, she ripped it to shreds and threw it to the ground. Everyone cried out in astonishment.

'The shroud for my father's fourth wife will cost more than that! Who knows why people even have children; they should just raise puppies,' she cried. Then she sat down on the bed.

'Chammi! You've gone mad, you could have got such a nice suit for five rupees,' scolded Aunty, who jumped up and started gathering the shredded bits of the note in her palm as though she intended to save them.

'Who told you to speak?' retorted Chammi, standing up. 'If he were really worried about an outfit for me, wouldn't he have sent the money order earlier? Are fairies supposed to come in the middle of the night and stitch it for me?' She stomped off to her room.

Aunty blew on the shreds and scattered them, then sat down on the stool and opened the paan box.

Kareeman Bua finished scrubbing a pot, washed her hands and stood up. She picked up the scraps of the note, tied them into the border of her sari and sat back down to clean the grime off more pots. 'Allah take this useless paper! Back in the day, there were real silver rupees, golden ashrafis and guineas. I'd like to see anyone try ripping those up.'

Kareeman Bua continued to mutter and Aliya sat under the arch of the veranda, quietly listening. She kept glancing towards Chammi's room. Who knew what she was doing, lying alone in that desolate and dreary room, tormenting herself. That room gave Aliya the chills. So many days had passed since Granny's death, but she still felt she could see her wistful eyes darting about the room. She still felt the rasping of her sharp breaths. How could Chammi be made to see reason? Aliya was extremely displeased—*Really, Uncle Zafar, isn't Chammi your daughter? Do one's children die off with one's wife?*

She went upstairs to her room and began to flip through her course books. Try though she might, she just didn't feel like studying. Instead, she was troubled by thoughts of Chammi. One day, Chammi would finish herself off if she carried on like this.

The sun was sinking behind the school building outside the window. There was much commotion downstairs as the time for breaking the fast drew near. Aliya gathered her books together and piled them on the teapoy. She squatted in the window and began to look outside. Sugar-cane hawkers sang out, balancing metal trays on their heads adorned with garlands of flowers. Aliya didn't know why she enjoyed their crude voices so much, but suddenly she felt sad. Evenings always filled her with sorrow; she felt overwhelmed by a strange mood.

She jumped down from the window. It was nearly time to break the fast, so she went downstairs to help Kareeman Bua. She felt such compassion for her. Kareeman Bua's back had grown crooked from sitting doubled over the hearth all day. She often wondered why she wouldn't just run away. All she received in life was shabby cast-off clothing and the bread and salt of her master. With that much labour she could get a job for ten or fifteen rupees a month at any home. The fruit of one's labour is only money, but perhaps Kareeman Bua had never even dreamed such things. How proudly she used to declare that her mother had come with Mistress's dowry! Her mother had served her Mistress until her death, and now she prayed that she might be useful to Uncle. Aliya found it surprising that she'd never seen Kareeman Bua grow dissatisfied with this family. She never tired of her work. Even in these debased times, she was still respectful. She never spoke with a raised voice under any circumstances.

A bedspread covered the takht and the food for iftar had been set out. Aunty was squeezing lime over fried chana. Kareeman Bua rested limply, perhaps feeling weak from the fast. Uncle was seated on the bare string cot in the veranda. He'd taken his watch from his pocket and hung it across his chest, and Shakeel, who sat by him, leant over to check the time again and again. Jameel had cracked down on him recently, so he hadn't been able to leave the house for too long at a stretch. Chammi stood in the doorway of her room, her ankles visible below the torn filthy hem of her pyjamas. When she saw Aliya, she walked softly over and sat down next to Shakeel without saying anything.

Several of Uncle's guests were seated in the sitting room outside, and Asrar Miyan had already popped his head out several times to take a peek.

'Kareeman Bua, would you please send the iftari out a bit quickly? There are only two minutes left until the end of the fast,' said Uncle, glancing at the watch hanging across his chest. Kareeman Bua got up, her back crooked, picked up two plates from the takht and rushed towards the sitting room. Asrar Miyan awaited them eagerly—when there were guests, he got to enjoy the feast, otherwise the poor fellow would not get to break his fast until it was too late and the food was practically tainted.

Amma was seated on the takht in one corner chopping betel nut as though guarding the iftari. She had never performed menial tasks in her life. She did nothing here except for portioning out the food and drink, or criticizing the goods brought by Asrar Miyan, and suspiciously checking the bills he brought from the market.

Once they heard the crack of the small canon from the nearby mosque, the kettledrums began, and Amma started doling out everyone's portions on to their plates. Aliya picked up the carved copper jug and began pouring lemon sharbat into everyone's glasses. Chammi's plate lay untouched. She had only broken her fast with a few sips of sharbat.

'Chammi, do eat something; you'll get a tummy ache drinking sharbat on an empty stomach,' said Aunty, but when she picked up the plate and tried to put it in Chammi's hand, Chammi pushed it away.

'She'll eat of her own accord when she gets hungry,' said Amma. Chammi remained silent.

'She must still be upset about her note, the one Zafar Uncle sent. She tore it up and threw it away. She should have given it to me.' Shakeel had broken his fast and was already feeling giddy.

'I'd never give it to a beggar like you!' snapped Chammi.

'Good God, this girl is truly foul-mouthed,' declared Uncle, staring at Chammi in surprise. 'One of these days I'm going to pull her tongue right out.'

'I'd never even let you touch my tongue. You spend all your time hanging around with Kaffirs and keep the fast just for show, but let me tell you, there's a limit to hypocrisy!' hissed Chammi, scowling with hatred.

'Have you no shame? Does anyone speak to their uncle like this! Have you no respect!' Aunty immediately scolded her. Her face was turning red with rage at the thought that Chammi would speak this way in front of her uncle.

'I don't have any uncles,' said Chammi with complete indifference.

'Hush, dear, why are you even talking to that ignorant fool?' Uncle leant back on the large bolster and stretched his legs out.

'Yes, no one even talk to me, I'm an ignorant fool! I will eat up all your fancy degrees, and I won't even burp,' snapped Chammi, as she stomped off to her room.

'It's the fourteenth century—now the cow will balance the earth on her other horn and the Day of Judgement will come,' observed Kareeman Bua. She couldn't talk back to anyone, so she was thinking of the Day of Judgement instead.

'But really, there is a limit to foul language. You've raised a bull in the house, Sister-in-law,' said Amma, laying into Aunty.

'But now, see here, Mazhar's Bride, this was her father's fault. What will the child wear now?' Whenever someone started picking on Chammi, Aunty immediately came to her defence.

Everyone fell silent for a time. Uncle closed his eyes. Shakeel got involved with his schoolwork. Kareeman Bua began cleaning the lantern chimneys. But how could Chammi remain silent? She had not yet taken revenge for being given no new clothing. In her dark room she began to chirp out her doggerel:

> *Tulsi was planted in Kashi, the goats ate it all up*
> *Gandhi and Nehru mourn, the mother of Kashi has died*

Uncle suddenly started. 'Look, someone stop her,' he said. 'The Maulana Sahib and everyone are out there in the sitting room; what will they say? Her voice will reach them.' Uncle was fuming.

'Chammi, for God's sake, do think a bit. There are guests seated outside.' Aunty rushed towards Chammi's room.

'What's it to you? I'm singing in my own room, this is my room! If I come and sing in your room, go ahead and forbid me. If they hear it outside, let them! Then at least they'll find out that not everyone here is a Kaffir.'

She began to sing again just to tease Uncle:

Tulsi was planted . . .

'Good God, you ignorant fool! What a lunatic! I'm not saying a word, and here you are, out of control. Go ahead now, sing all you want.' Uncle rushed towards her room. 'Shut the sitting-room door, Shakeel,' he said, turning to Shakeel. Then he slapped Chammi vigorously several times. Shakeel shut the door and stood still as though he were watching a show.

'Tulsi was planted . . .' Chammi shrieked loudly. 'I will sing, I will sing!'

'Shut up!' Uncle pressed his hand against her mouth.

Aunty separated her husband from Chammi, and Aliya stood in the doorway staring at Uncle in astonishment. How strangely he was asserting his authority over the household today, and just because his political beliefs were being mocked. Right at this moment, Uncle seemed like a political thug to her.

'Glory be to God! You've raised your hand against a young girl, a motherless child!' Aunty cried tearfully. She dragged Uncle out of the room, and then Aliya ran in and embraced Chammi, who was lying on the old bed, sobbing.

'Bajiya, go outside,' cried Chammi. Then she fell completely silent and lay down perfectly still, as though deeply contented.

Aliya came outside and leant against the archway in the veranda.

Aunty was weeping bitterly. 'Now if you ever raise your hand against her again, remember I'll give my own life for her. My heart is broken—she's a motherless child! I raised her myself; I have affection for her in my heart.' At that moment she didn't even remember that poor Chammi had raised herself. Aunty had wanted to raise her, but she'd been so overwhelmed by endless work, she'd never even had the time to give Chammi her birthright.

'I don't speak to anyone in the house myself but this girl is exasperating. Tomorrow I'm writing a letter to my brother Zafar to get her married off to someone and get this cursed girl out of our house,' said Uncle, before turning over and closing his eyes. Aunty wiped away her tears and began to make paan. Amma was lounging comfortably as though nothing had even happened.

After the uproar, everything was silent. Uncle's face was enflamed. His eyes kept fluttering open, then closing again. Right at that moment Jameel arrived.

'Why is everyone so quiet? It's Eid tomorrow!' Jameel glanced over at Aliya, who looked as though she were dozing.

'She's been beaten,' Shakeel leant over and told Jameel.

'Who's been beaten?'

'Nothing, nothing, really, it's just that Chammi was chanting repeatedly, "Tulsi was planted . . ." There were guests in the sitting room, and then your father slapped her,' said Aunty, making light of the matter, and then quickly stuffed a paan into her month.

'But why did you beat her? You could have reasoned with her, you could have stopped her insolence, but what sort of justice is it to beat someone? She was just expressing her views.

Why does that annoy you so much? If you don't give people in your own house freedom of speech, how will you liberate your country? And even if your country gets freedom, how will you maintain it?' Jameel blurted all this out passionately in one breath.

'Son, don't you confuse household matters with national politics, and don't go about putting on intellectual airs. You know nothing,' Uncle retorted with a stern look, then closed his eyes again.

'And don't you talk down to me about my intellect; you only paid for my education through primary school, then left me to play *gulli–danda* and went off to liberate the country— as though I wasn't a citizen of your country, as though I had no right to live a good life too. I didn't just do a BA, I've suffered too. Why don't you tell me this: if you don't care about your own household, how can you care about such a big country with so many households? That was also really something that you sacrificed your own household to save all the others.'

'Good heavens, what a coarse speech! What are you prattling on about? The meaning of independence and sacrifice is beyond your comprehension; why don't you stick to your poetry, seek applause, bind the delicate wings of the nightingale with the veins of a flower and enjoy yourself?' Uncle turned over.

'Yes, sir, quite right. But . . .' How could Jameel admit defeat in front of Aliya? He wanted to say something more, but Aunty began to beat her brow.

'Oh dear, oh dear, this household is on the path to ruin. It's just too much that the eldest son quarrels with his father!

I swear to God, one of these days I'll go ahead and drink poison,' wailed Aunty.

'Look, what Jameel is saying is right,' said Amma in defence of Jameel, but he fell silent and went to sit helplessly on his metal chair, where he rubbed his hands together, lost in thought.

'The sun is setting, and these fights and squabbles! The sorrows of this country have ruined everything,' muttered Kareeman Bua as she walked around placing the lit lanterns all about.

'To hell with you, you sympathizer.' Chammi had noisily re-emerged and come to stand by Uncle's bed. 'Who can stop me? Yes, Tulsi was planted in Kashi and the goats ate it all!' she screamed loudly.

'My God,' Uncle burst out laughing. 'She's completely insane.'

As soon as Uncle laughed, Shakeel, Amma, Aunty and Jameel all began to laugh as well.

'Yes, now it's fine,' said Chammi, drawing close to Jameel. 'Go ahead and laugh, who told you to defend me? I won't even look at the likes of you, now I'll love people like *him*. You wasted your time kissing up to me to get your BA done.' She turned again to go back into the room but then sat down in the doorway.

For a few moments there was silence. Everyone stared at Jameel in surprise, and Amma stared the hardest. But Jameel simply sat flipping through the pages of Shakeel's book with his eyes down, and Uncle cleared his throat as though something was stuck in it.

'Today she even ripped up her five-rupee note; now, if she'd given it to me, I'd have had my Eid clothes stitched in minutes. I'm not going to carry her letters for her any more,' said Shakeel.

'And where did you take those letters?' Amma asked in surprise.

'I gave them to the son of the inspector, Manzoor Sahib,' said Shakeel very innocently, looking over at Chammi.

'Oh my, oh my!' cried out both Amma and Aunty, who were floored by this explosive revelation.

Everything was totally still. No one looked at anyone else. Chammi got up and nonchalantly walked up the stairs, ignoring their reactions. Aliya stared hard at Shakeel; she was afraid Uncle would now punish Chammi harshly. Suddenly eleven- or twelve-year-old Shakeel looked more like a knavish rascal to her.

When Uncle turned over, Aliya trembled from head to toe. She felt as though he was about to get up and attack Chammi. But when he merely stayed lying down silently and turned away, she breathed a sigh of relief.

'Well, this is too much, Big Brother, I must say,' fumed Amma. She looked over at Uncle. 'Did all the modesty in this home fly off with the money? Weren't things bad enough in this family without Chammi making things worse? You go beat the stuffing out of her—don't just lie there!'

Uncle sat up.

'Shakeel, bring the pen and paper from the sitting room. I'll write a letter to Zafar myself. If he gives permission for her marriage, I'll search for a boy.'

Shakeel ran off and got pen and paper and Uncle sat up to write the letter. Would he shove Chammi off somewhere dreadful as he had with his own daughter, Aliya wondered to herself with a heavy heart. She sat down with her face covered, trying to keep her tears under control.

'If I had my way, I'd break her bones. How happily the witch flitted out of here and went upstairs!' Amma murmured, enraged.

'Oh, look, everyone's forgotten to look for the Eid moon!' Shakeel started and used this as an excuse to jump up from the bed and run outside. Jameel was sitting still on his chair, completely unaware of Shakeel.

Just then there was a loud knock on the door. It was a telegram from Najma Aunty. She would arrive the next morning.

10

Najma Aunty had arrived, along with her piles of luggage. She embraced only Aunty and avoided everyone else. This was the first time Aliya had seen her since she was a baby. Najma Aunty's plucked eyebrows were sharp as the new crescent moon, she wore her short hair loose, and her true face could not be discerned beneath her make-up. Chammi forgot all else, and dressed up early in the morning, put on a decaying suit from her departed mother's dowry, and really looked quite beautiful. Najma Aunty ignored her, but nonetheless, she burrowed her way in by her side. After all, she knew that Amma and Aunty strongly disliked her.

Jameel sat silently on his metal chair; he was the one who'd gone to fetch Najma Aunty at the station. Uncle had gone off somewhere early in the morning after prayers.

'Najma Aunty, there are more people in the house than there used to be,' Jameel reminded her. Perhaps he was offended that she hadn't even said one word to Aliya and her mother.

'So I am seeing, my dear,' she replied. 'I'm absolutely worn out from such a long journey! And where is my brother? He must have gone off to pontificate about his politics somewhere . . . and you, Aliya, tell me, are you studying at all now . . . or no?'

'Yes, ma'am, I'm about to take the FA exam,' Aliya replied softly.

'Great, great!' Najma Aunty's face showed marked disdain.

'And you, Jameel, young man, what are you up to?' she asked Jameel.

'Nothing, I just finished the BA and now I'm sitting around,' he replied.

'Oh my, what can be accomplished with just a BA? One is still totally ignorant. A little education can be a dangerous thing. What you should do is an MA or a BT; now look at me—whatever college I teach at, I'll be embraced with open arms! But if you do an MA, do it in English; an Urdu MA any fool can do.'

'Well, that settles it. I'll also do an MA in English some day.'

'But really, what was brother Mazhar thinking, going off to jail like that? I mean, it's just too much! Has he even written any letters? Or is he silent out of shame? He's not written me a single letter.' Najma Aunty was addressing Amma, but Amma continued making paan as though she hadn't heard a thing.

Aliya felt wounded by the thought that even Abba's sister considered him a criminal. She wished she could cut off her tongue—it was right of Amma not to answer her.

'And oh, yes, little Chammi! Have you studied something as well, or no?' asked Najma Aunty. In return for Chammi's show of extreme love, she patted her on the back. Chammi hung her head in shame. She looked truly mortified at her ignorance.

'Now I'm here to get a job,' announced Najma Aunty. 'So, starting tomorrow, I'll begin teaching Chammi. The poor thing's been left ignorant and no one's paid her any attention. This is the reason for this family's ill fate—none of the girls have been educated.' Najma Aunty had lumped Aliya in with the other ignoramuses. 'So, Chammi, why don't you put away my towel, soap and so forth in the bathroom? I think I'll just wash my hands and face and then celebrate Eid a bit.'

Chammi raced after Najma Aunty when she stood up, but her foot got caught in the hem of her pyjama. Today she'd got all dressed up and totally ignored Jameel. She hadn't even looked in his direction once, as if to make it clear that her dressing up was not for him, but for Manzoor.

Kareeman Bua made tea for Najma Aunty and placed it on the takht very tastefully and then became engrossed in cooking noodles. 'We used to have vermicelli cooked by the maund on Eid, but those days are gone now. May Allah give our Master good sense, everything has been lost,' Kareeman Bua was muttering as she cooked the two seers of vermicelli with saffron.

'You change your clothes too, Aliya my child,' said Aunty. 'When the neighbourhood ladies start visiting, what will they say when they see you? You didn't even stitch your new clothes.'

'I didn't have time, Aunty,' she said softly. Jameel was looking at her reproachfully. 'I'll change my clothes right away.'

She stood up to go to her room. Najma Aunty had already come out of the bathroom and sat down to drink tea.

As she climbed the stairs, Aliya turned to see that Shakeel was entering the house chewing paan and wearing a garland around his neck, but when he saw Jameel was there, he pulled the garland off and crumpled it in his fist.

Aliya stayed sitting in her room after she changed her clothes. *How would Eid be for Abba, sitting in jail?* she wondered sadly.

'You won't embrace me on Eid, Aliya?' Jameel had come upstairs as well.

The children and the hawkers in the gali were growing louder and louder. She closed the shutters.

'So?'

'So, what? You won't give me a hug? This is the day when even enemies embrace, and I'm not your enemy.'

'I don't consider you anything at all.'

'Considering me nothing at all is extremely offensive.'

'Please, Jameel, don't say such twisted things to me, please be a good man. I have no interest in romance. I find men and women who deceive one another with love extremely annoying.'

'Have you found some book on this topic in Abba's library?' Jameel glanced at her sarcastically.

'Yes, I got it from the library for which you have not been given the key.' She laughed loudly and Jameel became suddenly serious.

'Aliya, the more you spurn me, the closer I feel to you. If you don't support me, I won't be able to do anything in the world.' His face turned red, and sorrow spilled from his eyes.

Aliya looked down. She felt right then that she must avoid looking in his eyes, or who knew what would happen.

'If I fall in love with someone else, then you can complain that I was not truthful.'

'All lies, a woman cannot keep from loving a man; according to tradition, she was even born of a man's rib,' replied Jameel excitedly.

'All right, now I get it.' She burst out laughing. 'That's why men deceive women, because they can't forget the pain in the rib of our first father, Adam.'

Jameel also laughed spontaneously but then became serious again. 'You are mine, Aliya. I speak truly when I say that I will do everything in life, I'm not like Safdar, who finished off Tehmina.' Then he whispered, 'Safdar is in Bombay, he's a member of the Communist Party. He's in jail these days.'

Aliya fell totally silent for a moment. She stared at Jameel with empty eyes. The past can come and ambush one's thoughts so quickly.

'Aliya, I will dedicate my entire life to you. Believe me, Aliya, I will do everything for you, but if you do not support me on the journey of life, I will grow weary, I won't be able to accomplish anything.'

She looked hard at him. *For heaven's sake, what insipid clichéd things he says*, she thought. *The same sorts of things my sister Tehmina read of in stories before she died. How adept lovers are at using their tools of deception.* She looked down. His eyes had a strange depth to them.

'Well then, Jameel, start growing weary today. Shall I arrange for tea and so on?' She laughed heartily. If she could turn the whole thing into a joke, maybe she'd escape, but Jameel's mood was still deadly serious.

'Look, Aliya,' he moved towards her, then froze in place.

'Oh here, please take your letter from the Muslim League office in Kanpur. I managed to snatch it up before Aunty saw it, because you know, Aunty doesn't need to cope with that shock as well.' Aliya took an envelope out of her notebook and placed it in Jameel's hand signalling that the conversation was finished.

He stood with his head hanging, like a criminal. All of a sudden, the secret he'd kept hidden for so long had come out.

'All right, then, happy Eid; please don't mention the letter to Amma,' he said and rushed away.

At that moment, Chammi was dragging Najma Aunty's bedroll up the stairs into the big room; the hem of the suit from her departed mother's bridal gift had torn in the effort.

Chammi, Najma Aunty will never appreciate this devotion from you. And why are you angry with me? Aliya wondered, gazing at Chammi affectionately. Then she closed her door again.

The neighbourhood children were now kicking up a huge ruckus as they returned from the Eidgah.

'Kareeman Bua,' called out Asrar Miyan, 'please convey my greetings to my sisters-in-law and please wish them both a happy Eid as well.'

Aliya could hear the voice of Asrar Miyan shaking with joy as she walked down the stairs. How she wished she could say hello to him today. It was Eid, after all.

'Be patient; I'll send in vermicelli for you as well,' Kareeman Bua replied light-heartedly.

Najma Aunty handed Kareeman Bua one rupee as a holiday gift. When she looked up at Aliya, Aliya turned around and walked back up to her room.

11

It was Sunday. After drinking tea, Uncle lay down on his bed before going into the sitting room. He looked a bit deflated. Aliya went and sat by him. She felt agitated seeing Uncle like this. *Oh, poor Uncle, no one cares about him*, she thought. If Aunty were not in this home, everyone would torment him. Everyone here cried only for their own troubles. No one asked about his troubles, and he was the one who put up with everything; his own sister made him feel ashamed, just because she had to contribute her own money towards food. Najma Aunty had forgotten that at one time it was thanks to Uncle's money that she'd attained her education at all.

'How are your studies going, my dear?'

'They're fine, Uncle, I hope you're feeling well?' She spoke with a heavy heart. 'You don't pay any attention to your health. You're getting so weak. Maybe you should think of yourself from time to time as well.'

'No worries, dear, I am quite well,' replied Uncle, staring at Aliya with surprise. 'But really, is there someone here who really cares for me? Can anyone even feel sympathetic towards me? I am the ghost of this house that has destroyed everything.'

She sensed a faint sadness in Uncle's eyes that she felt he was trying to hide with laughter.

'Oh my crazy girl, what do I need to rest for? I'm fit as a fiddle. No need to worry. Well, now tell me this, are you reading any books from my library?'

'I was reading them, Uncle, but my exam is coming up, so I stopped doing everything else.'

'It's very important for a girl like you to read these books.' Whenever Uncle was happy, he would start advising her to read the books in his library.

'Uncle, what will happen when we get independence?' she asked foolishly, trying to bring up his favourite topic. She'd never actually expressed her loathing for politics before him.

'When we get independence, our work will be done! Everything about life will become simple. Do pray for me that I won't die during the era of slavery.'

Uncle, may God always keep you well, she prayed to herself. Even after witnessing the destruction of these two households she still could not hate her father or her uncle.

Just then, the chain in the main door rattled loudly and she stood up quickly.

'Wait, don't you go, I'll look,' said Uncle. He went outside and returned promptly. Aunty was seated on the takht in the veranda with a small basket in front of her, sorting through spinach leaves. Uncle went over to her.

'I've been summoned,' he announced to her. He looked a bit worried.

'Where to?'

'To the English rulers. I'll be back in four or five months. Please pack my bags.'

Aliya stood stock-still. Aunty threw the basket aside and got up quickly. Kareeman Bua rose up from among the dirty pots and pans and began to stare absent-mindedly at everyone. Aunty went into their room and began stuffing Uncle's clothes into a suitcase.

'What did anyone ever do to those bastards? Why must they go about arresting people every day? What will they do once they've got him? It's not like they can keep everyone from speaking.' Aunty was saying this as she looked over at Amma, and Amma, assigning blame for this new disaster to Uncle, gazed back scornfully.

'Big Brother, you should repent now,' she admonished. 'Look after your own home and your children, everything has been ruined.'

But Uncle didn't say a thing. He picked up his cane from the corner of the veranda and held the suitcase in his other hand.

'Have I struggled through adversity my entire life so that he should repent? After all, what has he done wrong?' Aunty wept with rage and sorrow.

The chain rattled loudly again and Uncle rushed over to the door.

'Make your aunty see some sense, dear. I had raised the question of Chammi's engagement; when you receive an answer from Zafar Uncle, make the decision,' he said, patting Aliya on the back, then went outside.

After Uncle had left, the house was filled with silence. Aliya stood still, frozen, between the two open doors. Uncle was surrounded by eight men in the gali outside—he looked exactly like a groom to her. But what sort of wedding procession was this that seemed to squeeze her heart?

Aunty had picked up the basket of spinach again; Kareeman Bua again became lost in her pile of pots. A thin stream of water flowed from the faucet to fill the flower beds. The marigolds swayed in the light breeze. Oh, if only Aliya had picked just one flower to give to Uncle as a spring gift! But now it was too late.

On hearing that her husband was going to jail, Aunty began praying that the arms of the arresters would break. Aliya was astonished that Aunty was neither crying nor beating her breast, even as her own heart shook. She was remembering the time of her father's arrest. Perhaps Aunty didn't even know the meaning of jail and police. She well remembered one incident from her childhood. Once two police officers had come to Dinu's quarters. All the low-born people who lived there had hid fearfully in their homes and the women had begun to weep in lament. So was Aunty not afraid at all? Did she know nothing?

By now, the sunlight had descended from higher up the walls and crept into the yard.

'Such tales have no impact on me, Sister-in-law,' said Amma excitedly. 'If you had stopped him from his activities, a prosperous household wouldn't have been ruined. If you hadn't supported him, he wouldn't have had the nerve— really, I mean to say, it's just too much!'

Aliya had dropped into the metal chair in the yard as though someone had knocked her over, and Aunty gave Amma no reply. Who knew what she was thinking? Then she spoke.

'Mazhar's Bride,' Aunty said slowly. 'When you were strict with your husband, what happened? No one can get in the way of another's passion. I have put up with everything.

Now, God willing, Jameel will bring me happiness. I have spent my entire life like this with my husband; he didn't even have a chance to fully appreciate his wife.' Aunty suddenly burst into tears and Amma hid her face in her knees.

'Allah, only You can guide the raft of this household safely across. My life be sacrificed to Your glory. You do whatever You wish,' sighed Kareeman Bua.

'Kareeman Bua, if . . .' Asrar Miyan called out weakly from the sitting room and Kareeman Bua interrupted him with a shriek.

'Would it kill you not to drink tea for just one day! Pathetic thing, obsessed with his tea.' Kareeman Bua poured Asrar Miyan's tea out in the drain. 'This wretch, this ill-omened one! He just won't go away.'

'Kareeman Bua, I was just going to say, if my brother's bags didn't travel with him, should I deliver them?'

'They all went,' snapped Kareeman Bua, who began sweeping the hearth.

So whatever happens, only Asrar Miyan is responsible—why can't that poor worm born of a downpour of sins die quickly? Asrar Miyan, now you must take your time and wander about hungry until two o'clock, Aliya said to herself, and then she got up from her chair and hurried up the stairs. She could hardly make tea for Asrar Miyan in the presence of Amma and Kareeman Bua, so what was the point of sitting there? Her exams would start in four days, but she couldn't imagine how she could study now.

03

It was after two in the afternoon. An owl hooted from a dead tree on the other side of the gali and its call only made the emptiness inside her grow. But all the same she was beginning to feel wretchedly hungry. Despite the fact that her heart was breaking with the shock, her hunger still would not stop. Though she was deeply saddened by Uncle's departure today, her stomach refused to pay any heed.

She got up from her bed and went downstairs. The plates were set out on the takht. Amma was seated by the drain spitting out her paan, rinsing out the red juice, and Aunty was reclining near the tablecloth, perhaps dozing. Chammi and Najma Aunty had been off to the bazaar since morning and had not yet returned.

'Why don't you eat? How long are we going to wait for everyone else?' asked Aunty, and Aliya sat down next to her. In the meantime, Jameel came into the house, dragging Shakeel after him. The moment they entered the house, Jameel began to shower Shakeel with blows.

'He doesn't study at all! He just wanders about all day like a bum. I just saw him roaming around with some serious loafers.'

'Beat the rascal some more,' cried Aunty angrily. 'How else are we to keep the household under control with things as they are!'

'They lend me their books to study!' whimpered Shakeel, as he jumped about trying to avoid his brother's blows and looking over at Aliya beseechingly.

'Enough! Please stop, Jameel, he won't stray any more,' Aliya cried out, taking Shakeel's side. Jameel stepped aside and began to wash his hands under the tap.

'Really, why are you protecting him? He'll never improve—I shall die wishing for it. He belongs in jail too,' moaned Aunty.

'Has Abba gone to jail again?' asked Jameel, forgetting to wash his hands.

'What else? The police came this morning at nine and took him away. Allah have mercy on us now,' Amma replied immediately.

'Great!' Jameel began washing his hands again. 'These Congress leaders can't seem to do a thing without going to jail. Who knows what he'll get out of making all these sacrifices for an all-Hindu party. And what a Hindu temperament he has too. Even these violent Hindu–Muslim riots have had no impact on him at all.'

'Have you no shame, calling your father a Hindu? If he were a Hindu, how is it you were born a Muslim?' cried Aunty, livid with anger. How could her husband be called a Hindu when she'd never even tasted the portions sent to them for Hindu holy days? How could the husband of a woman like that be a Hindu?

'Okay, he's not a strict Hindu; he's a Muslim, but . . . ,' giggled Jameel. His food was just sitting there, growing cold.

'Now you must take care of this household. Are you waiting for my death?' asked Aunty. She couldn't even eat her meal peacefully.

'I . . . I . . . that's it, that's what I'm thinking of,' Jameel burst out. 'I'm going to Lahore in a couple of days. When I get back, I'll get a job,' he said as he ate pensively.

All was silent for a while, but when Najma Aunty and Chammi entered loaded down with bundles, the silence was broken.

'Oh, Shakeel, can you just get change for this rupee from somewhere and give the fare to the tonga driver?' asked

Najma Aunty, taking a rupee from her purse and holding it out to him. Shakeel was still sitting on the metal chair in the courtyard. No one had even asked him if he wanted anything to eat.

'Wash your hands and eat first,' said Aunty, but Najma Aunty was eager to open all the bundles and show everyone.

'Really, I must say, prices have gone up on every fabric. Now can someone tell me if this silken fabric is going to be used as shrouds for white people?' Najma Aunty looked at everyone, expecting praise for her joke. But they were all lost in their own sorrows. Chammi laughed heartily.

'What will you do in Lahore? Are you planning on getting a job there?' Aunty asked, looking over at Jameel.

'There's going to be an enormous Muslim League rally there. I'm just going to participate in that,' said Jameel absent-mindedly.

'What did you say? A rally?' Aunty leapt up from her seat. 'What, you too? I pinned all my hopes on you, and now you too?' Aunty stared at Jameel like a madwoman. It seemed from her eyes that she might jump up and strangle him.

'Stop! Enough! Only God can save this home now,' cried Amma, setting down her food. Her hope of marrying Aliya to Jameel was perhaps dashed now, and Jameel sat quietly eating with his head down. His arrow had already left the bow.

'If you too have got into politics, I might as well kill myself. I'll eat poison one day! I've spent my life worrying; now I want some rest. I want everything, you crackpot! You may not go into politics.' Aunty was slowly calming down. Jameel left his meal and put his arms around his mother's neck, laughing.

'Okay, that's enough, Amma,' he said.

Najma Aunty gathered up her bundles of fabric and placed them on the bed. None of these losers were even paying attention. She was livid. Kareeman Bua put food on the tray and set it before her, and she sat right where she was, by her bundles, and began to eat half-heartedly. Najma Aunty's face was full of hatred, but today, Chammi, after a long time, was gazing at Jameel with great longing.

'Didn't I say every Muslim should join the Muslim League? Long live the Muslim League!' shouted Chammi. But at that moment no one paid any attention to her joyful shouting of the slogan, now that Aunty had lost control. Aunty's eyes were red from crying. Jameel patted her and gave her water, but nothing seemed to console her.

Aliya stared at Aunty with astonishment. My goodness, was this that same Aunty who had supported Uncle's political life for so many years? She was always the first to defend him. Yes, she always gave him an earful when her patience ran out, but she wouldn't hear a word of criticism against him from anyone else. She was always tolerant of whatever Uncle was up to, and always cursed at the soldiers who came to arrest him, instead of growing weary. Was all that patience and control because she had pinned her hopes and desires on Jameel?

'Amma, just you wait and see what a grand job I get. I'll seat you on a silver throne, and your only job will be to eat paan, and my bride will wash your paan and bring it to you,' said Jameel, trying to make his mother laugh at his promises of such pampering. But for some reason, when the word 'bride' was mentioned, Aliya felt him look up at her and she lowered her eyes.

'Absurd! Who gets a job like that? No one gets a silver throne just like that! He's got no training, no MA in English,' said Najma Aunty scornfully, and Chammi began to laugh again. She felt so proud to be eating with Najma Aunty.

'Hah! He was beating me, and now look, his own son has joined the League!' cried Chammi, recalling the beating Uncle had given her. No one seemed to be feeling any sympathy for Aunty right then.

'MA-pass people know nothing, Amma, I'm going to get a really grand job,' retorted Jameel, fighting back.

Najma Aunty was enraged. 'Good God, such people have the nerve to call an MA-pass ignorant these days? Well, it certainly is true that a little education is a dangerous thing. If such people didn't take part in politics, they'd have nothing else to do. My big brother has accomplished something amazing, and what else could the poor thing do?' She left off eating and gathered up her bundles. She'd said many sarcastic things about Uncle before. She'd joked about him knowing Arabic and Farsi and remarked several times that only people who are incapable of getting a degree study Arabic and Farsi.

'Najma Aunty, your big brother went off to jail this morning at nine; when he returns, please do ask him where the arrow he shot has landed,' Jameel replied sarcastically as he turned to look at her. For a moment she went pale.

'What! Big brother has gone to jail again!' She clutched her head. 'What a bad reputation our family is getting! Everywhere you look, people are doing jail time!'

By now, Jameel had managed to calm Aunty down, and she was watching the argument between him and Najma Aunty. No one responded to Najma Aunty at all. She loaded

Chammi down with bundles of fabric and went upstairs to her room.

As soon as she'd left, silence fell again. Aliya saw that Jameel sat hugging his mother, and looking very nice, and Shakeel had still not returned from paying the fare to the tonga driver. Aliya quietly got up and went to her room.

12

It had been four days since Jameel had gone to Lahore. Before his departure, Aunty had been in quite a state. It seemed she could accomplish absolutely nothing—how could she avoid this catastrophe? But Jameel had left all the same and she couldn't do a thing about it. Since he'd left, the news in the papers had been painful to read. The newspaper salesmen were busting their guts out-shouting one another: 'CLASH BETWEEN POLICE AND THE KHAKSARS!' shouted one. So many of the Khaksars had been the targets of bullets these days. 'POSSIBILITY OF OBSTRUCTION IN THE MUSLIM LEAGUE ASSEMBLY!' cried another.

Aunty listened to the voices of the newspaper sellers with her hand to her heart. Aliya would try to encourage her in every way, reason with her a thousand times that Jameel was a Muslim League supporter, not a Khaksar, but Aunty could find no peace. Chammi also became very quiet. She'd go early in the morning and ask for the paper from the neighbours and read it very attentively, then lie face down on her bed for hours. Ever since Uncle had left, the paper had stopped coming. And now who had the money to spend on it? If Chammi was in a generous mood, she would lend out the paper she'd borrowed, and Aunty would put on her thick glasses and read it, but she wouldn't let anyone else touch the paper. 'It's not ours—it will get torn,' she'd say.

In those days, Chammi also abandoned her studies. No matter what Najma Aunty said, she would not pick up a book and look at it, whereas before, if Najma Aunty gave her a lesson to study, she would stroll about memorizing it for hours, and glance over at Aliya as if to say: *If I don't come out ahead of you, my name's not Chammi!*

Every day, after coming home from teaching at the college, Najma Aunty would affectionately teach Chammi a few words, and in exchange, Chammi would be asked to do heaps of chores. After memorizing the lesson, Chammi had nothing to do but chores. If there weren't clothes to iron, there were sandals to be polished to a shine. She'd dye the dupattas and pleat them so fine it made the skin on her fingers peel.

'I'm going to hire a boy now to work for me,' Najma Aunty would say insincerely after watching her work so hard.

'What! What else am I good for, stop it! I'm not speaking to you any more,' Chammi would cry, and wrap her arms around Najma Aunty's neck earnestly. Najma would be pleased and give her another task that very moment.

Six days had gone by, but Jameel still had not returned. Aunty wandered about anxiously and Amma kept blowing up at her agitation.

'Really, Sister-in-law, why are you driving yourself mad? The son will follow in his father's footsteps; just wash your hands of him now.'

'But he was to be my protector,' Aunty would lament; she could no longer tolerate the harsh reality of life.

Aunty spent those six nights chopping betel nut. Aliya tossed and turned in her bed when she heard the crunch of the betel-nut cracker from the veranda. Night's silence grew deeper. Her heart was heavy for Aunty. *What is all this, what is this passion which leaves loved ones to roast in an oven of sorrow?*

The Lahore Resolution was accepted and eight crore Muslims would get their right. At the crack of dawn the newspaper seller came running, screaming, 'NEWSPAPER MAN! NEWSPAPER MAN!' People peered from their windows and doors and called out to him. Today the whole neighbourhood was up to buy the paper. Aliya peered out of the window. How bright the morning was. A man with a sacred thread about his neck and a small shiny brass pot in his hands was walking to the street-side tap to bathe. Now he would bathe and pray, hands clasped before an idol of God. *Why do Hindus look so lovely when they pray?* she wondered as she recalled Kusum.

No one even looked in her direction as she passed through Najma Aunty's room to go downstairs. Najma Aunty was busy getting ready to go to the college, and Chammi was picking things up and giving them to her, like a servant girl. *God willing, Najma Aunty will actually teach you something, Chammi,* Aliya prayed to herself. Poor Chammi had to pay such a steep price just to learn a few words.

Tea was ready. Kareeman Bua was removing hot, ghee-smeared rotis from the pan. Aliya sat by Amma and Aunty on the takht and began drinking her tea. Shakeel was still sleeping; he'd get up a few minutes before going to school—and only because Aunty had forced him to get up for the past few days. Aliya's tea was not even finished when the chain on the main door started to clank loudly and Kareeman Bua started and rushed over to it.

It was a telegram from Jameel. He was fine and coming home soon. Aunty snatched up the telegram and hid it in one of the cups of the paandaan, then made a second cup of tea out of happiness.

Aliya finished breakfast and went into the sitting room. This was the first time she was setting foot in there since Uncle had gone to jail. The table, chairs and glass-fronted cabinets were thick with dust. The large portrait of Gandhiji was growing dim. The white cover of the takht and the bolster cases had grown dirty. Fragments of Asrar Miyan's smoked beedis were scattered everywhere. She tucked the end of her sari into her waistband and began tidying the room. Then she swept the floor, sat down on the takht and leant against the bolster. She kept feeling as though the door would open and Uncle would enter.

After he'd gone to jail, he'd even written to her saying he was quite happy. The government's bread was so delicious, he felt as though he were eating Kareeman Bua's parathas. Despite recalling Uncle's amusing letter, the sitting room felt deserted to her. She took a book from the shelf and went outside again.

Najma Aunty had gone off to the college and for the first time in several days, Chammi was memorizing her lessons as she strolled about the yard.

Aunty spent the day chattering, and that night, the sound of her betel-nut cracker retired early. Aliya studied peacefully until one o'clock in the morning.

13

Her exams were over. Now she wanted to take a vacation for a little while. How tired she was. She was sick of her course books. She spent her afternoons and evenings reading the books from Uncle's library. All day long the hot summer wind blew and an owl hooted in the trees in front of the school. The afternoons were endless, and the scorching heat relentless. If it weren't for Uncle's books, she would have gone mad lying on her bed during those long afternoons, thinking and thinking. Also, she worried about the exam results. She was terrified at the mere thought of failing. If she failed, Najma Aunty would no longer have the slightest doubt about her complete ignorance. Even so, she kept taunting Aliya.

'How easy people have made it to take the exams while sitting at home. The rest of us had to suffer through colleges and universities to take them. Now all you have to do is hire a teacher for fifteen rupees a month and cram what you need to.'

Even after saying all these wonderful things, she continued to teach Chammi at home, but Chammi had not yet finished her primer, though several months had gone by.

In those days, Jameel had taken an ordinary job. He handed over all his pay to Aunty and was the only person providing financial help in the house. The rest of his time was taken up with Muslim League activities. In those days, Aliya fled even his shadow, but that shadow was growing longer. The sunlight of his love for her was on the rise.

Today a letter had come from Abba. He had written that he was waiting to hear about her results. He was well and fit as a fiddle. Sometimes he suffered from palpitations, which had perhaps been brought on by the heat. The jail doctor had given him medicine, which had cured him completely. After Aliya read her this letter, Amma worried for a little while, and Aliya closed the door to her own room and wept for a long time. She could not even imagine her father being unwell, let alone him falling ill, and that too far from her eyes in a jail cell.

The last days of June were terribly hot. A furious silence enveloped the afternoons. The voices of the hawkers were not even heard, but Chammi studied during those afternoons as if possessed. It was as though she'd vowed in her heart that either she would study until she became learned or she would remain ignorant forever. But even after so much labour, she wasn't anywhere near finishing her second primer. Her fingers would cramp from writing. She could recite the entire lesson without hesitation but Najma Aunty's criticisms never ended. Then Chammi would yawn and yawn, but she stubbornly continued to try to memorize it. Occasionally she would also glance over at Aliya through half-closed doors. Growing exhausted from reading, she'd put the book down on the table.

'Najma Aunty, I've memorized the entire primer, shouldn't we start the third one now?'

'Not yet, you must study exactly as I teach; this is not Urdu that any fool can learn it—this is English,' she'd snap indignantly.

'But I don't want to study any more, this primer will never be finished, will it? My teacher thinks she's so smart . . . as though I'm an idiot. Why don't you just keep a servant to do your work? Najma Aunty, Allah created me to be a fool,' cried Chammi, flinging the book, notebook and pen into the air.

'My goodness, what nonsense are you talking, Chammi! How difficult it is to reason with fools. Remember, if the first and second primers are weak, it becomes difficult to study ahead. Study quickly tomorrow, and I will bring the third primer for you,' said Najma with agitation and sat up. Her free servant was slipping from her grasp.

'I've had enough, Najma Aunty! If I become worthy, whom will you call a fool!' yelled Chammi, as she went stomping downstairs.

'Well, that really is the limit! The ignorance in this family will never end; no one here is worth talking to or is any fun to talk to,' Najma muttered to herself.

Aliya got up and slammed the door to her room. 'Oh, Najma Aunty, I know you full well,' she murmured to herself, and then picked up her book and lay down again.

Today, suddenly, clouds had begun to cover the sky. When a puff of cool, moist breeze blew in through the window, Aliya put down her book. She'd spent all the afternoons of the hot season awake and in pain. In this house, they didn't have cane-and-cloth fans in the upstairs rooms at all. But of course, what servants were there here to pull the fans all afternoon?

Ever since Chammi had stopped studying, her true form had come out. Storms kept erupting in the house. She quarrelled with everyone, or she'd wrap herself in a burqa and disappear into the mohalla. Everyone was disgusted with her, but Amma hated the very sight of her. 'God knows where the messenger for her wedding has gone and died,' she'd mutter.

'Chammi, do you want me to teach you?' asked Aliya, going into her room for the first time in many days. The moment her eyes fell on Granny's empty bed she began to feel depressed.

'But then Jameel Sahib will get angry with you,' Chammi chuckled loudly.

'For God's sake, Chammi, don't say such things.'

'Okay, then, forget him. I too dislike mentioning his disgusting name. No one compares with Manzoor now. I swear to God he loves me so much.' Chammi closed her eyes delightedly.

'Chammi, no man truly loves anyone. Love yourself, why don't you?'

'Oh my, what a pretty lesson you teach! Jameel Sahib follows you around like a madman for no reason. This is the only love in the world, as long as there is love, if it stops, the game is over; listen to her—"love yourself". In a few days you'll say "love your father and all his wives". This love of fathers and brothers is nothing, they're all just a bunch of idiots, the bastards.'

Realizing Chammi was beyond the pale, Aliya began to look around. A picture of Anwar Kamal Pasha and that year's calendar had been added to the room. Who knows who had given them to her? She got up quietly and went away.

Chammi had not even asked her to sit down. She was walking across the yard when she nearly ran into Najma Aunty on her way to Chammi's room. She was absolutely shocked—it was an outrage! An ignorant girl had stopped doing her chores—her chores!—when she herself was such an educated woman. Aliya had to laugh.

Chammi could not be won back, and now Najma Aunty had to huff and puff and iron her own saris. She had to burn her own coals. Tears started in her smarting eyes, and as she polished her sandals, the lines on her palms turned black.

'Why doesn't my brother Zafar even worry about whom to marry his daughter to? It's not like he has to search for someone with an MA; he can do just as my brother did when he married off Sajidah,' Najma would say. If Najma Aunty had anything to do with it, she would have married Chammi off to some desert of a household. The useless girl could die of thirst there for all she cared.

'First you please get married yourself, Najma Aunty, you're getting old,' Chammi replied, twisting the knife.

'Never! Why would I need to do that? People will beg for me, but no matter how much you beg, you won't even bag a fifteen-rupee-a-month soldier.'

Chammi laughed just to goad her. 'If I get a soldier I'd have him arrest Najma Aunty first of all.'

Najma Aunty would run off angrily to her room, because who needs an ignorant girl like Chammi? After raising a storm in the house, Chammi would wrap herself in her burqa and go out visiting from house to house in the mohalla, and when she returned, she'd be wildly enthusiastic and full of gossip.

'Oh, remember Kallu's mother's other son?' she'd blurt out. 'He joined a labour party, and it's *underground*. Good God, how can they possibly live beneath the ground?' Chammi had learnt a few words of beginner's English from Najma Aunty which she always translated literally.

'Oh, the poor widow,' Aunty sighed deeply. 'That's why that unlucky woman has stopped coming over here for quite a while; it used to be that she'd leave the house every six months.'

'And, Aunty, Mahmud's mother was sobbing. Mahmud's gone off to war. What could have possessed the bastard to be so heartless to his mother?'

'Oh dear, oh dear, how sad the poor thing must be feeling!'

'Humph.' Who knows why Chammi's mood would always sour as she relayed all the news. 'What I'm saying is, that beloved son of yours who wanders around like a vagrant night and day—why not send him to war? That jerk Shakeel filched a one-anna coin from under my pillow at some point yesterday. May God break his hands.'

Aunty would purse her lips with restraint and keep so quiet that everyone would be surprised. She was the only one who was willing to put up with Chammi. She never complained, and when Chammi couldn't get a rise out of her, she'd go lie down in her room with her face covered.

14

That day there had been quite an uproar in the house. Asrar Miyan had asked for tea early in the morning, but that day even Kareeman Bua forgave him this transgression. For perhaps the very first time in her life, she had actually handed him his tea tray before everyone else. That was because Uncle had been released from Allahabad Jail and was to arrive in the station at eight that morning. Aunty was beaming. She shook Jameel, who was sleeping, again and again, so that he too could welcome his father at the station. But every time she woke him, he made up some excuse: He couldn't sleep at night because of the thunder, or he had a headache. Today he could not even go to the office—and he was also running a bit of a fever. And when the time to go to the station was past, Jameel got up, quickly drank tea, got dressed and flew to his office.

'Shakeel, my brother, go buy four garlands for Uncle,' said Aliya, placing a two-anna piece in his hand. He didn't look at all happy. Though he had very little to do with his father, he was already feeling more restricted.

'Get twenty or twenty-five garlands for me from somewhere as well, Shakeel; Uncle is coming here after performing a great feat,' interjected Chammi, giggling, and she went and sat in the rope swing hanging from the ring in her doorway and began to swing back and forth. This swing had been installed there during the rainy season and hadn't been taken down yet. To the annoyance of everyone, she sang:

> *Place the palanquin beneath the neem tree, oh, traveller*
> *The joyous month of Saavan is here, is here*

Shakeel went out. Kareeman Bua was measuring a quarter seer of wheat into the small basket so that she could give alms on behalf of Uncle.

Oh! What will it be like to see Uncle again? wondered Aliya, and her heart leapt with happiness. She went quickly up to her room and began to peer into the gali from her window. Time was passing sluggishly. One day, Abba too would come home this way, she thought, and a sharp pain of sorrow pierced her heart. But there were still five years left to go.

A sadhu walked down the street covered in ash, wrapped in a red loin cloth, holding a pair of tongs.

'Give alms, child, and all your dreams will come true,' he called out, standing in the doorway.

'Forgive me, Baba,' said Kareeman Bua, glancing outside and then quickly pulling her head back in. 'He probably doesn't even notice whose house it is; he just stands outside stark naked, the imbecile,' she said loudly and burst out laughing.

'Oh, go on, Kareeman Bua, just give Uncle's alms to some Hindu,' Chammi immediately advised and then began to sing:

I used to play with dolls in my palace
But, O, now my husband has sent the palanquin bearers!

'May Allah keep you,' said another fakir wearing a necklace of thick beads who came to stand before the door.

Kareeman Bua held out the half-anna coin to him. 'Come after a little while and take grains as well, Babaji,' she said. Ever since the war had started, the ranks of the fakirs had swelled.

And now they could hear the rumbling of tonga wheels in the paved gali. Uncle was coming. He was seated up front, wearing a garland. Asrar Miyan was by his side and a few of his friends sat in back.

'Uncle has come,' Aliya shrieked to the whole house. Kareeman Bua picked up the basket of wheat and stood at the door. Chammi got down from the swing and went into her room.

Allah, where was Shakeel? Now how could she garland Uncle? For the first time, Aliya felt angry at Shakeel's dishonesty. When Uncle set foot inside, the very first thing Kareeman Bua did was to touch the basket of wheat to his hand; and then she began to give blessings. Uncle gazed about at everyone like a victorious hero.

'Are you preparing for the BA now?' he asked.

'Yes, Uncle. I asked Shakeel to get me a garland for you, but he hasn't come back yet. When he does, I want to put a garland on you too.'

'Yes, that Shakeel isn't anywhere to be seen. How is he?' Uncle asked as if for the sake of formality. As he sat down on the stool to remove his shoes, Kareeman Bua filled a large copper pot with water for him to wash his face. Aliya watched him quietly. Uncle looked so weak to her. His belly had shrunk and more than half the hair in his beard had turned white.

'Your son comes home at midnight, and sometimes he's missing all night long. He doesn't study—but what does it matter to you? You went off to jail and forgot us all. And even if you're here, you seem like a stranger! And on top of that, your elder son has taken to participating in Muslim League rallies.' Aunty only paused to take a breath when she was done with all her complaints. Although Uncle already looked ashamed, he was completely taken aback at this last item.

'Great! Great! So my son and heir has become a Muslim Leaguer?' he exclaimed. Uncle tucked a pillow under his head and lay down for a while. The all-night journey had exhausted him.

'Let's see if you have the guts to mess with your son and heir now!' challenged Chammi, who had emerged from her room and stood nearby with her back against the wall. She'd already begun to take vengeance on Uncle without even saying hello.

Aliya wished she could hide Uncle away somewhere at that moment so that no one could say anything to him right then, so that no one could remind him of old matters. He'd come home after such a long time. Jail had broken him; he needed rest.

'Ah, Chammi, how are you?' asked Uncle, smiling and deflecting her sarcasm. This annoyed Chammi and she went off to her room in a huff.

'Tell me this, Big Brother,' asked Amma, 'where have these people gone and died who were supposed to bring a proposal for that witch Chammi? It's been four whole months that we've been waiting.' Amma sat next to him and began pouring his tea into a cup.

Uncle hadn't even had time to finish his tea when friends began knocking on the door of the sitting room. Uncle went out to see them, and Aliya was left longing to sit by him and discuss heaps of things. There was so much she wanted to talk with him about right now. She wanted to praise his deeds. Everyone was worried for him in the house, but no one had welcomed him at all. Jameel pretended to have fallen ill. Chammi had needled him, and Aunty had opened up a complaints shop. *Oh, Uncle, what did you get from doing all this, from dedicating yourself to the country, besides living frugally— what has been accomplished other than destruction? Not even your own family respects you. Oh, if only today everyone would be happy and praise him. Oh, if only . . .*

15

It had been getting foggier since early evening. Kareeman Bua settled into the womb of the hearth as she cooked dinner. Aliya began to worry her clothes might go up in flames; in just a little while she'd roast and turn to ash, which wouldn't be so unlikely, after all, as she couldn't even see clearly any more.

'Kareeman Bua, why don't you sit a bit further from the fire?' asked Aliya nervously.

'I only have one life left; let it burn. My fate has already burnt up, Aliya dear. In this very house in the winter time I used to build fires with maunds of wood with my own hands. Do you know, this freezing cold veranda used to be fiery hot? Now all we have for warmth in this hearth, Aliya, is a couple of pieces of wood. How could that possibly burn me?' asked Kareeman Bua morosely. She'd seemed despondent for a few days now. Memories of bygone days constantly plagued her. Even after speaking so much, she did not stop. 'God curse all these rallies and marches,' she muttered softly. 'They've taken over everything. The fat-bellied ones have consumed everything. What I want to know is, will anyone really get independence by destroying a household? May God protect Master.'

Aunty and Amma were sitting on the takht, warming their hands over a small clay oven filled with coals, now caked with ash. Aunty sighed deeply and slightly raised the wick on the lantern set out on one corner of the takht. There was perhaps little oil left in the lantern, making the flame burn lower and lower. Somehow they eked out their expenses by economizing on everything. The war had been going on for a few years now and inflation had completely destroyed their household. Everyone worried all the time. Even if they got enough to eat, their clothing barely covered their bodies. Jameel's income amounted to nothing more than salt in the dal, and on top of that, the earnings from Uncle's shop did not even enter the household. It was all spent outside the house. Aunty was always berating Jameel to do something more. But now he too was involved in the movement to free the country. Shakeel had sprouted an early moustache and would spend all night and several days outside the house, supposedly reading the course books of others. Everyone considered him a good-for-nothing and he was resigned to it.

Kareeman Bua seemed truly determined to light herself on fire today. She was practically sitting in the hearth. Aliya felt she would go mad.

'Sit a bit further away, just one spark is more than enough to set you on fire,' Aliya entreated as she warmed her hands over the coals in the clay pan by the takht. My, how cold it was, and her stupid sweater had grown so old that it gave no warmth at all. After toasting her hands, her body felt a little warmer, and she too settled down by Aunty's side. The frozen voice of the revari seller slowly receded into the distance in the gali outside. How deserted that foggy night felt.

'We all used to sit on this takht during the winter and eat handfuls of revaris. Your mouth would tire from all the chewing; but now winter goes by like this, and there's not one revari in our fates. Oh, the times, oh, the times,' lamented Kareeman Bua as she shifted the wood in the fire. She'd developed a bad habit of talking all the time.

Aunty sighed deeply again and raised the flame of the lantern.

'Goodness, Kareeman Bua, how can you even talk when it's this cold out?' Aliya asked irritably. In the dim yellow light Aunty's face looked like the skull of a dead person. If she had any money, she'd ask Kareeman Bua to buy some revaris and feed them to Aunty to remind her of bygone days. Aunty grew so weary with these conversations.

Aliya suppressed a sigh. If she got dinner quickly tonight, she'd be able to study for a little while. The whole day had passed by but she hadn't touched a single book. She'd spent her time dozing in the sun on the bare cot.

Everyone sat there quietly. Aliya stared glumly at the walls of the veranda and ceiling; it had been ages since the electricity had been cut off, but there were still fuse bulbs in a bracket on the veranda that were now completely blackened by the smoke. No one had the nerve to take out the black bulbs and throw them away; Kareeman Bua wouldn't let anybody touch them. Aliya grew abstracted as she pointlessly clung to signs of the old days and then looked down.

'Kareeman Bua, is dinner ready? It's so cold tonight,' Asrar Miyan called out for the second time from the chilly sitting room, where he was huddled.

'Hold on, Commander,' Kareeman Bua responded irritably. 'Will he starve to death? He doesn't have a bit of patience.'

'Ridiculous, how he's always dying for food—so greedy! What sort of people does Big Brother take in.' Amma had been sitting silently for quite a while, warming her hands, but now she spoke out angrily. Aliya was furious, but what could she say to Amma? Nobody was even thinking about how terribly cold it really was. Asrar Miyan was human too; he wasn't made of stone, thought Aliya. What a dismal life he led. Ever since she'd come, she'd seen how he wore Uncle's cast-off kurtas and pyjamas and went about performing insignificant tasks. He spent both winters and summers this way. There was never one warm piece of clothing in his fate. How must he feel in this chill?

'All right, dinner is ready, Asrar Miyan,' Aliya called out weakly, as she glanced over at Amma nervously.

'Who told you to respond to him? Have you too taken leave of your modesty?' scolded Amma immediately.

Aliya didn't reply. She did not want to hurt Amma's feelings. Old habits die hard. Amma was the only one left to uphold the old grandeur.

'What was wrong with her replying, Mazhar's Bride? After all, Asrar is also the offspring of your father-in-law,' said Aunty, chuckling at her own joke.

'Certainly he is, but he should never forget his low status,' retorted Amma, making a face. Then the thought of Chammi's wedding began to eat at her. 'Sister-in-law, do set a date whenever you hear back. Look how long that girl's been out in the mohalla; she's not even back yet.'

'What do you mean she's not back? She's in her room,' said Aliya quickly.

'But the five hundred her father sent for the wedding, how will that be enough for everything?' asked Amma, who had now moved on to another worry.

'Well, it will have to do,' said Aunty, looking down.

'It'll do the way it does in low-class homes,' said Amma.

'Well, where are we supposed to get thousands?' asked Aliya, who could not stand listening to her mother today.

'It costs five hundred to let off fireworks alone. These eyes have seen it all in the weddings of our household,' remarked Kareeman Bua as she quickly toasted the rotis.

Chammi lifted the curtain and entered, sitting down by the hearth next to Kareeman Bua, so the talk of her wedding ended there. Everyone fell silent. They were hiding everything from her. Her father had sent money for a dowry and one day she'd be carried off in a palanquin. Everyone worried she'd start some sort of storm; there was no telling with her.

There were huge holes in the canvas curtains hanging in the veranda now. The sun and rain had destroyed them. And now it was as breezy by those holes as it would be before an open window. Aliya, growing tired of the silence, began to count the holes.

'Big Brother has gone to Kanpur in such bitter cold, and he hates even English clothing! How could a sherwani fend off the kind of cold where you feel every little breeze? I mean, really, what harm would it do to wear a coat? May Allah alone show mercy,' said Amma, starting up the conversation again. 'Who knows where this family's habits came from.'

'Well, this is how he lives, Allah will take care of him; may God protect him from the cold. He's never worn English clothing, of course, always hated it. And then, ever since his warm sherwani tore, there wasn't enough money to buy another. I'm sure his old one doesn't hold any heat at all,' said Aunty, as she began to scrape at the ashes stuck to the coals with a thin stick.

Aliya hid her head in her arms and closed her eyes. Red and yellow spots began to dance and jump about in the darkness, and then she saw iron bars in her mind's eye, and the face of her father shimmering behind them. *How cold Abba must be in there*, she thought. *There's probably no one there to light coals and keep the room warm, and his warm clothes must also be old by now. How does he pass the nights?* She shuddered and opened her eyes. Why did her heart ache so?

'Kareeman Bua, you can keep toasting rotis, but will you feed me first today? I have to study,' said Aliya.

'Sweetie, have some piping hot rotis—Chammi can also eat with you,' said Kareeman Bua.

'I have nothing to study—why should I sit down and eat piping hot rotis?' asked Chammi, frowning and hiding her face in her arms as she scooted closer to the hearth.

Aliya ate dinner apathetically. At that moment everyone was sitting around silently again. It was hard to find signs of life even though there were so many people. If Uncle were there, at least the sitting room would be occupied until ten or eleven at night, she thought, and who knows where Jameel had gone. What activities was he busy with? And God only knew where Shakeel was off to, wandering about like a bum.

'Kareeman Bua, send the food out to Asrar Miyan now too,' said Aliya as she stood up. But on such occasions Kareeman Bua always became deaf and dumb.

'It will be sent, once someone gives Kareeman Bua ten hands,' replied Amma bitterly.

'Yes, just look, Mazhar's Bride,' Kareeman Bua interjected quickly. 'What times those were, when . . .'

Aliya quickly pulled the curtain aside and went out into the courtyard. How dark it was. You couldn't even see objects that were close by. She bumped into the metal chair. A thin shaft of light coming from Chammi's room was all she could see on the other side of the wall of mist. She crossed the courtyard and quickly climbed the stairs. The thought of Kareeman Bua's ten hands made her terribly furious.

As she walked through Najma Aunty's room, she saw from lowered eyes that her aunt was reclining in her easy chair, lost in a book twice her size, and that a silken quilt exquisitely embroidered with silver lace was draped stylishly over her legs. As was her habit, Najma Aunty did not even look up. But how was Aliya supposed to stop using this route? Flying through the air to her room was beyond her.

The moment she entered her tiny room, she opened the shutters of the window into the gali. She made her bed in the strong electric light and then wrapped herself in her quilt and lay down. When her hands had regained some warmth, she picked up one of Uncle's books and began to read.

It had got much colder with the window open, but if she closed it she would be plunged into darkness. She always felt restless in the thin, sickly light of the lantern. And anyway, there was once a time when a large part of her life had been spent in the glow of the thirsty lantern. How much fun she used to have in the monsoon when the moths would gather around the lantern. 'Look, a moth just hit its head on the glass and is lying on its back! Now a second, now a third!' She used to fall asleep counting moths in this way, but now she couldn't study even for a minute without this free electricity.

Only the early part of the night had passed, but complete silence had descended over the gali. The school building and the dense trees around it were cloaked in mist. She could still hear the sound of loud conversation from downstairs and Asrar Miyan's reedy voice mingled with the others.

'Kareeman Bua, if dinner is finished, please send some in to me.'

'Eat, Asrar Miyan. If you eat late, you'll be really hungry. If your hunger has not been sharpened in this expensive age, what will we all do?' Chammi teased in her inimitable style, and the sound of her laughter pierced Aliya's ears.

Aliya lay the book down on her chest. A twinge of compassion pierced her heart. Really, how was it the poor man's fault? Why were all these people so hard-hearted towards him? After all, he didn't enter this world of his own accord—why should everyone be a stranger to him? He was no one's beloved uncle, no one's brother, no one's father—in fact, who would even think such a thing? How could he become anyone's father when he had no father himself?

How she wished she could run downstairs just this once, arrange a tray with her own hands, then place it before Asrar Miyan, and stand by his side like an obedient niece as long as he kept eating. But all of this was completely unfeasible. It would injure her mother's beliefs in the old ways, and Kareeman Bua would surely begin to lament the era gone by. 'Well, it's not my home,' she muttered.

She picked up her book again. Her heart pounded with horror as she read about the atrocities of Ghengis Khan. She put down the book and covered her face with the quilt. Mankind, the noblest of all God's creatures, had fashioned history from such hideous crimes, she thought. She was becoming something of a philosopher these days.

The will to power is never quenched. Countless civilizations are born but none survive. Power burns all to ash. Despite this, it is claimed that now we have become civilized. The idea of erecting towers made of heads, and putting men in cages, brings up memories of centuries-old barbarism, but in this war that was happening now, they would take a single bomb—each even more amazing than the last—a single bomb that could kill the largest number of innocent people, and that was considered the most advanced weapon of all. And then there was the story of Jallianwala Bagh—that was hardly ancient history! It was this civilization that gave birth to that incident. And then she thought of Kusum—her corpse floated before her eyes in the dark. Drops of water fell from Kusum's yellow sari into Aliya's heart.

Someone softly slid the quilt off her, and she started and sat up.

'Oh, I frightened you,' said Jameel, who stood by the head of her bed.

'Yes, I truly did get frightened, just a little while ago I was reading about Ghengis Khan's atrocities.'

'And it's also possible that you think I am like Ghengis Khan, even though I hardly have his nerve,' Jameel said with a laugh.

'How could I say that? You are civilized, and also a poet— did Asrar Miyan get his food?'

'I don't interfere in Kareeman Bua's business,' replied Jameel insipidly. 'But right now, I've come to talk to you, and . . .'

Jameel was clearly not in the mood for chit-chat at this time. He had something else on his mind. She'd already figured out what that was, and what he wanted to say, now in particular, when he'd come into her room in the dead of night after everyone was nestled safely in their beds. Then suddenly she worried that Najma Aunty might begin to suspect something.

Jameel pulled up a chair and sat by her bedside and began to stare at her deeply. She looked about, trying to put him off.

'Your eyes are so beautiful. The poet must have been thinking of just such eyes when he compared them to paradise.'

'Thank you, cousin Jameel,' she said with a loud laugh. 'This is not true paradise. Perhaps it is the false paradise of King Shaddad.'

'Aliya Madam, making minarets of heads is not so great a crime as making fun of emotions.'

'Is this also one of the finer points of poetry? Oh, I am sorry, instead of making fun of feelings, now I'll go ahead and make towers out of heads,' she retorted. She hid her hands under her quilt. 'Jameel, if I pass the exam this time, it will be great, Najma Aunty's erudition would get quite a shove,' she said, trying to change the topic, but Jameel took no interest in it. He just sat silently with his head down. Chill air blew in through the open window, but she couldn't even close it. Darkness snatches all light from emotions.

'I know you don't want to talk to me. You're putting me off, Aliya. Can you not even respect my love?'

'What are you talking about, I—I . . .' She was startled to see tears in Jameel's eyes and was stunned into silence.

'Aliya!' cried Jameel, and he lifted her up abruptly. She felt as though the shutters had closed and burning embers had been placed on her lips. All this had happened so fast, she couldn't do a thing. She couldn't even think, and when she tried to shove him away from her, he rested his head on her arm and sobbed like a baby, and she felt each tear like a boiling raindrop falling on her heart. She could even hear the sound of the drops falling. The light of those drops spread all about the room. She could see a clear path on which to run.

She sat senseless and Jameel had lifted his head and stared at her with great sweetness. There was much pride and peace in that smile.

'Enough, now please leave, Jameel Sahib,' snapped Aliya, looking at him like a witch. 'Please go make a fool of someone else. I am Aliya. Please go away, please, or I'll scream so loudly that . . .'

Jameel leant against the wall, staring at her. His eyes were screaming, *You can't love anyone, Aliya Begum, you truly are a witch.*

After he had left abruptly, Aliya closed the shutters again and began to sob.

Jameel, you've poked magic needles into my body! What prince will come now and pull them out, she thought. After her heart felt lighter from crying, she began to laugh at her own idiocy. Enough, just stop it! Was she any better than Tehmina or Kusum—humph! Who knows how she had gone so mad. She picked up her course book and began to study peacefully. At some point the book fell from her hand on to her chest and she awoke suddenly from a shallow sleep.

Why was Chammi standing right by her, barefoot, on such a cold night? Aliya put the book down on the table.

'So, are you still awake, Bajiya?' Chammi asked, hesitating on her way to the window.

'But what are you doing wandering around in the cold like this?' asked Aliya. 'Come, get under the quilt, Chammi.'

'Actually Manzoor said he'd be standing by the street lamp at midnight in the gali below. He asked me to stand in the window. You just go to sleep, I disturbed your sleep for no reason . . .' blurted out Chammi, as she opened the door and rushed back out.

'Oh, Chammi,' Aliya called out but she must have already run down the stairs and into her room.

She opened the shutters again and peered down into the gali. The fog had lifted. The dingy light of the moon covered the ground, but there was nothing else there.

16

The war continued on. Inflation had swept the house clean. In truth, Jameel's tiny salary couldn't have filled anyone's stomach. How selfish everyone in the household had become. Amma's brow was always creased. She'd come to hate the very sight of Uncle. She had a strong feeling that if the money from the shop were to come into the house, everything would be changed instantly. They would have the good fortune to eat in style. She was always threatening to leave for her brother's house, and then Aunty would worry that this would bring dishonour to their household. Everyone would say that Uncle wasn't even able to feed them. Meanwhile, Chammi was intent on quarrelling all the time. She'd secretly snatch Shakeel's food from the hanging storage basket and eat it all up, and when he'd retaliate with insults, she'd laugh with glee or try to hit him. Najma Aunty would watch these altercations and turn her face away in disgust.

'This is all the result of ignorance; if everyone were educated, would they be dying of hunger as they are now?' she'd remark proudly as she gazed down on them from the throne of her spectacular education.

Jameel would see and hear all this and look on in helpless silence. But despite those desperate times, Kareeman Bua hadn't changed a bit. Great droves of fakirs had cropped up thanks to the war. Kareeman Bua would mourn the grand alms given out in old days, and slice away at bits and pieces of Asrar Miyan's meals to hand out alms to them.

Aliya felt nauseated by these shabby gifts. Oh dear, why was Asrar Miyan so pathetic? Couldn't he at least lift a rupee or two from the shop? What would he get from his self-mortification by being so selfless and decent? After all, by behaving like this, he would hardly be called his father's legitimate son. No matter what he did, he'd be called the child of the mistress. No one would remember him by his father's name. Every day in this world would always remain a Day of Judgement for him.

Even after seeing the household in such a terrible state, Uncle did not have a change of heart. The arrows of his objectives had damaged him so terribly that all other sorrows and pains seemed insignificant. 'The war has brought independence very close,' he'd say, looking around at everyone, but no one would answer. He would grow ashamed and look down, breaking off bits of roti and eating furtively like a criminal, and then make for the sitting room.

The harsh cold of winter had abated. Aliya continued to prepare for her exam by keeping the gali window open until deep into the night and reading by the streetlight. In those days she had just completely left off thinking too hard about anything. Abba's letters still gave her courage.

CB

It was late in the afternoon, and the sunlight had receded. Even though she had studied all afternoon, she didn't leave the roof. Aliya was starting to feel the chill of the advancing shadows. She was studying hard, and when she lifted her head, she saw that Chammi stood near her. She'd been very quiet since the night before, and she'd walked by Aliya several times since morning. Aliya felt as though Chammi wanted to say something to her, but whenever Aliya looked towards her, she went away.

'What is it, Chammi?'

'Nothing at all, Bajiya, I just feel like sitting near you,' she said, plopping down on the chair near her.

This was the first time in so long that Chammi had affectionately called her Bajiya. She looked so adorable to Aliya. Chammi sat there looking lost and staring at her vacantly.

'Well, there must be something, Chammi, otherwise why would you look at me like that?' asked Aliya, pulling her near. Chammi laid her head down on her shoulder and began to weep.

'That idiot Manzoor has enlisted in the army, Bajiya. He was someone I could lean on, but now he's gone too,' wept Chammi.

'What! If he loved you, why would he go to war, silly? And now you're missing him and crying; don't be foolish, Chammi,' said Aliya, hugging her.

'Oh, I just suddenly started to cry for no reason. I was hardly in love with him. He loved me, so I started to like him, but on the bright side, someone did love me,' said Chammi, laughing helplessly as she wiped away her tears.

Aliya couldn't think of anything to say. After all, what could she? 'What about me, don't I love you?' she asked.

'You? Do you love me, Bajiya?' Chammi laughed loudly. Such ridicule there was in that reckless laugh. How could Aliya make her believe that she loved her? She sympathized with her. She was startled by Chammi's laughter and stared at her.

'Look at this, Bajiya, the cuff of my pyjama is horribly ripped. I'm going downstairs to sew it up, then I'll be back.'

Chammi went thumping down the stairs and Aliya was left sitting with her book in her lap like an idiot. What she'd said was so unimportant to Chammi that Chammi had suddenly remembered she needed to stitch up the cuff of her pyjama. Chammi didn't trust in her love one bit. The world had simply killed off her ability to trust. Aliya grieved for her.

A crow perched on the roof wall cawed and flew away. The sunlight had climbed up the walls and disappeared. Now it was getting quite chilly. She gathered up her books and put them back in her room. After Chammi had left, she'd not been able to read even one word. She closed her eyes for a little while as she lay on her bed and then went downstairs. The marigolds and the gul-e-abbasis were showing signs of spring in the flower beds.

Aliya plucked one flower and placed it in her hair, but when she saw Jameel standing under the archway of the veranda, staring at her amorously, she started and tossed the flower back into the bed. Somehow she sensed that adorning one's self reveals feelings of love.

After throwing away the flower she saw that Jameel's eyes had lost their lustre. He sat down dejectedly on the metal chair.

Amma was sitting on the takht chopping betel nut and Aunty was sorting through the split chickpeas. Her face

was lined with hardship. All those sorrows, all those pains
had marred the elegance of her face and they continued
to leave their mark. Moreover, for the last few days, she'd
been overwhelmed by a new sorrow. Shakeel hadn't come
home in two days. Jameel had searched for him but learnt
nothing. Who knows how far he had wandered in search
of books.

'Evenings are always sad,' remarked Jameel, looking over
at Aliya.

'That's just poetry, I'm not feeling any kind of sadness.'
Aliya laughed and went and sat by Amma on the takht and
began to clean out the cups of the paandaan.

'I have such a lovely, finely crafted ghazal before me that
now all my poetry seems meaningless; I've given up all this
poetry business. Have you read Faiz and Nadeem?' he asked.

Aliya remained silent. Really, how could she consider
herself a ghazal? This Jameel was really something, always
finding his own meanings in everything—now she was
starting to feel angry.

'You'd never find Faiz or Nadeem in your uncle's library,'
he laughed. 'Tell me, have any more books on Gandhi been
published then?' Jameel was perhaps taking revenge on her
for throwing away the flower. She continued to clean out the
paandaan diligently. She didn't even look up, as if she wasn't
even aware that anyone was addressing her. She hadn't been
thinking about Jameel at all, but for some reason she had
begun to feel nervous around him.

'Did you search for Shakeel today as well? But then when
would you ever have time for your Muslim League?' asked
Aunty, looking up from picking pebbles from the dal.

'Amma, don't you worry about him now. He's gone to Bombay; he'll make lots of money there and eat well,' answered Jameel, to everyone's surprise.

'In Bombay? So far?' Aunty's voice quavered. 'What, isn't he ashamed to run off! He didn't even think of his own mother!' She clutched at her heart and began to weep.

Aliya jumped from the takht, rushed over to Aunty and took her in her arms.

'Please don't cry, Aunty, he'll come back.'

'Why would he come back, Aliya Madam?' asked Jameel. 'What is there here for him? And now he'll hardly worry about us. He's gone to make his own way or ruin himself; but he must have thought there was nothing left for him in this troublesome way of life.' Sarcasm flashed from Jameel's eyes.

'Jameel Miyan, what can anyone do, it was his father's responsibility to worry about the household, to watch after his children, put them through school, get them training. The poor thing wandered about like a bum; your father never bothered to look around and find out what was going on,' said Amma, taking the opportunity to cast aspersions against Uncle. She was just forced to keep her mouth shut when he was present. Nobody could snatch from her the belief that Uncle was solely responsible for all the destruction in their family. Everyone else was innocent. She averred with great faith that if the foundation is laid crooked the whole house will follow suit.

Jameel was lost in thought, his head bowed. Aunty continued to weep, her head hidden in her dupatta. The child born of her womb had spit on her sorrows and abandoned her. No matter how much of a wastrel he'd become, she was his mother, and still had some hope in him.

'Please don't cry, Sister-in-law. When the country becomes free, Shakeel will also surely return,' joked Amma.

'And when our country becomes free, all the English people will tuck their tails between their legs and flee the country; there won't be a single English person left in our Pakistan,' interjected Chammi, coming out of her room.

'My God, if Aunty hears one more time about Shakeel running away, her heart will burst from the shock,' Aliya muttered softly. 'Can't everyone just drop the topic for a short while?' she asked sternly.

Everyone fell silent. The evening was growing lonely and sad, and it seemed to Aliya that Shakeel had not merely run away but that his funeral procession had just left the house. How Aunty wept and wailed.

'Amma, don't cry for him, he's really not worth it,' said Jameel, going over to his mother. 'After all, I'm still here— your caretaker.'

'You go on and abandon me too,' sobbed Aunty.

'Where would I go, Amma? I'll stay with you from this lifetime to the next—I have no other companion in this world,' he said, glancing stealthily over at Aliya. This made her nervous and she took shelter behind Aunty.

Aunty quieted down with just the slightest encouragement from Jameel. What else could she do? She'd led her entire life against her own wishes. She'd always followed the whims of others, bearing her tolerance upon her bosom.

'May God protect this house from destruction,' Kareeman Bua prayed as she lit the lanterns. Everyone else listened to the sound of the call to prayer with great reverence. Najma Aunty peered out of her window and looked down, then stepped back as though to say, 'Die, fools, you will all be punished like this. Everyone will starve to death until they run away.'

Around eight o'clock that night, when Uncle entered the house, a deep silence had spread throughout. Kareeman Bua had covered the takht with a tablecloth and set out the food.

'Shakeel has run away; he's in Bombay,' Aunty announced to him tearfully.

'What! He ran away? But why did he do it, the dog?' Uncle's face was turning red with rage. 'If he comes back, I'll break all his bones. Has he no shame?'

'Why would you break his bones? What have you done for him? You didn't even remember that Shakeel was also your child,' Aunty fired back. Today for the first time she was intent on a fight with Uncle in front of everyone.

'He . . . he . . . I had said that he shouldn't have done that,' Uncle snapped and then bowed his head and began to eat quickly. When Chammi started to laugh with her hand over her mouth in her typical manner, Aunty stared at her hard and she went back into her room.

Aliya listened and watched unhappily and was left pining. Seeing Uncle's head bowed, her heart was filled with compassion. If only everyone would leave him alone. They should let him enjoy himself. But no one here was prepared to forgive him.

After dinner, when Uncle went into the sitting room, Aliya managed to get Aunty to eat after much pleading. Today Aunty didn't even have it in her to fill her empty belly.

As Aliya was lying down on her bed, Asrar Miyan's shaky voice pierced her heart: 'Kareeman Bua, ask Shakeel's mother if I should to go to Bombay and look for him.' Was that really his voice? She couldn't believe it.

17

When Aliya finally lifted her head to look around after the exam, spring had already departed, and summer's heat had settled into the air. No matter how much they watered the flower beds the plants looked lacklustre. Their leaves withered and fell, baby birds gasped with thirst, and Kareeman Bua never stopped fanning herself as she cooked. No matter how many buckets of water were sprinkled about the courtyard to cool it down in the evening, no one found any relief from the heat. Everything burned.

During those hot, empty days, Aunty had entrusted Aliya with enough fabric for five suits of clothing for Chammi's dowry. In the afternoons, when all was still, Aliya would sit at the sewing machine to stitch the fabric. Aunty couldn't accomplish anything any more. She was subdued all the time and enjoyed nothing at all, and of course, Amma couldn't stand Chammi. If it were up to her, she'd have used the dowry fabric to sew a shroud for Chammi. That left Aliya to throw her heart into stitching the dowry and pray throughout that Chammi would meet with a good fortune.

And then there was Chammi herself, unaware of the turn her fate was about to take, running about the house raising hell. Whatever small degree of gravity Manzoor's love had produced in her had now evaporated. Whenever she saw Uncle, she could think of nothing but Pakistan. She'd hurl abuses at the British until Amma was beside herself, and when she'd grown exhausted from tormenting absolutely everyone, she'd come to Aliya.

'Oh, Bajiya, whose clothes are you sewing? My God, how lovely they are! But who will wear them?' she would ask coquettishly.

'These belong to *someone*, Chammi.' Aliya would make excuses uncertainly, hoping Chammi would not guess the truth.

'Give me one of these dupattas—I'll sew tinsel on to it and wear it,' she said, lifting the pleated dupatta and twisting it. 'Look how wrinkled my dupatta is becoming.'

'Let go, Chammi, the pleats will come out,' said Aliya, trying to pull the dupatta back.

'But whose dowry is this for? The poor thing can't tell me, my tongue grows tired.' Chammi was intent on fighting out of curiosity.

'I'll beat you, if you fight me.' When Aliya very sweetly attempted to pull rank, Chammi began to laugh.

There was a heavy silence that afternoon. Aliya was stitching metallic tasselled lace on to Chammi's dupatta and speculating about her own future. If she were to fail her exams, what would happen? And if she passed, she had only one option—to get a BT and become a teacher. But would she be able to do a BT? Would Amma allow her to go to Aligarh and would Mamoo continue to send her the same amount of money?

A cuckoo warbled incessantly in the mango tree in the yard of the high school, and Najma Aunty's snores were raising the roof in the next room. Aliya wished she could go to sleep as well, and snore that loudly. Then Najma Aunty would be startled out of her worry-free sleep and would have to sit around the whole afternoon waiting for time to pass.

Come, oh Lord, reside in my heart

A passer-by in search of the shadow of the Lord was walking through the gali to avoid the scorching sunshine.

She looked out into the gali for a moment and then began to stitch on the tassels again—many centuries had passed by but not much had changed in the attire of the Lord. How many he had laid to rest in their graves while never seeing the face of death himself.

'What's happening?' asked Jameel, appearing suddenly.

Today he had come again to sit by her side after such a long time. Lo, another Lord had arrived. Aliya jumped and began stitching haphazardly.

'I'm decorating Chammi's dupatta.'

He picked up one end of the dupatta and began to flip it back and forth listlessly. Aliya saw from downcast eyes a certain madness had returned to his gaze. His face showed signs of fatigue with life. She could not comprehend the nature of this desire that simply wouldn't die after being rebuffed so many times.

'Oh, so you're preparing Miss Chammi's dowry?' he asked, for the sake of starting a conversation.

'Yes, Jameel, before it's too late. Think hard about it.'

'Aliya.' Jameel lapsed into an angry silence. When he spoke a few moments later there was a quaver in his voice. 'Are you happy tormenting me?'

'Enough, really, you get angry over the tiniest things.' She began to laugh. She thought that if the topic could be put off with a bit of laughter that would be the best, but Jameel was turning deadly serious again.

'Aliya!' he cried.

'Hmmm . . . ?' she murmured without even lifting her head.

'Please just try on this dupatta and show me how it looks,' he begged, his voice now heavy with desire.

'Why?'

'I just want to see what you will look like as a bride.'

'I'll stitch a dupatta like this for your bride as well.'

'I have no bride.'

'If you ask, I can bring you four wives.'

'How is it hard to get wives? I'll get plenty of those, but I'll never get the bride I want. If you won't bother to arrange my marriage, then fine.'

She was overwhelmed by the sadness in Jameel's eyes. She stretched the dupatta out in her hands as though she were about to put it on. This time she would definitely do as Jameel asked. He seemed to enjoy watching her so. Then she started. If she put it on that day, it would have become a veil she would never be able to remove. It would become a blinder and fall before her eyes. One more Aunty would be born to wander aimlessly down the path of life, as the country continued on its quest for independence.

'You want to put it on, but you're a coward,' said Jameel angrily. 'What kind of girl are you?'

'Cousin Jameel, take a lesson from your own mother's life, please. Marry an uncomplicated woman. That's all it takes; she'll put up with everything.'

Jameel stared at her hard; perhaps he'd understood the depth of her sarcasm.

'I don't know what earth my father is made from, but it's wrong to believe that sorrow for the nation delivers salvation from the sorrows of home, or that those participating in politics don't love anyone.' He stood to leave. 'You could never understand the sorrow of a man who has never fulfilled a single desire.'

He waited a while before leaving, but Aliya did not respond. She didn't want to either. At that moment, she didn't have the strength to say anything bold before Jameel. She felt his sorrow, but the remedy was not within her power to give. She tried to return to stitching the dupatta but she didn't feel like it. How weighty the silence felt after those hopeless words. For a long time she lay there staring about vacantly.

When she came downstairs in the evening, Kareeman Bua was sprinkling water in the garden. Jameel was seated on the metal chair, twisting his fingers about, and Uncle was pacing back and forth in the veranda as though waiting for something. His face was downcast and his eyes were red. Aunty was peeling potatoes on the takht, utterly unconcerned.

'How are you feeling, Uncle?' asked Aliya, drawing near to him.

'I have a headache, my dear.'

Aunty started and looked up at her husband.

'Kareeman Bua, quickly make up the bed, the courtyard is cooler now.'

'May your pain be destroyed,' prayed Kareeman Bua, taking the bed from the side of the veranda and setting it up in the courtyard.

Uncle lay down with his back to Jameel. Aliya felt aggrieved with his son for sitting nearby but not even asking after his father. All conversation between the two of them had ceased long ago.

'Why have you been sitting at home for two days?' Aunty asked, looking over at Jameel.

'I lost my job, Amma, political people have no chance for survival in government offices.'

Aliya looked over at Jameel angrily. *Oh, wonderful! And he was seeking a bride on this income?* she thought. She gave Jameel a murderous look, then turned her face away.

'Muslim Leaguers are most desired in the offices of the English Master,' remarked Uncle without turning around.

'That's completely wrong. The truth is that one can only get a job when Congress members give a recommendation.' Why should Jameel remain silent?

'Humph!'

Both father and son flamed out in their own sarcasm and turned their faces away as though they didn't consider one another worth talking to. Aliya looked over at Jameel reproachfully and began to softly massage Uncle's head as she sat by his side. Amma emerged from the bathroom shaking her wet hair and when she saw everyone gathered in one place, she picked up the paandaan moodily and went and sat on the last bed.

'Now what will happen?' Aunty asked Jameel.

'Don't worry, Amma, I'm about to get a really great job; you'll all live in luxury.'

'Has anyone heard how Shakeel is doing?' Aunty asked suddenly.

'Amma, please don't worry about him, he's having a great time. He's probably forgotten all about the hardships here,' said Jameel, clearly lying again. He'd told Aliya the entire truth—that he had absolutely no idea where Shakeel was.

'Well, may he be happy, wherever he is,' sighed Aunty deeply.

'Uncle, shall I set up your bed outside on the terrace, in the open air? That might help with the pain,' said Aliya. She felt fearful to be around two strongly contrary points of view in the same place.

'Yes, if you can get the bed set up there, that would be very nice.' Uncle looked at her gratefully and then he stood up to go outside.

A procession of Congress children passed by in the gali making a lot of noise in a clumsy fashion.

'May our flag fly high! Long live Congress! Gandhiji zindabad! Jawaharlal Nehru zindabad! Hindustan will not be divided! May our flag fly high!'

A faint smile crossed Uncle's lips. His eyes shone. Jameel was laughing and Amma, who had been sitting silently chopping betel for a long time, finally burst out talking: 'Let them get freedom in the first place and then these Hindustani people will have to learn how to rule.'

Everyone stayed silent. No one even responded to her. Uncle's bed had been set up outside. He went out and Jameel again began twisting his fingers. The sound of the procession was drawing near to their door. Chammi burst thumping out of her room like a madwoman.

'If the procession goes by my house, I'll lob lumps of dirt at them!' she cried, rushing towards the door.

'You watch your step! Don't go anywhere; sit down immediately,' thundered Jameel, cowing Chammi somehow. She stared at Jameel and began muttering, 'Humph! Poor guy thing thinks he's so great. If I don't start a Muslim League procession here today, my name's not Chammi!'

When the procession had passed by the door, Jameel changed his clothes and went out. It seemed Chammi had been waiting for him to leave; as soon as he was gone, she put on her burqa and went out herself. Aliya was not able to stop her.

'It's a sign of the times; before, if ladies left the house, three or four housemaids would be sent with them,' complained Kareeman Bua, always irked when Chammi went out like this.

Aliya peered outside from behind the shutters. Uncle lay peacefully with his legs stretched out on his nice, clean bed and Asrar Miyan sat near him in his easy chair, talking. The moon seemed to be rising out of the dense pipal tree in front. Aliya wished she too could go and sit outside on the terrace, listen to Asrar Miyan's words, and see him up close. How did he speak, what did he talk about? What must the eyes of this offspring of her grandfather's ignoble habits look like? His face must betray a recognition of his low status in the family, but what else must it express? Beyond recognizing himself for who he was, what other expressions must radiate from his face? What must he think about? And after learning all this, she would secretly call him 'Asrar Uncle', just once. She'd tell him that he too was dear to her, just like Uncle. That she had the greatest respect for him, and that she wanted just once to serve him, and she would pull from his heart all the arrows that Kareeman Bua had shot at him and throw them away. She'd tell him not to take offence at anything Kareeman Bua said. She would tell him that Kareeman Bua was no one's enemy and that she wouldn't say such things if it weren't for the horrid debt of the Master's salt.

'Aliya dear, would you make me a paan,' asked Aunty, and Aliya came and sat on the takht, opened the paandaan and began preparing paans. She couldn't go outside and sit on the terrace and this filled her with a strange sense of helplessness.

They could hear the call to prayer coming from the neighbourhood mosque. Out of deference, she pulled the edge of her sari over her head. Kareeman Bua was quickly lighting all the lanterns.

'May Allah keep Shakeel safe and sound,' Aunty prayed with both hands outstretched. How sad she was at that moment, and how full of maternal affection.

Darkness had settled in on all sides but Chammi had yet to return home. Aliya was needlessly worrying, of course; no one else in the house had even asked where she'd gone. A little while later, Chammi was back, out of breath, her face red.

'Oh, Bajiya, I've prepared such an amazing procession! You will be stunned! It's going to come by here in just a little while. Azra's mother made the flag, Tahira's mother gave a bottle of kerosene and I prepared the torches. We gathered all the boys in the neighbourhood. Oh my, when Uncle sees it, he will be stunned. I instructed all the children to shout slogans more loudly in front of my door.'

Chammi said all this in one breath. Then she threw her burqa to one side and began pacing about as she waited for the procession. Chammi's joy knew no bounds at that moment. Aliya said nothing to her. She worried that this procession of small children would cause a riot in their house. She thought it best to sneak up to her room. The sound of children calling out slogans was coming from far off.

As she passed through the large room, she saw that Najma Aunty lay on her neatly made bed, reading a thick book. When it was hot, the large roof was Najma Aunty's headquarters, so Aliya spent her time on the small roof next to her own room. How could she spend time with someone as important as Najma Aunty?

The procession had drawn near. The children cried out their slogans lustily: 'Long live the Muslim League! Quaid-e-Azam zindabad! Pakistan will be created! There will be no Hindu raj! There will be no Brahmin raj!' Aliya leant over the roof wall and peered into the gali. Two large boys holding torches aloft walked at the very front.

'The scoundrel didn't let me look!' cried Chammi, running upstairs. She stood next to Aliya, half hanging over the wall. 'Oh my, what a glorious procession it is! That uncle of yours didn't let me watch the procession. His Lordship burned up and turned to ash.'

'Chammi, stand back a bit and watch, otherwise your body could end up being paraded by the procession as well,' admonished Aliya, pulling Chammi's back from the ledge.

'Oh, Bajiya, didn't I make the most wonderful torches?' Chammi looked over at her, eager for praise. 'Today your uncle is going to stop dead in his tracks.'

'Chammi, what are you talking about? All I've learnt is that you are no Leaguer, you just cooked this ruse up to make him mad.'

'Oh, I certainly am a Leaguer,' she said, objecting in embarrassment. She threw her arm around Aliya's neck and swung about.

When the procession had disappeared round the bend of the gali, Chammi lay down exhausted on Aliya's bed and began to sigh deeply, and Aliya continued to pace silently—how long would Chammi stay here annoying everyone? After all, one day she would go to her own home, and who knew if that home would truly become hers or not, or whether Chammi would be loved there or not? Would she spend her life there thinking of ways to get revenge on everyone else?

'Aliya, dear! Chammi! Come down, both of you, and eat!' called Kareeman Bua.

18

She had passed the exam, but now an entire year was being wasted. She hadn't been able to go to Aligarh to do a BT, and it was all because she didn't want to write with her own pen to Mamoo to ask for more money. When she had discussed it with Amma, Amma had told her very affectionately to write to Mamoo and ask him to send more money. Aliya had absolutely refused, and even said that she didn't like writing him letters. From that day on, Amma had been cross with her. She was outraged to discover animosity for her brother and British sister-in-law in the heart of her only child. After that, she'd stopped speaking to Aliya, and thus a valuable year had been lost in the stand-off.

'But if she just did a BA in Urdu that would be quite something; what else can she do, the poor thing,' Najma Aunty had blurted out one day. Perhaps she'd become convinced that this was it for Aliya's education. When Aliya heard this, she turned her face away in disgust. Najma Aunty was her father's sister. She didn't want to argue with her. If things weren't so bad, she would even just do an MA in Urdu. Urdu was her mother tongue, after all. It was the language of her beloved uncle. Uncle hated even the language of the

English. It was on his recommendation that she had done her BA in Urdu as well. She herself did not hate the English language, nor was she incapable of studying it. She could do an MA in English and shove it in Najma Aunty's face, but to do that she'd have to circumvent Uncle's authority.

The twentieth of September had been fixed for Chammi's wedding. Despite Amma refusing over and over, Aliya had prepared Chammi's entire dowry. Asrar Miyan, had scoured the bazaar and brought back pots and pans for the dowry. An engraved lota, bowls, a jug, a spittoon, a paandaan, two pots and six plates. When all these were being placed in the large trunk, Kareeman Bua sat clutching her head for a long time. Her eyes were forced to witness an era when the granddaughter of her late master would be given such a paltry dowry. In better times, such a modest dowry would be given to the daughters of maidservants upon their departure. Really the only difference was that those pots and pans had not been engraved. When Aunty got up after packing up the pots, Kareeman Bua burst into floods of tears. Aunty reasoned with her and, with great difficulty, managed to calm her down. What would be the point if Chammi were to find out beforehand? Everyone was afraid of her. What if she were to refuse the marriage Uncle had arranged?

Aunty waited desperately for the wedding day to arrive. Her daughter Sajidah was also coming to take part in the wedding. It had been ages since Sajidah's own wedding, but Aunty had not been able to escape her household tasks for even one day to go visit her daughter. In the beginning, Sajidah had visited the house regularly. Then she finally gave up on everyone. Who was going to be excited on her behalf?

Aliya had only ever heard her mentioned a handful of times. And then who would give her gifts of clothing and jewellery at her parent's home if she returned triumphantly to her marital home? Of course, her husband had also avoided coming there ever since he'd quit the Congress party. And thus Uncle had been lost as well. How could he show his face around him?

As the wedding day approached, Aliya was tormented with worry about what gift to give Chammi. Amma had taken out a musty old suit from her own dowry and set it aside for Chammi, thus discharging her duty. She hadn't even taken Aliya's advice on this matter. Aliya keenly felt her mother's viciousness. And Aunty was no less anxious than Aliya. She gave Jameel daily nudges to arrange for money to go buy some clothing for Chammi. Jameel heard what she said but remained silent. Nowadays the house's expenses were somewhat taken care of by his tutoring jobs. He didn't seem especially concerned about his job prospects otherwise. Being a Muslim League worker had apparently freed him of the worries of the world, but Aunty was not yet willing to admit defeat when it came to Jameel. Whenever he came home, she'd start after him.

'When will you get a job? Inflation is destroying this household. We have hardly anything in the house and Chammi's wedding is coming soon. Has your Muslim League promised to give anything for that?'

'Everything will work out, Amma, don't you worry,' Jameel would say, ashamed. 'I'm not like Abba that I'll just sit by and watch the household get destroyed.'

'Don't insult your father. Do something yourself to show us.'

'Amma, I'm prepared to do anything, but no one will let me.' Then he'd glance over at Aliya, and she would look away.

'Who doesn't let you? I will have his head! It's them isn't it, your Muslim League?'

'No, Amma.' Jameel would laugh loudly, and Aliya would go and take refuge in her room. She was sick of listening to such pointless conversations.

In the meantime, Chammi had fallen totally silent for a few days. Who knows what had happened to her—if someone said something she'd answer in an irritated tone. She'd come out of her room to eat and then go back silently. The most she'd do was play a record on the gramophone. All the good cheer had disappeared from her face. Seeing her so quiet, Aliya nearly melted with worry. What if Chammi suspected something about her marriage? What if she ruined Uncle's honour? This was Chammi, not Sajidah. It could be that she was so quiet because she'd already spoken so much in her short life she was now exhausted, and who knows, perhaps she was mourning the separation from Manzoor. But since when had Chammi been in love with Manzoor? She only considered him a support; she enjoyed his love. Aliya wore herself out worrying about Chammi. She tried to make her speak, but Chammi always put her off.

❦

Uncle had gone off to Delhi. The sitting room lay deserted. Jameel had also disappeared since morning. Chammi was silent, and the day, heavy with clouds, had grown extremely depressing. There was nothing for Aliya to distract herself

with. Chammi's dowry had been prepared, she'd tired of
reading books from Uncle's library and she simply didn't
know what to do. If nothing else, at least Chammi could
annoy her and help her pass this day as it crept by. She could
fight with her, make some noise and somehow chase this
desolate silence away.

Aliya went and stood in Chammi's doorway. 'Won't you
come up to my room?' she asked.

'I'm feeling sleepy, Bajiya.' Chammi turned over. She
didn't even bother to get up from her bed.

But two or three hours of steady rain seemed to wash away
all the emptiness and boredom. When Jameel came home
that evening, he looked quite pleased. Aliya wondered what
on earth had made him so happy. What had he accomplished
that he did not look morose even after seeing her? She had
truly become a *tazia* for Jameel Bhai, a symbol of mourning.

'Amma, a letter has come from Zafar Uncle in Hyderabad,
and the funny thing is that it's addressed to me.' He sat down
on the metal chair and looked around at everyone and laughed.
'Who can it be that is writing to him and complaining about
me? Who was it that announced my unemployment to him?'

'Your Najma Aunty has been writing to him; she must
have said something, otherwise he doesn't even ask about
anyone else,' said Aunty.

'The letter must have been full of complaints against me,
but I'm not scared of anyone!' cried Chammi, seated in her
doorway.

'What did he write?' Amma asked.

'He's written telling me to come to Hyderabad. He says
there's no shortage of anything there—forget this whole

Hindustan–Pakistan drama; there's already a Pakistan right here.' Jameel began to laugh.

'Well, then, go; wherever there's money, there's everything else,' Amma advised.

'Then I will forget everything else. I won't remember any of you, that's what happens when you drink the water there.'

'Oh, he just keeps talking nonsense,' said Aunty angrily. 'Why don't you show us by getting some kind of job here?'

'I have got a job, Amma. In fact, I'm about to go do it now!' Jameel announced.

'Where?' Aunty's eyes widened with curiosity.

'I had requested to join the army, and I've been accepted and now your humble servant is about to send you piles of money.'

'The army?' Aunty's eyes froze as though she had died. 'Have you gone mad, my Jameel? Why don't you just give me poison instead?'

'Enough, Amma, thousands of men go into the army, but do they all die? And listen, if we don't challenge Hitler, things will go worse than with the English. It won't be easy to struggle against his slavery,' Jameel tried to explain, but Aunty was the very picture of helplessness. Aliya wished she could scream at Jameel and call him a stinker, a scoundrel. So, he wasn't going to make his unemployment go away; he was going to confront Hitler and he didn't even know what a huge Hitler he'd become for his mother.

'You should have your name removed, Jameel Miyan,' said Kareeman Bua beseechingly, and Jameel burst out laughing.

'Kareeman Bua, I'm going just for you! Your kitchen will be fully stocked, and you'll forget bygone days.'

Aunty was close to tears. 'I'd feel calmer if you just ran off like Shakeel, instead of going to war,' she wept.

'My dear Amma,' said Jameel, embracing her. 'Amma, it's not like I'll pick up a gun and fight! I'll be fighting with a pen. I'll just write propaganda against Hitler, and I'll be looking after my mother.'

'You won't fight?' Aunty asked, regarding him with suspicion.

'Absolutely not, Amma, I'll do other types of work instead.'

'What sort of work?' Najma Aunty asked. Somehow she'd slipped in to sit among them all at that moment.

'I'm going into the army,' Jameel responded immediately.

'That's a very good idea; there's really no other job you could get with so little education,' sighed Najma Aunty with contentment.

'Quite right. You should thank God so few women are educated around here, otherwise you'd be going about unemployed as well.'

Najma Aunty returned whence she came—how could she put up with these fools! There wasn't the slightest bit of respect worthy of someone like her. Aliya felt like laughing.

'Put your hand on my head and swear that you won't fight.' Aunty placed Jameel's hand on her head.

'On this beloved head I swear, Amma,' chuckled Jameel.

Then everyone else started laughing as well, and Chammi, who had been sitting silently for so long, suddenly went into her room, her face red.

19

Jameel was gone. He had come to take his leave of Aliya in her room in the middle of the night and sat by her on a chair for a long time, swinging his legs. Both were silent as it rained steadily outside. Aliya felt angry at her own weakness. Why didn't she speak? What sorrow did she announce by her silence? Time continued to pass by. The rain grew lighter. She felt suffocated by the silence and by Jameel's proximity.

'You're leaving in the morning?' she asked, gathering up the courage to speak.

'Yes, I am leaving. So?' he answered stiffly and began looking about. His eyes were filled with the pain of suppressed desire.

'Is it a crime to ask?' Aliya looked down. She felt injured by his reply.

'Aliya, will you think about me?' he asked, suddenly grabbing her hands.

'No! Why would I think about you? You're nothing more than a first cousin to me. I don't wish to consider you anything else. The truth is that I have no faith at all in the love of any man, and if at some point I do begin to have faith, it wouldn't be in someone like you. It wouldn't be in anyone like my father or yours. Those who are consumed by the needs of others are always unaware of their own households. And anyway, if I ever do fall in love, I have no way of telling you what sort of man he would be. I'm telling you all this so that you won't go far off and still think of me. When you live far from home and leave everyone behind, memories can become distressing. So please relieve yourself of that distress right here and now. This household and Aunty hold no importance for you. How many more days will she even live?' Tears had come to Aliya's eyes. She didn't know why she wanted to sob right now.

'It was good that you said all that. Even if you hadn't, I would have known. Anyway, I will tell you that my mother is very dear to me, and as far as the needs of others go, my own needs concern me more. This need consumes me like a fire, but I don't feel a thing. Indeed, I wish I had a companion to fan the flames. What is the difference between you, me and Chammi, after all? Well, goodbye.'

He stood up.

'But tell me one thing,' he added. 'Do you ever desire revenge? Because I believe that no matter what man does, he always wants revenge. I too want revenge before I leave. Perhaps this will act as a balm for me when I am far away.'

Jameel looked into her eyes and she began to tremble.

'What sort of revenge?' she asked, acting ignorant, as though she didn't know.

For a short while, silence reigned. Jameel was watching her. There was bitterness in his eyes, the sorrow of losing something, and yearning to gain something.

'What revenge can I offer you?' she asked, startling him, and now she was unable to meet his gaze.

'Just this . . .' He moved forward and grabbed her in his arms and began kissing her like a madman. He pressed her against his chest and she wasn't able to resist him at all. She wasn't even able to push him away angrily. She had no idea how all this had happened so fast and how she was allowing it, when suddenly he practically threw her on the bed and left, and she began to weep with despair. But what had she agreed to offer him as revenge? She fell asleep chastising herself.

Jameel left very early in the morning while she still slept. Chammi came and woke her up to complain.

'Bajiya, you just kept sleeping, you didn't even come down to say goodbye to Jameel. It would have been nice if he hadn't left for a few more days.'

'Why?' Aliya started as she got out of bed and looked at Chammi. What difference would a few more days have made to Chammi?

'He just shouldn't have gone,' replied Chammi, confused. 'Poor Aunty is so sad. Even Jameel has brought her no happiness. Why do mothers raise children? I'm the best one, since I raised myself. No one is sad for me.' Chammi sighed deeply.

'Yes, poor Aunty gets no happiness,' agreed Aliya, and she went downstairs holding Chammi's hand.

Shakeel was lost, Jameel had gone to war—poor Aunty looked like a parched bird in summer.

'May Allah keep him well; at least money will come into the house, Sister-in-law, that will give you some happiness,' Amma reasoned with Aunty, who sat sighing.

'It's a sign of the times, nowadays the descendants of my late Master are all scattered about looking for jobs. There once was a time when wealth came walking into our home and there was no one to pick it up and put it away,' lamented Kareeman Bua, her eyes darting about vacantly.

In the afternoon, Aunty handed Aliya a bundle of fabric.

'This is the cloth Jameel has given for Chammi; he wanted you to stitch it. He's considerate of everyone, but these bad times have forced him to go far away. If he had got some nice job here, he'd have had no reason to go.'

'God will bring him back safely, Aunty, don't you worry,' Aliya assured her, taking the fabric and going off to her room. She wished she could show Chammi these clothes and tell her that Jameel had left them for her, but for what? How could she answer that? She was scared of Chammi. There were only fifteen days left for the wedding.

That evening, Uncle returned from Delhi. When he learnt that Jameel had joined the army, he immediately began to lament.

'Good God, what else could have happened with that worthless fool, he will only create Pakistan with the help of the English. They are all sycophants when it comes to the British.'

'So, do you think he should have helped the cursed kaffirs?' Amma immediately retorted. Uncle hung his head.

'Please change your clothes and freshen up, Uncle, you must be tired from your journey. Why don't you rest a while?' suggested Aliya, trying to change the subject. Her heart ached on seeing Uncle's tired face. He'd come home after so many days, and needed to rest now.

Kareeman Bua was preparing tea and Aunty was unpacking his box. Aliya picked up his things and put them away in his room. After changing his clothes, Uncle lay down on the bed in Aunty's room. Perhaps he was so tired he didn't even feel like going into the sitting room. Kareeman Bua placed a lantern on the teapoy by the head of the bed. Aliya sat by his side and began massaging his head.

'I'm afraid these Leaguers will divide the country,' Uncle said sadly.

'Yes, I am too,' agreed Aliya to put him at ease.

'As you've seen, Jameel went into the army—my own child!'

'It was horrible what he did, Uncle,' she agreed. How could she tell him that if Jameel had not gone to war, there would be no other way to feed their bellies?

'Has Mazhar sent a letter?'

'Nothing has come for a few days,' she said sorrowfully. How she longed for Abba's letters. She started twisting the end of her sari so hard the fabric began to unravel.

'It's got very old,' she laughed sadly.

'Oh yes, your clothes must be getting quite old. You've had nothing new made, after all.' Uncle also laughed with embarrassment.

'Actually I have some new outfits set aside,' she lied boldly. For some reason she couldn't bear to see Uncle ashamed for even one moment.

Uncle began to think about something, and closed his eyes as if he was sleeping. Aliya tiptoed back to the veranda. How quickly night had come to the room, while outside the Maghrib prayer had not yet arrived. Kareeman Bua was cleaning the chimneys of the lanterns and Chammi was seated on the chair in the yard feeding stale bread to a beggar boy about ten years old.

As soon as she saw Aliya, Chammi began to praise him. 'He sings really well, Bajiya, I heard him sing at Zeenat's mother's house. Okay, sing now,' Chammi ordered him. After cleaning his hands and face on the hem of his shirt, the boy closed his eyes and began to sing:

The birds have destroyed the garden, they pecked every leaf

Aliya liked his voice very much. She was listening happily, but who knows what happened to Chammi—she suddenly began sobbing and ran into her room, and the boy got nervous and glanced around at everyone. Then he gathered up his begging bundle and ran off frightened. Aliya was left agitated. What did Chammi hear in his singing that caused her to weep? Then she saw that Aunty was also wiping her tears away.

'The times are such that beggar boys can sit beside respectable young ladies and sing,' Kareeman Bua muttered as she hung a lantern in the archway of the veranda.

'Kareeman Bua, make me a cup of tea, my head has begun to ache from reading,' ordered Najma Aunty, peering out of her window, so Kareeman Bua scooted over to the hearth.

Aliya looked up at Najma Aunty and then away. Such dark circles had developed under her eyes from reading thick books in English all the time. Really, why was she reading them; what use would they come to? She just did it so that she could be proud of speaking proper English.

Now darkness was falling and the metal chair in the yard was plunged into gloom. *Would Jameel have arrived by now?* Aliya kept wondering.

'Kareeman Bua, Prakash Babu has come, please tell my brother,' called Asrar Miyan from the sitting room.

'They never let him have a moment's rest. He's sleeping; he won't come right now!' Kareeman Bua told him angrily, but Uncle seemed to have been waiting for Asrar Miyan's call.

20

Four days before the wedding, Sajidah arrived with her four children in tow. Aunty embraced her long-lost daughter and wept for a long time, before filling her in on all the important news: of Shakeel's running away, of Jameel joining the army and of hiding the wedding from Chammi. Hearing so much painful news, Sajidah went pale and sat a long time lamenting her separation from her brothers.

Aliya had heard from her mother that Sajidah was extremely beautiful, but she saw no signs of that beauty now. Sajidah was a pile of bones gathered up in a sack of pale skin. She behaved so affectionately towards Aliya that Aliya was constantly reminded of Tehmina.

When Sajidah arrived, even Najma Aunty was forced to come down to greet her. Instead of embracing her, she remained aloof.

'You look quite unhealthy, Sajidah,' Najma Aunty remarked after examining her carefully.

'The children torment me, Najma Aunty, and on top of that, I have heaps of housework, and have to look after two water buffalo.'

'So does your husband plough?' Najma Aunty asked contemptuously.

'Yes, he does, Najma Aunty.'

'How educated is he?'

'To class ten, Najma Aunty,' replied Sajidah proudly.

'Well, then, that's fine; what else could he do with so little studying, poor thing? And Sajidah, your children look naughty—educate them well, at the very least have them do an MA in English.'

'I'll definitely educate them, Najma Aunty.'

Sajidah's face fell and Najma Aunty retreated back upstairs. Aliya sat on the takht listening to the whole dialogue in distress.

Ever since Sajidah had come home, Kareeman Bua looked quite cheerful. The children were kicking up a ruckus all around the house and Kareeman Bua happily washed the dirty hand of one, then the face of another, while giving a piece of roti to a third to calm the child down.

When Uncle came home at night, he stuck by his daughter. He was in the midst of speaking delightedly when Chammi all at once became very excited. All her seriousness was upended and she gathered all the children together and made them chant slogans: 'Long live the Muslim League! Pakistan will be created! No Hindu rule, no Brahmin rule!' The children gathered around Chammi, joining in. Uncle silently slipped into the sitting room.

'May these cursed slogans go to hell! Come here, all of you! Watch out, whoever makes noise! How can you think of shouting such things in a wedding house?' Sajidah began pulling her children away and sitting them down.

'But who is getting married?' Chammi laughed victoriously.

'You are, who else?' snapped Amma in Chammi's general direction. Everyone looked nervously at Chammi. Aliya felt alarmed. Chammi looked around at everyone, flabbergasted, and then went into her room with her head down. Aunty took a deep sigh of relief. Whatever she had feared from Chammi had not occurred. She didn't say a word—contrary to all expectations, she simply hung her head in surrender.

'Girls, no matter how mischievous, truly are the cows of God: you may drive them where you want, but they won't say a word,' observed Aunty, wiping away her tears.

Aliya went into Chammi's room a little while later and found her lying on her bed, lost in thought.

'Why didn't you tell me before, Bajiya?' Chammi glowered at her, her eyes damp. 'Well, it doesn't matter. Ever since Sajidah came, I could see myself in her.'

'Oh, silly! I only didn't tell you because you'd get embarrassed and shut yourself up in your room. I can't stand such shyness. Today you will get your mehndi. You'll be seated in *maiyon*; so you can just start your shyness from today.'

'All right then.' Chammi stared at her wildly. There wasn't the slightest bit of shyness there. She got up and squatted in the doorway of her room, and Aliya was reminded of Tehmina. She felt terribly anxious. What if Chammi also went crazy? She decided she would become Chammi's shadow during this time. She wouldn't let her do a thing.

And Aliya did stick to Chammi. Evening was approaching on tiptoe; Chammi sat about vacantly, as if defeated, and everyone else was busy. The children were making a lot of noise, Kareeman Bua was grinding up the Vazirabad mehndi, but Aliya felt stillness all around. Sita must have passed evenings like these in her forest exile. Oh, dear, why was a small pink hand taking shape out of the mehndi stone? Aliya covered her face in terror and then hugged Chammi and sat down as though that hand was pulling Chammi away from her.

After the evening prayer, Asrar Miyan called for the mirasis. Their harsh clanging voices could be heard in the courtyard. She got up from Chammi's side and came out. The anguish of bitter past memories had already descended upon her and passed her by. On seeing her, the mirasis began to ask blessings:

Long life to the bride's sister
Long life to the bride's aunt

Sajidah was seated on the stool, arranging the mehndi on a tray. Amma and Aunty had dragged everything from the veranda and were unrolling the borrowed dhurrie, and Sajidah's children crowded around attempting to run off with the mehndi. Aliya stood and watched the show for a little while and then went back to Chammi. She sat on her bed like a stranger, her feet dangling.

'Bajiya, who will live in this room after I leave?' Chammi asked when she saw her.

'I'll stay here, I'll clean it every day and whenever you come, I'll run off and leave it for you.'

Chammi suddenly got up and taking her dirty kurta from the hook, began to dust the bed and the table and chair. Aliya sat and watched her silently. Humans love their own spaces so much, but Chammi had no place of her own. She couldn't call any place home. After cleaning up, Chammi sat down, covered her face with her hands and began to sob. Aliya hugged her.

'What is this foolishness, Chammi? Everyone gets married some day.'

'It's true, Aliya Bajiya, but I will get married and no one will know.' Chammi wept on and on.

'If you had told me, I could have talked about getting you married to Manzoor, but he didn't send a message either, Chammi, and then he left you heartlessly and went to war. So why are you thinking of him now?'

Chammi gave Aliya a strange look she could not understand.

'What is it, Chammi?' she asked with confusion.

'It's nothing, Bajiya.' Chammi wiped her eyes and began laughing.

'Take this gaslight inside, Kareeman Bua, and if everyone has had their tea, then . . .' Asrar Miyan called out from the sitting room. Aliya felt sad. There was no reason to hope Kareeman Bua would give him any tea today.

'Why don't you try forgetting about tea sometime, Asrar Miyan—drink a glass of water today,' Kareeman Bua answered with a laugh, and the mirasis grinned with her. *Oh my, this Asrar Miyan seems to be an open secret*, she thought.

Aliya wished she could claw all their faces off.

When Aunty, Sajidah and Amma came in with the mehndi tray and a yellow outfit, Chammi looked down and covered her face in her dupatta. According to custom, this suit and the mehndi should have come from the groom's family but that had not happened. Who would come from so far away for that?

The beggar boy was singing outside main entrance:

The birds have destroyed the garden . . .

'Run away, you evil little thing, shoo!' growled Kareeman Bua.

Chammi silently put on her yellow suit beneath a sheet, and Sajidah applied mehndi to her hands and wiped away her tears.

May elephants sway at the door of the father-in-law

the mirasis began to sing and Aliya realized that she had asked Sajidah absolutely nothing about Chammi's groom and his family.

Everyone came outside after applying the mehndi. Chammi did not lift her eyes even then.

'Jameel had a very lovely suit made for your dowry,' Aliya told her.

'I see.' Chammi glanced at her carelessly and began picking at her mehndi.

Oh, oh, there's a thief in the attic, sister-in-law! Light the lamp

The mirasis continued to sing lustily. Seeing how listless the rituals were, they began singing popular gramophone hits instead of tired old traditional wedding songs.

'Chammi, you'll invite me to your new home, won't you?'
Aliya asked, trying to distract her.

Look how beautifully the secret of hidden sorrow is kept
The arrow is in my heart but the archer hides behind the curtain

The mirasis were now singing qawwali songs non-stop.

'How should I know!' Chammi replied softly.

'Okay, so you won't invite me—now I know how much
you love me,' Aliya said, pretending to be put out. But
Chammi didn't really seem to be listening to anything at all.

If you are coming, come quickly, this is my last call to you

The mirasis were finally done singing. Chammi just sat there
gazing emptily about the room. '*If you are coming, come quickly,
this is my last call to you,*' Chammi began to sing softly as Aliya
watched her.

'Why do you like this particular qawwali so much,
Chammi?' she asked sharply.

'Really, it's not like I'm calling out to anyone,' Chammi
snapped back. Aliya wished she could smack her. *And if the
one you wish would come never gets here, what will you do? Eat
opium, you crazy girl? Die and go to your grave, leaving him to
thrash about the bosom of the earth?*

For a long time, neither spoke to the other, and when the
mirasis had gone home, Chammi lay down on her bed. 'You
go upstairs and sleep in your own room now. You've been
sitting here for ages with nothing to do,' she said stiffly as she
closed her eyes.

'I'll lie right here, by your side,' said Aliya, hugging her affectionately. It was wrong of her to snap at Chammi; as it was, the poor thing's heart was broken.

The day after tomorrow the groom's procession would come, but Chammi's father still had not arrived, and in the meantime, Uncle seemed to have no free time. Kareeman Bua was getting extremely worried.

'Will Asrar Miyan have to greet the groom's party? What will they say if they find out who he is? They will find out, won't they?' she kept muttering.

Aliya felt angry as she listened to her words and thought, 'And if they didn't find out, you would tell them, Kareeman Bua. You are the one who tells everyone about him, after all.'

∞

There'd been quite a hustle and bustle since morning. The groom's procession was coming at four o'clock in the afternoon. Aliya helped Kareeman Bua clean the sitting room. The white sheet covering the takht and the cases for the bolster had been changed for the groom to sit on. Outside, Asrar Miyan rushed about making arrangements. The schoolyard across the gali had been rented for a day. Tents had already been set up and the cauldrons of pulao and zardah were clanking away.

At around two o'clock, Aliya sat down by Amma, exhausted. The mirasis were singing at the top of their lungs.

Oh the beautiful young bridegroom has come, oh he has come

Amma and Aunty were serving the lady guests paan and such. Sajidah was dressing her children in new clothes, and Kareeman Bua, free of the worry of roti and pots, was rushing about clucking and chattering.

'In Master's day, there'd be *mujra*s for ten days outside the house. All the very best courtesans came. The mirasis would come a whole month beforehand and sit with their drums, and when they left, their bags would be heavy with rupees. Oh my, what times those were.'

Aliya felt that the metal chair looked lonely and sad despite all the hubbub. Even today it sat in the yard, as before. Sajidah's children had jumped all over it in their bare feet and covered it in dirt. When Aliya was going to sit with Chammi, she was suddenly possessed by some strange emotion and went and stood by it. She wiped off the dirt with the end of her sari and then walked away.

'My father didn't come, Bajiya?' Chammi asked Aliya as soon as she saw her. She placed her hennaed hand on Aliya's.

'He didn't come, Chammi; he's sick. He sent two hundred rupees more for the food and so on,' Aliya lied.

'Perhaps the poor thing will come down with the sickness of death,' Chammi muttered, looking about her with hatred. Then she lowered her head.

Aliya stayed silent. After all, what could she say? Liars don't have a leg to stand on. Would it have hurt Zafar Uncle to come? But then, why would he—it would disturb his peace. Why should he stir from his Hyderabadi paradise?

Only a little time now remained before the procession arrived. She looked hard at Chammi, who sat still, looking shy. She saw no signs of danger on her face. She stood up, because she too needed to get ready.

'Kareeman Bua, listen to something I have to say, Kareeman Bua!' called out Asrar Miyan, but Kareeman Bua had fallen deaf. Really, was she not going to do anything for Asrar Miyan on this special day?

Aliya screwed up her courage and called back to Asrar Miyan herself.

'I brought these clothes for little Chammi; please give them to her for me, I couldn't do any more than this.' Asrar Miyan's voice was flooded in tears and his outstretched hand trembled. Kareeman Bua's hearing suddenly became sharp— 'This is not for you to do, Aliya,' she said, taking the bundle from Aliya's hand.

Amma and Aunty looked the clothing over. 'My, what nice fabric it is, this is what Asrar Miyan has given to Chammi,' Aliya said proudly.

'Asrar Miyan has? Well, well, isn't that amazing, to be generous with another's money,' Kareeman Bua fussed. 'It's a sign of the times, that Asrar Miyan would give suits to the girls of this household. May Allah keep Mistress in heaven— she used to give her old clothes to Asrar Miyan's mother.'

'Well, now the clothing has come, after all. We'll say this suit has come from her uncle. Asrar Miyan must have cut the money from his shop, after all,' Amma immediately decided.

'All right, Mazhar's Bride,' said Kareeman Bua, sighing with relief.

Aliya picked up the bundle of clothing as though she were touching some immensely sacred object. She wished she could scream out loud, tell everyone that Asrar Miyan brought it, that this was a gift of his love out of the goodness of his heart, but she couldn't say anything at all. She softly put the clothing on the bed and went upstairs to her room.

Najma Aunty was sitting in her room doing her make-up. She wore a gold-embroidered sari and looked extremely disgusted. Until then she had not taken part in anything, but today she felt forced to say farewell to Chammi.

Aliya changed her sari and went downstairs again. The sunlight had turned yellow and climbed the walls. Everyone awaited the groom's procession. She went and sat by Chammi. When they heard the commotion of the approaching procession, Chammi blanched.

'Bajiya!' she called out as though frightened of something.

'What is it, Chammi?' Aliya hugged her.

'It's nothing. You won't leave my side, will you? I feel scared.'

'I'm not going anywhere, Chammi,' she said, wrapping her arms around her trembling cousin. But what was happening to her? She was trembling herself as well.

Amma, Aunty, Sajidah and Kareeman Bua all came into the room. Kareeman Bua held a tray arranged with the wedding suit, a gift from the in-laws, jewellery and a wedding garland.

'Pull across the curtain, they're coming for the nikah,' Asrar Miyan called out, and Kareeman Bua stretched out the curtain, putting everyone in purdah. They sat down silently behind it.

'At least today the big Master should have been at home, to read out the nikah for his niece. What a tragedy—it's God's will that Asrar Miyan is having it read out. God, please keep her happy,' Kareeman Bua wept.

Chammi replied, 'Yes,' so easily that Aliya was astonished. She had worried that the groom's party would be left standing in the doorway until the Day of Judgement. The witnesses would have to wait centuries to hear that word, and not even a mighty storm could have pushed aside the curtain.

The witnesses went back and the mirasis began to sing the congratulations:

> *Oh, congratulations, the wedding garland has come from your in-laws!*

And Aliya was left feeling as though the singing voices were coming from miles away.

Sajidah dressed Chammi in a red suit and made a bride of her in that short time. Aliya stayed seated to one side as though paralysed. When everyone had left the room, she flipped up Chammi's veil. Was she truly this beautiful?

'The wedding had to happen, so it happened, game over, money gone,' Chammi whispered, opening her eyes. Aliya said nothing. What sort of mood was this that made it impossible to speak or listen until the end of time?

Aliya went outside silently. Chammi's female in-laws were seated proudly on the white sheet of the takht in the milky-white light of the gas lamp, consuming paan after paan and chewing great quantities of tobacco. In the midst of them all sat Najma Aunty, the heroine of her time.

'How educated is the groom?' she asked them.

'To class eight—no need for him to be educated, he has twenty bighas of land and two buffalo, thanks be to Allah,' Chammi's mother-in-law told her proudly.

'Fine, what more could Chammi need?' remarked Najma Aunty smiling scornfully at the ignorant farm women.

Then a mirasi lifted Chammi and brought her outside, causing a huge stir among the women. Everyone fell upon her. Outside, the groom had arrived with the little boy who would be his best man, his rugged country complexion showing clearly beneath his flipped-up wedding garland.

Aliya wished she could hide her face. This was Chammi's groom! Chammi who used to be in love with Jameel and was bursting with pride at attracting Manzoor. And this was all she got in return. The way Chammi looked at her groom when the mirasis began to perform the ritual of the mirror made the mirasis cover their mouths in shock.

After dinner, Chammi's luggage was prepared for departure. The dowry items were being loaded on to tongas in the gali and the mirasis sang tearfully:

You gave my brothers a palace and two-storey house and to me
you gave a foreign country, oh my rich father!

Aunty and Kareeman Bua both wept. Amma was lost in thought, her head down, and Najma Aunty waited disgustedly for the fools' party to end.

'Oh, my, Bajiya, where did Uncle find such a wonderful groom?' asked Chammi. She placed her head in Aliya's lap and began to sob softly. Aliya hugged her and wanted to say something comforting, but she did not get the chance, for it was then that the very fine groom lifted Chammi up among the cackles of the mirasis and seated her in the curtained tonga. Aliya stifled her screams—Ravana had carried off Sita. *Jameel, if only you could have been Ram.*

21

After Chammi left, the house became utterly wretched. The Muslim League and Congress parties had departed from the household. No one needled anyone else. Everyone was as peaceful as a still pond. Uncle happily came and went from the house. There was no longer any need to close the door of the sitting room. No slogans against the blasted Congress party echoed in the courtyard. Aunty lowered the curtains and sat on the takht. The coals continued to crackle in the clay oven. Amma and Aunty sat and warmed their hands, lost in thought. No one spoke of Chammi. No one waited for her letters. It was as though she had never lived in that house.

The household was in good shape in those days. Jameel's salary had put a bit of life back in the hearth, and Kareeman Bua was so busy, she spoke little of bygone days. Now what troubled her was that Uncle insisted on having his food cooked in a separate pot. He had very clearly refused to have even one paisa of Jameel's salary spent on him. In taking this job, Jameel had sided with the British. 'I did not know that Jameel, my own child, would one day become my enemy,' Uncle had said several times to Aliya, and she was stunned at his agitation. She'd sit and wonder for hours where all these separate streams of thought come from that consume mankind, and how these prompt people to cut all ties and bonds and throw them away. Uncle was the father of no one, nor the uncle, nor the husband, and this was why Chammi had been shipped off to Lanka with Ravana. Sajidah was now occupied with slapping all her family's greatness and wealth together with cow dung and shaping it into patties. Shakeel had run away and Jameel had fanned the fire of his love in his mother's heart and then gone off to extinguish the flames of fascism.

It was getting very cold out. Aliya would either lie in the sun on the roof and distract herself with books from Uncle's library or else wander about like a lost soul. Amma stayed engrossed in herself. Lengthy letters drowning in love continued to arrive from Mamoo. Aliya tried to avoid reading those letters as much as possible. She had not even mentioned going to Aligarh next year to Amma; all the same, she had decided that she would definitely go. Every now and then, letters also came from Abba; reading these would fill her with new life, and she'd restlessly begin to count the days until his release.

How does one fill empty time? Whom should she speak to? Sometimes Aliya felt so confused she burst into tears. If only Najma Aunty considered her worthy of conversation. But she'd only done a BA in Urdu, so she was a complete fool in Najma Aunty's eyes.

ঙ

All night a light rain fell and the clouds thundered so loudly, the heart shook with fear. For a while hail fell, and when it hit the closed shutters on the window it felt as though someone was hurling clods of earth at the house. She finally fell asleep as the rain grew lighter, but it was a very shallow sleep. In her dream she saw Jameel. He was fleeing somewhere, trying to avoid getting hit by hail. When Aliya called out to him loudly, he stopped. 'I'm not speaking to you, Aliya,' he said, and then her eyes opened. The thunder rumbled loudly. 'May God bring him back safely,' Aliya restlessly murmured in prayer. 'May Jameel remain safe and may Aunty's love not suffer.' But she avoided thinking about how Jameel had forced his way into her dreams.

It was extremely cold that morning. The wall around the rooftop terrace and the courtyard were still wet from the night's rain. She opened the shutters. Wails of mourning came from somewhere far off. Who had died? She got out of bed. Several men had recently been killed in the war. But there had been no wailing all the way out here; they had just happened to hear the news. Of course now the whole mohalla had been cut off from their home; when Chammi used to wander about the neighbourhood, she'd always come home and tell them all the news: who had been killed on the front, whose daughter was getting married, where a boy had been born, who had gone to jail for their party and which old man had succumbed to a lengthy illness.

She went downstairs quickly. The metal chair in the courtyard shone after being washed clean by the night's rain, and the plants in the flower beds sagged from being pelted with hail. She went and sat quietly on the takht where Amma and Aunty were silently listening to the sounds of weeping and drinking their tea. Kareeman Bua was frying parathas and asking blessings for the welfare of their home.

'Who died?' Aunty asked as though speaking to herself.

The front door banged open and a sweeperess came into the courtyard with a large open basket hanging from her waist. 'The inspector's eldest son Manzoor was killed at war. Mercy, what a strong young man he was, his mother is devastated,' she announced standing in the courtyard. Then she got to work.

'Take me, I'm going,' Aunty put her hands on her chest and bent over. 'Oh, my Jameel.'

'He'll be fine, Aunty; he'll be completely safe. He won't go to the front, he's doing other work.' Aliya held on to her. The paratha burned on the pan as Kareeman Bua gave Aunty some water to drink.

'Try to be brave, Sister-in-law; if Allah wishes it, Jameel will be fine. Calcutta isn't far from here; you can send Asrar Miyan there to find out how he's doing,' said Amma, in an attempt to soothe her, but Aunty would not calm down.

'Did Manzoor die?' Uncle asked. He had slept late and was just getting up. His face was turning red. 'These English rulers are playing Holi with our blood, just for the sake of their own interests.'

Amma grimaced but did not say anything at that moment. Aunty had by now brought herself under control and sat up. The sound of weeping had faded away, then disappeared.

'And I heard that Zainab Begum's boy has been captured by the Germans,' the sweeper announced on her way out.

Uncle was seated on the stool, washing his face and hands. When Aliya saw his hands trembling, she panicked.

'Do you feel all right, Uncle?' she asked, drawing close to him.

'I'm perfectly fine,' he laughed weakly.

'So many days with no letter from Jameel,' complained Aunty in a voice quavering with foreboding.

The weak sunlight of winter had climbed down the walls and spread into the courtyard. When Najma Aunty came downstairs to go to the college, Kareeman Bua told her the news. 'Najma dear, the eldest son of the inspector was killed at war, may Allah bring Jameel Miyan back safely.'

'What is the ill fate of this household that no one can get enough education to comfortably earn a living?' asked Najma Aunty anxiously.

'Yes, and since you received the very best education, you are winning the greatest battles,' retorted Aliya, getting up the nerve to speak in English.

'Oh! And who told you to go ahead and speak bad English? You did a BA sitting at home, so you think, oh, I am worthy,' said Najma Aunty, attacking her viciously. She sounded so contemptuous that Aliya wished she could be buried in the earth right then and there.

'Now, Najma, don't put on airs. Whose money did you use to become so admirable? You were given this reward after you cut the throats of your sisters-in-law. As long as my brother is alive I will not sit idly by and listen to people like you . . .' Amma stopped herself from saying more.

'Ridiculous! I don't even want to look at you people. The Farsi writer Sa'di Sahib has said that one should flee from fools as though they were flying arrows.' With this, she abandoned her breakfast and went outside to go to the college.

'Kareeman Bua, tell Mazhar's Bride not to worry, I will find out how Jameel Miyan is doing. And if everyone has had their breakfast, then . . .' Asrar Miyan called out weakly from the sitting room.

'You go ahead and let everyone do their worrying, Asrar Miyan, and here you go, eat your breakfast . . .' Kareeman Bua took the cup of tea and ghee-smeared roti and lunged towards him as though she were throwing them in his face.

'Do tell him to go and find out how Jameel is. What else is this good-for-nothing fit for,' Amma said to Kareeman Bua, but Kareeman Bua continued to gather up the dirty dishes and pots in deep silence.

The mourning from Manzoor's house had grown loud again. Aunty sat around sadly. When a fakir passed through the gali calling out, she took a paisa from the little cup in the paandaan and handed it to Kareeman Bua.

In the afternoon a letter and money order arrived from Jameel. Aunty trembled with joy and the intermittent sounds of mourning no longer seemed so heart-rending. She spoke constantly about Jameel as Kareeman Bua prepared maleedah to place as an offering on the tomb. God had fulfilled her prayer. A letter had come from Jameel.

22

The pleasant days of February brought tidings of spring, but why did Uncle's face look so pale? His hands and feet were withered and his belly was bloated. Gandhiji had fasted in jail for twenty-one days. He'd risked his life for independence, and as a result, Uncle had given up all comforts as well. He was always off, wandering about, or else entertaining a crowd of friends in the sitting room. They were constantly cooking up new schemes. Aliya was pained to see Uncle's poor health. Allah, what sort of man was Uncle? He never asked after Jameel. He had no idea if Shakeel was dead or alive. Aunty was drowning in her sorrows but Uncle never turned around to look. He was consumed with fear that Gandhiji would die. For several days Aliya had been trying to figure out how to make Uncle pay heed to his own ill health.

One night, when everyone had emptied the sitting room, she went to sit by him. He was lying down exhausted. In the yellow light of the lantern, he looked even weaker than usual.

'You do know that Gandhiji has been fasting in jail? I know he'll never die, but . . .'

'Yes, Uncle, I know, I read it in the newspaper, but . . .' She choked on her words.

'If, God forbid, anything should happen to him, the British rulers will forget all their craftiness. A great storm will erupt that will cost them even more than war,' said Uncle, sitting up with excitement.

'That's good, Uncle, that's good,' she said weakly. Now, how could she reason with him, what could she say? She began to caress his head gently. 'Uncle, you don't ever worry about your own health, but we all depend on you.'

'Oh, yes, that. I've told Asrar Miyan to get Hakim Mahmud Sahib to mix a herbal electuary for me. After that it will take no time for my health to return. He's a very reputable hakim and very advanced in his ideas about independence for our nation. I've also noticed that I've been feeling a bit weak these days. Could you just raise the flame in the lamp a bit? As soon as we get freedom, I'll get the electricity connected again. This lantern light does not allow me read at night.'

Aliya rose and raised the wick of the lantern. Who knew what would happen after independence? But then it would be time to serve the nation—and when would there be time to reconnect the electricity? *This household will continue to drown in darkness*, Aliya thought to herself. She went and sat at the head of Uncle's bed again. There was such joy on his face at that moment. Perhaps fancies of independence danced in his head.

'Then everything will be wonderful, Uncle,' she said, defeated.

'You read my books, right?' he asked.

'Yes, I read them, Uncle.'

'How is Najma? I haven't seen her for many days.'

'She doesn't sit among fools, but she is fine.'

'Despite all her studying, that girl is hollow as a dome. That is the precise aim of British education.' Uncle sighed deeply. Aliya did not respond. He had closed his eyes and was perhaps preparing to sleep. When he began snoring after just a short while, Aliya tiptoed away to her own room.

Outside, a chill breeze moaned and a few patches of cloud blew about. Amma and Aunty must have been sleeping in their rooms but Kareeman Bua still sat by the hearth, warming her old bones. Aliya quietly climbed the stairs.

Najma Aunty was still up reading. Aliya closed the door between their rooms and lay down on her bed. The hooting of an owl came from the direction of the high school and some stray dogs fought and howled in the gali. The night felt frightening to her and she recalled what Kareeman Bua had once said: 'When dogs howl, a calamity is near.' Now what calamity was left to come, and how must Abba be spending his days in jail?

How did she pass the night? It seemed instead that the night had passed her by. Such agitation, such anxiety—as she lay there awake, she began to feel a burning in her eyes. 'Allah-Allah,' she moaned softly over and over, and the dogs continued their howling in the gali. In the last watch of the night, a deep darkness spread about the room after the street lamps went out. When the roosters began to crow at dawn, she fell asleep peacefully. Thoughts of morning drove all dread from her mind.

Her eyes opened suddenly when she heard someone rattling the chain on the door. Then the trembling voice of Najma Aunty pierced her ears.

'Oh God! My brother Mazhar has died in jail!'

With this, Amma began to scream. Aunty wailed, and Aliya could clearly hear Kareeman Bua beating her chest. All the same, she remained lying on her bed perfectly still. She stared all about her, eyes wide open. How had this morning turned to night? Where had the sun disappeared to? Had Abba truly died?

She wanted to weep, to scream. She could feel her heart breaking, but she could do nothing, and when Kareeman Bua came to her side, beating her breast, she held Aliya tightly to her bosom and brought her downstairs, practically pulling her along. Where was the life in her legs?

Uncle stood in the courtyard. Was that really Uncle? Was he really alive? What had happened to him? Uncle didn't even look at her. She stood right next to him. Amma wept uncontrollably and thrashed about, her eyes filled with a strange helplessness, tinged with pain. Her face radiated wretchedness.

Aliya walked unsteadily towards Amma and embraced her. And it was then that she felt she too could weep.

'The British must have killed him, he didn't die on his own, he couldn't die, he's my brother . . .' Uncle clutched at the metal chair and sat down. 'I'm going to get him,' he said, placing his hands on his knees and then standing up laboriously.

'Let's go quickly, Big Brother,' Asrar Miyan called out tearfully from the sitting room; at that moment, Kareeman Bua did not even hear his voice.

ॐ

Everyone was worn out from crying. By now they were seated as mourners on the dhurrie spread out in the veranda. The sunlight had climbed from the courtyard up the walls and the crows cawed continuously. Really, whose arrival could they be announcing now? Proverbs mean nothing. Aliya wished she could smack the crows sitting on the wall and make them fly away.

Everyone's eyes were glued to the front door. It was evening-prayer time and Uncle had still not returned with Abba. Whenever there was the slightest sound of footsteps in the gali everyone would start. When a fakir walked by crying out, he seemed to wail in mourning.

Kareeman Bua prepared a hearth in the courtyard and put a large pot of water on the fire. She read from the holy Quran in her lap as she blew on the damp sticks of wood. How chill the wind felt in the courtyard.

Now they heard the sound of many footsteps in the gali and the voice of Asrar Miyan calling out, 'Pull across the curtain, Brother Mazhar has come.'

The storm broke afresh. When the men went into the sitting room after placing Abba's body on the bed set out in the veranda, Aliya ran over. Amma wept as she banged her head against the bed frame. Najma Aunty cried out for her beloved brother. Aunty sat with her arms around Amma, and Kareeman Bua continued to read from the holy Quran with her head bowed.

Aliya slipped the sheet from Abba's face. Was this really him? She tried to recognize her father, but jail had left nothing behind. 'Uncle,' Aliya pulled at her uncle's hand. He stood at the head of his brother's bed in silence, his head down.

'They murdered my brother, he did not even earn a reward for killing an English ruler and they gave him such a great punishment. I'll tell everyone I am carrying out his bier as a protest procession,' Uncle cried out excitedly.

'Who will stage a protest?' Amma suddenly tensed and stood up. 'When he lived, he belonged to you; he was your shadow. Now he's mine, and no one can commit any sacrilege against his body.'

Uncle bowed his head, deflated.

They took Abba away. There was an uproar, then a tapering off. In the final sight, what desire there is—she was stunned as she wondered why she could not imagine Abba when she closed her eyes.

That night, at around eleven, Asrar Miyan and Uncle returned from the cemetery. By then the tears had abated and the burden of patience had settled on their chests.

'Kareeman Bua, tell Mazhar's Bride that if I could die in his stead I would assuredly do so, but humans are helpless before the will of God.' Asrar Miyan's voice ripped through the silence.

'You cannot die, Asrar Miyan, you will remain alive, you cannot die!' screamed Kareeman Bua, cursing Asrar Miyan's very existence as she read from the holy Quran.

On the third day, in the evening, Zafar Uncle and Mamoo both arrived from Hyderabad. Amma was overcome with emotion when she saw her brother. She seemed to implore him with her eyes, but Mamoo looked away—he didn't want to see anything. After all, his English wife would hardly consent to the suicidal act of supporting her husband's family.

Zafar Uncle was crushed by the shock and said again and again that if his brother had lived in Hyderabad, this calamity would never have happened. That very evening he set out again for the protected territory of his kingdom. He promised to help Amma in every way.

Several days later, a letter came from Chammi. Perhaps she'd written it weeping. The tears had spread ink everywhere. At the end she'd written that she didn't want to come back— what connection could there be between the small village where she now lived and her former home? Even now she wrote nothing of herself. A letter also came from Jameel, saying that his Uncle Mazhar could never die. He would live on forever. He wrote that he would visit home on a two-day vacation.

23

How quickly spring flew by that year. Loads of gul-e-abbasis and sunflowers bloomed but somehow none looked attractive. As soon as the mango trees blossomed, the cuckoos began to sing. But Aliya felt too despondent to enjoy all this. She'd become inconsolable since Abba's death.

Amma was always lost in thought, her head bowed, and Aunty would try to divert her by talking about all sorts of things, but nothing could dim Amma's worries; who knows what she was thinking about? Aliya would sit by her side for hours but she never said what was on her mind.

It had started to get extremely hot. In the early evenings, when the sky grew yellow, the children outside would start making a racket, crying out, 'A yellow dust storm is coming, a yellow dust storm is coming!' There were hardly any days without dust storms. The loo wind blew all day, with whirlwinds spinning about, and Aliya lay in her tiny room and pondered her future. The days dragged on and on. Now she wished she could flee. Every single thing in this house had become nightmarish for her. Whenever she entered Granny's old room, she imagined she could hear her rapid breathing. She saw Abba's body lying on every single bed in the courtyard and when she set eyes on the metal chair, for some reason she felt she was going mad, and the desire to flee would take hold of her. Jameel also did not come to give her encouragement, as though the death of her father had been such an ordinary thing to him; she had begun to hate him.

When the sunlight had climbed up the walls and disappeared, Aliya came out of her room on to the roof. Najma Aunty was still dozing in her room. Recently, she too had seemed changed. She lay about with an open book on her chest thinking about God knows what. Aliya wondered if Najma Aunty's English would grow weak if this continued.

Boys flew red and yellow kites on nearby roofs, shouting out in glee, 'I cut one down!' The candy hawker selling rose-scented sugar-cane pieces seemed to have parked himself down below in the gali. Aliya sat watching and counting kites with interest for a while but soon tired of it. Today she felt listless and upset. She lay down on the bed that had roasted all day in the sun and covered her face.

'Aliya!'

'Amma,' Aliya started and got up. She was stunned to see that Amma had come upstairs. It had been ages since she'd even set foot on the stairs. She never came to talk to her alone. And since Abba's death, she'd been completely vacant and lost.

'Will you go to Aligarh to do your BT?' Amma asked, sitting by Aliya.

'I will definitely go; please write to Mamoo and ask him to start sending more money.'

Amma looked at her hard and then became lost in thought. Birds seeking shelter flew about in lines. Aliya watched them with indifference, and then began to stare at Amma. Despite being deep in thought, she seemed very peaceful at that moment.

'Aliya, what will become of us now, child? The truth is that we have already been destroyed. If you were a boy, I wouldn't be so depressed, but now you're all I've got, and you will have to do everything.' Amma's eyes shone.

'It only takes one year, Amma, then I'll be able to stand on my own two feet.'

'What I'm saying is now you need to let go of the idea of going to Aligarh. May God bring Jameel back safely—I will get all our money from Mamoo and give it to Jameel. Then these shops of your uncle's will take off in just a few days. Jameel is a very good boy and he has always respected me, may God keep him happy. What I think is that if I say so, after he returns from the war, your Mamoo will surely give him a fine position somewhere. That leaves your Uncle and Asrar: I will quickly get rid of them. It's a good house— almost a haveli. I'll have all the property written out in your name. We might as well consider Shakeel dead, or he'd have written some sort of letter to his mother.' After she'd finished, Amma looked hard at Aliya.

Aliya had understood everything. She stared at Amma in shock. She felt as though the witch she'd heard of in childhood stories was hiding in Amma's face and wriggling and prancing before her.

'I will go to Aligarh,' Aliya said sternly. 'May this house remain auspicious for Uncle. It would be better if you did not

think about such things.' With that, she turned her face away
to show that she didn't wish to hear anything further.

'You are exactly the same as your father. I know you can't
bear to see me happy. You want me to be homeless forever.
Now I will never get back my lost kingdom.' Amma covered
her face in the end of her dupatta and began to sob.

Aliya sat and watched her cry as though she were a
stranger—she did feel sympathy for her mother's ruined
life. She wanted to give her happiness, but Amma didn't
understand anything; what a dangerous scheme she'd
planned to completely ruin Aliya's life. She was her own
mother, and she was pushing her. Jameel had never once
tried to live a happy life alone for a moment and even
now when he'd gone to earn money, his goal was to end
fascism. She would never live a wretched life like Aunty
and Amma . . . What sort of life had Amma lived herself?
Abba had not been able to belong to the household for even
a moment. Could Amma not think of all this? Was this
truly her mother? She looked at her mother through dim
eyes. Amma had wiped away her tears, turned away from
her and stood up.

'You go to Aligarh. I'll write to my brother. I have no
hopes from you. Do as you wish.'

Aliya watched her mother leave. Amma was so proud of
her brother. Aliya wished she could laugh loudly, but as soon
as Amma left, she burst into tears. At this helpless moment,
she felt very much alone. After she finished crying, she felt
lighter and lay down on the bare string bed and watched the
birds fly over her in formation.

'Kareeman Bua, has everyone finished drinking tea?' Hearing Asrar Miyan's weak voice made her feel even sadder. *Asrar Miyan, you're still waiting for tea.* Today, Kareeman Bua gave no reply at all. *You won't get tea until the Day of Judgement.* Aliya sighed deeply. How many days left until college opened? She began to count them down in her mind.

24

She had returned from Aligarh after a full ten months away. She had not even come home for Christmas vacation. And Amma had not asked her to either. Several letters had come from Aunty urging her to come, and Aunty had been the only one to write to her of everyone's news as well. Amma had stayed angry that long, and over that entire period, she had not written a single letter. How could Amma know that the one she was so angry with spent her lonely nights fretting at thoughts of Amma's suffering? She had not been able to remove Amma from her thoughts for even one minute. Besides Amma, if there was anyone she strongly missed, it was Uncle. She always connected fresh news and unusual happenings with thoughts of him. She had also written Uncle several setters but never got a reply. The very first person she saw after getting down from the tonga was Aunty, and full of joy, she melted into Amma's embrace and made her chest all damp with her weeping.

The contours of the house had been worn down terribly—dust storms and rains had peeled the colour from the walls, and the whitewash in the rooms looked yellow and sickly. The curtains in the veranda had torn in several places and hung limp. Kareeman Bua was now completely bent over with the burden of her memories. And many white hairs now peeped out along Amma's hairline. Aunty's mournful mood had made her a living tazia, and the legs of the metal chair in the courtyard had grown rusty.

'Chammi has had a daughter; a letter came from Sajidah,' Aunty announced.

'Oh! So, darling Chammi is a mother now,' Aliya cried, leaping with happiness. But who among them could bring the baby a new kurta and cap? By now all the customs had died out in their household, she thought sadly.

'Have you heard anything from Shakeel, Aunty?' Aliya asked.

'Your cousin Jameel had written that he's doing very well; he's earning loads of money and spending it all. He thinks of no one and everyone is dead to him. Your cousin Jameel had gone to Bombay, you know.' At Shakeel's name, Aunty went into a state, as though she was walking with bare feet in scorching sunlight. 'Look, he's forgotten the one who gave birth to him; he's just having fun all by himself,' she sighed deeply.

'There once was a time when all the little ones would get up in the morning and greet their elders; at least, their parents controlled everything,' muttered Kareeman Bua.

My, how innocent Aunty is, Aliya thought. Really, why would Jameel run around looking for Shakeel in Bombay? Who knew where Shakeel was; but thankfully, Jameel was looking after his mother's heart. Goodness, why was Shakeel so hard-hearted?

The upstairs window opened and Najma Aunty's head popped out. Even Najma Aunty looked depleted. Aliya wished she could greet her as well, but she completely ignored her. She didn't even look at her. She'd still have to do an MA in English to be able to greet her.

Kareeman Bua had made her tea with great care. Eating her brittle handmade parathas after all this time gave her such pleasure.

'Where is Uncle?' she asked after drinking her tea.

'He's out—somewhere—must be planting the flag of independence,' said Amma grimacing, and Aunty looked around anxiously.

'He hasn't gone away, has he?' she asked again. She was extremely eager to see him.

'No, Aliya, he is home these days,' Aunty replied.

'Now all you need to do is start applying for jobs quickly; I've had enough of all these disasters. Who knows how we make it through the day in this benighted home. I've never even eaten a full meal here!' Amma said boldly, a haughty look on her face.

'What! Mazhar's Bride, I look after you more than my own life, and . . .' Aunty was speechless.

'That's enough, dear, thank you for your care, but now you people can give me back my life, and don't talk about the favours you've bestowed on me. I knew that one day I would have to hear this.'

'Amma!' cried Aliya, stunned, as she looked over at Aunty. She bowed her head. The results of the exam had not even come out yet. Had she longed to be able to stand on her own two feet just to hear all of this? Now she wished she could pray for a fail.

Aunty had turned her face away and wiped her tears with the edge of her dupatta.

'Aliya has come home after such a long time, talk to her . . .' she laboured to get up. 'Oh dear, all the work has been piled up since morning; I haven't done anything at all.'

When God was giving out hearts, he gave the largest one to Aunty. Aliya watched quietly as Aunty walked away.

'Aliya dear, may God give you a pass, may you spend your days happily. When I think of the old days, my heart is overcome,' added Kareeman Bua. Perhaps she hadn't heard what Amma had said. A thick stream of water splashed on to the hard ground of the courtyard and spilled into the flower beds. The red, yellow and purple spring blossoms were now withered.

'Well, well, at last I have peace. Now our luck will surely change,' said Amma, looking at Aliya happily.

Would Aunty keep to her room all day today? Aliya was still focused on Aunty; she wasn't listening to anything Amma said.

Uncle finally came home. Amma turned her face away from him in loathing, but Aliya rushed towards him, ignoring her mother's behaviour.

'It's been so long since I've seen you, Uncle!' she cried as she hugged him.

'How was the exam?' he asked, patting her on the head.

'It was very good, I have every hope of success.'

'Then you should read a lot during this waiting period; do keep my library key with you.' He began feeling around in the pocket of his sherwani. 'I've just ordered Gandhiji's memoir—you should definitely read it.'

'Now you'll ruin her too! It wasn't enough for you to make me a widow. Go ahead and leave me with nothing at all,' complained Amma, who was bent on confronting everyone today. She was behaving like a pauper who has suddenly got his hands on a bit of money.

'Humph—where is Jameel's mother, anyway? We need dinner for two—go ahead and arrange for it,' said Uncle, perplexed, as he went into the sitting room.

'I'll definitely read it, Uncle, my goodness, what a good book it must be,' said Aliya, ignoring Amma, and she walked up the stairs with tired feet.

'Kareeman Bua, give my blessings to dear Aliya, and tell her I pray that Allah may bring her success. Elder Brother said her exam results must have been very good,' called out Asrar Miyan, at which Kareeman Bua's tongs clacked loudly.

'Asrar Miyan, can you never keep quiet! Whenever there's some auspicious occasion, you make sure to butt in.'

For a moment Aliya stood frozen on the stairs, and then she rushed up to her room. *Kareeman Bua, you got hit so hard in the stomach that you even forgot the enjoyment of tasty things, and all you remember is the bitterness of the fruit of your late Master's infidelity. All the failure and slavery of your entire life has turned you into Asrar Miyan's enemy, and now you pursue him relentlessly. How can he go on living this way! Some dog or cat must have been allowed to die in his place.* She lay down and wept for so long her pillow became damp.

25

After many days, a letter finally came from Jameel. Aunty was hopping all about like a tiny bird and Amma was gazing at Aliya with longing, but somehow Aliya was suddenly reminded of all the important chores she had to do at that very moment. She was well acquainted with Amma's terrifying plan that was the cause of her longing. Amma had been thwarted from her ambition to be made the mistress of the ancestral haveli; she would never be called the feudal mistress, but now she was trying to make the most of whatever she could lay her hands on; and of course, she also really did like Jameel. Hadn't he proudly and openly defied his father and then run off to save the British from defeat?

'Aliya dear, could you just read the letter to me one more time? My eyes are not working very well; they water so much—everything looks blurry,' asked Aunty, taking the letter from the paandaan and holding it out to Aliya.

'*My darling Amma,*' Aliya read out, '*I've been so busy, I haven't been able to write you a letter, but that doesn't mean I've forgotten you. I think of you all the time, Amma. Aliya Bibi must have returned home by now. God willing, she will be successful. I have nothing to send her as a gift, and . . .*'

Aliya felt she couldn't read the rest of the letter, as though there were thorns sticking in her throat. She read out the remainder with much difficulty.

'After we leave this house, we will be forever homeless, Aliya darling,' Amma said softly as soon as Aunty got up.

'Then, Amma, I will go somewhere else. Why do you want to throw me into hell?' asked Aliya defiantly, in the manner of an independent girl, and then looked down. Ah, even the walls of this house were corroding. How much longer could this remain Amma's feudal estate?

Amma stared at her silently without getting angry. She had a look of defeat in her eyes. She had lost the chance to own a haveli and an estate, and now she couldn't even make this wretched home her own.

'Is this flour edible? It has worms in it. Allah, that we even had to live to see this day! There was a time when our lands produced gold,' murmured Kareeman Bua, as she sifted through the flour, picking out thread-like worms and throwing them away. The long war had made finding a single clean grain of wheat a dream. Kareeman Bua was constantly afflicted with dysentery.

'If our government wins, then Kareeman Bua, we will get whatever we want to eat. Everyone else has lost, just one country is left: Japan. Allah only knows what rock they're made of,' said Amma encouragingly to Kareeman Bua.

'Bygone days never return, Mazhar's Bride,' observed Kareeman Bua. She looked around at everyone after this profound utterance, then heaved a deep sigh and covered the tray of dough. 'Who knows how dear Chammi must be, and that Shakeel . . .'

'Do be quiet, Kareeman Bua, don't mention Shakeel. If Aunty hears, she'll start to cry again,' interrupted Aliya.

When the washerwoman came inside to take their bundle, Aunty began to gather up everyone's dirty clothing, and the washerwoman came huffing and puffing and sat down on the ground by the takht.

'Ah, Mazhar's Bride, it's certainly the Kali Yug these days. Give me a bit of tobacco, my throat is drying out.' The washerwoman held out her hand.

'What do you mean it's the Kali Yug?' Amma put a piece of paan in her hand.

'You know how Haji Sahib's son was killed in the war? Now the son's wife has run off with someone. It's been three years since Haji Sahib's son was killed. She used to lie at home weeping so innocently everyone was amazed. She was always bursting into tears—how could anyone have known she was up to no good?'

'Outrageous! If ever I meet her, I'd dig a hole and bury her, that bitch,' said Amma, making a face.

'It's the fourteenth century—time was if a twelve- or thirteen-year-old girl became a widow she'd just sit by, never see the face of anyone else to the grave—but now everything is coming to an end. It's true what the elders have said, that in the fourteenth century cows will eat dung and virgins will choose their own grooms.' Kareeman Bua could hardly keep quiet.

'Kareeman Bua don't say such things about cows; if the Hindus heard, they'd come after you. There's no longer that sense of brotherhood; everyone you see is against Pakistan; even women don't miss a chance to taunt. I just quietly pick up the bundle of clothes and come away. May Allah save us from these people—such riots keep happening in Kanpur!' The washerwoman clutched her head. 'Several of our dear ones were killed in the Kanpur riot.'

'Everything is fine, the times have changed,' remarked Kareeman Bua, and she began gathering up the dirty dishes as though bored with the conversation.

26

It had rained continuously all night long. The rain fell in torrents, and when morning came, the sky was still not clear. Fragments of black clouds wafted through the sky. Aliya swung open her shutters. The tree in the schoolyard had been washed sparkling clean by the rain and a hidden cuckoo perched somewhere warbled on and on. The air was filled with the scent of the mango seeds and peels that littered the streets, and the newspaper man passing quickly through the gali shouted: 'A horrifying bomb! Japan's back is broken! Hiroshima has been destroyed! Allied victory is imminent! Today's paper is here, it's here! Hiroshima . . .'

So an entire city had been destroyed by a bomb. Now what? Jameel would return. The British rulers would no longer need to generate propaganda, and all their scribes would now return home empty-handed. But those poor people who had died in the fires of war—what would now happen to those awaiting them? Aliya could think of no answer to that question, so she got out of bed. Today, she was truly anxious to read the newspaper.

Uncle had already gone into the sitting room and the pages of the paper lay about on his bed. She eagerly gathered them up: Hiroshima appeared to be nothing more than flames now. She put down the paper and sat there silently. *Allah, why do these governments target cities? What have they done wrong, why are they sentenced to death? But this is what always happens. Will history ever turn out happy? Each and every word in the newspaper seems to be written in blood. Could there be anything left that hadn't burnt down in Hiroshima? Who knows what state the people must be in? They must be worrying about accomplishing so many different life tasks coming to an end right now. They must have left their homes to do something, and, who knows, maybe there were children standing at shops to buy Japanese dolls, and right at that moment, that horrifying bomb had exploded—and . . .*

'Quick, quick! Drink your tea, Aliya dear, the school tonga must almost be here. What are you thinking, just sitting there?' Kareeman Bua interrupted her thoughts. Aliya quickly sat down to drink her tea. She had yet to get ready.

'Japan is also about to lose. An entire city of theirs has been destroyed,' announced Amma contentedly as she emerged from the bathroom.

'Yes, it has!' Aliya drank her tea and went out into the yard. Aunty was seated by the tap, washing her face and hands. All the plants in the beds had been weighed down by the rain and bowed to the ground.

Aliya had changed her clothes and was fixing her hair when a voice came from outside.

'Teacher Madam, tonga's here!'

As Aliya was walking downstairs, burqa in hand, Najma Aunty was also teetering down the stairs in her high-heeled sandals.

'*Teacher Madam, tonga's here,*' Najma Aunty turned and said with a mocking smile.

'We do the same work, but you are called a lecturer and I am called a teacher. Even if the difference didn't disappear, would that be the end of the world, Najma Aunty?' Aliya responded tartly.

'Hah! How could that difference ever disappear? Have you done an MA in English? Surely there's a difference between a donkey and a horse,' retorted Najma Aunty, as she sat down to drink tea.

'Teacher Madam, tonga's here from the college,' called another voice from outside.

'You and I are exactly the same to the tonga driver.' Aliya laughed loudly. 'Why don't you explain it to them?' As she went out and sat in the tonga, she didn't even hear what Najma Aunty had to say in reply.

When she returned home from school, Aliya saw someone standing in the courtyard. She couldn't recognize her from the back but when she stepped forward, Chammi turned around and embraced her.

'Oh, my! Chammi! You're here!' Aliya squeezed her tightly. 'And who's that lying in the cradle in the veranda?'

'I don't know, Bajiya,' Chammi replied bashfully.

'It's Chammi's little girl, who else?' said Aunty happily.

'Oh!' Aliya ran towards the baby, forgetting to take off her burqa. 'Oh, how sweet she is, exactly like Chammi!' Aliya wished she could pick the sleeping baby up and cover it with kisses. She realized that if Tehmina were still alive, she too would probably have a couple of children by now.

The dupatta had slipped from the baby's face and a fly came to rest on her cheek. Aliya shooed it away and covered her face.

'Tomorrow on my way home from school, I'll buy her a tiny mosquito net, then she'll be protected from flies,' she said.

'But who can really avoid flies! They're seasonal butterflies at our place, Bajiya.' Chammi laughed. 'If anyone says things like that in our village, everyone starts making fun of them, because how could anyone avoid flies!' She started laughing again—there was such sorrow in her laughter. She'd grown quite thin and looked very beautiful. *Jameel has certainly made a mistake letting her go*, Aliya thought, as she began to remove her burqa.

'Did you see Uncle?' she asked as she folded it up.

'Where? He hasn't even come home,' said Chammi, and she turned towards Aunty. 'Is Uncle well?' she asked the way grown-ups do.

'Oh yes, he's fine, but he's become a bit weak,' Aunty replied.

'Did you eat yet, Chammi?' Aliya asked.

'No, I was waiting for you, Bajiya.'

When Chammi's baby awoke and began to cry, Aunty picked her up and held her to her shoulder and began to pat her lovingly. Amma was seated on the takht, chopping betel. She did not even look once at Chammi or the baby. Ever since Aliya had been employed at the school, she looked down on everything in the house. And she'd always been enemies with Chammi.

'Your mister didn't come, Chammi?'

'No, Bajiya, how could he? His buffalo was ill. He seated me in the lady's compartment and told an old woman to look after me . . .' She laughed.

'I missed you so much, Chammi.' Aliya looked at her affectionately. Chammi was not satisfied with her environment and that thought made Aliya sad.

'I also came just to see you.'

'Humph! Things have got more peaceful in the house since you left. That's why she missed you.' Amma glared at Chammi with cutting eyes.

'Oh, really!' Chammi laughed at her sarcasm.

Goodness, had Chammi really cooled down this much? Aliya could not believe it. How serious and dignified she seemed.

'Chammi, do give her to me. Bringing her up will help me pass the days,' Aunty said as she kissed the baby.

'Please take her, Aunty,' said Chammi, for the sake of it, but her face went white. Perhaps she was recalling her own upbringing. She too had been left here to be brought up.

Chammi's baby had been whimpering with hunger but now she began to bawl, so Chammi stopped eating, washed her hands and took the baby into her lap. Aunty went to her room. Amma had already gone into Chammi's room with the paandaan. Perhaps she feared Chammi would try to set up camp in her old room.

It was very hot. Since there was no breeze, everything felt suffocating. Afternoons were so difficult to get through.

'Kareeman Bua, take these toys for the little princess, and give dear Chammi my blessings, and if everyone has finished eating, then . . .' Asrar Miyan called out from behind the door panels to the sitting room, and Kareeman Bua gathered the leftover gravy into a cup as if to give him cholera.

When Aliya held out her hand to take the toys, Kareeman Bua whimpered, 'Glory be to God! It's a sign of the times—to think that Asrar Miyan has brought toys for our Chammi's daughter.' And she slammed the dish of gravy and the rotis into his outstretched hand.

'These toys are gifts from Asrar Miyan, and he sends his blessings,' said Aliya, shaking the rattle like a child.

'This is not going to make him high and mighty, that Asrar Miyan! He goes around all puffed up. Doesn't even recognize his own status,' Kareeman Bua was still muttering in the veranda.

Kareeman Bua, may Allah make you dumb or please just let Asrar Miyan die, Aliya prayed in her heart as she went to sit by Aunty. Aunty was opening a bundle of fabrics and her needle case and picking out silken scraps to stitch Chammi's daughter a kurta and cap, talking all the while.

'Chammi, how is your mother-in-law? She doesn't quarrel too much, does she? Your husband must love you very much.'

Chammi was laughing and agreeing with everything she said, but Aliya could see that she was avoiding everyone's eyes.

'Why do I adore her so much, Bajiya?' Chammi asked, to avoid the topic.

'Because she is your daughter.'

'Ever since she came along, the rest of the world has seemed insignificant.' Chammi sighed deeply as she lay down, holding her baby to her breast. 'Her father and grandmother have no love for her at all, they wanted a son.'

In just a little while, Chammi had fallen asleep and as she slept, she sighed deeply, but Aliya spent the entire afternoon stitching the kurta and cap with Aunty.

It was in the evening when everyone was seated and drinking tea that Uncle finally came home. Chammi looked at him and then looked away.

'Uncle is standing right here, Chammi,' said Aliya, glancing at her reproachfully.

'Oh, it's Uncle, I didn't recognize him.' She laughed sarcastically. 'Greetings, Uncle, tell me, how is your Congress party? Praise be to God, that Mr Gandhi is living too long.'

So this was the same old Chammi, the only difference being that she had a baby in her arms now. Aliya stared at her in astonishment.

'Everything well in your home, then?' snapped Uncle as he turned towards the sitting room. 'Kareeman Bua, send my tea in there.'

'If he's not getting old, what else is he doing—the poor thing dreams of ruling Hindustan, ha! As if he can rule in a loincloth.' Amma was quite pleased and started speaking to Chammi. In such matters, she was one hundred per cent on Chammi's side. And anyway, of late she was prepared to sacrifice her life for British rule, because ever since Aliya had become employed, her English sister-in-law had begun writing her affectionate letters. She wrote many exciting things in those letters, for example, that if every woman in Hindustan learnt to stand on her own two feet, this country too could become an equal to England.

'Chammi, now that you're so grown up and you've become a mother, try to have some respect for Uncle,' Aliya scolded Chammi though she tried to restrain herself.

'I'm sorry, I don't know what happened; I'll beg forgiveness of him, Bajiya,' said Chammi looking down thoughtfully. 'I'll be leaving in the morning,' she added, and turning towards

Kareeman Bua, she asked, 'Kareeman Bua, please tell Asrar Miyan to bring a tonga over in the morning and take me to the train.'

'What, you're leaving so quickly, Chammi? Are you angry?' Aliya scooted over to her side.

'What! Now you stop! How could I be angry with you? You have no idea how hard it was to get permission to come here for one day. You don't know, Aliya Bajiya, you don't know.' Tears came to her eyes. 'My heart wants to stay here, but now this daughter of mine, oh! Tell me a good name for her, Bajiya! Her grandmother has given her the name Tameezan.' Chammi burst out laughing at the name.

'Why can't you stay for a while? Stay for nine or ten days. The house seems so nice now, it's like spring has come,' said Aliya, becoming emotional. 'How empty it's been since you left, Chammi, I feel so bored in this silence.'

'I'll come again, Bajiya,' said Chammi, patting her baby intently.

A tonga stopped in the gali and Najma Aunty appeared in the house smoothing out the end of her sari.

'Well, well, Chammi's here! How's it going, and is this your daughter? She's very sweet. She doesn't look a bit like her father.' She patted the baby's cheek affectionately. 'Make sure to educate her well, Chammi, otherwise she too will turn out a fool like everyone else.'

'I'll send her to you. You will teach her, won't you?' Chammi shot back.

Najma Aunty frowned. 'All right, well, we'll talk again, won't we?' she said. 'Right now, I'm exhausted.' And she went clacking up the stairs in her high heels.

'Have you heard anything about Shakeel?' Chammi whispered.

'No, Chammi,' Aliya replied quietly.

'And has my father written any letters?'

Aliya did not reply. She continued to stroke the baby's cheek. Receiving no response, Chammi began to look around. She'd asked about everyone but forgotten Jameel. There was no truth in that love. Aliya felt strange.

That night the sky was so clear the moonlight made everything look like it was bathed in milk. A tiny cradle had been added alongside the row of beds in the courtyard and the gurgles from the tiny baby in that cradle made the night all the lovelier. Torrents of rain the night before had given this night a slight chill. Tonight, Aliya had her bed set up next to Chammi's in the courtyard instead of sleeping on the roof. There was an odd sense of excitement in the household. Everyone was gathered in one place talking, while Chammi's baby cooed. Only Najma Aunty lay alone on the roof, away from the company of fools. Yes, Uncle had also not set foot inside the courtyard since seeing Chammi. He'd eaten in the sitting room and then had his bed set up outside on the terrace where he was talking to someone.

Now that she was free of all her tasks, Kareeman Bua sat down near Amma on the ground and began to sing lullabies to Chammi's baby.

Come, O sleep, why don't you come?

'Kareeman Bua, tell me a good story,' begged Chammi. She was feeling like a little girl at that moment.

'I don't even remember any more, Chammi dear.' Kareeman Bua began to think.

'Tell any story, Kareeman Bua! How fun all those stories were,' insisted Chammi and Aliya as well. She'd grown tired of the world of books. At this moment all she wanted to hear was an innocent story.

'Oh, tell that story, Kareeman Bua, the one where there once was a king. He had seven daughters. Then one day he called for all seven and asked them, "Whose fate do you depend on?" Then they all said, "Your fate, father." But the very smallest one said, "I live my own fate!" And so, the king had her thrown into the jungle and declared, "Now you can live your own fate." And then, as the daughter sat alone in the forest weeping, a jinn came and he made a palace for the girl and—just tell that same story, Kareeman Bua, I reminded you of so much of it,' said Chammi, sitting up.

'Okay, well, then listen: There once was a king, a king of my god and your god, yes. So this king had seven daughters. One day, that king called all seven of his daughters before him and asked . . .'

Kareeman Bua was telling the story but Aliya did not hear a single word. Instead she began to wonder what it was that made Chammi think of this story. Did she hold out any hope for her own fate? She'd been wandering in the jungle of her own ill fortune for so long, but no jinn had yet appeared. *Chammi, people while away their time listening to innocent stories filled with longing, but there is no truth in them.*

The story had not even come to an end before the sleep fairy had carried Chammi off. Who knew which palace it took her to, and to which prince's side?

In the morning, Chammi left, and as Aliya went off to school, she felt quite sad. Today she would not be able to teach from the heart. What harm could there have been in Chammi staying a few more days?

27

As soon as the bomb fell on Nagasaki the war had ended. Japan laid down its arms. A letter had come from Delhi, from Jameel, saying that he would soon return. His work had ended now, and when Aliya awoke from a nap at four o'clock one evening, she saw that Jameel truly had come. She wasn't sure what to do. Should she immediately run downstairs, or stay sitting where she was? But that might upset Aunty, and after all, why should she keep sitting there?

She went downstairs. Amma and Aunty were sitting with Jameel. Kareeman Bua was preparing the tea things. Aunty's face was wreathed in smiles for the first time in so long.

'But why were you all afraid? I was just sitting in Delhi, fighting the war with my pen. What use was I on the front?' Jameel laughed.

'I was just afraid you might be sent off to fight too. Whenever something happened I would get nervous. You didn't write back right away, and when there was a delay I would think you'd been sent off to fight as well.' Aunty was embarrassed at her foolishness. 'And then you never came home either. After all, it's not like Delhi is so very far.'

'And my father never explained what my work was? Where would I have gone? There was no reason to worry.' Jameel hugged Aunty. 'So what if I didn't come for a long time—I'm here now.' He turned and looked around. 'Oh, Aliya Bibi.' He stood up. 'Are you well? You've become an important person now—and I've just stayed the same old fool. Will you teach me too, or no?'

'Why are you making these distinctions? Tell me, how have you been?'

Aliya attempted to look him in the eye as she spoke, but quickly looked down. Jameel was looking exceptionally handsome in his army uniform.

'This uniform suits me, doesn't it? I look silly, don't I, or else, handsome?' Jameel seemed to be teasing her.

'Can any symbol of war be handsome?' she asked gravely.

'Oh, good lord, Amma, hurry up, let me get this uniform off so that I can try to look a bit handsome. Where is my trunk? Please get out my clothes.' Jameel laughed loudly.

'I'm so happy to be home; I'm seeing everyone after so long.' He looked meaningfully in Aliya's direction. 'How patient man gets when he lives far away,' he said seriously. 'Listen, did you ever even miss me?' he asked Aliya.

'Yes, when Aunty would weep from missing you, I too would think of you,' she replied indifferently.

'You haven't changed a bit; you're exactly the same.'

'Tell me something about yourself,' she said, changing the subject.

'What's to tell? I've come home after being released from my job; now the same old unemployment awaits me,' he said in a subdued tone.

'Then why did you leave your job, Jameel? It's clear you will have to stare unemployment in the face now. And how could you have accepted this employment in the first place? You did it to defy Uncle, didn't you?'

'Oh! Why would I defy him?' There was intense disgust in his tone. 'After I achieved my goal, my employment ended. What need was there for me to establish myself in what I was doing? Now I will only be employed after independence.'

'Look, Jameel Miyan, don't speak that way, now you've seen how even big important countries have paid the price for fighting the English—so let go of that dream,' Amma told Jameel.

'You're right, now I've let go of everything.' He bowed his head dutifully and sat down.

'Did you see Shakeel?' Aunty asked as she handed Jameel his clothing.

'I saw him, Amma, but he ignored me. He's become an important man; he wants nothing to do with us. He's not worth asking about.'

'Go ahead and wash up,' said Aunty, sighing deeply.

'Amma, where is my father?'

'He's been out somewhere, since morning, he'll probably be back soon,' Aunty told him.

'Did you ever miss Uncle?' asked Aliya, laughing.

'Did he ever miss me?' Jameel laughed as well and then turned towards her. 'And you, I'm sure you never missed me.' He looked at her hopefully.

'I have no interest in missing people and such,' she said, avoiding his gaze.

He fell silent. He thought for a few minutes, then hugged Kareeman Bua and stood up. 'But you missed me, my Kareeman Bua, didn't you? What are you cooking for me today?'

'I've passed the days in agony, and I am your humble servant, Jameel Miyan.' Kareeman Bua touched her curled hands to his temples and then touched her own to remove all evil influences from him. 'I am making pulao for my Jameel Miyan.'

When Jameel glanced over at Aliya from the corner of his eye, she looked away. If only she didn't have the day off today, she could bother her head with the girls in school.

'Oh, and yes, where is my Najma Aunty, Amma?' asked Jameel.

'She is utterly bored in this house now, so she goes and whiles away her time over at her girlfriend's house—she teaches at the same college as her,' Aunty replied.

'So she must surely be an English MA as well, otherwise how could they be friends?' Jameel chuckled and, picking up his clothes, went into the bathroom.

Aunty was extremely busy tidying up Jameel's trunk, Amma was spreading out the cloth on the takht, and Aliya was racking her brains wondering how she would be able to live in the house now. How could she tolerate this mental torture every moment? The war was over and Jameel had come home, but what atom bomb could finish off the war that would take place in her mind?

'How nice the house seems now that Jameel has come,' said Aunty looking towards Amma.

'The joy in a house is all thanks to the master,' said Amma happily.

'But the master of this house is Uncle,' said Aliya, needlessly jumping into the middle of the conversation.

Amma did not respond. Ever since Aliya had started earning money, Amma had put up with everything she said.

Aliya began to pine for Uncle. Who knows where he'd been off wandering since morning? He didn't eat at the right time or rest properly. How weak he'd become, and now Jameel was back, and there would be conflict all the time. It was impossible to say how father and son would behave when they met after being separated for so long.

Jameel had bathed and re-emerged. Amma was trying to gather him to her side like he was her territory. Aliya felt irritated. She was not responsible for this affection of her mother's. It was impossible for her to give her mother a wonderful son-in-law like Jameel.

After sitting by Amma a few minutes, Jameel began to pace about and when he passed near Aliya, she announced, 'Chammi came to visit.'

'Oh really?' Jameel kept going, his head down, and when he passed by her on his second loop, she could no longer remain silent. 'She didn't mention your name at all, and she had an adorable baby girl.'

'Great. But since when did I ask you to tell me the entire story, and since when did I want her to mention me?' he grumbled, and went over to sit by Amma.

She was feeling quite pleased at having annoyed Jameel; she had entirely ruined the fun of his pacing back and forth and touching her as he went by.

'Kareeman Bua, get my food ready quickly; I'll be going out after I eat. I need to get out and about.' Jameel was now in a terrible mood.

'What? You want to go out so soon?' Aunty gazed at him with loving reproach.

'He has business to attend to, Aunty,' said Aliya sarcastically. But everyone was in such a good mood, they didn't really understand, and all began to laugh. Jameel stared at her darkly. After dinner, Jameel went out and Aliya went upstairs to her room.

ᴄᴈ

The season had changed. It was no longer exceptionally hot during the day. All the same, she felt as though it was intensely hot today. Her whole body was burning, and she wasn't able to rest. She spent the afternoon tossing and turning on her bed. She'd grown exhausted thinking about herself.

In the evening, when Aliya came downstairs for tea, Jameel was sitting on his metal chair, perhaps waiting for his tea. 'Aliya Bibi!' he called out softly.

'Yes!' She stopped walking.

'Since I've come back, I've been having a strange experience. Distance is a good thing, really. Distances can erase a great many things,' he said with a long sigh.

'That's right, Jameel,' she responded with downcast eyes and quickly went on to the veranda.

Amma had not yet come out of her room and Aunty was busy with something or other. Right at the moment when Kareeman Bua warmed the tea and placed it on the teapoy, Uncle entered the house unbuttoning his sherwani. Aliya was fixing the tea in cups when she left off suddenly, panicked and stood up.

'Assalam aleikum' said Jameel, standing up.

Uncle seemed startled when he saw Jameel. 'Waleikum assalam,' he replied, sitting down on the stool to wash his face and hands. 'Everything is well?'

'Everything is well.' Jameel picked up his cup of tea and went back to his chair.

Aliya went back to preparing the tea. *Ya Allah, what kind of father and son are these! They can actually meet this way after so long?* The ideological gulf between the two of them was an impediment, as neither was prepared to budge at all; all the same, thankfully Jameel did not turn his face away like Chammi.

Uncle washed his face and hands and went into the sitting room, and Kareeman Bua sent his tea in there.

'Life is tough, but simple too. It's all in man's hands, how he wishes to lead his own life. What do you think?' Jameel held out his empty teacup to her. 'Make me one more cup, Aliya Bibi.' He seemed very serious at that moment.

'That's what I think too, you can make your life simple if you wish.' Aliya held out his cup to him. 'Here, drink.' She handed him the cup, then stood up and rushed off to her room to escape the delicate conversation. Amma and Aunty were coming out to drink tea.

The oncoming night was etched with despair as the sun sank behind the dense pipal trees. Slowly she began to pace about the roof. Haze filled the air as smoke rose from nearby homes, and the breeze were redolent with the fragrance of frying spices.

When she had tired of pacing, she sat down in the doorway to her room. As soon as the sun set, the breeze became cool.

She was feeling a chill running through her hands. Since the moment he'd arrived, Jameel had started to bother her and disturb her peace. She began to wonder why he had such faith in love even though he believed in no worldly ties. *These exalted humans are really something,* she thought, *when they don't believe in God they even consider the very word 'God' to be false, but when they do come around to believing, they begin to see divinity even in the threshold beneath the feet of saints. Jameel, what confusion have you got me tangled up in?* She began to mutter to herself.

There was a clatter on the stairs and Najma Aunty came in and stretched out on the easy chair. She'd come home after enjoying her friend's company all day long, so she looked exceptionally tired. Aliya was just about to get up from her doorstep when Najma cleared her throat and called out to her.

'Come here, Aliya.'

She started and looked over at Najma Aunty. She was so surprised, she couldn't stand. This was the first time Najma was calling her to her side.

'What is it?' Aliya came and leant against the bed near her.

'There's no one worth talking to in this house. Although you were only educated at home, at least you've studied a little, so maybe you can give me some advice.' Najma Aunty looked at her carefully.

'I don't have the capacity to give advice, but all the same, perhaps I can think a little,' she replied, keeping her anger in check.

'What are your views on marriage? All the lecturers I work with are getting married.'

'You should too, I imagine marriage must be a good thing, especially for you,' she replied seriously.

'You mean just for me? What a silly thing to say; won't you get married?' she retorted, a trifle annoyed. 'Well, you can just marry someone in the household, Jameel or somebody; what more could you get than that anyway? But it would be hard for me to find a man my equal.'

Aliya felt like spitting in Najma Aunty's face, but she managed to restrain herself. If she spat, the conversation would be over, and she didn't want it to be over; she wanted it to be completely frank.

'Look, Najma Aunty, as far as the question of Jameel's worthiness goes, no one in this home can be his equal. But I don't like him as a man. He is my cousin and that's it, so don't you worry about other people's engagements. Speak for yourself instead. In my opinion, there must be someone else in a country this large who has done an MA in English, and he can become your husband. For this task you should have a public announcement made.'

'What is this nonsense you are spouting? Everyone in this house is an utter fool! Oh, God, who can give me advice?'

'Even after getting such a grand degree you find it necessary to get someone else's advice?' Aliya shot back. She got up and went on to the roof. Whatever Najma Aunty said next she didn't hear.

'Time for dinner!' Kareeman Bua called out from below in the courtyard.

28

Time passed with difficulty in that household. Life is just another word for our passage over the *Pul-e-Sirat*, the narrow bridge that separates this existence from Paradise. How wonderful it would be if she could flee from there. She could leave Jameel behind. But all of this was unfeasible. If she were to leave, what would Uncle say? He'd say, wouldn't he, that she had no interest in them now that she could stand on her own two feet? And now the household fortunes had reverted to the state they'd been in before. Jameel had been let go from his job and was yet again unemployed. Aunty had saved up a bit of money, but that had been finished off in this new era of Jameel's unemployment. Aliya would have so liked to give money regularly to Aunty, as a secret from Amma, but Aunty had affectionately refused. Perhaps she feared Amma. Ever since Aliya had been employed, Amma's taunts had become so horrible; Amma had come to loathe the household.

Each day dragged by like a night of agonizing sickness. The bitter cold of December was at its height. It stayed dark until nine or ten in the morning due to the fog: the veranda curtains had lost all their integrity due to the dust storms, rains and sunlight. Now, in winter, the wind whipped through the curtains as though it were galloping across the plains. Kareeman Bua's weak bones rattled in the cold, and she would slip into the womb of the hearth and murmur about bygone days: 'Mercy, what a time that was when the veranda curtains were changed every other year! If just a couple of holes appeared, they'd be divided up and given to the servants. But will that time ever return?'

Aliya had given Kareeman Bua one of her old sweaters, but instead of wearing it in this bitter cold she'd set it aside for later. 'If this sweater wears out too, what will I wear next winter?' observed Kareeman Bua feeling rather wise.

Uncle had gone to Delhi for a while and Asrar Miyan had been suffering from fever for two or three days. No one knew what sort of state he was in, lying in the sitting room. Who had time for his medical treatment—Jameel had no time off from his rallies and processions. Whenever he did come home, he'd roast in the agonizing fires of love. Now was he going to quench those fires, or would he sit about sprinkling medicines on the feverish body of Asrar Miyan?

Aliya was extremely worried about Asrar Miyan. She worried about his health all the time—*How ill he must be if we don't hear his voice asking for tea, nor see his outstretched hand waiting for food!* Kareeman Bua would mutter and get up of her own accord to go into the sitting room and set out food and water. When Aliya asked about his health, she'd snap: 'Everything is fine. He's got a fever, not some grand illness.'

God, please don't let him suffer from some grand illness, Aliya would pray, her heart in agony. How she wished she could go sit by the head of his bed, massage his head and feed him medicine with her own hands; but how could she break

such ancient customs before Amma's harsh gaze? None of
the women in this family had ever come before these bastard
offspring. Najma Aunty did not even observe purdah, but
despite this she had never come before Asrar Miyan. When
the tonga came for college, he got out of the way on his own;
if he saw her on the way, he'd turn his face. Once, Aliya had
gone into the sitting room when Asrar Miyan was there. She
didn't even have time to get a look at his face before he'd got
up and fled. 'There's purdah between us, little one,' he had
said, as she stood there gaping. Under such circumstances
how could she even think of caring for Asrar Miyan when
he was ill? Who knows, perhaps even now, he'd say, 'There's
purdah between us, little one,' and run out. And then, what
would it do to Amma's heart to see her do such a thing?
What would she say? By now her mother had renounced
both the house and Jameel for her sake. She had hung her
head helplessly before Aliya. Now that she'd lost everything,
she considered Aliya her only support. What was the point,
then, of hurting her mother's feelings? What was the point
of overturning the ancient customs? She must defer to her
mother as well, after all.

❃

That night, when Jameel returned home to eat dinner, the
clouds were gathering, and the thunder was so loud it shook
the soul.

'Hail may fall,' Kareeman Bua kept saying.

'What makes you so certain it will hail, Kareeman Bua—
does someone have a freshly shaven head?' Jameel laughed.

Today for the first time in many days he looked like he was in a cheerful mood, while in the interim he had been so silent you'd have thought he had no tongue in his mouth.

'Oh, Master, who needs their head shaved, it's my topknot that's being shaved, with all this, "Please go check on Asrar Miyan, he's coming down with a fever." I have to deliver all the food and water to him,' complained Kareeman Bua, looking extremely out of sorts.

'What's happened to Asrar Miyan?' asked Jameel, startled.

'I already told you, he has a fever. Master has gone to Delhi, otherwise he'd get the medicine and take care of him. How did I end up in the middle of it? Now if something happens to Asrar Miyan, he'll get angry with me when he comes back.'

'I'll take a look at him, Kareeman Bua, even though I utterly despise the man.'

'Is it because the poor thing is not one of us?' Aliya asked sharply.

'It's not that, Aliya Bibi, I just hate him because he's become like Abba from living with him for so long. And I also know that he sits with Abba and criticizes me. Things have got so bad with them, that all they have left is to start putting tilaks on their foreheads.' He laughed bitterly. 'Anyway, you listen to me, Aliya Bibi, I have absolutely no thought about his illegitimacy.'

'Well, he may be the equivalent to an uncle for you, but what's the point of this useless debate now?' Amma said with disgust.

'May God not make it so! May that be the fate of our enemies—that Asrar Miyan could be the equivalent to an uncle.' Kareeman Bua blew up, not comprehending Amma's sarcasm. 'It's a sign of the times, that today queens in palaces could make him an uncle,' snarled Kareeman Bua, behaving rudely for the first time in her life.

When Amma, Aunty and Jameel all laughed at her misunderstanding, Kareeman Bua was flustered and began rolling out the rotis, and Jameel got up and went into the sitting room. There was a loud clap of thunder, and lightning flashed in such a way that everyone shrank back and put their fingers in their ears. 'God, you are great, please save us from this calamity,' Kareeman Bua began reciting at the top of her lungs.

'Lightning has struck somewhere,' said Aunty anxiously.

A fierce wind lifted the curtain. Jameel had emerged from the sitting room and was in the middle of the courtyard when lighting flashed once more, fiercely, and Aliya fairly shrieked, 'Run inside quickly, Jameel!'

Jameel came inside laughing. 'Hail is falling, but why were you afraid, Aliya Bibi?'

'I wasn't afraid, I was just telling you there was lightning,' hedged Aliya foolishly. She felt embarrassed. Really, why had she screamed? Was Jameel actually about to be struck by lightning?

'It's really difficult to understand humans; when they think they are enlightened, they are in the dark, and when they are in the dark they announce they are enlightened,' said Jameel, gazing at Aliya affectionately. At that moment, how happy and contented he looked.

'Fine, Jameel, just as it is hard to understand humans, it's also hard to understand why man's actions are sometimes unconnected to his thoughts. Who knows why he sometimes does things with no goal in mind,' she replied, looking him in the eyes. She knew that after hearing her shriek, Jameel wanted to capture the fugitive secret in her heart and bring it into the light.

'That's fine too, Aliya Bibi,' he said, deflated all at once, and then for a little while silence fell again.

Where must Uncle be right now, and what must he be doing? Aliya began to wonder in order to distract herself.

When dinner was over, everyone rushed to their own beds for fear of the cold, but Aliya did not get up from her seat. She had to go upstairs to her room, and despite the rain abating, lightning still flashed. How could she cross the courtyard in this state? She'd always feared thunder and lightning.

She pulled the curtain aside and looked out. She saw nothing but darkness and black clouds. She gathered her courage and went out into the courtyard.

'Come, I'll take you upstairs,' said Jameel, walking out of the veranda behind her. 'You're afraid of lightning?' he asked as they climbed the stairs.

She continued to walk upstairs silently. Bringing up the topic of lightning was a seriously dangerous business. Najma Aunty was asleep with her face wrapped in her quilt. Aliya tiptoed into her room. Jameel stayed standing in the doorway.

'Okay, good evening. You go and sleep too,' she said softly.

'Shall I sit by you for a little while? Who knows, maybe lightning will flash again. You'll definitely be frightened all alone.' He came forward.

'I am not at all frightened, you go to sleep,' she said brusquely, and sank into her quilt.

Jameel gave no reply. What he was thinking as he stood there and she trembled inside her quilt? What would he say now? Fifteen or twenty minutes passed like fifteen or twenty centuries, then he suddenly went away. He had said nothing. After those centuries had passed, she took a sigh of relief, wondering what harm there would have been if Jameel had sat here just a little while longer and spoken a bit.

In order to save herself from this maddening thought, Aliya thought of Asrar Miyan—*What must his condition be right now? Mustn't he feel the needs of an ailing person? His head must be bursting with fever, and how he must wish someone would sit by him, someone would ask after him, someone would look at him with love at this moment. But he had no one; he had dropped from the sky totally alone. What must he be thinking about today when he was so ill and so lonely?* Sighing for Asrar Miyan, she fell into a deep sleep.

In the morning the sky was completely clear. The sun looked shiny, and when she was preparing to go to school, she heard Asrar Miyan's trembling voice for the first time in three days: 'Kareeman Bua, if everyone else has drunk tea, then give me some as well, I'm feeling weak.'

29

Day followed day and suddenly spring rushed in and made the flowers bloom. A month and a half before, Kareeman Bua had cleaned out the planting beds and dug them up on her knees, then planted seeds and breathed a sigh of relief. Now Aliya felt happy gazing at the blooming flowers, but Aunty could not even bring herself to pick two blossoms, clean off the dusty vase and arrange them in it. She did not feel the coming of spring in her heart. She felt no joy from flowers. Shakeel had planted a seed of eternal autumn in her soul, Jameel was watering it, and Uncle—but no, she shouldn't think ill of Uncle, she reproached herself.

The state of the household had worsened. Jameel didn't even try to get a job, and instead worked all day in the Muslim League office, receiving a small compensation. He'd give his wages to Aunty and then disappear for the rest of the month, and the entire month would pass by in taking revenge on Aunty.

In those days Uncle was cursed by the ill luck of Saturn. Today here, tomorrow there. England's Labour government had decided to grant India independence, and Amma heard this news as though it were the sort of rumour spread in an opium den.

Ever since the decision to grant independence, father and son had begun to feel disgusted at the mere sight of one another. *Pakistan will be created, Pakistan will not be created!* And in the midst of this conflict, Aliya kept thinking of Chammi. What would have happened if she were still living in the house today? Everyone would have died and gone to heaven before independence came along.

Today when Uncle entered the house after being away for more than two weeks, he lay down peacefully on the bed near the veranda and stroked his head. After seeing him relaxing in the house after so many days away, Aliya got a cup of tea and sat near him. Uncle sat up and began drinking tea.

'And so the English are saying that Hindustan will be free?' Aunty also came over laughing.

'Yes, all they have to do is make it free, but they'll just mess things up for a little while longer—such a dishonest nation,' said Uncle animatedly.

'Then when we get independence, will you come back and sit at your shops?' Aunty asked, her eyes burning with desire.

'I'll sit there, why not? You wait and see how the shops run after independence! Also, we will get assistance from our government to run our shop.'

'Oh, our government will give assistance too? Oh, how lovely that will be.' Aunty's eyes shone.

'Uncle, it's so nice to have you here in the house today. When you're here I feel as though . . .' Aliya couldn't say anything, her voice choked up.

'And if I'm not your father, what am I, crazy girl?' Uncle hugged her head to his chest. 'When we get independence, I'll make my daughter a bride, and I will bring her a

magnificent educated groom, hmm?' He looked over at
Aunty and they both began to laugh, but Aliya, feeling the
warmth of love against Uncle's chest, began softly crying.
She was praying to herself that Allah would quickly make
this country independent and that Uncle would come back
home, and then in the evenings he'd lie here and chat
with Aunty, and he'd ask after Chammi, and he'd write
for Sajidah to come to visit, and he'd look for a bride for
Jameel, and he'd search for Shakeel and bring him home.

'Silly girl! You're crying.' Uncle had felt the dampness
of her tears through his homespun kurta. 'Don't cry, my
daughter.'

'Kareeman Bua, tell my brother that Hakim Sahib and
Hardayal Babu have come.' When Asrar Miyan called out,
Uncle got up immediately. He even forgot that he was calming
Aliya. She wiped away her tears on her own. How her heart
overflowed. Now she wished she could weep in earnest.

That night, Jameel spoke animatedly while everyone ate
dinner.

'Pakistan is as real as you and me sitting right here. No
matter how many obstacles the Congress put in the way,
they won't be able to do a thing. How can anyone stop the
demands of ten crore Muslims?'

'So will all the Muslims go live in Pakistan?' Aunty asked.

'Of course not! What need would there be for that?
Everyone will stay right where they are.'

'But why would the Hindus let us stay, won't they say,
"Go to your own country!"'

'But they will have Hindus living in our Pakistan as well.
We won't tell them to leave.'

Once Aunty had understood Jameel's argument she breathed a sigh of relief.

'Yes, Jameel Miyan, this whole leaving thing is bad, I also could not leave this home.' Kareeman Bua finally spoke up.

'And since when am I leaving my home? I'll just send Asrar Miyan to Pakistan.' Jameel laughed cheerfully, and Kareeman Bua grinned with embarrassment and began clearing up the pots and pans.

'Then you should take over one of your shops; Abba is so tired now. You will show him respect, won't you?'

'I'll do anything you want, Amma; whatever you tell me to do, I'll make it happen. Just let Pakistan be created first.' As Jameel spoke, he looked in Aliya's direction again and again and she continued to sit and eat on her own. For some reason she was very hungry these days.

'Oh, enough! Always the same old story, eating and drinking have become impossible!' Amma had become infuriated as she listened. 'Now you only believe people of your own community have any intelligence. Do you think the poor English are simply idiots—that they'll just hand over independence and quietly go back to their own country? Go ahead and do all that nonsense for many more years, and you still won't get freedom.'

'Who thinks they are idiots? But now time is making them look like idiots; if they don't leave, they'll be thrown out all the same.' Jameel was on a tear as well.

'Glory be to God, what drivel are you on about!' Amma got up in a huff. 'Kareeman Bua, send my food to my room.' As Amma started to leave, Jameel caught her.

'Come on, forget it, Aunty, if I ever mention the word "independence" again, may I receive the punishment of a thief.'

The conversation had turned humorous, but Amma's mood had not been righted. As soon as she finished eating, she went into her room.

Now that the cold of winter had dissipated they had begun to sleep on the veranda. The battered curtains had long since been wrapped up and stowed away. At this time of night, the moonlight shone into the veranda and gambolled about on the beds.

Jameel was pacing around the courtyard after talking so much, Aliya was seated by Aunty chopping betel nut and Amma was off sulking in her room doing God knows what.

'Where is my brother?' asked Najma Aunty, who had come downstairs and perched next to Aunty. She looked a bit worried.

'He must be in the sitting room, have him called in here,' Aunty replied.

'Look, Kareeman Bua, if there's no one there with him, then call him in here,' said Najma Aunty wearily.

As soon as Uncle entered, Jameel went off to his own room. Aliya could not figure out what Najma Aunty could want to discuss that was making her so worried.

'Brother,' she began, 'the thing is, I have found a life partner for myself, and I've come to inform you of that,' she said brazenly.

Everyone stared at her in astonishment. Uncle remained seated, his eyes downcast. Does a person simply abandon her manners when she does an MA in English? Najma Aunty could also have communicated through Aunty. Aliya glared at her with loathing.

'Then go ahead and get married; just tell us the details, and we'll immediately make arrangements.' Aunty grinned sheepishly and began to laugh.

'What arrangements will you make, exactly? Am I Chammi that the mirasis will be invited to my marriage? That drums will be played, and my dowry must be stitched? I myself am the dowry,' retorted Najma Aunty haughtily.

'I will take part whenever you wish,' remarked Uncle. He stood up again and went back outside.

'The ceremony can take place during summer vacation; after that we shall go to Simla,' Najma Aunty announced to Aunty, and she too stood up.

'But who is this gentleman?' Aunty could not help but ask.

'He is the brother of a lecturer at my college. He has also done an MA in English. He's a very important businessman,' she replied, as she went clacking up the stairs.

Everyone was silent for a little while. But as soon as Jameel returned and began pacing again, Aunty announced softly, 'Your Najma Aunty is getting married.'

'Ah, so that's what she just came to tell you?'

'Humph!' said Aunty, who looked down and began making paan.

'She won't have drums, she won't be made a bride of; what sort of a wedding is that? The times have changed. We used to have the girls sit in maiyon for a quarter of a month. They didn't even see the shadows of their father or brothers,' muttered Kareeman Bua as she washed the dishes.

'She did all that studying and this is what she learns. Tell the qazi he better read the vows in English,' joked Jameel, laughing out loud. 'Truly it was the ill fate of the girls in this

family that they weren't given an education. Najma Aunty
was the first girl in our family to be educated. Clearly, vanity
made her turn out like this. The other educated girl here is
our Aliya Bibi, and there's a defect in her after all,' he said,
looking over at her in hope of praise.

Aliya understood what defect he was signalling towards
and she was enraged.

'Yes,' she snapped back, 'if a woman attempts to move
beyond the status of puppet, her brain is clearly defective. A
man feels true joy on seeing a woman stupid. Najma Aunty's
way of doing things is wrong, but she has the right to arrange
her own marriage.'

'Who's getting married?' Amma asked, popping out of
her room.

'Najma Aunty,' Aliya replied.

'Where did Big Brother arrange it?'

'Big Brother did not, she arranged it herself,' Aunty
informed her.

'Oh, enough, enough! Her older sister got married
according to her own wishes and thanks to that, her fabulous
son Safdar now sashays about on the bosom of the earth.'
Amma's anger was in full force.

No one gave any response. Aliya regretted Amma's bitter
tone. Amma went back into her room, and Jameel got up and
started pacing and humming:

My heart was not soothed, nor did the darkness of the mournful
   night disappear
If I had known this, I wouldn't have set my house on fire

Ah, so he was bemoaning the defect in her mind, and she wasn't able to soothe his heart. *I never gave him colourful evenings.* What greater defect could there be?

'I'm just going out, Amma, I have some important work to do. I'll be back late, so please lock the door,' said Jameel as he went towards the door. '*My heart was not soothed, nor did the darkness of the mournful night disappear*'—even as he walked out of the door he continued to hum that song.

Just then, Asrar Miyan's gloomy voice emerged with fanfare in the bright moonlight: 'Kareeman Bua, if everyone has eaten dinner . . .'

Aliya climbed the stairs to her room.

30

It was extremely hot. Najma Aunty had already departed for Simla with her businessman. At her wedding, neither were drums played, nor did mirasis sing. Kareeman Bua's heart was broken. What must one endure in these wretched times! Amma was constantly reminded of the late Salma Aunty after the wedding, which brought out her prayers for the death of Safdar. In the meantime there was an uproar all about the country. The Cabinet Mission had raised a ruckus and then returned home. The Muslim Leaguers had grown more important. If Uncle could help it, he'd never look at Jameel's face at all; he'd begun to consider him a snake nurtured in his own sleeve. If at any time they came face-to-face, they'd taunt one another—'All Muslim Leaguers are the sycophants of the British,' Uncle would huff.

'There's no doubt about that, but since when has this friendship between your exalted Nehru and Lord Mountbatten been going on? And why is there such a special friendship between your Nehru and fair Lady Mountbatten,' shot back Jameel, not one to back down.

'You would ask such a question in your ignorance.'

'Really, Jameel, don't you tire of having debates outside the house?' Aliya would say, jumping into the middle, and then Jameel would feel unable to stand up to his father.

'Bah! The blood of every single Muslim being killed in the riots falls squarely at the door of the Muslim Leaguers.' Uncle would sigh deeply.

Jameel would stare at Aliya and remain silent. He was dying to respond, but he couldn't say anything.

Aunty continued to worry about Shakeel.

'God knows where he must be! Hindus and Muslims are thirsting for one another's blood,' she would lament. In those days Aunty was tortured by her worries for Shakeel.

ᘓ

Early that evening, a dust storm arose. Kareeman Bua was lighting the lanterns. Every single one had gone out simultaneously.

'May they be destroyed, these dust storms,' she muttered as she gathered the lanterns together and went into her room.

'Garlands! Jasmine! *Moti* and *chameli*!' called out the garland seller as he dashed through the gali.

The storm was over in just a short while. A few drops of rain had fallen and released the fragrance of sweet earth, and songs played on gramophone records could be heard from the roofs of the mohalla.

Father, my parents' home slips away from me

'Everyone eat dinner! Who knows if it will start to rain again—it's still quite cloudy,' called Kareeman Bua, and then she began to wipe the storm dust from the pots and pans. 'Who knows why these blasted storms keep coming,' she mumbled to herself.

'In the old days there must not have been as many dust storms, Kareeman Bua?' Jameel asked laughingly.

'These dust storms always came, Jameel Miyan. They carried off all manner of precious things,' Kareeman Bua responded seriously, not understanding his joke. 'Once a storm carried off my georgette dupatta; I'd just washed it and hung it out on the clothes line.' Kareeman Bua began to adjust the tattered dupatta on her head. 'May these dust storms be destroyed,' she repeated, as she picked up the plates and went out on to the veranda.

'It may rain tonight as well,' said Jameel, looking over at Aliya.

'God willing; then we'll get a break from this heat.'

After dinner, Amma and Aunty opened up the paandaan. Kareeman Bua was gathering the leftover gravy from the other plates into a cup for Asrar Miyan. Jameel had gone back to sit on his chair.

Where is Uncle? thought Aliya as she climbed the stairs. *This cold food will only ruin his health further. At the very least, he should come home early at night.*

The night was damp as tear-stained eyes. After making up her bed on the roof, Aliya began to stroll slowly about. 'Oh, Allah, the time simply doesn't pass,' she murmured. The gramophone records played continuously:

In vain I was dishonoured, darling, just for you

'Oh, there's a very nice breeze up here,' observed Jameel, coming upstairs as well. He began strolling with her.

She stayed quiet. Night, solitude, the swelling clouds and now Jameel. Her heart felt weighed down, as though she were trapped in a storm. What was this strange terror? She wished she could pick Jameel up and toss him into the gali below. She leant over the wall and began peering down, where the sugar-cane hawker walked by, shouting out, his tray illuminated by a lamp with two wicks.

'Aliya,' Jameel addressed her in an emotional voice.

'What is it?' She turned indignantly.

'So many things—but you have become so deaf to me.'

'What's left to say? You've already said everything and I've already listened. Don't you ever tire of repeating these things over and over?'

Jameel stood next to her and leant over to peer at her in the dark. He was so close that she could feel his breath on her face and she felt as though her face was being torched by the hot June wind. She moved away and went and sat on her bed and rubbed her face with both her hands.

'Why are you so cruel and unfeeling towards me?' he asked, drawing near again. What was this huge gulf that could not be bridged? He leant over and looked into her eyes. Aliya saw a darkness even blacker than clouds shrouding his eyes, but despite those clouds a hot summer wind blew. Aliya felt her heart would melt.

'Please sit down,' she said, sliding to one side.

'May I sit on your bed? On your bed I'll feel as though . . .'

Aliya had the sensation of being embraced by a cloud of hornets.

'Jameel Sahib, you have become stubborn when it comes to me. You senselessly wish to prove that if you don't get me, you will die, you'll be destroyed, you'll never find a more wonderful girl in this lifetime than me, but I know that if I leave your sight this very day, you'll find someone else. You must have once felt something like this for Chammi, and . . .' Her voice became tearful and she hid her face in her knees and began to weep. Right at that moment, she was feeling extremely weak.

'What? Are you really so disgusted with me that—don't cry, Aliya.' Jameel panicked and placed his hands on her shoulders. 'Calm down now, I won't say anything, I want to make you smile throughout your life; I don't mean to make you cry.' He took his hands away from her shoulders. 'Now I won't demand anything of you, I don't even have the right. I swear you won't be troubled by me any more. There, you're happy now, right?'

What could she say? She continued to sob.

'Don't cry, Aliya Bibi.' He stood far from her, like a criminal. 'If you don't want to be my life companion, that's fine. Life will continue on. How many people really live a happy life, anyway? But for now, do calm down; I won't say anything to you any more.' His voice shook.

For a few minutes he stood there silently and then went quickly downstairs.

'Kareeman Bua, my brother will be home by midnight; if everyone has eaten please send some dinner for me too.' Asrar Miyan's voice rent the stillness of the night.

Aliya wiped away her tears and lay down perfectly still. It was very dark. The gathering clouds looked menacing. Would it rain so hard tonight a deluge would come? Tonight she would surely drown. She hadn't even fashioned a boat to protect herself! She closed her eyes.

31

Pakistan had been created. The League leaders had already departed for Karachi, the capital of the country. In Punjab a bloody Holi was being played out. Uncle seemed felled by the shock. He lay like an invalid in his sitting room, asking everyone, 'What has happened? What is happening? How did Hindus and Muslims suddenly become mortal enemies? Who taught them to do this? Who snatched the love from their hearts?'

When he asked these questions Aliya would stroke his head, saying, 'Uncle, please rest; you're tired, Uncle.' And he would close his eyes as though he saw a river of blood flowing before his very eyes.

'It's a sign of the times; time was if Hindus saw peril coming to the Muslims of their village, they would risk their lives to save them, and a Muslim laid down his life to protect the honour of a Hindu; there was such brotherhood they seemed to have been born from the same womb. But now what's left? Both hold daggers in their hands.' Kareeman Bua would sigh deeply on hearing news of the riots. There had been no riots in their own city, but everyone constantly worried about what would happen next.

'Where must he be, my Shakeel?' Aunty would weep on hearing news of riots in Bombay. 'Your Pakistan has been created, Jameel, your father's country has also become free, but now who will bring home my Shakeel?'

'Everything will be fine, Amma, I'm sure he's well. All these riots and such will be over in a few days,' Jameel would reason with her, but his face remained pale with shock.

One evening everyone sat silently drinking tea, when a letter came from Mamoo. He had written to Amma that he had committed his services to Pakistan and was soon to move there: *If you two wish to come as well, respond immediately, and prepare for the journey.*

'Oh, just send a telegram right away, Jameel Miyan, what will it take for us to get ready? We are already completely prepared. Gracious! He is my brother after all, surely he can't just leave me here alone.' Amma's face went pink with glee.

Jameel panicked and looked around at everyone as though the rioters had just arrived at his door.

'But why would you go, Aunty? You're safe here. I would give my life for you.' Today he looked at Aliya after a very long time. What beseeching eyes these were—but Aliya looked down.

'If I don't go, am I to live in Hindu cities? In Pakistan at least it will be our own government. Also, I can't for one minute live without my brother, of course.' Amma was so pleased she couldn't contain herself.

'Aliya won't agree to go, Aunty, she won't go, she just can't go,' said Jameel as though half mad.

'You certainly have become quite the authority over her—
who exactly is it that won't go?' Amma snapped. 'Who are
you to stop her?'

'Do go, Aunty,' said Jameel. He looked down, and Aliya
felt suddenly as though she couldn't go. Centuries would pass
but she would not be able to stir from there.

'I'll go send a telegram right away saying that everyone is
ready,' he said, getting up and going outside.

Aliya wished she could announce to everyone at the top
of her lungs that she wouldn't go—she couldn't go, no one
could make her! But she felt her throat pricked by hundreds of
thorns. She couldn't even speak one word; she just looked all
around and then down. *But to stay here—for what, for whom?*
she wondered, and then she began to chop betel nuts very
calmly. *Aliya Begum, if you were to stay, you would be stuck for
ever in this swamp,* she told herself.

'Kareeman Bua, if everyone has finished drinking tea . . .'
Asrar Miyan called out from the sitting room and today
Kareeman Bua began screaming at him like a witch:

'My Gawwwwd, would someone please send this Asrar
Miyan off to Pakistan as well! Everyone's left and everyone
will leave, but this one never goes anywhere!'

The sound of Asrar Miyan coughing came from the
sitting room and then all fell quiet

'Will you truly go, Mazhar's Bride?' Aunty asked after a
while.

'Obviously,' Amma replied abruptly.

'But this is your home, Mazhar's Bride, don't leave me
alone.' Aunty closed her eyes brimming with tears; perhaps
she feared the ghost of solitude.

Aliya ran upstairs in search of refuge. The sunlight had turned yellow and climbed the high wall of the house across the way. Nesting birds in the schoolyard kicked up a constant din. Coming out into the open air, she breathed a sigh of relief and began pacing about and wondering, as travellers do, what would happen next. Maybe it would even be good; she would surely be happy after leaving here.

When she returned downstairs everyone was sitting lost in their own thoughts. Only Kareeman Bua was muttering about something or other as she briskly toasted rotis. Where had Jameel gone? Why had he not yet returned? Aliya glanced over at the empty chair. Would this madman remember her or forget her, she wondered. The wick of the lantern was defective so two flames rose from it, and the chimney had gone black on one side. In the dim light, the faces of Amma, Aunty and Kareeman Bua all looked distorted.

Jameel finally re-entered the house and sat down on his chair. 'I've sent out the telegram, Aunty,' he said softly.

'Don't stay outside the house for so long; come back in the evenings. Who knows when things will turn bad here as well,' said Aunty.

'I have to go outside; Muslims are scared, but they have to be made to understand that they should stay put here and keep the situation peaceful here. I can't get anything done by staying at home.'

'For God's sake, now that the country has become free, this new work has begun. Well, what's it to me, anyway—you did put the right address on the telegram, didn't you?' Amma asked.

'Rest assured, the address was correct.'

'Well, anyway, we are going to Pakistan now, but you should worry about your own home, Jameel Miyan, look how bad it's got already, and look at your mother too,' said Amma, glancing sympathetically over at Aunty.

'Who's going to Pakistan?' asked Uncle agitatedly the moment he set foot in the courtyard. He'd heard what Amma had said.

'Aliya and I, who else?' Amma snapped back.

'No one can go, no one can set foot out of here without my permission! Why would you go to Pakistan? This is our country, we've made sacrifices, and now we'll just leave it behind? Our time for enjoying it is about to arrive,' cried Uncle with intense passion.

'Mashallah, what a great protector you've turned out to be—you can't support us, what hardships have we not endured since coming here? You were the one who snatched away my husband; you were the one who killed him! You made my daughter an orphan and now you have the gall to assert your authority.' Amma's voice trembled with rage.

'Kareeman Bua, send my dinner into the sitting room,' said Uncle, walking into the other room, head down.

'Do you really want to take this revenge on Uncle before leaving? Uncle didn't destroy anyone. Uncle didn't invite anyone to join him. You listen to me today and listen well: I love Uncle just as much as I did Abba,' Aliya declared, abandoning her dinner. She got up, washed her hands and went off to the sitting room. Whatever Amma may have said in reply, she did not hear.

'Are you really going, dear?'

'Yes, Uncle, since Amma wishes it,' she replied helplessly.

'These British have laid a trap for us: they've displaced
people even as they left! All the same, don't leave, daughter—
try to reason with your mother, our time of happiness has
come now.'

'Uncle, I am all the support Amma has in the world, how
can I abandon her? She is intent on going, but you don't know
how much I will suffer on leaving this house, you . . . you
are . . .' She covered her face in her hands and began to sob.

'Your amma loathes me intensely, certainly, and I didn't do
anything for the two of you either, but now the time has come
for the old joy to return, I am getting a really excellent job;
then I hope to get a subsidy of ten to fifteen thousand rupees
to run the shops, and I will resolve all of her complaints,' he
said, patting Aliya lovingly. 'Has the oil run out in the house?
The light from the lantern is growing dim; of course, now,
inshallah, in a few days I'll have the electricity reconnected.
And why don't you enrol in the MA programme now? I think
I'll definitely have you enrolled next year.'

Aliya felt her heart breaking. She wiped her tears away
and sat in silence. Deep down, she was suffocating, but she
couldn't even say one word. *God grant you happiness, Uncle,*
she asked for blessings in her heart of hearts, *may God fulfil all
your pleasant dreams.* How could she explain to Uncle that she
too wished to flee from here?

Asrar Miyan was opening the door panels to enter.
Aliya got up and went into the courtyard, where Amma and
Aunty were discussing something or other. Jameel still sat
on his chair, twisting his fingers. She stood for a moment in
the courtyard, then went upstairs. The dew-drenched night
looked bright as the moon sparkled in the centre of the sky.

And tonight, as on every night, a gramophone record played on some nearby roof:

A thief has been in your bundle, traveller, do wake up

Slowly she began to stroll about the roof. How strange she felt—as though someone had snatched away all her capacity for thought and understanding. 'Is this me?' she asked herself, and hearing her own voice, she was astonished. Had she gone mad? To whom was she speaking? Once, as she turned, she saw Jameel standing mutely before her like a statue. She began to walk more rapidly. What had he come to say now? He had forgotten his promise.

'Have you truly decided to go?' he asked softly.

'Yes,' she replied, as she paced.

'You're making a mistake in leaving here. Didn't you once say that distance makes memories more distressing? I don't think you'll be happy there.'

'I can be happy anywhere. But you had promised that you would never speak of such things to me.'

'What things am I speaking of?'

'Nothing!'

'You are indebted to me—do remember that you will have to repay this debt,' he said as he turned to leave. 'You will be happy there, right?' he stopped and asked.

She was silent. Jameel stood there for a little while and then he left, and she felt that this time she'd truly lost everything.

When she grew tired from pacing, she sat down to write Chammi a letter. She had to inform her of their departure.

32

This night shoulders the burden of mountains—someone please make it pass. When would she receive tidings of morning? In the morning, she was to leave and free herself of this agony. Everyone was talking, everyone spoke at once—yet all the same there was silence everywhere! What lunar date was it? So far the moon had not come out. Aliya watched everyone as she chopped betel nuts. Jameel, weary of conversation, was seated on his chair humming a melody:

> Give me more life—my story is still incomplete
> My death will not truly express my sorrow

Jameel had not left the house all day. That day he had nothing but leisure, as though all work was done, and now he had nothing to do at all.

'Sister-in-law, I'm leaving—but remember one thing for me: if you don't get Big Brother and Jameel Miyan under control, your entire life will pass you by like this. Now that independence has been achieved, what excuse do they have! Father and son both still wander about all day like bums.' Amma was lecturing Aunty.

Give me more life—my story is still incomplete . . . my story is still incomplete

Jameel kept repeating the same couplet.

What was he trying to point out by reciting those same lines again and again? What was he saying to her? Aliya began cracking the betel nuts rapidly. How wonderful it would be if Allah could make her deaf right now.

'Mazhar's Bride, I feel my heart sinking; this used to be a full household. Then everything fell apart as we watched. It's a sign of the times. No one can do anything about it. May I be sacrificed to that Master who made one country out of two; our Muslims have their own government, but we are left behind,' said Kareeman Bua, beside herself with the shock of separation.

'You come too, Kareeman Bua,' said Amma with great sincerity.

'Mazhar's Bride, I pray that only my dead body will leave this house. If I were to leave today, how could I show my face to my late mistress after dying? Why would I ever stir from the place where I've been set down?'

When Sita set foot outside the line drawn by Ram, Ravana carried her away, thought Aliya. *Sita knowingly disobeyed Ram's orders when he was still living, but you, Kareeman Bua, you cannot disobey the command of your departed mistress. All the same, Sita remained Sita, and you will remain Kareeman Bua. Who will know your story? Who will write your tale?* Aliya glanced tearfully at Kareeman Bua. How vivid was the sorrow of separation etched on her face in the dim yellow lantern light!

'Mazhar's Bride, even now you can change your decision. Don't go.' Aunty's voice was growing tearful.

Give me more life—my story is still incomplete

Jameel, totally indifferent to all their conversation, seemed lost in his passion for that couplet.

'Allah, please make this night pass, or I will not survive,' prayed Aliya. She set aside her betel-nut cracker and looked around. The moon was rising, lighting up the night sky.

'A letter has come from Chammi—what has she written, Aliya?' asked Aunty.

'She has written, *Congratulations on going to Pakistan, definitely do go. Please kiss that pure land for me, and send me a bit of earth from there. I will smear it in the parting of my hair. It is my misfortune that I can't go there myself. Send everyone my blessings and greetings,*' Aliya recited everything she remembered of the letter.

'Did she write anything else?' Aunty asked.

'Just hello to everyone, I have the letter upstairs.'

My death will not truly express my sorrow

Jameel continued to recite his couplet, still ignoring them all.

'Who knows what our Muslim country will be like, whether you'll get a home quickly or not? Don't stay in a hotel, Mazhar's Bride! You'll get sick from the food there,' advised Kareeman Bua, anxious about their future.

'Don't you worry, Kareeman Bua, I will write a letter as soon as I get there,' Amma said.

It was now striking midnight. The night was growing cold, but everyone stayed up. Aliya wished she could just run upstairs somehow.

'All right then, I'm going to sleep now, goodbye,' said Jameel, standing up from his chair. '*Give me more life*,' he recited, as he went into his room.

The outside door to the sitting room opened and closed. Uncle hadn't come in even for a moment, though Aliya had been waiting for him. The stray dogs howled in the gali. If only sleep would come. She felt as though there were hot peppers pricking her eyes. The day she had first come here and spent the night in that same room, she hadn't been able to sleep all night long, and tonight, now that she was leaving, sleep had again forsaken her. So many feelings tore at her heart—Jameel had said not one word to her. Would he not even speak to her as she left? Was there nothing left to say now? Allah, what must Uncle be thinking? She was going away and leaving him. And Chammi, may God grant her the good fortune of going to Pakistan.

Morning came and found her still awake. The sounds of clanking of pots and conversation drifted upstairs. She looked around the room with a farewell glance, then went downstairs.

Breakfast was ready. She sat down with Amma and Aunty. From the open doors of the room, she saw Jameel was still asleep with the sheet pulled over his face. Really, he was so uncivil. It was too much. Here she was leaving, and he hadn't even opened his eyes—as though he was sleeping the sleep of death. How his pompous slumber grieved her! He could always go back to sleep again once she left, after all.

After breakfast, Amma began to arrange all the luggage. Except for their clothing and two light blankets, they'd filled Chammi's room with rest of the luggage for whenever a good time came for them to take it all away.

'The tongas have come,' Asrar Miyan called from outside.

She quickly ran to the sitting room. Would Uncle also stay asleep today?

'Your Uncle went somewhere very early this morning. He said that he had work to do, and he also said he wouldn't be able to see everyone off,' said Kareeman Bua tearfully.

'Kareeman Bua, he should have said that there was no time to waste sitting around, waiting to say goodbye to us,' said Amma, making a face. 'Sister-in-law, please keep my luggage safe, please keep a lock on that room,' Amma instructed her once more.

Allah, if only their seats today were not reserved, if only she could stay today, how could she leave without saying goodbye to Uncle? Aliya sat down exhausted.

'Get up, Jameel, your sister and aunt are leaving. Come bid farewell to them,' Aunty called out to Jameel for the third time but he didn't move a bit.

'Hurry up, Kareeman Bua, aeroplane don't wait for anyone. It will fly away on time,' Asrar Miyan called out again.

'God forbid. My brother will be waiting for us today at the Lahore airport; if he doesn't find us, his heart will break,' Amma said nervously, wrapping herself in a burqa. 'Now hurry up, will you?' she snapped, looking over at Aliya who still sat, unable to think.

'It's getting quite late! It would be better to get them there earlier.' Asrar Miyan just would not stop.

'Please, will someone send this Asrar Miyan to Pakistan as well!' cried Kareeman Bua, weeping copious tears.

Kareeman Bua and Aunty were embracing Amma and weeping, but Aliya just stood there dumbstruck, not even crying.

'If you see Shakeel over there, definitely write and tell me,' whispered Aunty as she hugged Aliya. 'Remember me! Now go, I'm entrusting you to God,' she said, her voice shaking. 'Oh, Jameel, hey! Get up now!' she yelled loudly.

'I'm leaving. I'll go see him myself,' said Aliya.

'Why will you go see him? He doesn't want to see us off, out of hatred,' said Amma with a frown. 'Now let's just go quickly.'

'I'm going, goodbye,' said Aliya, pulling the sheet off Jameel's face. Then she stepped back with embarrassment. His swollen, damp eyes told their own tale. She panicked and shut her eyes. But even with her eyes shut, his eyes managed to make their way into her vision.

'Why don't you leave, silly girl? Did you wake me to see this? Goodbye,' he said, hiding his face again.

'Come quickly, Aliya,' called Amma. Then Aliya realized that she really must go, that the tonga was waiting—but why wouldn't her feet move? Why wasn't she leaving, and why was there such darkness in this room?

'Kareeman Bua, hurry up, it's getting very late! And do give my blessings to Mazhar's Bride and Aliya Bibi and tell them to forgive me if I've offended them in any way, and tell them that . . .' Asrar Miyan's voice trailed off.

'God willing, your tongue will tire, Asrar Miyan!' prayed Kareeman Bua angrily.

Aliya could hear everything that was being said, but her feet! Oh, if only someone would pull her away from there. If only she could leave this room.

'You're dragging your feet so that the aeroplane will fly off and leave us behind! The money my brother spent on the tickets will be wasted, and he will go mad when he doesn't find us on the aeroplane!' God only knows what else Amma would have said, when Aliya came running out of that room like a madwoman.

'Your brother and sister-in-law couldn't even wait for you for four or five days so that they could travel with us, and now you're saying they'll go mad because of us, humph!' Aliya cried out, and then she hugged Aunty and began to sob.

33

After arriving in Lahore they had to stay with Mamoo for a few days at his government house. Things were such that Aliya had to spend all day shut up in a small room. All the time she kept wondering how she could spend her whole life in this vexing atmosphere. Of course, Amma was thrilled. Her long-standing desire to live with her brother and her British sister-in-law had now been fulfilled. She intended to live with them her entire life, and was offended when Aliya remained aloof from everyone else. If nothing else, she should at least practise speaking fluent English with her aunt, but Aliya performed only one task during those four days, which was to write long letters to Aunty and Uncle.

On the fifth day, Mamoo had the lock broken on a small vacant bungalow and forced Amma to move into her own home. He quietly explained to her that Englishwomen didn't even like to live with their own mothers. Amma wanted to hide that conversation from Aliya, but when Aliya was moving to their new home, her aunt explained in broken Urdu that it was best for everyone to live apart. Living together was just so messy.

Everything was in its place in the new house. The dishes were lined up in order on the dining table, their patterns shrouded in dust. It felt as though someone was just about to emerge from behind the curtain and sit down to eat. The metal pots and pans were lined up in the cupboard in the kitchen and a few had rolled on to the floor and lay scattered about. Dust coated the rug and sofa in the drawing room and the flowers in the vase had withered and lay strewn about the table. Now only the dry black stems remained crammed into the vase. In the bedroom, the bed was made and the lamp on the bedside table lay on its side. In the small room next to this, there was a statue of Lord Krishna above the fireplace. His garland of flowers lay littered all about; only a yellow thread hung about his neck now.

'Do get that out of here, dear; give it to the children outside, they can play with it,' Amma had said several times since they'd arrived.

Aliya did not respond. The Krishna idol stayed there for several days. When it was no longer possible for Amma to manage things without using that room, Aliya picked it up and hid it in her trunk.

The days passed by monotonously. She'd grown bored from sitting around with nothing to do. No one had replied to her letters either. Who says distance renders memories all the more painful? Everyone had forgotten her. The memories were painful only for her.

Evenings were torment. Aid committees walked from house to house. 'Help your refugee brothers,' they'd say, 'the caravans of refugees are coming, please help them.' And Amma would weep, 'But we are refugees ourselves!' The committee members would go away again, but Aliya wished she could kick dust into Amma's eyes and give them everything.

When Mamoo and his wife would sometimes come over in the evenings, Aliya wished she could go hide in a mouse hole. Amma would be flustered, she could not understand how to receive her sister-in-law properly.

After sitting idly at home for a while, she applied for a job at a high school. Her application was quickly accepted, and having something to do saved her from much torture and sadness. All the same, as soon as she reached home from school every day, she'd ask if any letters had come from Uncle and Aunty. Amma was deeply annoyed by her daily questioning, and would blow up at her in reply.

One day, when Mamoo had come to visit alone, he told them that he'd had the bungalow allotted in Amma's name. Now they would not have to leave under any circumstances. Then he gave them a few receipts for the furniture and so forth, so that if anyone asked, they could show these and say they had come here and bought everything; that this house had just been full of junk.

Amma continued to be pleased by her brother's actions. 'If you have a brother, he should be like him. He thinks only of my comfort. Among the English they don't follow the custom of everyone descending on one another's heads all the time. If they had a custom like that my brother would not separate from me for one minute.'

Aliya listened quietly. She couldn't understand what was going on. Who was making off with whose rights? Where did these receipts come from, and how had this house come to be hers? But whom could Aliya ask all this? Amma was just Amma. Now that she received Aliya's salary and had become a homeowner, she was just as arrogant and self-satisfied as before.

Time dragged by. Aliya would wander about agitated when she got home from school. There was no one to visit in the nearby homes either. Where had all these people come from to settle here? No one knew anything about anyone else.

Amma did not even have the time to look in her direction. The entire day was spent in looking after the house. They had hired a maid for ten rupees a month; if she put something down a little too hard, Amma would be enraged—'We've bought all these very expensive things and you can't control yourself! Try to do things sensibly.'

Not long after, Mamoo was transferred to Karachi. Amma wept and wept and was in a terrible state as he bid them farewell. Her sister-in-law smiled when she saw Amma's agitation: 'Even our children goes very far from home, but no one every cries.'

Aliya felt neither shock nor joy at their leaving. If they left they left. What connection did she really have to those people? Since coming here, Mamoo had said several times that Aliya, like her father, disliked him deeply. When she heard this, she laughed. At this time she strongly missed Abba. But now she'd left even his grave behind in another country. All links had been broken. No one had even answered her letters.

34

The riots had ended. One just read of a few incidents here and there. Now both countries were insisting on establishing peace. Aliya wasn't interested in this at all. Really, what was the point of such innocence?

After Mamoo's departure, Aliya gave up purdah. She knew no one here; what was the point of clutching on to old customs? In order to fill her idle time, she had started volunteering at the Walton Camp for refugees. She'd rest a bit after coming home from school and then leave by bus. Teaching the children there for free made her feel oddly contented. The dust of all her activity helped dim the old memories.

Amma was extremely disgruntled about Aliya's visits to the Walton Camp; whenever she came home, some unpleasant thing or another would happen. On such occasions Aliya would remain silent. She did not wish to make things worse on her part.

One day, when she returned at six in the evening, Amma was seated on a chair on the dry lawn as if waiting for her.

'Why do you go there?' she demanded harshly. 'What do you get out of that useless work?'

'I get peace,' Aliya answered gently.

'Like father, like daughter; do you wish to ruin me now as well?'

'If you are ruined by me teaching children, there's nothing I can do about it,' she replied in annoyance.

'There's nothing you can do?' Amma asked angrily.

'Yes, there's nothing I can do.' She got up and went inside. She didn't even turn around to look and see that Amma was crying into her sari border.

Once she was alone in her room, she thought for a long time about what she should do. She couldn't make Amma happy; to keep her happy she would have to stay in this home that belonged to someone else. How would she rid herself of the loneliness that tormented her? Where could she flee to escape the ghosts of memories that hovered about all around her? Time could just continue to pass; she needed help. As she was thinking this, the doctor at the Walton Camp came to mind for some reason. He was a good man, poor thing.

That night Amma ate dinner alone. She didn't even complain.

The next day when Aliya came home from school, she felt sad. She felt as though her heart would sink. The weather was growing warmer but somehow it felt very cold to her. She decided she would rest; today she wouldn't go anywhere. After eating she shut the door and lay down to sleep. She tossed and turned for a long time, but sleep just wouldn't come. Growing weary, she picked up a newspaper. Today she hadn't even given the paper a cursory glance before going to school; she just hadn't felt like it.

After glancing over two or three large headlines, her eyes froze on one news item—about a famous Muslim Congress leader who had been killed. Nehru had expressed his condolences and donated a three thousand–rupee gift to the family of the deceased. He had severely censured Hindu–Muslim hatred. When she read Uncle's name in the article, she hid her face in her hands. She stood up like a madwoman, then fell upon her bed. She felt such pain in her heart. She hadn't even seen him before she left, and now he was gone forever. She pounded her head against the bedrail and wept for a long time. Now she would never see Uncle again. This feeling tortured her so terribly that she couldn't think of anything else.

Evening had fallen, and darkness crept into the room. She'd grown exhausted from weeping. Amma had knocked on the door several times and gone away. She opened her swollen eyes with difficulty and came out of the room, trampling over the scattered pages of the newspaper.

'Goodness, what has happened to you?' asked Amma in alarm when she saw Aliya's red face and swollen eyes.

'Some Hindu has ambushed Uncle and murdered him,' she said quietly. All that crying had calmed her.

'Oh my, oh my! This is what he gets in exchange for being a slave to the Hindus his entire life?' Amma cried tearfully. She dried her tears in her sari. 'Oh dear, my poor sister-in-law, how must she feel now? She didn't even inform us.'

Aliya left Amma to her own devices and went out on to the lawn. Was that all, Uncle? Was this the end that such a magnificent life came to? A three thousand–rupee grant and condolences? Who knew if he had ever got the ten- or fifteen-thousand rupees for the cloth shops or not. Had the electricity been reconnected? Was everyone weeping over Uncle's body in that same yellow lantern light? How must Jameel be feeling? Had death scrubbed away all their differences?

She spent a long time bent over at the table in the lamplight writing a letter to Aunty that night, and Amma talked and talked: How must Sister-in-law be feeling? And Big Brother, he had never rested in his lifetime and never let others rest either. He had destroyed a prosperous home. What did they get? The very people whom he helped killed him in a foreign land. Oh dear! They should come to Pakistan from that land of unbelievers. What was the point of staying there, really? And now there's that Jameel Miyan; he's sure to turn out just as fantastic.

When Aliya had finished the letter, she sealed it in the envelope.

'Go to sleep, Amma,' she said, turning off the lamp and lying down on her bed. A little while later, she could hear Amma snoring, but she continued to stare into the darkness at nothing, her eyes wide open. Who had brought Uncle's shrouded body from so far away and placed it here? *Asrar Miyan, don't you touch Uncle, Kareeman Bua will get angry! Kareeman Bua, don't read the Quran Sharif so loudly. It aggravates our grief. One feels as though it's not just Uncle who has died, but a whole world. Read quietly, Kareeman Bua* . . . She felt alarmed and closed her eyes, but how could she shut her ears? She could hear Kareeman Bua reading the holy Quran continuously from far, far away, from Uncle's country, and Aunty's keening tore at her ears.

'Oh, Allah, please make this night pass,' she murmured as she sat up. They say that people even fall asleep at the gallows, so why couldn't she? How is it that such false sayings have been made famous, yet no one corrects them?

When she got up in the morning, she felt exhausted with fatigue and shock. Sunlight had entered the veranda and Amma was busy preparing breakfast with the maid. Aliya began to get ready for school as usual. Amma glanced at her as though to ask what the need was for such shock. Despite Amma's and the maid's insistence, she departed for school without eating breakfast.

When she returned at one o'clock, she practically fell on to the easy chair that lay in the sunlight, and when the maid placed her food in front of her, she began to eat as though she was swallowing bitter bread. Amma was still busy with her housework.

'Gracious, the whole day passes by but the work doesn't end; there's so much work to do in a bungalow. Maid, water the plants on the veranda, they're getting dry.' Amma was speaking continuously. 'Maid, why didn't you just put the food on the table in the room? If there's a table and chair, a person can eat happily. We had a terrible habit in our old home of sitting and eating on the takht.'

Today you die, tomorrow is another day, but no one weeps for you any more? Today Amma was exposing the flaws of the customs of the place she came from. If they hadn't got this bungalow, how would all these secrets have been revealed?

After eating, Aliya got up to go to the Walton Camp. Amma turned to look at her, then again became engaged in her work, without making any objection.

When Aliya returned in the evening, she was somewhat calmer. At the camp, the doctor had encouraged her affectionately. He had made her leave early, given her two sleeping pills and advised her to take them that night, definitely. She had an extreme need for sleep. He was a good and kind man, Aliya decided, as she took the sleeping pills before going to sleep that night.

35

When she came home from school she saw an envelope lying on her bed. Aunty had at last sent a reply. She had despaired of ever getting one.

She opened the envelope and began to read the letter quickly:

Dearest Aliya,

I received your letter, but was too upset to reply right away. You saw how unkind Uncle turned out; I supported him my entire life and now he has left me all alone. How can I explain to you how it all happened? I tried to stop him from going to Delhi. Who knew what things were like there? But he didn't listen, and went off to meet with Nehru. Some Hindu ambushed him and made a martyr of him there. He left talking and laughing, and when he returned a lock had already been affixed to his lips. Thankfully, people there who knew him recognized his body and brought him here with respect, otherwise we would have missed even a chance to see him one last time. Daughter, please pray that now Allah will preserve the honour of your Aunty and quickly carry her away as well.

Nehru had announced that he planned to give us a gift of three thousand rupees but your cousin Jameel refused to accept the donation. Jameel was so upset by his father's death that he still turns pale when he hears his name. Jameel remained unemployed for quite a long time. He did look for work but found nothing. We began to starve at home. Thanks be to God that your Uncle's Congress friends forced your cousin Jameel to take a job as assistant jailer. He secured this job with much pleading, and that too because of the services your Uncle had rendered. May God reward those friends of his.

It's been many days now since your Uncle passed away, but I keep imagining he's just about to come out of the sitting room. Kareeman Bua misses you and your mother very much. She's become very weak. As soon as she heard the news of your Uncle's death, she shoved Asrar Miyan right out of the house. Who knows where he went? He hasn't returned yet.

If you see Shakeel anywhere, please tell him how his mother's heart breaks for him. Who knows how many more days I will live, Aliya? May I just see his face one more time.

As soon as Hindustan seized Hyderabad, your Uncle Zafar moved to Karachi. He has written that he still hasn't even found a place to stay. May Allah be merciful, your Najma Aunty is not happy in her new home, and she's thinking of getting divorced. I tried to reason with her, but she doesn't listen; she says her husband is a fool, that he can't even speak two words of English properly. She is extremely embarrassed to be married to such a man. Her friend tricked her into marrying him; he has only studied till class twelve.

Please send my blessings to your mother. I'm just surviving now, this treacherous world won't quit me, otherwise I'd have died along with your uncle. Please do keep writing to us.

Yours,
Aunty

After reading the letter, Aliya leant back against the chair. If only Uncle had taken Asrar Miyan with him to Delhi. Maybe someone would have had mercy on him and slit his throat with a sharp knife as well. She closed her eyes to hide her tears from Amma.

'Who is the letter from?' Amma asked.

'Aunty. She sends you her blessings.'

'That is really too much, writing after so many days! She hardly considers us part of the family. Tell me what she's written.'

'Read it yourself, Amma, I'm tired,' she replied without opening her eyes.

Amma read the letter, put it down and sighed deeply. 'How foolish it was of them to return the three thousand rupees; if they'd invested it in a shop, it would have worked out better for them.'

Where must you be now, Asrar Miyan? Aliya asked deep in her heart.

'Well, it was great that Kareeman Bua kicked that lout Asrar Miyan out. That freeloader was no use at all, he destroyed everything, the ill-omened man.'

'Amma,' Aliya called out, opening her red eyes.

'What is it?'

'Nothing.' She closed her eyes again. She wished she could ask who had brought about the destruction of their own home. Had there been an Asrar Miyan there too? Who had destroyed Abba? Who made Abba yearn for happiness? But she couldn't ask any of this. After all, she was her own mother. She lay there sighing deeply. Amma filled up some lotas and began to water the flower beds.

Had Jameel completely forgotten her? He had not even answered her letter. But why was she complaining now? Fine, so he didn't reply, he must not miss her. Distance makes everyone forget. Some emotion began gnawing at her heart.

When she heard Amma's voice, she got up to eat—Aunty had written nothing at all about Chammi. Who knew how she must be. Her daughter must easily be able to sit up by now. After eating, she got ready to go to the Walton Camp. Who knew what shape Zafar Uncle must be in after departing from his paradise of Hyderabad.

'What I say is, stay at home once in a while. After all, how long will this absurd state of affairs continue?' Amma suddenly blew up as she placed a lota on the ground.

'This absurd state of affairs will continue as is,' Aliya replied abruptly. Amma was always engrossed in her own condition, she didn't even notice that today a letter had come from Aunty, that today Aliya's heart was slashed with knives.

'Peace? You get peace from it? You get peace from serving those beggars for no money? What do they give you that makes you go off running about like this?' Amma's face was turning red with anger.

'I want nothing from them. What can those poor devastated people give me? It makes me happy to serve them. When I'm there, I forget the entire world.' Aliya closed her eyes as if it took all her strength. She was thinking right now of the little girl whose books were back in Amritsar, who still cried when she thought of them. She had given her several books to take their place, but the little girl still hadn't forgotten her own books.

'Humph! Your father used to say the same thing, that he got happiness from his useless work. "I find peace," he'd say, and your uncle said the same thing too.' Amma was glaring at her.

'I am not Abba, nor can I be like Uncle. It would be better if you did not mention their names. Just think of me as your daughter and that's it.' As she started to leave quickly, Amma picked up the lota again.

Spring had put some life into the dried-up plants. Tiny little buds were bursting out and two large blossoms swayed from the rose bushes. Aliya was suddenly reminded of how she had once plucked a flower from the beds and put it in her hair, but when Jameel had looked at her amorously, she'd pulled the flower from her hair and thrown it back in the beds.

As she went through the gate she picked a flower and put it in her hair.

In the evening, when she returned from the Walton Camp, she changed her clothes and came on to the lawn.

Amma was extremely angry; she turned her face away as soon
as she saw Aliya. Cars and tongas drove by noisily on the
other side of the gate. All the same Aliya felt as though there
was silence all around. She felt anxious and began to pace.
The dry leaves from autumn still lay on the grass, and when
she stepped on them in her sandals, she thought of last fall.

'Will you just stay sitting out here today?' asked Amma,
stepping out on to the veranda when it began to grow dark.
Then she retreated inside.

Amma's mood was improving apparently. Aliya sat back
on the old reed chair, exhausted. It was quite dark by now,
but she didn't even consider getting up. This whole exchange
of letters should end now. What was the point of enduring
continuous torture? Memories are the most cruel of all,
and . . .

Suddenly the gate came crashing open and a man rushed
headlong inside.

'Who's there?' she called out, panicking.

The fleeing person stopped for a moment. 'You are my
mother, my sister—please let me hide! I am a poor refugee,
and the cruel police are trying to catch me for no good reason.
I'll leave very soon.' The man ran and hid behind the hedge.

Aliya was frozen in her chair with fear. She tried to call
out to Amma, but try as she might, she couldn't make a
peep. Right at that moment, Amma came on to the porch
and turned on the light. 'Come and eat dinner,' she called
out sternly. Aliya looked all around in the light, but she still
couldn't get herself to speak. Then Amma went away and
Aliya held out her hand and froze. She wanted to get up and
run inside but her legs wouldn't cooperate.

It was completely silent behind the hedge. Aliya's heart was pounding hard. What if a thief had hidden in their garden? She got up with great difficulty and was about to go inside when there was a commotion and the man emerged. He was about to run out of the yard when his eyes met Aliya's.

'What, Aliya Bajiya, is that you?' It was Shakeel. He lowered his red eyes. 'They realized I was poor and thought I was a pickpocket, but I'm not like that, Bajiya.'

Aliya could not believe her eyes: Shakeel was standing right before her. His shirt was torn at the shoulder, and his long hair hung tangled across his forehead.

'I'll go right away, Bajiya, what if they come in looking for me?'

'Where will you go, Shakeel, my brother?' Aliya asked, overwhelmed by grief as she embraced him. Then she sat him down in the chair and quickly turned out the light in the veranda. 'Now you won't go anywhere. What if those scoundrels capture you? You come into my room.'

She dragged him into her room and locked the door that opened out on to the veranda.

'Please let me go, Bajiya,' he said anxiously.

'I won't let you go anywhere. What have you done to yourself, my brother?' She wept as she beheld Shakeel's torn clothing and emaciated face. 'You're wandering about in this condition, and back home, Aunty is half dead from missing you.' She sat Shakeel down on the bed.

'Oh, so Amma misses me? Who else misses me? I doubt Abba does, he doesn't care about anyone, and Chammi and Jameel, I'm sure they only have bad things to say about me,' he asked with yearning in his eyes. 'I'm extremely hungry, Bajiya,' he added. 'I haven't eaten anything since yesterday.'

'Uncle doesn't miss you at all, you're right, brother,' she replied tearfully. 'Come let me feed you, then we'll talk.' She grabbed him by the hand.

'When did you come here, Bajiya?' Shakeel asked, going along with her.

'I came shortly after Pakistan was created.'

She took him into the dining room where Amma sat alone sulking. She ate her dinner very daintily, while the maid stared at Shakeel with bulging eyes. Amma did not even look up.

'Amma, Shakeel is here.'

'Shakeel who?' Amma looked up. 'Aha! When did you come to Pakistan?' Amma asked happily as she looked at him.

'A few days ago, Aunty—and it's all wrong what those irrational people—they just thought I wasn't from around here and . . .' Shakeel began defending himself to Amma. Perhaps he thought that Aliya would surely tell all, but she quickly interrupted him.

'Amma, poor Shakeel came with the refugee caravans. He was staying somewhere deep inside the city, but right now the poor thing doesn't know anything about this place. So he's doing manual labour here and there to fill his belly. That's what happens if you have no one.' She pulled up a chair for Shakeel.

'Now, if we had room, we'd ask you to stay, but it's such a small house,' said Amma in a tone of severe disinterest, making a six-room bungalow sound tiny. She stared at Shakeel with critical eyes.

'Now he will stay here with me for a long time,' Aliya said sternly and decisively.

Amma glared at Aliya and began to eat. Shakeel wolfed down his food like a starving man. He grabbed his roti as if pouncing on it. 'I'm getting home-cooked food after a long time, it's wonderful, Bajiya,' he said.

Amma was the first to get up and leave. She didn't even bother to look at Shakeel and Aliya as she left. Aliya sat and watched Shakeel eat, and she trembled as she wondered what would happen if the police captured him right at this moment. After dinner she took Shakeel to her room.

'Lock the door, Bajiya, I'm scared,' he said, lying back comfortably on Aliya's bed.

'This will be your room, is that all right with you?' she asked.

'Now that Abba's country has become free, what is he doing?' asked Shakeel. 'What fiefdom has Nehru given him?' There was such loathing in his eyes.

'Uncle?' Aliya's voice trembled. 'Uncle has departed from this world, Shakeel, my brother. A Hindu made him a martyr in the riots.'

'What?' Shakeel hid his face in the pillow and his whole body began to shake softly.

A little while later when Aliya wiped her eyes and lifted his head, the entire pillow was damp.

'I'm missing Amma right now, Bajiya,' he whimpered like a two-year-old child.

'Go to her now, Shakeel. It will bring spring into her life. Uncle's death has unmoored her. If she sees you, she'll live a little longer.'

'It was right for Abba to die, Bajiya, he didn't do anything for anyone. And what would I do if I went home now? Jameel would taunt me and make my life miserable. There would still be nothing for me in that house. I'll make my living here.' He sighed deeply.

'But don't make your living in such a way that the police run after you. You are very hard-hearted, Shakeel, my brother.'

'I didn't do anything, Bajiya, it's the police who are hard-hearted. They don't allow the poor to live . . . oh, I'm missing Amma so much.'

'If you won't go to Aunty, you'll have to live with me. I won't let you go away now. I'm employed—I'll have you enrolled in school. You'll study in comfort; that way you'll make something of your life. I'll write to Aunty tomorrow and tell her you're with me, and we are living happily together as brother and sister.

'What will I study now, Bajiya? I've forgotten what I did study, and, Bajiya, the high school across from our house—was it still the same as when I left?'

'Yes, it was—when you start studying, everything will come back to you.'

'Let's talk more in the morning, Bajiya, I'm feeling sleepy,' yawned Shakeel, exhausted.

'Go to sleep, but listen: I won't let you go, you will stay with me.'

'Go to sleep now, Bajiya, I'm extremely sleepy.' He lay back down. 'Now you go, I'll lock the door from the inside.'

'If you shut the door won't you get hot?'

'No, Bajiya, I need to lock the door, I'm frightened.'

Aliya came out and lay down on a bed in the veranda. Amma was sleeping soundly on the nearby bed. She began to feel pity for her. There had been no need to speak to her so harshly today. For a long time she lay there glancing about in the dark. The spectacle of Shakeel running in and hiding had robbed her of her sleep. She understood everything. She decided that she wouldn't let Shakeel leave under any circumstances, no matter how much animosity she'd have to put up with from Amma.

Late that night she finally fell asleep, and when she awoke the next morning, the door to Shakeel's room was open.

'Is Shakeel in the bathroom?' she asked Amma.

'I didn't see him when I got up this morning—maybe he left. He must have had work to do, being a labourer and all,' Amma replied calmly.

It was all a lie.

'He must have told you he was leaving and you must have gladly given him permission,' said Aliya angrily.

'You have gone crazy, don't talk to me, or I'll beat my head in,' retorted Amma, going into the kitchen.

Who knows when he will come back? He must have been so depressed by Amma's permission to leave. What a crime Amma has committed. She doesn't have a heart in her breast, just a stone, thought Aliya, sitting silently on the bed for a while, her feet dangling.

When she went into her room after washing her face and hands, she didn't have to open the lock on the cupboard. It was broken, and opened when she touched it. Her purse lay open and fifty rupees were missing from her store of savings.

Shakeel, my brother, I will not see you again. Now you are lost forever, who can reach you now?

36

A new letter from Aunty lay before her, and yet again Aliya sat wrapped in melancholy. She had no idea what would now become of Chammi's life. Really, why had she refused to come to Pakistan with her mother-in-law and husband? Why on earth had she not come to Pakistan, the cause for which she'd waved her hands in the air and yelled slogans?

She picked up the letter one more time and began reading the part about Chammi: Chammi had refused to go to Pakistan with her husband, and when he'd insisted, she got ready for a fight. The fight had progressed so far that Chammi had grabbed her mother-in-law's hair and hit her hard, and that very instant her mother-in-law demanded that her son give Chammi a divorce and sent her home to Aunty with her daughter. *Before leaving*, Aunty wrote, *the mother-in-law sent me a telegram telling me to marry off our out-of-control girl to some sweeper. She said her son would get himself a bride like the moon in Karachi. Since coming here, Chammi has been totally silent, and she just lies still and dumbstruck with her baby to her breast. Our Chammi has always made enemies. I can't imagine what will happen to her now. When I look at her I feel terrified.*

'Amma, Chammi's husband divorced her and came to Karachi,' Aliya announced when Amma came nearby.

'What!' Amma looked at Aliya with astonishment and then picked up the letter and began to read.

'Now what will poor Chammi do?' Aliya wondered.

'Those people did the right thing. After all, who can manage a girl like that? It's the wrath of God, she beat both her husband and her mother-in-law.' Amma tossed the letter on to the table and began to tidy up the room.

'Humph!' Aliya came out of the room. She hadn't even changed her clothes since returning from the Walton Camp. The maid handed her a cup of tea and she began to drink it standing up. What had become of her, everything was scattered about the room and Amma was tidying it all up. What was the point of such carelessness—what must Amma think of her?

Aliya handed her empty teacup to the maid and came out on to the lawn. It was so hot in June even in the evening. The tall, stately trees stood totally still. Not a leaf stirred. She began to stroll about on the dry grass. Now it seemed solitude and sorrow plagued her all the time. How tired she'd grown of this dreary life of hers.

Now that she'd mourned Chammi's ruined life, she began to think of her own. What would she do now? How would she spend her life? She considered the doctor for a moment as she thought about it. She tried to recall the things he'd said to her today, and then she felt so disgusted, as if she were doing something strange—what was he even talking about! Yes, he was a good man, but he was shallow. His bungalow, his car, the state of his practice; that was it. A bungalow Mamoo had also given her, and as for a car, she travelled every day by bus. The only difference between a car and a bus was that the bus was bigger and wasn't private property.

'Now eat, what are you doing, sitting alone in the dark?'
Amma had come over and stood near her, and now she felt
that truly the darkness had spread. She went inside with
Amma.

'You're silent all the time, I've written to your Mamoo
that . . .' Amma said as she walked along, '. . . that now he
should arrange your marriage.'

'Oh, I see, this is the first I've heard that that's the reason
why I am sad.' She was enraged by this revelation. 'But since
when did you give Mamoo this right? I don't even consider
him my uncle; he means nothing to me! I will not get married.'

Amma gazed at her reproachfully but said nothing. Of
late, she had stopped scolding Aliya and quarrelling with her.
The two of them ate in silence. Aliya felt overwhelmed with
sadness. All the same she kept control and continued to eat
while Amma sat lost in thought.

37

On her return from school, she saw that a letter from Chammi lay on the table, and that Amma had already opened it and read it. One page lay on the floor. She felt a bit angry and quickly began to read it.

Dearest Bajiya,

Greetings to you! It's been nearly a year, but you haven't missed me at all. That's fine, I haven't written you either, but I never forgot you. I've thought of you during all the ups and downs, and even now, when I am so happy and spring has come into my life. I'm still thinking of you, Bajiya. If only you were here, you would see how happy I am! Our cousin Jameel has made me his own. I still can't believe that I belong to him now. After my divorce, when I landed back in this house, I never would have imagined such a thing. Long ago, when he first looked away from me, I became convinced I would always be unlucky, Bajiya—but now I will tell you, this was why I didn't go to Pakistan. They were taking me so far away, where I would never be able to turn back and see Jameel again. Those cruel people were snatching everything from me.

Bajiya, the funny thing is that Aunty was already looking for a bride for Jameel. I had thought that I would pass my life serving Jameel's wife. Some day Jameel would regret what he had done, and that would be the only way I would feel I had found some success in love. That I had won him. But that's not how it turned out, Bajiya, and the night before Aunty was to take the final answer to the girl's house, Jameel came and sat by me, and he picked up my little girl and began to feed her. I sat by quietly. Ever since my husband divorced me and I came here, he hadn't said even one word to me. How could I talk to him? And he himself asked why I didn't go to Pakistan. Bajiya, what reply could I give him? My heart was bursting with the knowledge that the person for whom I did all this had absolutely no idea. I started to cry, and then he became agitated and hugged me and began asking my little girl, 'Shall I be your father?' Then he told me, 'Chammi, your love weighs on me like a debt. Now I will rid myself of that debt.' He wiped away my tears and went downstairs, and the next day Aunty dyed my hands with mehndi and made me a bride.

Now I am very happy, Bajiya. Jameel fusses over me, he loves my daughter very much, Bajiya, and can I tell you something? When I had my baby girl, I never even thought she was anyone but Jameel's.

Aunty is very happy, and I'm looking after her very well. Kareeman Bua is also very happy; she says our own blood has come back among us. She goes around all the time holding the baby. She misses you very much. Now the house is in very nice shape. Only Aunty misses Shakeel so much. Okay, Bajiya, now I'll be taking my leave. May Allah find a groom as handsome as the moon for my bajiya. Bajiya, now you get married too— very soon. Please give my regards to Aunty.

Yours,
Chammi

When she'd finished the letter, she began to look about. How empty and deserted she felt right now. 'It's a good thing that Chammi's life has turned out well,' she said in a voice that was not her own.

'Who else would Jameel Miyan get, besides used-up old Chammi?' Amma asked smugly.

Aliya went silently to her room and lay down and began to look about aimlessly. A little while later, she got up and prepared to go to the Walton Camp.

38

That day the doctor had begged her to marry him. He had said he would put everything in her name—the land and the house. He pledged to spend his entire life as her humble servant, and when he was saying all this, she felt like saying yes for a moment—she would bask in that protection he had to offer—but when she tried to agree, it felt very strange to her. A car, a house, a bank balance and this doctor who earns money curing the poor people of the Walton Camp— was that all she wanted? Was this person her only choice? Something possessed her to run from there crying, 'No, no!' and now she lay at home wondering what it was that she actually wanted. It had been a long time since she'd even thought of Jameel. She hadn't responded to Aunty's letters. She'd broken all bonds with them. Now she felt nothing for them.

Clouds had gathered thickly above. She came out of her room on to the lawn. The rains had turned the grass lush and green. As she strolled about in the damp air, she suddenly saw a person standing by the gate gazing at her.

'May I come in, Aliya Bibi?' he asked, and walked forward.

An attractive man of forty or so stood before her. Aliya stared at him in alarm. Where had she seen him before? Whom did he resemble? She tried to remember.

'Who are you?' she finally asked.

'I am Safdar. You didn't recognize me, Aliya Bibi? I often visit the house across the way. Today they mentioned your Mamoo and said that his sister lived right across the street. I couldn't control myself, I longed to see you. Where is your mother? But actually, don't inform her of my arrival,' he murmured.

'Safdar!' Aliya spoke with difficulty. The past emerged before her, keening. 'Oh, so now you've come. Please sit, what do you need?' Aliya asked coldly.

'Aliya Bibi, so much time has passed—twelve or thirteen years—even after all this time, you still hate me. Oh, but I'm wrong. You didn't hate me. You remember, don't you? You haven't forgotten?'

Even after the passage of twelve or thirteen years, his voice hadn't changed at all. It had the same humility, the same vulnerability.

'Where do you live? Where are your wife and children?' she asked, finding herself forced to talk with him. The vulnerability in his voice had melted her heart. She was remembering how once this person had spent the worst days of his life in her house.

'My wife and children?' He laughed sadly. 'No woman has entered my life since Tehmina. Tell me about her, Aliya Bibi.'

'After you left Tehmina and went away, and never asked after her, and wrote only one letter, forcing her to die? After that what is there to tell you? Now you want to cheer yourself up by learning that she ate poison. She refused to be married to Jameel. She was an idiot, so she died. You were wise, so you stayed alive, and now after such a long time, you are sitting before me in order to remind me of the past.'

'I may be alive but I'm worse than dead. Do you think that if I'd stayed there, Aunty would have accepted me? That would have been impossible. A prosperous household would have been destroyed. That's why I removed myself from her path. I even stopped taking any money. You can't imagine what I had to do after that just to stay alive. My conscience is clear, however. I continued to do honest work, and in exchange for that, like Uncle, I spent time in jail. I didn't know that Tehmina wouldn't just forget me and give up her life.' His voice began to shake with the weight of memories, and he fell silent and began to look about him.

'What are you doing here now? Tell me something about yourself. Let's not dig up old matters, I don't have the strength to bear it,' she said, trying to stop her tears.

For a short while there was complete silence. Aliya sat with her head down. She was remembering every single detail of bygone days. She was extremely sympathetic towards Safdar for no good reason. After all, how was it his fault? Tehmina had been weak; she didn't have the courage to have things done according to her wishes. That's how Amma had destroyed their home.

When Aliya looked up, Safdar was gazing at her with great desire and love. So much so that Aliya lowered her gaze, and he too started.

'Tell me about yourself,' she said again.

'What is there to say? I've already been jailed again under the Safety Act since coming here, and now I feel quite exhausted. But now what I want is not to be exhausted, and to continue the struggle to stay alive and . . .' He stopped in the middle of what he was saying.

For a little while, silence again reigned. It was quite an ungainly silence, as though no one knew what to say . . . today the man who had endured tortures in her home for ages sat before Aliya. He'd lived through hell before he committed any sins, was fed scrap meat and milk mixed with heaps of water; he was fed stale, rotten leftovers from several meals back, as prayers were made to hasten his death. His only fault was to be born of a poor father. They say that on the Day of Judgement, he will be called by his mother's name. If only this world could be the Day of Judgement every day for Safdar, so that he might be remembered by the name of Salma Aunty, the landowner's daughter. Surely then his value would increase.

As she thought about all this, she looked over at Safdar. What must he be thinking, leaning back in his chair with his eyes closed? At this moment, he looked tormented. Just like the old Safdar. She remembered that when she would feel defeated by squabbles of the house and wander about with a weepy face, this same Safdar would show her the path to happiness and, for her sake, would bear Amma's sharp glares that pierced his heart.

When she looked up at him again, she saw that he was gazing at her affectionately. Such strange glances that she felt agitated, and Safdar reddened with embarrassment. 'Aliya Bibi, I still love Tehmina today as I always did. Today, I'm remembering all sorts of things as I sit here. Now that you've grown up, you look just like her. You're exactly like her. Looking at you, it doesn't even seem like she has died.'

She couldn't respond at all. The cloud-weighted sky appeared so melancholy. She stared hard at him. Two tears had rolled from his eyes and down his cheeks. Did he really still love Tehmina the same way he always had? And was that why no other woman could come into his life? And today, was he only looking at her so lovingly because she looked like her sister? Aliya remembered how Safdar used to stare at Tehmina secretly, in just this way. Can love really survive so long? And now Safdar was so worn out; so much of his hair had gone white. Perhaps he'd never even taken a happy breath in his life.

'Safdar, do I really look like Tehmina?' she asked suddenly, and then felt alarmed at her own question.

'Yes, yes, exactly like her,' he said, again gazing at her strangely.

'I keep forgetting that you are not her; if you were Tehmina, you would hide me in your heart, you'd give me all life's happiness.' He began to speak as if in a dream. 'Become Tehmina, Aliya, become mine, I'm so very tired.' He got up and leant over her. 'Support me; Tehmina used to say that whatever I did, she would support me, and she said so many other things.' He sat down again, as though he'd suddenly come to his senses.

Aliya closed her eyes. She was sinking into the sort of state that could carry a bride away, the first time she's brought into the groom's room. Her ears echoed with the howling of a windstorm. She had no idea what Safdar went on to say after sitting back in his chair—she didn't hear a bit of it; she was completely deaf to his words.

'Do you simply not plan to get up from here today?' Amma called, coming out on to the veranda. 'And who is that sitting over there?' She walked over.

Aliya came to her senses and looked up at her. Amma was trying to recognize Safdar.

'Assalam Aleikum, Aunty,' Safdar mumbled, his face suddenly pale.

'You . . . ?' On recognizing him, Amma began gesticulating wildly. 'Why have you come here? Will you never leave this household alone? Everything has been destroyed! What have you left to destroy now?'

'I . . . I came to see you, I wanted to see you all, but now I will leave, Aunty.' When he looked at Aliya with farewell eyes she felt her heart would burst.

'He will not leave, Amma. I have decided that he will stay with me forever. Please make us two one,' Aliya said with determination, her eyes downcast.

'God forbid! Shame on you for sitting out here so long with Aliya, seducing her like this!' Amma's eyes boiled with rage. 'You get out of here right now!'

'I'm not mute like Tehmina, Amma. He will not go.' Aliya felt thorns prick her throat.

Amma stared at her with bulging eyes. 'Did you get all this education just so this could happen?'

'I am doing nothing wrong,' she replied composedly. Safdar sat before her, a picture of vulnerability. Aliya looked at him affectionately. He had dedicated his whole life to others, but no one had become his, no one had supported him; now she would definitely support him.

'Yes, certainly, get married, you have my permission, I'll go to my brother's house tomorrow; even if I'm dying, I won't waive the mother's milk right you owe me. I'll rejoice at that moment when you ruined yourself during my lifetime. Just like Salma. May this man spend his life in jail, and may you languish at home.'

'I will wait for him, Amma, and I won't languish. I will also not die like Salma Aunty,' she replied softly.

Amma placed her sari border on her eyes. Her body was shaking.

'Aunty, you won't go anywhere,' Safdar said beseechingly. 'I will look after you. I've changed the direction of my life—if the world is destroyed, so be it, it has nothing to do with me. I will just earn money now, enjoy myself; now I will fulfil the dreams of owning a car and a house. I cannot go to jail now. Right now I'm trying to get an import–export licence. I'll get it very soon. Aunty, I'm going to become an important man now, please do accept me.'

'What?' Aliya stared at Safdar as though he were a stranger.

What, is this now your life's goal, such a tiny thing? Aliya felt as though she had travelled here from far off, through desert lands. Flat-out exhausted. Thirsty for many lifetimes. Please, could someone pour just a few drops of water down her throat?

'First you make something of yourself, then we'll see. Only then will I fulfil Aliya's desire,' Amma said very craftily to put the matter off.

'I'm not getting married, Amma. You listen too, Safdar, I'm not getting married.' Aliya stood up from her chair. 'Now when you come here, please keep in mind that I still miss my sister, Tehmina. I wish to be released from that memory!'

She ran quickly to her room. 'Goodbye!' she called.

And as she lay stricken on her bed, she felt Chammi running—*thump thump thump*—across her chest, crying, 'I won, Bajiya, I won!' And she wrapped her arms tightly across her bosom.

Afterword

'If you think . . . that anything like romance is preparing for you, reader, you never were more mistaken. Do you anticipate sentiment, and poetry, and reverie? Do you expect passion, and stimulus, and melodrama? Calm your expectations; reduce them to a lowly standard. Something real, cool, and solid, lies before you; something unromantic as Monday morning, when all who have work wake with the consciousness that they must rise and betake themselves thereto.'

—Charlotte Brontë, *Shirley*

I. The Brontë Sisters of Urdu Literature

Khadija Mastur and her sister, Hajira Masroor, have been called the Brontë sisters of Urdu literature. This comparison seems to have been made primarily on a biographical basis— they'd led tragic lives, were meek and unassuming in person, but wrote with conviction. But from a feminist perspective, the comparison is quite apt. Khadija Mastur wrote two novels and five collections of short stories in her fifty-five

years, and it is a rare story that does not contain a critique
of patriarchy, chauvinism and misogyny. Happy endings are
few and far between.

Though the Brontës' books are often described as
romances, they too took a bleak view of male behaviour. The
Brontës sometimes came up with a 'happy' ending, though
it often feels tacked on, for the sake of the formula. 'Reader,
I married him'—Charlotte Brontë's famous last line in *Jane
Eyre* cannot be seen as a truly happy ending to the brutal tale.
After all, our romantic hero is by now old, blind, disabled
and semi-homeless. Mr Rochester, as has been explored in
countless retellings and analyses, is not a very nice man: one
who locked up his mentally ill Creole first wife in the attic,
and then lied about her very existence. It is only when Mr
Rochester is tragically maimed and reduced in the eyes of
society that Jane Eyre can hope for a relationship built on
trust and mutual respect. In fact, throughout their works,
it is clear that the Brontës did not have a high opinion of
male motivations and behaviour—as with Anne Brontë's
description of married life in *The Tenant of Wildfell Hall*,
in which even the supposedly positive character of the male
narrator often behaves poorly himself; or the unappealing
and disappointing male love interests in Charlotte Brontë's
Villette.

Unlike the Brontës, Mastur and Masroor came of
age writing at a time when there was a strong progressive
writers' movement. Though they could have chosen to write
romances, they were politically engaged, Mastur for a time
serving as the head of the Pakistani Progressive Writers'
Association. Because of her political views, shaped in part

by a youth marked by poverty and deprivation, Mastur felt no obligation to deliver happy endings to her readers. It is clear from her writings that she saw patriarchy and classism as systemic poisons that destroy and kill women intellectually, emotionally and physically.

Not that Mastur treated her female characters with unstinting kindness either. Far from it. In characters such as Aliya's mother and grandmother in *The Women's Courtyard*, Mastur paints a detailed and unforgiving portrait of the role that women play in perpetuating the rigid bonds of patriarchy and class hierarchy. Indeed, Aliya's mother and grandmother play active roles in destroying the lives of those who dare step outside the boundaries of tradition. The behaviour of these women is so brutal at times that they end up looking far worse than the actual patriarchs in the family, whom Aliya regards with love and respect despite their neglect of their families in favour of outside political involvement. Aliya's mother is by far the most toxic character in the novel; she makes it clear that she considers her mother-in-law a flawed role model, one who ruined the family by failing to poison her own daughter when she was discovered in a romantic liaison with a lower-class man.

Aliya herself wonders what it is that makes her so forgiving of her father's and uncle's neglect of their families' welfare:

> How she wished that Amma hadn't driven anyone from the house; it was Safdar who had divided everyone, and then Abba was so busy with his animosity towards the English that he wouldn't even turn and look at anyone. He didn't even acknowledge her love. But she

couldn't say any of this out loud. She herself wondered why, despite Abba's indifference, she still loved him the most. Abba's affectionate eyes were so expressive. She'd never been able to say even one word against him (see p. 77).

Aliya sees her father and uncle as brilliant, politically principled men, even as their families are slowly wiped out financially and emotionally by their failure to step into their roles as patriarchs. But Aliya's love is an intrinsic part of patriarchy as well—she has infinite forgiveness for her male elders, but little sympathy for the shrewish women who work desperately to keep the family and class structure in place.

Still, Aliya knows that the worst thing she can do to perpetuate the system is to step into the role awaiting her as a wife—specifically as wife to her cousin Jameel. Despite her suppressed love for Jameel, and a certain physical attraction to him, she sees capitulation to his advances as a sure way to end up just like her mother and aunt: a whinging housewife with a neglectful and politically active husband. The only way she can see clear to break the cycle is by refusing to marry. Implicit in this choice is the belief that marriage is a tool to perpetuate the system of patriarchy, a notion that is still radical more than fifty years after the publication of the novel.

II. A Claustrophobic Life

When we consider the setting of *The Women's Courtyard*, and many other stories by Mastur, the Brontë comparison breaks down. Brontë heroines may live bleak lives, but they are also proto-flâneuses. An unhappy Brontë heroine is always free to walk out of the door and go charging off across the moors. Lucy Snowe walks all over the town of Villette, night and day, when she is upset. If one is poor, one might take a horrible position as a governess in a rich family and earn a meagre living, away from unpleasant family. Certainly, there are barriers to what they can do in their lives, but those are nothing like the virtual imprisonment of the courtyard, or *āngan*, in a traditional South Asian home.

The courtyard is a central open space where women gather to cook, prepare paan, talk, garden, sew and often live out their entire lives. It is surrounded on three sides by a covered veranda, and along the veranda are doors to individual rooms. The fourth side would often be a wall, with a door to the outside. A room near the wall would be a sitting room for male members of the family to receive guests, and that room would have a door on to the street as well, so that strange men could not accidentally enter the women's space. Only approved men from the family would be allowed into the courtyard, and on the rare occasions that outsider men showed up, women would retreat to a part of the veranda that had a large heavy curtain, or *pardā* (this is where the English term 'purdah' comes from), that could be lowered to protect the women from view. A richer home would have another storey above the first one, with additional rooms, and rooftop terraces, where women could also move about freely.

It should be noted that despite all these precautions taken to protect the women of the family and preserve their purity, male cousins are not considered outside the core family group, and first cousin marriage is still preferred in many South Asian Muslim communities. Because of this tradition, the only men that a young woman is not barred from interacting with are her cousins, even if they are cousins that the girl's parents do not think suitable for marriage, as in the case of Safdar. This social reality leads to the peculiar situation in which many Mastur protagonists find themselves. Romances, tragedies, love triangles, sexual harassment and even assault occur almost always between cousins. Cousins in love are surprisingly under-chaperoned; stalker cousins have easy access to their prey and sexual assault can be carried out relatively easily without anyone noticing. Women are virtually imprisoned with their cousins whether they like it or not. And yet, purdah from 'outsider' men is observed so strictly that Aliya—or, for that matter, any woman in her family—has never spoken with her pathetic uncle Asrar Miyan, because, as the illegitimate son of her grandfather, he is deemed an outsider. Thus Asrar Miyan is relegated to the men's sitting room and can only be fed or given tea by the unwilling family servant, Kareeman Bua.

The Urdu title of *The Women's Courtyard* is simply *Āngan*. For Mastur, the courtyard is not merely the setting of the novel, it is a rigid delimitation for all the action of the entire book, apart from a few scenes at the very beginning when Aliya recollects life as a small child when she could run about freely outside with neighbour children. Interestingly, unlike her mother and aunt, Aliya is not literally a prisoner in the courtyard, in that she attends school outside of the house in the section 'Past', and later even spends a year in Aligarh getting a teaching degree, after which she works outside of the house as a teacher for the remainder of the book. But whenever Aliya leaves the home, we do not see her again until she returns. This strict adherence to the mise en scène makes the novel resemble a play, a form that demands relatively static locations due to the restrictions of the stage and sets.

Limiting the narrative and dialogue to the courtyard can also be seen as a formal feminist experiment on the part of the author. In a men's world, during a tremendously active political moment—the Independence movement in the United Provinces in the 1930s and '40s—how can you keep the story focused on women's lives, without allowing male dialogue and male activities to hijack it? Indeed, in novels by men in Hindi and Urdu that cover this period, there are endless political debates, speeches, rallies and excerpts from newspapers. The men are scarcely ever inside their homes. The national political moment is important, indeed critical, to the story of *The Women's Courtyard*, but if the narration were to follow the men out of the door to rallies, processions, prison or even men's talk in the sitting room, the voices of women would immediately become marginalized.

In 1985, the American cartoonist Alison Bechdel created a comic strip depicting a conversation between two women complaining about the male-centric nature of most Hollywood films. One woman tells the other she will only go to movies that 1) have at least two women with distinct identities in them; 2) feature women talking to one another; and 3) portray women talking to each other about something besides a man.* This set of three criteria has come to be

---

* See Bechdel's discussion on her blog, http://dykestowatchoutfor. com/testy

known as the Bechdel Test, and most films and many books the world over continue to be so infused with patriarchy that they do not pass muster in these terms.

Thanks to Mastur's formal experiment, *The Women's Courtyard* passes the Bechdel Test with flying colours, despite being set in a strongly patriarchal milieu. Mastur does not eliminate male voices; far from it—the men in the family all play prominent roles in the narrative. But her choice makes it possible to privilege women's voices. In this way she also foregrounds an anti-patriarchal feminist politics. The men in the family are obsessed with independence from British rule, and endlessly argue about Congress versus Muslim League ideologies, yet fail to see how the change of rulers on a national level has virtually no impact on the lives of the women in the courtyard. Independence from foreign rule is vastly more important for the men than for the women—not because women have no political beliefs, but because it is men who will step into positions of increased power. Women are not automatically emancipated from male dominance by a change in rulers.

III. A Different Kind of Partition Novel

Despite *The Women's Courtyard*'s strengths as a feminist novel, it is most often referred to as a Partition novel. The 1947 partition of India and Pakistan, which coincided with the end of British rule in the subcontinent, was marked by massive upheaval and movement of peoples, loss of life and the rape and abduction of women. The events of Partition gave rise to numerous works of fiction, particularly in Hindi, Urdu,

Punjabi and Bengali, and later in English as well. Partition literature, as a genre, is quite varied, with some authors focusing on the violence and inhumanity on display during the days immediately preceding and following Partition, and others turning their attentions to the sense of nostalgia and loss for those who lost their homes, ancestral lands and family members.

The short-story writer Sa'adat Hasan Manto (1912–55) is perhaps the best-known Urdu author to write about Partition in numerous scathing short and very short stories describing, in his classic ironic style, unspeakable acts of cruelty and stupidity and man's inhumanity to man (and even more so to women). Manto's stories depict horrifying violence against women in skin-crawling detail, a quality that has led many to laud him as a feminist, though the case can be made that the obsessive detail of his descriptions of rape and assault can shade into a kind of voyeurism. Qurratulain Hyder (1927–2007), another famed Urdu author, is known for her lengthy novel *Āg kā Dariyā* (1959—'River of Fire'). *River of Fire*, which follows a series of characters over millennia in the Indo-Gangetic Plain, starting with the era of the Buddha and ending in a post-1947 era with a diaspora that leaves the characters isolated and lost, in England, Pakistan, India and Bangladesh. Where Manto's stories focus on violence and inhumanity, Hyder's novel is concerned with Partition as a destroyer of a syncretic and harmonious civilization. Her characters are centred around Lucknow, not Punjab (or Bengal), where the most brutal violence occurred. They are erudite, learned and imbued with the multiple layers of culture that have existed over the history of the Gangetic plain.

Mastur's novel takes a different course from either Manto or Hyder. Partition occurs late in the novel, and the main characters, who live somewhere in the United Provinces, are far from the bloody events taking place at the new Punjab border between India and Pakistan (Hyder's characters all enjoy a greater degree of privilege than Aliya's family, and many are in London during Partition, whilst Manto's are in the thick of the violence). The riots and atrocities are mentioned in *The Women's Courtyard*, but only in the context of newspaper stories and a general atmosphere of fear. Aliya and her mother—who has decided to follow her brother's family to Pakistan—take a plane to Lahore, thus avoiding the disasters unfolding at the border at the land-crossing point.

Mastur thus takes a subtler approach to depicting displacement and loss, as the characters are not subjected to bodily harm by Partition, and their sense of bereavement comes from their separation from the family members they have been confined with for many years. At the same time they are not of the socio-economic class as Hyder's characters; no one could possibly afford to travel to England. On their arrival in Lahore, Aliya's maternal uncle has them assigned to a house abandoned by Hindus who have fled to India. The lock is broken for them and they enter a new home that is fully furnished but covered in a thin layer of dust. Aliya's mother tells her to give the Hindu idols they find in the house to neighbourhood children to play with, but Aliya cannot bring herself to desecrate another person's holy objects and hides them away:

> In the small room . . . there was a statue of Lord
> Krishna above the fireplace. His garland of flowers lay

littered all about; only a yellow thread hung about his neck now.

'Do get that out of here, dear; give it to the children outside, they can play with it,' Amma had said several times since they'd arrived.

Aliya did not respond. The Krishna idol stayed there for several days. When it was no longer possible for Amma to manage things without using that room, Aliya picked it up and hid it in her trunk (see p. 336).

Such minimal descriptions are hallmarks of the spare writing style of Mastur, who often opts for a gestural description over baroque details. Thus, the abandoned Hindu gods, and Aliya's attachment to them, stand in for her empathy towards the refugees who have fled to India. Whereas Hyder's characters will be given pages and pages of dialogue and interior monologue regarding their feelings on everything from the personal to the political, Mastur's characters express their views sometimes with only a single gesture.

Interestingly, it is only by moving to Pakistan that Aliya and her mother end up leaving the sphere of male-dominated households. In their new home, Aliya becomes the primary breadwinner, abandons the burqa and begins to stay outside the house more and more. She teaches during the day and volunteers at Lahore's crowded Walton refugee camp in the evenings. Her mother is enraged, and accuses her of being just like her father, always focused on what's outside the house:

One day, when she returned at six in the evening, Amma was seated on a chair on the dry lawn as if waiting for her.

'Why do you go there?' she demanded harshly.
'What do you get out of that useless work?'

'I get peace,' Aliya answered gently.

'Like father, like daughter; do you wish to ruin me
now as well?'

'If you are ruined by me teaching children, there's
nothing I can do about it,' she replied in annoyance.

'There's nothing you can do?' Amma asked angrily.

'Yes, there's nothing I can do.' She got up and went
inside. She didn't even turn around to look and see that
Amma was crying into her sari border (see pp. 339–40).

Does Amma think her daughter takes after her late husband,
or does she object to her actions because she is behaving
as men do? While the stories of rape, abduction and
abandonment of women during Partition are important to
tell, Mastur's quieter narrative tells a tale of liberation tinged
with loneliness and loss. Migration, Mastur reminds us, does
not always result in trauma, and for women, it can sometimes
disrupt a patriarchal milieu and lead to a quiet empowerment.
In this way, *The Women's Courtyard* is reminiscent of Hindi
writer Yashpal's two-volume 1958–60 novel *Jhūṭhā Sach*
(translation published by Penguin Classics as *This Is Not
That Dawn*, 2010).

Though Yashpal's woman protagonist, Tara, is abducted
during the riots of Lahore, her subsequent repatriation to
India leads eventually to employment, independence and
emancipation. For both Aliya and Tara, the disruptions
and migrations of Partition create new possibilities to
find independence from traditional family structures and

patriarchal hierarchies. This same formulation occurs in Krishna Sobti's recent autobiographical Hindi novel *Gujarat Pakistan se Gujarat Hindustan* (forthcoming in my translation as *A Gujarat Here, a Gujarat There*, Penguin India). Set in the years immediately following Partition, Sobti's novel depicts a young woman embarking on a quest for a career in education in independent India. Despite the challenges she faces, she finds no small degree of success and independence. *A Gujarat Here, a Gujarat There* is written more in the classic style of a Bildungsroman about a male protagonist, setting out on the threshold of adulthood, ready to take on the world. Sobti's autobiographical character feels her future is full of possibilities, and she has only to scan the 'help wanted' sections of the newspaper to find her next adventure.

Narratives of rape and abduction during Partition, and tales of women's post-Partition emancipation from traditional patriarchal family structures can be read as two sides of the same coin. During the chaos of Partition, women were literally forced out of the safe space of the home, out of the courtyards that protected them. But those courtyards were also prisons for some. As Mastur shows us throughout her oeuvre, sexual violence existed even within the friendly confines of the āngan. The rupture of those walls led to worse violence and imprisonment for some, but liberation for others. When we think of women in Partition we are more likely to think of Bhisham Sahni's village women committing suicide by jumping in wells in *Tamas*, or Manto's horrendous rapes, than we are of Yashpal's Tara, Mastur's Aliya and Sobti's heroine finding personal independence.

IV. In Praise of Unhappy Endings

After Tehmina's suicide, Aliya looks through the books her elder sister had been reading—romances given to her by Safdar. She blames this genre for Tehmina and Kusum's unrealistic expectations for love and romance:

> One day, she began to leaf through Tehmina's books absent-mindedly. Such tales of love and fancy! Women would commit suicide for love and depart as examples of perfect fidelity, and then, some dark night, men would appear to momentarily light a lamp over a tomb, then leave, and that was that. She threw the books back in the cupboard and cried tears of rage, as she felt Tehmina watching her with disdain from the other side of her curtain of tears (see p. 78).

Aliya is intent on avoiding love herself. Love makes people do ridiculous things and foster unrealistic expectations. Love is not the same thing as marriage, which is also to be avoided, because it brings disappointment and dependence. Even her vain, educated, English-speaking aunt Najma is deceived in marriage, and forced to contemplate divorce. Love is for fools, marriage is for slaves, in Aliya's view.

But Mastur knows that women's investment in popular tales of romance, betrayal and true love help perpetuate the patriarchal system and it is with these tales and the expectations they create that Mastur wishes to engage. Narratives of eternal love, overcoming all odds and romantic bliss are exactly what Aliya becomes sceptical of after the suicides of Kusum and

Tehmina. She has heard of the suffering and death of her aunt, Safdar's mother, because of her forbidden love. Aliya wants nothing to do with love—she makes this clear. She knows that those who believe in true love seem to end up dead. And those who believe in tradition, hierarchy and class end up like her mother's generation. Alive, but twisted and gnarled beyond recognition.

But these are Aliya's intellectual views. Mastur's depiction of the battle between Aliya's emotions and intellect is artfully done—her romantic feelings for Jameel distress her, but she is able to master them to the end, when she and her mother depart for Pakistan and leave behind Jameel and his family forever. And the way Mastur writes about this inner conflict seems designed to produce confusion in the reader as well. From a certain perspective, nothing Jameel says or does is out of character for the genre of literature that Tehmina and Kusum consumed. His passionate avowals of love, his stormy speeches, his brooding good looks and yes, even his physical assaults on her would all be expected in a romance novel, an epic love story, a contemporary Bollywood film and even (or especially) a Brontë hero.

Thus, despite Aliya's very explicit interior monologues about her reasons for distrusting Jameel and rejecting his advances, a reader's instincts for the romantic genre will tell them that she will 'come around' in the end, accept his love and live happily ever after. Every heroine protests for a certain period, but then she gives in and we all cheer. Yet Aliya is right. Jameel is not particularly bright. He writes bad poetry. He pretends not to have manipulated or seduced Chammi to get her to pay for his education. He is unable to get a job, and he is in all likelihood going to follow in the footsteps of his father, despite his loathing for him, ignoring his family and hanging around with his political friends outside the house. And no means no.

All the same, Mastur knows that we, her readers, are also deeply conditioned in the cult of romantic narratives, whether through literature, song or film. It is somehow easier to process the tragic deaths of star-crossed lovers than the deeply uncomfortable love triangle of Jameel, Aliya and Chammi, an unpleasant dynamic that damages all involved and drags on for years and years. In current terminology, Jameel is a stalker, a sexual harasser and a gaslighter. He assaults Aliya, does not respect her wishes and manipulates her. She never believes in him, even when his performance of true love for her is the most credible.

But it is not just Jameel whom Aliya refuses to marry. Once in Pakistan, a doctor at the refugee camp where she volunteers asks her to marry him. She considers it, but then feels that all he is offering her is material wealth and status symbols: a fine house, a car, a comfortable income. She already had a house and a good income and doesn't see the point of the car. She will not marry for material benefit, because she already supports herself. Finally, in a surprise entrance at the end of the novel, Safdar reappears. He too wishes to marry Aliya; his approach again fulfils the requirements of romance writing: he sees in Aliya her dead sister; they share a bond of nostalgia. For a moment she is tempted, until Safdar tells her mother that he is no longer an activist and plans to set up an import–export business. Another illusion is broken: Safdar is not a romantic hero, but an insufferable romantic who drove her sister to suicide and now wishes to renounce his political ideals in favour of pursuing wealth.

Is this an unhappy ending? Has Chammi indeed won? Will Aliya lead a depressing life alone with her unpleasant mother? All of these scenarios are possible, but at the same time, I would argue that Mastur is offering us an opportunity to embrace romantic ambivalence and grapple with the reality of Aliya's life: as a woman, she is offered a buffet of poor choices. She chooses independence from the imprisoning influence of patriarchy but has not found a path to emotional contentment through companionship or friendship that will fill the gaping hole left behind by male control. Yet.

V. A Note on This Translation

The Women's Courtyard has been translated before as *The Inner Courtyard*, by Neelam Hussain, and published by Kali for Women in 2001. Retranslation is still a rarity in the context of modern South Asian literature but the practice enriches the field of translation, offering readers different prisms through which to read a text. When I choose to retranslate a work, it is usually because I feel I have something substantially different to offer from the previous translator or translators. All the same, I draw comfort and inspiration from the work of previous translators, who may have seen things differently than I did and send me scurrying back to my dictionaries and expert friends for more information.

Khadija Mastur's writing style is spare and elegant. Unlike many Urdu authors she does not favour heavily ornamented writing and turns of phrase full of literary allusions. I felt inspired to reproduce this clarity in English, after seeing that Hussain's translation struggled with this quality, attempting to elevate the language to a more formal register of English than was used in Urdu. See, for example, Mastur's description of Safdar Bhai, and the two contrasting translations, below:

> Mastur: *Safdar Bhai kitne vajīha magar kaisī maskīn sūrat ke the.*

> Rockwell: Safdar looked so handsome, but so meek.

> Hussain: How tall and well built Safdar Bhai had been and yet how diffident his mien.

Not only does Hussain divide descriptive adjectives into phrases, but in the case of the second phrase, *maskīn sūrat ke*, she introduces a flowery and somewhat archaic-sounding descriptor, 'how diffident his mien'.

These embroideries of the original, in which Hussain seeks to somehow augment the original text, stretch even to ordinary narrative sentences, such as the following:

> Mastur: *Dūr kahīñ se ghaṛiyāl ke gyārah bajāne kī āvāz ā rahī thī.*

> Rockwell: From somewhere far off came the sound of the bell striking eleven.

> Hussain: A distant clock struck the hour. The sound of its measured strokes rolled over her. It was the eleventh hour of the night.

Here, Hussain's rendition conveys a breathless dramatic tension that is absent from the original, which merely alerts us to the passage of time.

Hussain also occasionally inserts new ideas into the text, such as below, where she actually adds foreshadowing to the original sentence that describes Aliya worrying about her sister Tehmina Apa:

Mastur: *Rāt kā qissā bār bār yād ātā aur voh anjām ke khauf se ek lafz bhī na paṛh saktī thī.*

Rockwell: She kept thinking about what had occurred the night before, and was so fearful of what might happen she couldn't read a single word.

Hussain: The inexorable end of Apa's fated love was before her eyes and she was unable to concentrate on her work.

Mastur merely writes of Aliya's *'anjām kā khauf,'* her fear of the outcome, whereas Hussain announces to us that Tehmina's 'fated love' is coming to an 'inexorable end'. This embellishment on the original text both spoils the suspense of the story and romanticizes Tehmina's love for Safdar by referring to it as a 'fated love'.

Strangely—perhaps by accident—a pivotal passage is missing from Hussain's translation. I can attest as a translator that it is far too easy to drop bits of a text in the course of translation. The phone rings, the dog must be let out, one's attention is divided—and there goes a paragraph. Usually these mistakes can be rectified in editing, when one notices that something is missing or when a transition between paragraphs makes no sense. An extra set of eyes helps too. In this case, the passage in question is Jameel's first physical assault on Aliya. Aliya has been reading about the horrors of Ghengis Khan and his army, when Jameel comes to speak with her. She tries to make him go away, or stick to the topic of her exams, when he grabs her and kisses her (or more—the text is not entirely clear on this point, but it reads clearly as sexual assault). After this she feels shaken and defiled.

Finally, language changes, cultural norms change and politics change. All great works deserve multiple translations, and English can only be enriched by multiple versions of classic South Asian texts. With this fresh translation, a new generation of readers will be introduced to *The Women's Courtyard*, and perhaps a few who know some Urdu will take the plunge and try reading the book in the original.

Daisy Rockwell

Further Reading:

Hyder, Qurratulain. *River of Fire*. Delhi: Kali for Women, 1998. (Translated by the author.)

Manto, Sa'adat Hasan. *My Name Is Radha: The Essential Manto*. Delhi: Penguin, 2015. (Introduced and translated by Muhammad Umar Memon.)

Mastur, Khadija. *Cool, Sweet Water*. Delhi: Kali for Women, 1999. (Introduced and translated by Tahira Naqvi.)

Sahni, Bhisham. *Tamas*. Delhi: Penguin, 2016. (Introduced and translated by Daisy Rockwell.)

Sobti, Krishna. *A Gujarat Here, a Gujarat There*. Delhi: Penguin. (Introduced and translated by Daisy Rockwell.)

Yashpal. *This Is Not That Dawn*. Delhi: Penguin, 2010. (Translated by Anand.)

Acknowledgements

Many thanks are due to my wonderful editor, Ambar Sahil Chatterjee, for agreeing to take on this project, and to Cibani Premkumar, my ingenious copy editor, for her rigorous editing. Thanks also to Ali Kamran of Sang-e-Meel Publications for granting me permission to translate this work. This has been my first full-length Urdu book translation and Aftab Ahmad, translator and Urdu scholar extraordinaire, has my eternal gratitude for meticulously going through every line of this translation and answering my constant barrage of questions. Naveed Tahir, Khadija Mastur's niece, has been amazingly helpful in supplying me with beautiful photographs of Mastur and Hajira Masroor (Tahir's mother), as well as a treasure trove of archival materials. Thanks are also due to Dr Asif Aslam Farrukhi for introducing me to Naveed Tahir. I am grateful to my husband and daughter for their patience through it all, and to my cats, who have quietly overseen the project from the sidelines. Last, but not least, I am very grateful to my friend Manan Ahmed for suggesting that I consider translating this novel and helping me through the proposal stage. To him I dedicate this translation.